The Autobiography of Maria Callas: A Novel

The Autobiography of Maria Callas *is dedicated to my dear daughter*
Janet Bond Brill, who gave me the idea for the book.

First Edition
Library of Congress Catalog Card Number: 97-077319
ISBN: 0-913559-49-0 (Hardcover)
ISBN: 0-913559-48-2 (Softcover)

Artwork by Frank C. Eckmair

Although factual information is at the core of this book, The Autobiography of Maria
Callas: A Novel *is a work of fiction, and is not intended to present a complete or historically
precise rendering of the life of the artist. This work draws upon some of the well-known details
of Callas' life, some of the speculation that has appeared in print, as well as impressions of the
great diva gathered by the author, who has admired Maria Callas for many years. It was this
admiration that led to the writing of this novel.*

Published in the United States of America by

Birch Brook Press
PO Box 81
Delhi, NY 13753

(212) 353-3326 (in NYC)

Write or call for free catalog of books and printed art.

Composition by
Pro•To•Type
Middletown, NY

Printing by
Royal Fireworks Press
Unionville, NY

Hardcover binding by
Spectrum Bindery
Florida, NY

The Autobiography of Maria Callas: A Novel

Alma H. Bond

BIRCH
BROOK
PRESS

About the Book

A brief note in answer to queries of how I went about writing this book. I listened and researched and remembered and dreamed, and wove a tapestry of impressions that seem to me more real than life. Although the facts of Maria Callas's life and career are historically correct in this book, it is essentially a work of fiction. I do not wish to imply that it is any more than an effort to present my ideas of what it was like to be Maria Callas. In all humility, I have tried to depict the life and times of a great genius who was also a vulnerable human being. I have taken a great risk in doing so, and wish to apologize to the memory of Maria, as well as to my readers, for my arrogance in presuming to think that one person can genuinely understand the heart and soul of another.

— Alma H. Bond

Introduction

ON THE SIXTEENTH OF SEPTEMBER, 1977, I was surprised to receive by registered mail a huge bundle from France. It included the following letter:

Dr. Alma H. Bond
11 E. 87th Street
New York, New York 10128

Dear Dr. Bond:

We have never met, but you may well have heard of me. My name is Maria Callas. I am an opera singer.

I am taking the liberty of writing to you because a friend of mine who is your patient says you are a wonderful psychoanalyst. I must confess that for a time I considered coming to you for treatment, and indeed, if I had lived permanently in the United States I might well have done so. Also, friends who are better versed in literary matters than I admire the understanding of human nature evident in your writing. They particularly like your biography of Virginia Woolf, which they say is a sensitive, insightful portrait of a misunderstood woman. They believe you understood Woolf's relationship with her mother as no other writer has. Lord knows, my relationship with *my* mother could use some insight!

I have investigated your background, and appreciate that you are my age, and, like me, grew up in a large city in the United States. Under other circumstances, we could easily have sat side by side in elementary school. You will understand the times I grew up in and the difficulties that faced a struggling artist of our day.

I, like Woolf, am misunderstood, though many biographies and newspaper articles proclaiming to expose the "real Callas" have been published. My mother has written one (Lord help me), as has my sister, my ex-husband, Giovanni Battista Meneghini, and even my cousin Steven Linakis, whom I only met once and hardly ever talked to. I am especially annoyed by those, and there are many, who speculate publicly on the source of my "genius." How could they know? Most of them have never even met me. Not a one has understood me or the wellsprings of my art. I do not like being called *La Divina*. I am only a woman. That is the source of my art.

I have kept a sort of diary of my life since I was a child. I did it to make sense out of a confusing and often disorganized life. No one but me has ever seen it. Like me, the diary is in scraps and pieces, but for the astute psychoanalyst you are, it will tell the true story of Callas, the woman and the artist.

I have sorted the material into four piles. Since my rejection of my mother mystifies everyone including the press, the first heap of papers tells of our relationship from the moment I was born to the present day. I am angry with her for many reasons, but most of all because she took over my childhood and kept me from knowing who I am. It has been said I am a singer with a thousand voices. I think I am a soul with a thousand selves. Hopefully, this potpourri of paper will cast some light on why I feel so nonexistent except when I am on the stage.

The second group of memoirs deals with my marriage to the "old man," Giovanni Battista Meneghini, and how he nurtured me and helped launch the development of my incredible career. People wonder why I married a man so much older than I, but they fail to realize that without him I never could have become Maria Callas.

The third selection chronicles the rise and fall of my operatic career, my triumphs and heartbreaks. It tells about my mentors, the marvelous conductor Tullio Serafin, and how he shaped my talent and my art, and Luchino Visconti, the famous producer and screen director who expanded my musical horizons at the same time he introduced me to a whole new way of life. Sometimes I think Maria Callas was born under the tutelage of these remarkable men.

The fourth and most important assortment of papers divulges how I lost my identity when I lost my voice. It gives the details of my affair with Aristotle Onassis and illustrates how I found a whole new identity as his mistress. I trust you will understand this kind of connection and not be offended by the graphic details of our love life. Such a description is necessary if one is to understand my obsession with him. This section also discusses the manner in which I dealt with his marriage to Jackie Kennedy and how his death affected me as nothing else in my life.

Last of all, Dr. Bond, I am writing to ask you to set straight to the world the real nature of my relationship with Onassis, and to clear him of the charge that he destroyed my career. I am sending you the diary because I want to make sure the book is edited and presented to the public by someone who can understand the psychology behind our relationship.

Why didn't I write the book myself, you may ask? I have never been able to communicate well through words. You might say my communications for the most part were sung rather than spoken. And in particular, I have always disliked writing, perhaps because I do not feel I am an educated woman. But I do wish to be understood, and now when it is almost too late, this is the only way I know to do it.

Will you take these fragments of my life and turn them into an autobiography, in order to set to rest for once and for all who I am? Please?

As you may have heard by now, I am . . . unavailable for conferences or corrections. Nor will I ever be again. But I have always trusted my instincts, and they tell me that in you I have made the right choice.

My best wishes to you, Alma Bond. And may God be with us both.

The Early Years

ℳy DISASTROUS RELATIONSHIP with my mother began a few minutes after I was born. According to both parents, the nurse reached out to Evangelica and said, "Here is your beautiful twelve and a half pound baby girl!" My dear mother muttered, "A girl? I already have a girl. I need my baby boy. Take her away, I don't want her." Then she turned her back on me and refused to see me for four whole days. I wasn't Vasily; therefore I didn't exist.

People say a little baby doesn't know anything, but I've always been a sensitive person, and know how I must have felt. Here I had knocked myself out pushing my way out of my mother—if it was like everything else she did my whole life, she didn't make it easy—and nobody was there to greet me when I arrived. Like when you sing a beautiful aria and nobody claps or says a word. You are met by a vacuum and it hurts.

I try to understand how she felt. She and my father had lost my little three-year-old brother Vasily to a typhoid epidemic in Greece, and had run away to Astoria, Long Island to escape their heartache. Liska, as she was known, was hoping to replace Vasily with me, and had knitted beautiful little blue clothes to take the new baby home in. I can sympathize with her that she did not give birth to the boy she wanted, and that she had lost her beautiful son who was not even to have a namesake. I, too, have lost someone I love, and know the agony of it. I knew it even when I was little and wished I had died instead of Vasily. Then she would have been happy.

Yes, I can understand her pain. But I cannot forgive her, ever.

I read in my favorite magazine, *Reader's Digest*, that the first meeting of a mother and her new baby is extremely important. They call it "bonding." I am an emotional person and have always known intuitively whether a person likes me or not. I am sure my mother did not want me, even though she denied it. After the first four days, she relented enough to breast feed me for the twelve months Greeks consider essential for a child's future well being. After all, what would the neighbors have thought if she hadn't nursed me? She fed me, dressed me, and saw to the necessities of my life. I guess you could say she did everything she was supposed to. But I don't believe we ever bonded. I never felt I had a mother who loved me.

Would you believe she doesn't even know the date I was born? Dr. Leonides Lantzounis, the godfather I love, who was present at my birth, says it was December second, 1923. At school, the date is registered as December third, and there is no record of it at the Flower Hospital, where I was born, or the New York Department of Health. But my mother insists I was born on December fourth. I celebrate my birthday on December second.

Even the matter of my naming was confused. When the nurse asked my mother what name to put on the baby's bead bracelet, she was stunned into silence. They had not prepared any name for a girl. While the impatient nurse stood by, my parents, who never agreed about anything, argued about my name. My mother finally answered, "Sophia." "No," my father said, "it is Cecilia," the name of his sister. After much debate, they managed to agree on Maria. Three years later I was christened in the Greek Orthodox cathedral on East Seventy-fourth Street as Cecilia Sophia Anna Maria Kalogeropoulos, so everybody was happy. Except me. No wonder I never know who I am. How can anyone without a name know who she is?

My mother says I was a sweet and placid baby, a nice little girl who tried hard to win her affections. I don't believe it for a minute. I think I was a good actress even then and behaved the way I thought she wanted me to. I can't believe I really was sweet and placid or I wouldn't be so . . . so unquiet now. But whatever I did, I never was able to penetrate her closed heart. I grew into a lonely, unhappy child who gobbled food as a substitute for love.

We owned three canaries, Stephanakos, David, and Elmina, whom I loved and watched by the hour to learn how David sang so beautifully. But what I really wanted was a little dog. I thought having a companion to be with all the time would make me less lonely, and begged to have one throughout my childhood. But no, Liska would not permit it. She never let me have anything I wanted unless she wanted it, too. As she carefully explained and explained and explained, by tradition Greeks allow no pets in their homes except canaries. But I knew what the real reason was. She just doesn't like animals. So one of the first things my husband Battista did after we were married was to get me a dog, Toy. I have never been without one since.

"Why are you so fat, Maria?" my mother would say in her flat, dry voice, and then follow it by urging me to eat more homemade bread, macaronada (an Italian macaroni with Mother's own sauce of fried onions and chopped meat), fried potatoes, saganaki (two fried eggs with a mild cheese on top), candy, cake, and ice cream. The refrigerator was always well stocked with meat, which I devoured raw all my life. This resulted in at least two tape worms when I was older. Although Liska stuffed me with food, I must say I made my own contribution to my corpulence. I was a passionate eater, wolfing and stuffing down the food, and then grabbing for more. My mother says I was always standing up in my crib reaching out for a cookie when I was a baby. I can see I needed something, anything, because I certainly didn't get much from her. But why was I always in my crib, I want to know? What I needed was not a cookie but to be picked up and hugged. Or to have a dog.

Before I was eleven, I had developed into a fat, pimply adolescent. "Her nose is always buried in homework or opera recordings," my mother would complain to anyone who would listen. If I was miserable as a child, you can imagine how I was as a teenager. I felt myself an ugly duckling, overweight, clumsy, and unpopular. Eventually, I turned into the "elephant who would like to sing Butterfly," as a critic cruelly put it later in my life.

On the other hand, my sister Jackie was tall, slender, and gentle. When I didn't love her, I wished she was dead. I guess I'm a little mixed up about the feelings I had for Jackie when I was a child. On the one hand, I looked up to her and wanted to be beautiful and have beaux like her. On the other hand, her syrupy cow-towing to Mother made me nauseous. She spent most of her time trying to please Liska. "Certainly I'll do the dishes, Mother. Can I do anything else for you?" So of course, she was the favorite. It would kill me when I saw the two of them talking, always whispering together like girlfriends. The only time my mother talked to me was to order me to practice or to criticize me. It didn't help that Jackie had many beaux while I remained friendless and isolated. Every time one of her boyfriends rang the doorbell an arrow of pain shot through my heart. The house was filled with boys, but none of them were ever for me. I felt like the *Ancient Mariner*, "Water, water everywhere and not a drop to drink."

"No boy will ever love me," I cried in my bed at night when no one could hear me. "I'll be an old maid, stuck with mother forever."

Do you know what it is like to have a gorgeous, popular older sister when you are fat, pimply, and ignored by the boys? One of the worst moments of my life was when Vasso, a gangly young man with a huge Adam's Apple, rang the doorbell. Our neighbor Marina called out, "Maria, there is a beau at the door for you." I was humiliated to have to tell her that Vasso, despite his youthful looks, had come to visit Jackie, not me.

Jackie and I used to fight all the time. The only consolation in being fat was that, despite the six years between us, I weighed as much as she and managed to sneak in a few good clouts whenever I could. That always made me feel good—until my mother walloped me on the behind or rushed in to put pepper in my mouth and on my lips. Somehow Jackie never got the pepper treatment; to Liska, everything was my fault.

But I guess I loved Jackie after all. She used to teach me to play the piano and to sing. She would teach me a song and I would practice it for hours, and was so proud when I could play it for her without looking at the music when she came home from school. She was my first music teacher, and I've always loved anybody who has anything to teach me. I liked to look at her too, much as I hate to admit it. She was so graceful and pretty. I thought she could have been a movie star, like Constance Bennett.

I remember something dreadful that happened when I was five years old. I guess it taught me it's dangerous to love, so I've been careful whom I love ever since. Not that my caution has helped me much.

I was walking down the street wearing a little pink summer dress and holding my mother's hand when I saw Jackie across the street. According to Mother, I yanked my hand away and bolted across the street, yelling "Jackie, Jackie, it's me, it's me, Maria. Wait for me!" The next thing I knew I woke up in Fort Washington Hospital. I had a concussion and had been in a coma. The only thing I remember about that stay in the hospital was that I was delirious, and thought there were shelves on the wall with all kinds of toys on them. I recall in particular a large stuffed dog I named Toy. When it disappeared, I cried and tried to make it come back, but it paid no attention to me. As far as I can remember, that was the worst part of the hospital visit for me, not getting my dog.

My parents were told my chances of surviving were slim, but I fooled them. I've always been a fighter. I came home from the hospital after twenty-two days, and except for being a bit more irritable than before, proved none the worse for the experience. Except I imagine I was disillusioned, not for the first time nor the last, about not having my wishes come true.

My mother said in her book that she thinks the accident injured my brain and that that is why we are estranged. How obtuse can a person be? She has no idea that it is impossible to be her daughter and remain oneself. I'll have nothing to do with her, because even though she doesn't love me, she acts like she owns me. She takes me over and tries to keep me her baby.

She chose all my clothes until I was a grown woman. No wonder I didn't know how to dress at the start of my career! I'll never forget a hat she bought me when I was seventeen. Did you ever see one of those white baby bonnets that have a lace brim around them? That's the kind of hat she got for me when I was seventeen! My sister's boyfriend Milton saw it and burst out laughing. "What are you trying to do, Liska?" he asked. "Make her a baby again?"

The one thing I did to rebel against her tyranny when I became an adolescent was not to show up for meals unless I felt like it. It made Mother furious, because there was nothing she could do about it. You would have thought I had murdered the Queen of England, for all the yelling Liska did. But it made me feel great to have power over her, little as it was. That wasn't so terrible, was it? When I see what is happening to teenagers these days, I think Mother was lucky.

When people speak of being suffocated by another person, I know what they mean. It was her pushing me to practice and dragging me around to contests that made me a singer, she said over and over again. Forget the fact that I was born with God's gifts of voice and character and have worked at singing night and day for more years than I care to remember. But I can't explain it to her now any more than I ever could tell her anything and have her understand. She would only blame me for not thinking differently. She believes there is only one way to think; her way.

Girls didn't have any independence in Greece, at least when my mother was growing up. I'm sorry about that. But I want to say here in black and white that the only way I can be Maria Callas is to refuse to recognize Liska Kalogeropoulos as my mother. The media is forever asking what kind of cruel and heartless daughter would do such a thing to her poor old mother. They don't understand that it is a matter of survival.

The worst thing about my mother, however, is not that she is controlling but that she is mean. I think she got a kick out of hurting me. She got a funny look in her eyes and a tight little smile when she deprived me of something I wanted. I remember once I asked her for a Baby Ruth Bar like one of the children in school brought for lunch. She said, "Just because you want it you can't have it!" Is that any way to treat a child?

But the lickings were even worse. She used to turn me over her knee and paddle me on my bare behind. I can still smell the slightly acid odor of her body through her house dress and feel the imprint of her hot hand across my buttocks. I would scream and holler and cry as I rubbed up and down, up and down, against her warm legs every time she hit me, but she never stopped until she decided it was enough. My crime was usually something horrible, like maybe I wouldn't finish my spinach. Down would come my pants and up would go my bottom, no matter who was around!

Once a group of Jackie's friends trooped in after her and stood watching the performance. I froze with horror. If there is anything more mortifying than being spanked, it is being spanked in front of others.

Sometimes, after it was over, she would come and soothe me, hold me in her arms and stroke my hair. Oh, how sweet it was! I would overlook everything else for the moment.

Even my sister thought Liska was a perpetually dissatisfied woman who subjected every member of the family to endless fault-finding. Jackie soon learned to stay out of Mother's hair, for she always found something she felt could be improved upon. Whatever anyone did, Liska could always do it better. Sometimes I realize how ridiculous it is that a woman with no musical training whatever gave me advice on how to sing. But do you know, I always listened to her as if she knew better than I?

I saw a postcard once in which a huge, menacing woman is looming up over a tiny cowering child. That's how I feel about Mother, despite being taller than she and a world famous diva.

Jackie says when Mother was young, she was crazy about anything to do with the stage. She and Father would go from where they lived in Meligala, in the Peloponnese, to Kalamata, on the coast. Kalamata, the closest town of any size, boasted a real theatre where they could see traveling companies touring plays from the previous season in Athens. My sister says the only time she remembers Mother being happy was after visiting the theatre in the nearby town.

Liska had wanted to go on the stage herself. That's why she pushed me so savagely to become a famous singer. It infuriates me that she tried to get through me what she didn't have the guts to do herself. Who knows what I would have chosen to do if she hadn't pushed me to be a singer? I might have been a famous actress or perhaps a concert pianist.

When I was four years old, I found the way to my mother's attention, if not her heart. My family owned a pianola that played perforated rolls of music and was pumped by pedals. It was black and gleaming and always smelled of furniture polish. I loved it and listened to it all the time. One day when Jackie was in school my mother heard some music in the parlor and rushed in from the kitchen where she was baking bread to see who was playing the pianola. She found me crunched down under it, pressing the pedals with my hands. I still remember the wonder I felt when I realized I could "make music" all by myself. Time seemed to stop as I thought, "I'll never have to ask anyone to play for me again." My mother grabbed me and carried me to the kitchen but I crept back under the pianola to make music whenever she let me.

By the time I was seven I was taking real piano lessons from Signorina Santrina, to the despair of my father, who resented every penny he had to pay her. "Two dollars a lesson, four times a week," my mother bragged. That was a lot of money for those days. My classmate Ariadne Theopoulos took lessons that cost only fifty cents apiece. "Why are you throwing my money away?" my father would shout at her. I was torn in two. Was my mother right, and my music worth all she was putting into it? Or was my father correct in thinking I was wasting his hard-earned money? I didn't know then, and sometimes I still don't know.

The Signorina was a tall bony lady of indeterminate years, as they say. My mother and I called her "the old maid." She was very strict, and made me curl my fingers around an apple to show me how to hold them when I played. Andros, who sat next to me in school, told me she swatted his fingers with a ruler when they drooped over the keyboard, but she never had to hit me because I always practiced until I got it perfect. Even then I was a perfectionist. She taught me the Czerny exercises, the Leschetizky method, and Breithaupt's principles of relaxation. Sometimes she would blindfold me, making me feel the music with the tips of my fingers, in my arms, and up and down my spine. I'm happy she was such a taskmaster, because she taught me well from the beginning. That is one reason I love to play the piano, because I know I play it well.

An incident that was to change my life forever happened the year I began my lessons. My sister says up to this time both of us had pleasant voices and neither one was considered better than the other. I was playing the piano and singing my favorite song, "La Paloma," when it happened. Years later, my mother remembered every detail. The windows were open, she said in her book. "And a little wind was stirring the lace curtains. Children were playing in the street, and not far away on the Hudson a boat was tooting its way up the river. I looked out on the street and saw it was crowded. A great crowd of people were gathering outside our apartment to listen to my daughter Maria singing. They were standing there listening and clapping their hands; only when she stopped singing did they go away." I found out then that when I sang people loved me.

From that moment on, Mother really took over my soul. Gone were the moments I could sit and daydream at the piano or look out the window until I felt like stopping. "Why are you loafing, Maria?" she would demand, with that peculiar look in her eyes and that mean little smile on her face. "You missed three notes on "La Paloma" yesterday, and if you do that on the

Major Bowes program, you will lose the contest!" If I had been her personal property before, she now treated me as if I were an attachment she could push and pull whichever way she pleased, like her arm or leg. She had a new ambition in life; I was to be a great opera star. She was going to see to it if it killed her. And me: I was never allowed to play with other children I could have compared myself to; I had no chance to discover what it was like to be a normal girl. I was in a daze at the blaze of activity that followed the discovery of my gift, and began to feel a strange sensation in my head. It was as if something was pulling inside me, pulling, pulling, I knew not where. It was distressing, because when I felt that way it was as if I wasn't all there. The sensation lasted until I began to study with de Hidalgo in Greece and then it went away without my hardly noticing. I don't mean to imply that I didn't like all the attention my singing got me. Insignificant little Maria had the power to make people clap. Of course I was pleased, and if Mother said I was going to be an opera singer, well, I didn't know any better than to go along with her. But it was not my decision: It only became so after I began to study with de Hidalgo.

The applause of our neighbors brought back to my mother another moment on a warm evening many years before when she had sat at her father's feet and listened spellbound to him singing. She adored her father and never got tired of talking about him. I know the stories by heart. In fact, I grew sick of hearing them. Her favorite was the time he was sitting on the porch of his little house in Stylis, across the Gulf of Lamia from Thermopylae, nestled among tiny cottages and white churches with roofs of blue. He was surrounded by his seven children and numerous guests. Soon a swarm of applauding peasants were chanting, "Colonel Petro, give us a song," and the children joined in with "Sing to us, Daddy." Petro rested his arm on the ledge of the porch and burst into "Questo o quello", one of his most beloved arias. (No wonder I love Verdi so much!) The audience was spellbound and remained there until his last note died away. I know how he felt. There is no pleasure like hearing the applause of an audience when you know you have sung your best. The clapping of the crowd outside our window had shown Liska the way to achieve her unfulfilled ambitions. And I had found the way to become central in her life, and to make up for the fact that I hadn't been born a boy. I have no doubt that moment was the turning point of my life.

Around the same time, something similar happened to me in music class in school. It was one of those brown double rooms that have sliding doors, where two classes could be combined for a lesson. I remember the smell of chalk dust, and the drawings of colored stick figures tacked to the walls. Forty or fifty students were standing up to sing "The Star Spangled

Banner." The teacher blew her round black pitch pipe for us to begin the
national anthem. I remember Grace Demitriades sounding horribly off
pitch until Miss Sugar came up and asked her to just make the motions of
the song with her lips and not to sing. Little Harry Hershberger with his
squeaky voice stood squirming next to me. I guess I must have been singing
louder than the rest of the children in the high soprano part "and the rockets'
red glare" that nobody can sing in tune. All of a sudden I realized that
everyone else had stopped singing and was listening to me. When I finished
"and the home of the brave," the teacher and all the children applauded. It
was the only time any of them had paid attention to me. It was the highlight
of my school career.

I don't know why that should have surprised me. My sister and I often
sang together and I always drowned out her voice. "Do you have to sing so
loud?" she would complain. "Nobody can hear me at all." "Sing louder!" I
answered.

Soon I was winning singing prizes at Public School 164 in Washington
Heights and taking leading parts in school plays and concerts. Mother
treated these as if I were making my debut at Carnegie Hall. A national
amateur talent contest on the Mutual Radio Network brought me first prize,
a Bulova watch. I remember telling the children in school, "I feel so warm
in my new watch!" My second public appearance was in a children's show
in Chicago. I only won second prize, but since Jack Benny presented it to me
it almost made up for my defeat.

Then Mother really got down to business and dragged me around to
every children's show, radio program, and contest she could dig up. She
was frantic to make me a famous singer. If she had been able to see me at all,
she would have known I was miserable. What I needed was to be loved
unconditionally, not hauled around to satisfy my mother's thwarted ambitions. The pulling in my head got worse. I felt as if I was on a pulley with no
will of my own. A child treated like that has no insides.

Although I had never met my grandfather, Liska's love for him influ-
enced my entire life. To develop a talent like his was the only way I knew
to pierce my mother's heart. So long as she was hopeful I would fulfill her
ambitions, I had a hold on her that nothing could break. I worked as hard
as I could to make her happy with me. But I always felt her love was strictly
conditional, and should I ever lapse into being fat, pimply Maria, God
forbid, her interests would quickly revert to Jackie. While I was singing I felt
like an adored child. It was enough to keep me plodding away every waking
hour. But the moment I stopped singing, the fear froze my mind and I felt
shy and unlovable. So pretty soon I began to take a score to the dinner table

and into the bathroom with me to keep away the unpleasant feelings. Nobody seemed to care. Mother and Father were too busy fighting or she and Jackie were too wrapped up in talking about Jackie's beaux to notice.

Sometimes I think my father could have saved me from Liska if only he had been a different kind of person. I loved him so much (I can see him now twirling his cane and stroking his dyed black mustache) that even a small amount of attention would have made up for my mother.

I didn't have many toys as a child, and the few I had were given to me by neighbors or sewed by my mother on our black-wheeled, hand-operated Singer Sewing Machine. Once my father brought home from the pharmacy where he worked a little kewpie doll made of a kind of hard, pink plastic called cellophane. If you held it up to your face it felt cool to your skin. It had a slight smell, like, well, maybe acetone, but I must say I don't know anything that smells exactly like cellophane did. I named the doll Lovey. She wore a little stiff purple skirt that looked like a tutu. You could move her head and arms and legs, which were attached to her body by an elastic string. I was heartbroken when the string broke and one of her arms fell off. I glued it back on, but it never could move again. I wasn't a child who played with dolls, but I kept Lovey on the top of my bureau until we went to Greece. My mother didn't want to bother packing it and threw it away. Do you know, I still look for a doll like Lovey whenever I go by a toy store window? I swear I would buy one if I found it.

But much as I loved my father, he faded away when Liska was at her most powerful and left me to cope with her alone.

I remember one occasion in particular when I appealed to him to intervene. It was my turn to stay late after school and help the teacher clean the blackboards. We were supposed to take the erasers out on the fire escape and bang them together to beat the chalk out of them. It was fun to watch the white dust go up into the air in clouds. All the kids took turns doing it, and it was a job everybody wanted. I loved my teacher, Miss Sugar, and wanted to be "teacher's pet." Would you believe, my mother used to take me to school and come for me when classes were over even when I was twelve and thirteen years old! She wouldn't let me stay late to take my turn at cleaning the erasers like the others. I was terribly upset and asked my father if I could stay late the next day. Guess what he answered? Right. "Ask your mother." After a while I stopped appealing to him for anything. What was the point? My father was a gentle and loving man but Liska's contempt kept him powerless in the family. Their difficulties started soon after they were married. My grandfather had been against the marriage from the beginning; he felt Georges Kologeropoulos at thirty-three was too old for his eighteen-year-old daughter. He also felt Georges was their social inferior. It took Liska only six months to come to agree with her father.

My father had been a successful pharmacist in Meligala, and he soon made enough money to buy his family the best house in town, complete with servants. As he often repeated, "the best house, the best servants, the best food." Liska loved the status his profession gave them, as well as the luxury it made possible. But when their son Vasily died, both were heartbroken about losing him. Seeing reminders of the child wherever he turned, Georges found the pain unbearable and secretly decided upon a plan of escape. He sold the pharmacy and their home, and bought three tickets to America. Unfortunately, he neglected to tell Liṣka about the plans until the day before they sailed. My mother always had to be in total command, and never accepted an idea anyone else had first. Of course Georges always wanted to be in control, too, and retaliated by retreating when he didn't get his way. This time he found a way around her stubbornness: He bought the tickets without telling her. After that, the clash of wills escalated and grew ever fiercer and more frequent. He won that round, but paid for it with his marriage. She never forgave him, nor did she ever let him forget it.

Only twenty-three years old with a five-and-a-half-year-old child, another on the way, and no way of making a living, Liska was forced to leave her country and family and accompany the husband she hated to a strange and bewildering land. Like me later on, she wasn't asked if she wanted to live far across the sea.

To make matters worse, my father never again was nearly as successful as he had been in Greece, and had to take a job in a pharmacy. We first lived in Little Athens in Astoria, Queens, where the food and customs were like the ones we had left behind. I don't remember it well, because we moved nine times in eight years from one walk-up to another, and finally settled in a middle-class neighborhood in Washington Heights where I spent most of my childhood. Once, the teacher asked me where I lived and I had to go through all the addresses we had lived in before I could remember which one we had moved to.

At one time Father opened a drugstore on Ninth Avenue and Thirty-seventh Street, a Greek area in Manhattan, but it failed during the depression. After that he went to work as a traveling salesman for a cosmetic firm. Our family's standard of living was severely reduced, and Mother never let him forget that either. Now that I have achieved some distance, I can't help but suspect my father's lack of success was at least in part an effort to spite and frustrate my mother. If so, he was successful at it.

Because my mother always lorded over everybody, my father slipped away from the family, even though he came home every night he wasn't on the road for the cosmetic company. It hurt to have him there but not there, and it left an empty place in my heart. I would stand and stare at him, mute with longing, but he just sat there reading his newspaper.

I remember once I got up enough nerve to ask him, "Papa, would you like to hear me sing 'La Paloma?'"

"Hmmmmm," he said, as he continued to read his paper.

"Would you like my special saganaki? You like the way I make the fried eggs and cheese."

"Yes, dear."

"Papa, would you like a wax-paper sandwich?"

"Yes, dear," he said. "Go on outside and play."

I cried out, "Papa, I need you. I love you. Why can't you ever talk to me?"

He briefly looked up from his paper, cleared his throat, and said, "Yes. Hmmmm. Did you say something, Maria?"

"Never mind, Papa," I said between sobs. "I . . . I just wanted to know what time it is." He went on reading his paper.

No, Father was no help. With him I didn't exist at all. Is it any wonder I never thought of myself as someone a man could love?

Sometimes I thought it was better when he was on the road, because then he didn't awaken my longing for him. Much as I love him, it still brings tears to my eyes to realize how much I yearned to have more of a father. I guess that's why I fell in love with Meneghini; he took care of me the way a father should.

I soon found out that Father had a girlfriend on the side. Mother screamed and yelled about it but it did no good. That's the only thing he ever stood up to her about in his life. And do you blame him? All he got at home was contempt and yelling. When he did express a wish, such as to drop music lessons for Jackie and me because of lack of funds, it was ignored by Mother. But I was grateful to him for the thought, because it showed that he, at least, did not value me for my talent.

Something occurred to me for the first time while writing this. Grandfathers were the big thing in my house, much more important than fathers. Didn't my mother teach me that old men are to be adored and younger men treated with contempt? Isn't that why I always hooked up with old men? I could have had a young and handsome man, especially after I got famous and lost weight. But no, I had to go for the old grandfather types.

I once made a joke about grandfathers, only about Jackie Kennedy, not me. I said it was nice of her to provide a grandfather for her children. But wasn't I on the right track?

Despite my longing to have more of a father, I desired my mother's love more. As an adolescent I used to beg our neighbor, Marina, to tell me why Liska loved Jackie more than me. When the neighbor reminded me I had a voice, it made me furious. "What is a voice?" I cried out. "I am a person, that's what matters."

Did you ever see the photograph of Liska and me when I was a gawky, plain teenager with bushy bobbed hair and wearing ankle socks? Ugh, I was ugly! We were sitting on a big old burgundy couch embellished with blowzy flowers. A whiff of the musty claw-footed sofa comes back to me now. I smile as I remember the rough feel of the velour when rubbing my fingers against the grain. The room was small and dark and cluttered with furniture covered with crocheted antimacassars. Icons and embroidered cushions were everywhere. In the picture I am leaning away from Liska and looking rather warily at her, as if to say, "I love you, Mother, but I mustn't get too close to you. It is too dangerous." Liska, beautiful and elegant in contrast to me, also seems to be leaning as far away from me as she could without falling off the sofa. She is looking at me rather skeptically, seeming to say, "You aren't much, but you're all I've got." That picture tells the whole story, two women who were stuck with each other and had to make the best of it.

Have you ever heard my recording of Carl Maria von Weber's "Ocean! Thou Mighty Monster?" I always think of my mother when I sing it. The words to the first verse are:

Ocean! thou mighty monster, that liest curl'd like a green serpent, round about the world,

To musing eye thou art an awful sight, When calmly sleeping in the morning light.

But when thou risest in thy wrath, as now, And fling'st thy folds around some fated prow,

Crushing the strong ribb'd bark as t'were a reed, then, Ocean, art thou terrible indeed!

Liska is a terrible monster like the ocean, uncaringly "crushing the strong ribb'd bark as t'were a reed" whenever she "risest in wrath." Of all the thousands of arias I have sung, "Ocean! thou mighty monster" is the only one I ever recorded in English. It gets the flavor of my mother better than gentle Italian.

Another thing I hold against my mother is that she didn't know how to help me get along in America. I guess that at least is not her fault. She was born in Greece, but that didn't make me feel any better when she gave me the wrong advice about things. Once we were going to have a school party after a play I was in and I asked my mother what to wear. She said my woolen gamp, a clumsy jumper-like skirt she had made which made me look even fatter than I was. When I got to the party all the other girls were wearing pretty dresses of voile or silk. I was humiliated. I felt so jealous when I asked a friend how she knew what to wear and she said, "I asked my mother." If Liska had only known what she was doing, she could have helped me to express myself through my clothing, instead of looking like a country bumpkin!

Another time I happened to be wearing a pretty camel's hair jacket a neighbor gave me when her daughter outgrew it. I wore it with a plaid skirt. A Jewish girl named Bella Aizen came up to me and said, "You look nice today . . . for a change." I try not to think of the incident, because it still hurts.

My mother knew even less about the ways of America than I did, so after a while I stopped asking her advice on anything. I pretended I wasn't interested in clothes, and was thirty years old and a famous diva before I learned how to dress. Can you blame me for going all out and buying two hundred dresses, a hundred hats, and two hundred forty pairs of shoes?

My sister knew a bit more of the ways of America than Liska, having gone through elementary school before me. So when I was little I found myself turning to her for answers. It was Jackie who explained menstruation to me, and told me about the birds and the bees. My mother was too embarrassed. But when Jackie was a teenager she became preoccupied with her beaux and had little time for a needy younger sister. So after a while, I quit asking her things, too, and got along with what I had picked up from listening to the girls talk at school. That's how I really learned about sex, by overhearing the girls talking. The ways of America were dark and strange to me, and I was always frightened when I was with people who were not Greek. To me being shy was the normal way to be, and I never really got over it, even when I became a world famous diva and people of all nationalities stood in line for four days to hear me sing. I was always afraid I would say or do something ridiculous and people would laugh at me. If you ever saw one of the TV programs I was on, like Edward R. Murrow's, you will know what I mean. I was stiff as a board, and about as appealing.

In 1950, when I was twenty-six years old and married, I decided to make one last effort to improve relations with my mother. I thought, whatever mixed feelings I have about her, she helped prepare me for my career and she *is* my mother. It was only right she enjoy my success, too. And, I must confess, sometimes I was lonely for her. Once when I was a little girl in school, I told her that, and she answered, "How can you be lonely? You have the other students all around you." I answered, "Without you, I'm lonely." It makes me cry to think of it. She was not there to soothe my childish fears and worries. When I got married, I had a husband to do that, but it's not the same thing. I missed her Greek cooking, which nobody else's can compare to, even the famous chefs of Greece. And I yearned for the times we had fun together, when she wasn't up on her high horse. We loved to talk about the people we knew. I must admit we enjoyed tearing them apart. My mother used to laughingly say, "Gossip takes precedence." After all, it never hurt anybody. They never even knew we were talking about them.

So after I got married I surprised Liska by inviting her to accompany me to Mexico City, where I was to give a series of concerts. My parents are not smilers, but when she first came to Mexico City she actually wore a smile on her face. In the beginning she was thrilled to enjoy the attentions my colleagues and the press heaped on the mother of the diva. Everywhere we went were cascades of flowers, parties, and receptions. She admired my fabulous theatrical wardrobe, chosen for me by the great conductor Serafin and paid for by my husband, Meneghini. I was treated like a queen, and it was fun for her to be the Queen Mother. Why wouldn't it be? Her lifetime dream had come true. Liska had waited many years for her reward, and I guess I'm glad somewhere in my heart that I could at least give her that before the blowup.

It just so happened I was between dressers at the time, and Mother stepped in to help me out. She made herself useful, although I didn't like it that she always found a better way for me to wear my costumes and constantly fiddled around with my hair and straps. When I returned to the hotel tired and exhausted she rubbed me down with alcohol and put me to bed as she had when I was a child. It felt heavenly and brought back memories of when I was sick and she took care of me. . . . I guess maybe I did love her a little after all.

When I sang *Aida*, Liska even washed my brassieres and underwear, which were black with dye from the makeup of the African heroine, and hung them to dry in the hotel bathroom. Yes, I'm glad that much of the time in Mexico City she enjoyed herself. It eases my conscience a bit. I owed her that, and even though I'm furious with her, I'm glad I could give it to her.

But Mother's idyll was short-lived. During much of the visit, I tried my best to be good to her, paying for her plane ticket and all her expenses and giving her money, even though I am known to be a bit of a tightwad. I even spent a whole morning between performances of *Tosca* and *Trovatore* buying her an expensive mink coat. The memory of its smell in the rain overcomes me now and makes me cry. But then I remember she has a way of taking over that I can't stand. My career becomes *her* accomplishment, and I'm only an instrument to get her what she wants. Don't get me wrong. Most of the time I love music. I just don't want her to take it away from me.

"Practice 'O patria mia,' " she would advise me during the weeks in Mexico City, even though I had rehearsed it to death. I knew what I needed to practice, and certainly didn't need my untrained, unmusical mother to tell me. But I would think, "Well, maybe she's right and I ought to go over 'O patria mia' again." So I would. She often irritated me badly, so that I couldn't help myself and burst out in a fit of rage. I remember once she put the lucky brassiere I wore in *Aida* in the wrong drawer and I couldn't find it in time for the performance. I lashed out at her as if she had twisted a knife in my throat. "You can't do anything right," I screamed at her. "You can't bear my success and do everything you can to ruin it." Other times when I wasn't being inordinately polite I was cold to her and ignored her as if she were the maid. Poor woman! I ruined the trip for her and I don't like myself for it. I know at least part of the time I kept her from enjoying the splendor around us, the glamour she had longed for all her life.

My sister Jackie once said that Mother and I are too alike to get along. She says Liska encouraged a spiteful streak in me like hers, and both of us have the instincts of a killer and an unflinching desire to have our own way. If so, they are qualities I certainly have needed as an opera singer. I doubt if I could have gotten where I was if I had been a sweet little pussy cat.

Maybe Jackie is right in part about why Mother and I can't get along. After all, there is only room for one queen! Neither of us is willing to adopt a position subordinate to another woman. When my mother helped me out after my performance as Aida by washing my underwear, I could let myself need her. But I should have known it couldn't last. Liska is unable to accept such a role on a permanent basis.

In her book, *My Daughter, Maria Callas*, (*Her* book? It is ghost written, of course. She never could write a grocery list without our help.) Liska gave the following account of an incident she said happened between us. One night, after a particularly strenuous performance of *Aida*, I was unable to sleep and began to cry. My mother heard me sobbing in my bed after I had turned off the lights. She rushed in and said, "What's the matter? Are you afraid the performance wasn't a big success?"

"No, Mother," I said, sobbing even louder. "I don't care about *Aida*!"

"Then what is it? What's the matter?"

"I want children . . . in fact, I want twins," I answered tearfully. "I want lots of children around me . . . and I want you to raise them."

I went on sobbing in my surprised mother's arms until I fell asleep.

The whole world is up in arms about the way I treat my mother. You can read about it in headlines in every civilized country. They say I am a cold, ungrateful daughter, but that's because they've only heard a distorted version of events.

What really happened that night? Did my mother report the scene correctly? If so why did I behave that way? Yes, the scene as she described it is fairly accurate, although I find it a bit mortifying to say so. But it was her power over me that kept me from taking time out to have the babies I wanted.

As I lay in her arms that night I had a dream that helped me make the fateful decision. Like many of my dreams, it was vivid and in color, and seemed as if it were real. I dreamed I was gliding through the turquoise sea. I have always loved the ocean, particularly the Aegean Sea. The water was sparkling and shimmering in the sunlight as I swam on top of the waves. Suddenly a huge lion leaped on me and pushed my head under the water. The lion's mane was auburn, the color of my mother's hair. The water went up my nose and filled my mouth and I knew I soon would suffocate if she didn't let me go. (Strains of "La Mamma Morta," where the heroine is being burnt up by fire are going through my head as I write this.) I struggled to break her grasp, but to no avail. Just as I was about to go under for the third time I woke up in terror, knowing I had to wield a knife like a surgeon and cut her out of my life.

The next morning I walked up to the table where Liska and Giulietta Simionato, another opera singer and my good friend, were having breakfast. My mother leaned over to give me a good morning kiss. I pushed her away. "Don't, Mother," I said. "I am no longer a child."

Simionato was horrified. "If I were your mother," she said, "I'd give you a good slap!" Even my good friend couldn't understand that I was struggling to save my life. If she couldn't, who would? So I stopped trying to explain to anyone and have suffered the abuse of the world in silence ever since.

The "wonderful" vacation with her daughter, the world famous diva, proved to be a parting gift for my mother, for it was the last time we were ever to meet. I never saw her again.

I must admit, I wavered for a while about sticking to my guns. My longing for her was as real as my fear of her, and kept me vacillating back and forth. In 1950 I came down with jaundice and had to leave in the middle of the *Don Carlos* rehearsals. The doctor gave no hope of me being well enough to return before the date of the production. I am certain the conflict about my mother made me ill.

I kept getting one letter after another from her in Athens. She found life with my father more and more unbearable, and her letters were filled with complaints against him. I didn't like to hear her attacks on him so I never answered her. She became increasingly angry with me, reminding me in every letter of how much she had done for me and that it was the duty of a daughter as successful as I, married to a millionaire, to take care of her poor old mother. Her every sentence was a denigration and an indictment against me, and gradually strengthened my determination to cut her out of my life.

Finally I got one complaining letter too many from her demanding money. It made me feel as if my chest were on fire. I stamped to my desk and impulsively wrote an answer that has followed me around the world ever since. I said I could give her nothing, that money is not like flowers growing in a garden, and I bark for my living. I also told her she was a young woman (she was only fifty-three) and she should go to work. Then in the *pièce de résistance* of the letter I said, "If you can't earn enough to live on, throw yourself out of the window."

It was rash, and I was young, and I suppose if I had it to do over again I wouldn't have included the last sentence. But I simply couldn't go on living with her constant complaints, assaults, and demands.

I have a confession to make, a sneaky little thought I never dared to have before. I see her holding my hand when I was little. Walking down the street, we pass a candy store. I ask her for a Baby Ruth Bar. "No, Maria," she said, "you cannot have one." "Why not?" I asked. "Just because you want it, you can't have it," she answered. After Mexico I took away the thing she wanted most in her whole life right after she had a taste of it. Through my mind went the refrain, "Serves you right, Liska! Just because you want it, you can't have it." She'll never stop thinking about me now. I've found the way to make sure she thinks about me more than Jackie, without having her around to suffocate me!

She is getting what she deserves. Over the years, I miss her less and less. But sometimes when I am troubled I still yearn for her sweet embrace. I must admit I do now, *especially* now, when I need all the comfort I can get.

That I was acting in the interests of self-preservation with Liska became clear many years later in my love affair with Aristotle Onassis, when I yielded to the submissive side of my nature. There is no question it ruined my life. When I am submissive, I lose Maria Callas. I was more decisive with my mother and did the right thing in ending my relationship with her.

At the time of the Mexico City performances, perhaps the fact that I was married and had a husband who stood up for me gave me the necessary strength to make the break. It is interesting, too, that it was only after this point that I was able to reestablish contact with my father. I could forgive him his shortcomings because I had a man of my own now. For the rest of his life I invited Father to attend my performances and concerts. He often came to them and seemed to enjoy being the father of the diva. I have to smile when I picture the pain and frustration this must have caused Liska, seeing her hated husband reaping the glory of the seeds of greatness she had sown in her daughter. My smile feels familiar to me. It is a mean, tight little smile, just like hers . . .

It cost me a great deal to reject my mother. It meant I had to stand alone at every step in my life. It was bad enough as a child when she didn't know things like what I should wear. But it was even more painful when I was trying to learn how to be a woman. I couldn't emulate her because I didn't want to be anything like her. Why would I? She had made a mess of her marriage, and didn't know anything about the world of opera. It is hard not to have footsteps to follow in. You are always confused and without any guidance about which way to turn. It is like hacking your way through a jungle, where nobody has walked before. People like my sister have it easier; if she doesn't know what to do she only has to look at Liska, or to ask herself what Mother would do in her place. Right or wrong, at least she never feels in the dark about things. That is the major reason I have always idolized the Spanish opera singer Maria Malibran.

In my living room hangs a large portrait of Malibran, the only other likeness in my home besides that of my teacher, Elvira de Hidalgo. Malibran was born in Paris in 1808. Many consider her the greatest diva who ever lived. She, like me, started singing when she was a little girl. She was taught by her father, the famous teacher and producer Manuel Garcia and sang Mozart and Rossini with his opera company. Imagine being taught by your own father and singing in his opera company! It would have made my whole life beautiful. I would have sung for him with pleasure! If I had been given one wish as a child, that would have been it.

Malibran's voice was a contralto with an added soprano register, but it is said she had an interval of dead notes in between which she learned to conceal. Anyone who has kept track of my reviews knows the same criticism has been made about me. There are so many other similarities in our lives that sometimes I believe I am Malibran reincarnated. She moved from Paris to Naples at age three, alternated among three languages, and always felt rootless and that she never really belonged to any country. She, too, was totally dedicated to the theatre and had no life outside of it. Besides her

talent, she had great courage and will power, which were at odds with her
delicate constitution. Like mine, her portrayals were passionate and un-
restrained and provoked sensations in her audiences ranging from terror to
sublimity. But strangest of all, she married a decent, middle-aged business-
man exactly *twenty-eight years older than she*, whom she loved in a friendly
but not erotic fashion. Isn't that uncanny? And to make the comparison even
more incredible, she eventually left him and fell passionately in love with
another man. She was famous for many of the roles I do best, including
Norma, Amina, and Leonore in *Fidelio*. My voice has often been likened to
hers, and it pleases me so much that I remember every word I have ever
heard or read comparing us.

Once, when I was learning *Aida*, I didn't like the lengthy recitative "Oh
patria mia" and puzzled a great deal over how to sing it in a way that didn't
bore me. That night I dreamed Malibran came to me holding a candle and
dressed in a gauzy white ankle-length dress with long sleeves. She had a
look on her face of gentle compassion and understanding. She put her hand
on my forehead and said, "Maria, think of Greece when you sing 'Oh patria
mia.'" I leapt out of bed and ran to the piano, knowing she was right. I never
had a problem with the aria again.

In January 1950 I sang *Norma* under Antonino Votto at La Fenice in
Venice. The tenor Giacomo Lauri-Volpi, one of the most respected commen-
tators on the opera, wrote in *A Viso Aperto*, "All those people who were
amazed the work had also been performed by Malibran should have heard
Maria Callas ..." And the critic Terdoro Calli emphasized in *Oggi* that Maria
Callas had resurrected the art of Malibran in giving life to the style of the
ottocento. Their words made me feel proud and happy.

In the last act of *I Puritani* Malibran is said to have filled the auditorium
with cries of emotional derangement, unheard of on the stage of her time—
or in ours either before me, I might add. Critics said her portrayal of Amina
in *La Sonnambula* possessed a "vehemence too nearly trenched on frenzy to
be true," and if you will excuse my lack of humility, such inspired cries of
rapture and terror accompanied my performances too.

It has been said I carry on where the singing of Malibran left off because
I, too, sing my roles as if I never had heard the words or music before. Like
her, I never copy other singers, but interpret the score through the use of the
composer's and my own imagination. After my radio broadcast of Elvira in
1949, Nazzareno de Angelis, one of the most outstanding bass voices in
Italy, sent a telegram saying, "After this radio program I dare to predict the
spirit of Maria Malibran will rise again in Maria Callas." I was ecstatic for
days after I read it, too happy to dwell on my usual post-performance post-

mortems. It is so good to have someone you want to be like. Believing I am like Malibran, I don't feel so confused about who I am.

Malibran was thrown from her horse in April of 1836 but concealed her injuries and insisted on singing in the Manchester Festival in September of that year. She was a plucky woman, with the kind of spirit I adore. She died from her injuries shortly thereafter. Especially tragic to me is that she had just ended her brief marriage to the elderly Francois Malibran and married the Belgian violinist De Beriot when she passed away. It seems great singing and success in love are mutually exclusive for the greatest among us.

I have said every girl needs to follow in the footsteps of another woman, but there was no one alive I felt able to model myself after. Surely not my mother or my sister; they were light years away from the person I wanted to be. My teacher, Elvira De Hidalgo, served this purpose for a while, but I went far beyond her a long time ago. My future was a blank page because no one I knew had ever lived the way I wanted to. There were no rules for me to follow, except those of a determined heart. Is it surprising that many of my colleagues didn't like me? I had to find my own way to success, and often it wasn't pretty. The solitary pilgrimage to the top of Mount Olympus has been a bleak and barren crusade.

Unfortunately, Malibran died at the age of twenty-eight, ending her career of only eleven years. We'll never know what she would have been like at age thirty, forty, or fifty. I'll never know how the great diva would have aged. Would her voice, unlike mine, have held out? If not, could she have lived with its loss? When would she have retired? Or would she have continued to sing until she died? Would her marriage have remained a happy one? I'll never know, so I am in the dark about what I should be like as I reach the milestones of middle age. I often imagine what further heights she would have scaled had she lived another decade or two. Opera might be quite different today. I suspect my professional life might have been easier, as she would have carved out some of my path before me. For however opera might have developed under her influence, I am sure it would have been closer to the kind I envision, and my career would not have been a constant struggle to bring about my ideals.

Once, on a plane between New York and Milan, I stopped in Brussels for a quick visit to pay homage at Maliban's gravesite. All seemed sanctified and still as I communed at the side of the majestic singer's grave. I was in the presence of the remains of my great forebear, and I drank in the awesome stillness to take out again on sleepless nights when I feel especially alone. I left the cemetery with a quiet center inside of me I had never known before. To my surprise, my eyes were streaming with tears.

The Greek Years
Part 1

WHEN I WAS THIRTEEN YEARS OLD and just graduating from elementary school, my mother yanked me out of school to take me and Jackie to Greece. She never asked if I wanted to go, but went ahead and made the plans as if I were a carved piece on a chess board. My sister and I needed musical training, she said, and my father couldn't afford to pay for it. Teachers were cheaper in Greece, and besides, her relatives with musical connections would help us out financially.

What finalized Liska's decision was a dream in which her father, the singer, came to her in the night. He looked much larger than she remembered and took up most of the room on the whitewashed porch where he sang Verdi to his family and friends. Also, his beard seemed to have grown thicker and more luxurious. In a mighty voice he proclaimed, "Leave New York, Liska. Take Maria to Greece. I am the patriarch of this family. I have always known what is best for you, and I say that is what you do now." There was no way Liska wouldn't listen to her father. Especially when he said what she wanted to hear.

I did my work well in school, got good grades, and liked my teacher, Miss Sugar, a lot. She was a kind lady and told my mother I was a hard worker and a pleasant, well-behaved girl. Nevertheless, I hated school. The children were mean to me and laughed at my fat, myopic, pimply face behind my back. No one asked me for dates after school, even if Mother would have let me go. Lunchtime was a nightmare. The children ignored me completely and talked right past me or across me as if I didn't exist. I ate alone in the crowded lunchroom, watching the other children laughing and whooping it up. It was hard to hold back the tears. Those were the only times in my life I couldn't wait to finish eating. I would gulp down the bread, macaronada, and cake Liska had packed for me, while the others ate baloney or peanut butter and jelly sandwiches, and rush off to the girls' room so no one would see me eating alone. I spent the rest of the lunch period crying and squeezing out my pustules in the toilet stall until they drew blood that edged my fingernails.

One Valentine's day, all the children were sending valentines to each other. I proudly addressed one to each child in the class. There were thirty-two of them, thirty-three counting me. One by one, the teacher called out the names of all the students to hand them their valentines. I waited, holding my breath, to the end of the roll call before I stopped hoping, but she never called my name. I was the only one in the class who got no valentines at all. It brings tears to my eyes even now when I think of it. Grace Demetriades asked, "How many valentines did you get?" I answered, "Three."

I have to laugh when I remember Edward R. Murrow's interview with me, in which he asked if I had a pleasant time in school. "Oh yes," I answered with a fake smile, "it was a pleasant, carefree time." I lied, of course. It was a sad, miserable time. To live is to suffer, and whoever tells children this is not so is dishonest—cruel. . . . If you live, you struggle from the time you are born to the time you die. It is the same for everybody. What matters are the weapons you have and the weapons used against you. If yours are strong enough to combat your enemies then perhaps you can get the best of fate.

When I sang in *The Mikado* at school, I knew I had found my weapon. The children applauded and complimented me and for a short time I was popular. But it was too late. I was too hurt and angry to accept their favor. I refused all invitations. "Sorry," I said, "I'm too busy studying opera to have time for superficial dates." When I got home, I looked deep into my eyes in our little steamed-up bathroom mirror and promised myself, "Maria, some day you will become the most famous singer in the world, the most celebrated, the most envied. Then they will be sorry!"

So except for not being consulted, I didn't mind leaving the United States. There wasn't much to leave behind. Despite my resentment at being pushed to be a singer, I really loved music. It was my whole life, and I thought about it every minute. I was delighted about studying in Greece and looked forward to seeing the beautiful land Liska had talked so much about.

I have only one regret at having left school at thirteen. When I graduated from the eighth grade, it was the last formal schooling I was ever to have. It is true I am multi-lingual and speak four languages like a native. And of course, I know music from the bottom up. I also learned a little history from my experiences in the war, as well as what one absorbs while studying roles of times past. And I picked up a little geography from performing all over the world. But I do not feel I am an educated women.

I rarely tell anyone this, but when friends and acquaintances speak of literature, they might as well be talking Sanskrit as far as I'm concerned. I just can't get interested in reading books. I have neither the patience nor the desire. When I was a young girl Mother took me to the library and tried to get me to read the works of Dostoyevsky, Tolstoy, and Victor Hugo that she had never read herself. But she could never tear me away from the shelf of opera records. I would spend hours listening to the records, and for ten cents each would borrow at least two at a time to take home and study. The energy for reading books all seems to go into working on my scores.

Maybe it's because my eyes are so bad and my ears so good that my knowledge about books is limited to magazines like *Vanity Fair* and *Readers' Digest*. I don't have to tell you how inferior it makes me feel when I am the only one at a cocktail party who is ignorant of the works of Shakespeare, except of course for Gounod's *Romeo et Juliette*, and Verdi's *Macbeth*. I would give anything to know as much about his works as some of my friends. But I disguise my ignorance fairly well: I either change the subject or dash off and talk to other people. I do like TV, but I'm afraid my impatience limits what I absorb there, too. I keep changing the channels so fast I couldn't learn anything even if there were something I wanted to watch.

My father had mixed feelings about our leaving the country. As I've said, Liska always acted as if he were not in the room when questions of our welfare came up, and he sank more and more into the woodwork. He never gave us guidance or advice as a father should. Mother treated him so badly he must have been relieved to get her off his back.

And me? I love my father. But I didn't miss him when I got to Greece, at least not in the beginning. I was so excited by the new life ahead of me I didn't give him much thought. But sometimes in the still of the night when I was trying to fall asleep, I was flooded with feelings of longing for him. I smile when I remember the expression of pride on his face when I caught him sneaking a quick look at me. In spite of his not talking to me, I always felt he loved me. I guess you can forgive a parent anything when you feel loved.

He always seemed the perfect gentleman. He had two neat suits, one brown, one navy blue. He wore them interchangeably over a fresh white shirt, with silver cuff links shaped like the head of Neptune. His elegant cane and dark handsome face with an Adolph Menjou mustache gave him a dapper look that I loved. I warmed inside at the thought of his gentle touch, scarcely a flutter, and his tiny smile that you could hardly see unless you were right up close. Then I would yearn to be with him and cry myself to

sleep. But in the morning I would forget all about him. I suppose if I had
known that eight years and a war would keep us apart, I would have felt
even worse about our separation.

A few days after graduation, my mother and I, loaded with canaries,
parcels, paper bags, and suitcases, struggled up the gangplank of the Italian
liner, *Saturnia*.

Jackie had been sent on ahead to get things ready for us. I missed her and
couldn't wait to see her again. Once on the boat I dreamed about her. She
looked lovely in a pink dotted swiss dress with rows of ruffles all around the
skirt. I pushed her face in.

I spent the first few days on the boat listening to the canaries singing and
chirping between the times I was throwing up. I've always loved the ocean
and this was my first sea voyage. Pretty soon I felt better and went round the
boat singing merrily, drinking in the crystal blue sky, the rolling waters, and
the fresh ocean smell. I was leaning up against the rail loudly singing "Ave
Maria" out over the waves when the captain passed by. He must have liked
what he heard, for he said, "Very beautiful, young lady. Will you sing it
again in church on Sunday?"

I have a personal approach to religion. Even as late as my last performance, I walked into the nearest Greek Orthodox Church, right foot first,
and lit a candle in front of the Madonna. I crossed myself Greek style, from
forehead to belly button, right to left, before every performance. But for
some reason I do not feel orthodox religion is exactly right for me and am
not a regular churchgoer. I am too much of an individualist to swallow any
philosophy whole, religious or otherwise. I am a mystical person, and in
part combine my beliefs with Greek mythology.

Also, if the truth be known, I suddenly felt shy on the ship and didn't
feel like singing in a strange church. So without giving it any thought I
refused the captain's request. But he didn't give up so easily, and a few
minutes later asked me to sing at a party he was giving for the officers and
crew and two Italian contessas from first class. I was flattered and even
though I was nervous, couldn't turn down the invitation.

When I sat down at the piano to accompany myself, I forgot all about my
fears and felt thrilled to be among such illustrious company. I had taken off
my glasses and felt pretty for a change, in my dark blue cotton dress with
a white collar. My pimples were covered with powder and my black hair
curled on my shoulders, with my bangs carefully combed on my forehead.
I remember thinking with a flush of pleasure, "Of all the places in the world,
this is where I most want to be." I sang my two favorites, "La Paloma" and

"Ave Maria," and finished off with the Habanera from *Carmen*. As you remember, she sings, "Et si je t'aime, prends garde à toi," and throws the flower in her hair to Don Jose. Well, something swelled up inside me and took me over. It was as if I became a vessel for some mysterious force that occupied me and directed my actions. At that moment, I knew who I was: I was Carmen and Carmen was me. There were no boundaries between us. This was to happen over and over again in my life as a singer, and resulted in my best performances and greatest happiness on the stage.

It was while I was singing for the captain on the boat that I first experienced such a thrill. I spontaneously pulled a carnation from a vase near the piano and tossed it to him. The audience applauded like mad, and the captain was so delighted he gave me a bouquet of flowers and an Italian doll. Imagine, a doll, when I thought I was being so sexy! I never even liked dolls when I was a child. But I loved it anyway because it reminded me of my triumph. I named her "Lovey Two" and packed her away in my suitcase. I kept her with me all the time I was in Greece.

The *Saturnia* docked at Patras and we took a long train ride from Patras to Athens. I loved everything about that trip as we roared through the land of blooming orange trees. With nose pressed against the small, dirty window, I savored the hills with their olive trees and the peasants riding their donkeys on the hillside, and devoured stuffed vine leaves and overcooked lamb in the dining car. I was thrilled to be on Greek soil at last. "I am a Greek," I shouted to the rushing air, my long hair blowing in the wind, as I stood outside astride two cars. "I am as Greek as the first stone Pyrra threw behind her from which sprang the Hellenic race. My blood is pure Greek. . . . I *am* a Greek." I knew I was a citizen of the United States where I was born, but it seemed all the years in America had passed me by and I had returned to the homeland of my heart.

It's a good thing I enjoyed the train ride, because it was the last Liska allowed me to relax for a long time. It was nightfall before we arrived in Athens. We were met at the station by a bewildering throng of relatives, including my mother's three sisters, her three brothers, and Jackie. My grandmother was sick in bed in her large baroque house behind the Acropolis where we were to spend the next month before we could move into our own home. Uncles and aunts, cousins, neighbors, friends, strangers, and colleagues all were corraled in the huge kitchen and forced to hear about thirteen-year-old Maria's talents and achievements, the prizes I had won, the audiences I had dazzled, the career Liska was planning to establish for me. Or perhaps I should say, for her. I was made to perform on demand for anyone she could persuade to listen. Every time I think of what she put me through I get that same pulling in my head, with muffled wadding around my brains. I got so sick of her ravings I never wanted to sing on demand again.

We had come to Greece because my mother believed her family would help me get a start. To her bitter disappointment, they were not impressed with my singing. Many of them were musical, as my grandfather had been, and various members played instruments and also had beautiful voices, so they were not carried away by the talents of a fat thirteen-year-old girl. I was too fed up to be interested in what they thought and only wanted to be left alone so the cotton batting in my head would melt.

A month after we arrived, we moved to a large, airy top floor apartment at Patission 61, with a balcony and six rooms. I thought it was much more elegant than our Washington Heights apartment. The living room was all decorated in blue, with a blue silk grosgrain couch and small blue rugs on the floor. What a coincidence that the living room of my Paris apartment is also decorated in blue!

But best of all, I had my own room, although I must say I missed having Jackie there to fight with. We even had a maid's room at the back of the apartment, where we kept the canaries. It was called "The Canary Room."

Uncle Efthimios was the only one in the family interested in my career. He arranged for me to have an audition with Maria Trivella, a woman who had never been a great success as a singer and was teaching at the National Conservatory in Athens. I was so nervous my teeth didn't stop chattering until I began to sing. Before I sing I know nothing, don't remember the part, don't know where to start. It is pure panic, not knowing one thing before you go on stage. But once I start singing, all the fear disappears and I get lost in the music.

I don't remember how or what I sang, but it must have impressed her, for when I finished she bellowed, "This is talent!" She promptly took me on as a student of music and French and helped me get a scholarship from the conservatory. The cutoff age of admission was sixteen, but she and Liska lied and said I was sixteen, not thirteen. I was so big and fat the conservatory had no difficulty believing them. I was still bewildered by all that was happening, but somewhere inside I always knew I had true ability and wasn't really surprised.

Nevertheless, the unloved little girl in me needed the constant reassurance that I was doing well. Trivella gave it to me. She believed from the beginning that I had the potential of greatness and reflected it back to me, "You will be a great singer some day, Maria, and I am proud of you." That always made me cry, because nobody before had ever said they were proud of me but only criticized me when I didn't do my best. Trivella made me feel good about myself and I loved her for it. She was the kind of mother I should have had, kind, sensitive to my needs, encouraging, and loving.

We worked long hours together, often eating lunch in her studio. Because I had Trivella to believe in me, Liska became less important and her constant criticism not as hurtful. My mother seemed to approve of something I was doing for a change; at least she held her tongue about it. She liked that I was working hard at becoming a singer and interfered relatively little, even though I knew she was jealous of my relationship with my teacher. I could tell by her grim mouth and the cold look around her eyes when I mentioned Trivella's name. But in spite of that she tried to be helpful. When I ate at home, she brought meals to my room, where I went on studying and practicing with my plate in my lap. All my energies were poured into my career. I had no social life and no friends, but I didn't mind much because I was doing exactly what I wanted. I was determined to be a great diva, and working hard was the only way I knew to do it. I studied with Trivella for two years, and began the magic transformation from a confused novice singer to a professional opera star.

This fruitful period ended just before I reached my fifteenth birthday, when I made my stage debut as Santuzza in a student production of *Cavaleria Rusticana* at the conservatory. I had worked night and day on my role and was hell bent on winning first prize in opera at the conservatory. I knew the awarding of the prize depended entirely on my performance in *Cavaleria*. Coming in first was so important to me that I told Trivella that if I didn't win I was going to give up singing. She said she knew beyond doubt I would win. And indeed, I did, partly because she had given me the confidence to do my best. I will always be grateful to her for it. Nevertheless, my victory marked the end of a glorious period in my life and hers. Sometimes I feel bad about that, but I needed to become a great singer, so what else could I do?

Elvira de Hidalgo had recently come to Greece from Spain to join the staff of the Odeon Athenon, Athen's leading conservatory. Liska, with her ear doggedly pressed to the musical grapevine, had heard of de Hidalgo's arrival and was determined to have me audition for her. I was terrified, for to me de Hidalgo was a dream figure who had sung successfully at the Met, Covent Garden, and La Scala. How could such a great star possibly be interested in a pimply, fat teenager from Washington Heights?

I pulled myself together long enough to sing Carl Maria von Weber's "Ocean! Thou Mighty Monster." As I said before, the aria always reminds me of Mother, with all the might and power she wields, along with her magnetic pull. In a thrilling vocal climax the aria covers in rapid succession the whole gauntlet of emotions from despair to triumph. It wasn't hard for me to get engrossed in the feelings the song inspired. I let the music take over until I lost all sense of where I was or who was listening to me. When I sang "It is a boat . . . My husband! My love! We are sav'd, we are sav'd, we are sav'd! sav'd! Hunon! We are saved!" I felt a deluge of sounds lift me off the ground and carry me up to the heavens.

Sometimes I think it is a good thing I have little sense of an identity of my own. What makes me weak as a person makes me strong as an artist. When I am working well I get so into the soul of the characters I play that nothing else remains of me. Perhaps it is this ability that most distinguishes me from other singers.

I wasn't aware of it at the time I was auditioning for de Hidalgo or I would have died, but I was right when I thought she wouldn't be interested in someone with a horrible figure like mine. She said later she kept staring at the fat, pimply creature wearing thick glasses, looking down at her shabby sandals, and biting her nails. She thought the very idea of me as a singer was laughable.

"But," de Hidalgo told me later, "a few moments after you began to sing I closed my eyes and was overcome with violent cascades of sound, full of drama and emotion." It's funny, but she was feeling exactly the way I did while I was singing. I wonder if everybody does, when I sing well. My heart fluttered with joy when she said she had been waiting for my voice for a long time, and her head had filled with visions of what my voice and I could become. She immediately arranged for me to be given a tuition-free scholarship as her personal student at Athens' leading conservatory.

Elvira de Hidalgo became my life. I adored her and lived for the time we spent together. She was my mentor, my teacher, my best friend, my confidant, my mother. She was my fairy godmother. For the five years I studied with her I knew who I was: I was Elvira de Hidalgo's pupil. Sometimes I used to daydream that a prankster angel had switched me at birth and Elvira was really my mother. She says I am her spiritual child, the daughter she always wanted. So I guess my fantasy was not so farfetched as it seems.

Liska became the wicked stepmother in my mind, so I went home as little as possible. Since I was getting the training she wanted for me, I guess she was afraid to protest too much, only now and then about the hours I spent away from home. But she was terribly jealous of de Hidalgo and got revenge on her in her book, where she says Trivella, not de Hidalgo, was my most important teacher. That's just Liska's customary spitefulness. As usual, she doesn't know what she's talking about.

For a poor love-starved girl with ambitions, Elvira was a dream come true. I remember being afraid to go to sleep at night, for fear I would wake up in the morning and find it was all a dream. She set me on the path to fame and fortune and gave me the sense of my own self-worth I had never gotten as a child. For the first time in my life, I was truly happy. I could say to myself, "Mother was wrong to reject me or Elvira wouldn't love me and believe in me."

"This is what I was born for," I said to her once. "I know what you mean," she responded. "You are my dream come true, too."

From the first class with her, I arrived at the studio at 10 o'clock. I didn't realize what I had been missing all my life until I saw Elvira's face light up every time I arrived. My mother's pinched face was always glowering at me. She didn't enjoy me; Elvira did. It was hard to believe somebody got pleasure just from seeing me. No wonder I didn't want to leave her apartment until eight o'clock at night. I didn't want to go home any earlier because I felt I *was* home at Elvira's.

We worked as hard as I ever worked in my life. Through her I began to discover undreamed of possibilities in my voice. It formerly was so narrow that many of the teachers at the conservatory thought I was a mezzo soprano. Elvira helped me develop my high notes and discover my low chest tones. I was like an athlete in training who develops muscles he didn't know he had. She taught me voice and theatre technique and then would delight me for hours with stories of her work with Caruso and Chaliapin. I had entered the enchanted world I'd day dreamed about since I was a child, and it became my spiritual home.

I remember the exact moment I knew I was a singer because I wanted to be, not because Mother had made me. I was singing "Vissi d'arte," as Elvira accompanied me on the piano. I stood looking out the window at the celestial blue of the Greek sky and was overcome by a feeling of rapture. I thought, "I love Elvira. At last I'm where I belong. Of all the moments of my life, this one is the most me." After that I never again fretted that I was singing because Liska wanted me to. I *knew* I wanted to be a singer.

Elvira was also a true mother to me in a personal sense. She taught me how to dress, how to walk on stage, and, what I later became famous for, how to move and stand tall inside myself at the same time. She was also the first to help me express music through my hands, "Those wonderful, eloquent hands," more than one reviewer said of them later. My love for her brought me an inner stillness that became my core.

Perhaps her greatest gift was to teach me the repertoire of the majestic, tragic heroines in opera, Norma, Elvira, Gioconda. With de Hidalgo, I learned the scores of many operas by heart long before I was ready to sing them on stage. She introduced me to the work of Rossini, Bellini, Donizetti, and Verdi, and instructed me in bel canto, which she defined as "the development of a specific training of the voice for making full use of it as a player of the violin or the flute is trained to make full use of his instrument." The works of the great composers of opera were written to demonstrate the glory of the human voice, the most beautiful, expressive musical instrument of all. De Hidalgo's relentless technical training was the groundwork for the artistry that was to mark my entire career. Without it, I never would have been able to sing the difficult roles I mastered within a few days later in my career.

Thank you, Elvira, spiritual mother and dearest of friends. I will always love you and be indebted to you for taking in a stray kitten and making a tiger of her.

When I was seventeen years old, I was thrilled to be given my first professional role, that of *Tosca* at the Royal Theatre. Seventeen years old and already a prima donna! Clumsy as I was, I twirled from room to room until I got so dizzy I had to stop. Then I laughed hysterically until de Hidalgo slapped my face. I still treasure the memory.

But unfortunately, the illusion of being a beautiful young woman wooed by a handsome young man was marred for me by the appearance of my Mario, Antonis Thellantas, a wonderful singer who was grotesquely fat. Can you picture me, no sylph myself, making love with a huge tub of lard before a grand audience? I can't imagine why they didn't laugh out loud. We must have looked like a couple of copulating whales. But no, the audience seemed to close their eyes to our appearance and enjoy the opera.

In the opera Mario Cavaradossi, an artist, has painted a blond Madonna in an old churchyard. He is deeply in love with black-haired, black-eyed Tosca, who he is afraid will be jealous of his Madonna. He knows his Tosca!

In the complicated ways of grand opera, Mario hides Angelotti, an escaped political prisoner, in the chapel, where he expects to flee in his sister's clothing.

Tosca arrives, sees the painting, and grouches, "She is far too lovely . . . Let her eyes be black!" Now some people are jealous types and some are not. Unfortunately, I belong in the first category, and am often tortured by its piercing pangs. I felt that part so genuinely that every time I looked at the portrait of the Madonna I experienced a stab in my heart. When Mario swears none but Tosca's eyes can charm him, she leaves reassured for the moment. Then he helps Angelotti to escape.

The treacherous chief of police, Scarpia, arrives in search of Angelotti. He discovers a dropped fan and suspects Mario had something to do with the prisoner's escape.

When Tosca returns, Scarpia makes a play for her. She is uninterested in his advances until he diabolically shows her the fan. This reawakens her jealous rage. "In my grief, here I languish, while Mario betrays me in her arms!" she sings.

Meanwhile Mario has been captured as a partisan of the republic and taken to the torture chamber to force him to reveal the whereabouts of Angelotti. The evil Scarpia sends Tosca a note saying he has news of Mario. When she arrives, Mario is bound hand and foot in the adjoining apartment, where an iron hook is twisted into his temples to make the blood spurt out all over him. Nevertheless he refuses to disclose his friend's hiding place. Tosca is unable to endure Mario's screams and blurts out that Angelotti is in a well in the garden.

Scarpia finds Tosca's tears get him strangely excited, so her hostility only heightens his wish to possess her. "Hatred and love," he shrewdly sings, "are never far apart!" He doesn't give a fig whether she detests him. "What does it matter," he asks, "spasms of rage or spasms of passion?" Ah, men! In what distant planet were they spawned?

Scarpia bargains with Tosca that he will spare Mario's life if only she will be his. Although she loathes him, she reluctantly agrees. No man has ever forced me to have sex with him, so I don't know how I would react if I were Tosca. But knowing how I get lost in the one I love, I can imagine behaving just as she did, with the same conflict, nervousness, submission, and rage. And yes, I can see myself killing Scarpia! I don't take well to being forced to do anything, let alone have sex. Come to think of it, I guess I played the situation exactly the way I would handle it in real life.

Scarpia tells her there will have to be a mock execution of Mario to make his escape possible, and writes a safe-conduct pass to enable them to leave Rome. While he is writing, Tosca surreptitiously seizes a knife on the table. He comes to embrace her and she stabs him full in the chest. Good for her! "This is the kiss of Tosca!" she sings out fiercely. "He is dead. Now I forgive him!"

After the mock execution is over, Tosca runs down to Mario. "Up, Mario. Quickly. Come, come quickly," she happily sings. She raises his cloak and screams in horror as she sees the execution was a real one and Mario is dead. I cry every time I listen to a recording of it.

When soldiers rush in to take Tosca prisoner, she breaks away from them and leaps to her death from the parapet, exclaiming, "Oh Scarpia, we meet before God!"

We ended the opera with explosive applause. I didn't receive a standing ovation, and it was not the reception of my dreams, but it was a very nice performance for a beginning young singer. Little did I know that, except for another Tosca at the Opera, and a German production of the nondescript opera *Tiefland*, it was to be my last major appearance for a long time, due to the turmoil of world events.

Part 2

While I was becoming more and more absorbed in my work with de Hidalgo, Greece was preparing for war. On October 28, 1940, war broke out between Italy and Greece. When Salonika in Northern Greece was bombed in April, 1941, even I could no longer deny that we were at war. On April 27, the most feared event in the minds of Greeks took place: The Germans occupied Athens, beginning a rule of oppression that was to leave its mark on me forever. I was determined not to let my fear of the bombs or of the Nazis interfere with my destiny, and continued my daily lessons with de Hidalgo, often hiding from German soldiers in almost deserted streets and picking my way over bodies lying in the gutter to get to her. Fortunately Athens was not bombed, but when bombs fell on the nearby port of Piraeus, the sirens shrieked in our ears and forced us to stay in the air raid shelter in our basement. Once I was safely hidden in the shelter, I always got violently ill and couldn't stop throwing up. Believe me, that didn't endear me to the others in the shelter.

Like a broken clock, everything stopped in the city of Athens. Stores, schools, and institutions were shut down. When I had to venture out into the streets, I saw only enemy soldiers and the bodies of the people who had starved to death and lay in the streets where they fell.

Getting enough to eat was one of our biggest problems. My father was no longer able to send money because of the war, and even if he had, there was little food to buy. What there was had to be rationed, and black markets sprang up all over the area. Most of them were up in the mountains, and my mother, sister, and I had to take long, exhausting walks in order to survive. We came home struggling with fruits, vegetables, and whatever sustenance we were lucky enough to find.

Everything changed overnight, the food we ate, where we slept, the state of my clothing, the look of my adopted country, my singing lessons. It was the worst thing that could have happened to a girl as insecure as I was.

Fortunately, the most important part of me remained intact: my voice. It was the main tool that enabled us to survive. It brought us food, friends, and protection. One Italian soldier heard me singing from the street. He waited until I came outside and with tears in his eyes talked of memories of home my singing brought back to him. He rewarded me with food from his rations. I was so famished that after he left I ducked into the nearest doorway, tore open the package, and gulped down its contents. My mother was upset that I never brought much home, but I was too starved to care.

Another friend my voice made was Colonel Mario Bovalti, a friendly Veronese officer who began calling on me and accompanying me on the piano. He always brought little gifts and shared his rations with us.

One day my voice saved our lives. A Greek friend of the family had brought two escaped British officers, a dark-haired Scotsman and a fair-haired Englishman, to stay with us. The penalty for aiding and abetting fugitives was death. After our friend had taken the men away, Italian soldiers came to search the house with drawn revolvers. I knew the British officers had left photos and letters behind, so I ran to the piano and started loudly singing *Tosca*, the part where she is pleading to save her lover's life. The soldiers forgot all about searching the house and gathered around the piano to listen. I probably never sang the aria better, for it was our lives I was singing to save.

Without my musical talent, I would be dead. It was my ability to survive through the use of my voice that consolidated my image of myself as a singer.

Much as I adored and looked up to de Hidalgo, the lush and fruitful time with her became a casualty of the war. But a promising turn of events brought a rush of hope to embattled Greeks.

When the Allies landed in Normandy on June 6, 1944, the end of the war was clearly in sight, and on October 12, Athens and the port of Piraeus were liberated by the Greek resistance troops. My first important new triumph came shortly before that in Beethoven's *Fidelio*, when the Italians took over the amphitheatre Herodes Atticus in Athens. It was a great stroke of luck for me that the soprano who had been hired to sing the role of Lenore was not able to learn it in time. I, always ready to step in, was cast as Leonore. I sang it in German under the German conductor Hans Horner. The theatre was jammed with joyous Athenians as well as occupying soldiers who knew the hour of liberation could not be far away. I sang the majestic finale, "Oh Nemenlose Freunde," with an exaltation that carried me and the audience to a pinnacle of rapture.

I know it is treasonous to say so, but the opera under the Germans was organized as it had never been before. It had been a disaster when run by the Greeks. The production of *Fidelio* surpassed any I had ever appeared in.

Leonore is known as an unsingable part, full of technical musical difficulties which demanded the most I was capable of giving. Besides the vocal challenges, Leonore dresses as a man. Fidelio must act the role so convincingly that the jailer's daughter Marzelline falls madly in love with her. I must say this aspect of the part embarrassed me at first because I cannot picture myself as a man, but I soon got so lost in the music that I played the male part as easily as the female. "After all, Maria," I consoled myself, "it is only an opera and not real life!" But as I got into the deeper aspects of the character, I realized why Beethoven had wanted to call the opera *Lenore* and not *Fidelio*. I think he didn't see the transsexual aspects of the part as primary. He meant to communicate the real woman underneath the masculine apparel, the heroic Lenore who dressed in male clothes to save her husband's life. After I realized that, I found myself enjoying dressing up like a man.

In the opera, the minister Don Florestan is thrown into a dungeon by his political enemy, Don Pizarro, the governor of the prison. Pizarro plans to allow his prisoner to die by starvation. He circulates the rumor that Florestan is dead, but his faithful wife, Leonore, does not believe it. Good for her! I wouldn't either. She disguises herself as the boy Fidelio and enters the service of Rocco, the jailer. There she discovers her intuition was right and her husband is not dead, but about to be starved to death. Leonore even agrees to marry the girl Marzelline, in order to stay near her husband. Word comes that Don Fernando, the minister of state, is arriving to inspect the prison. Don Pizarro decides to have Don Florestan murdered at once.

Fidelio gets permission for the prisoners to come outside for a little fresh air. They are taken half-blinded from the dungeon and brought out into the glaring sunlight. As they stagger into the brightness, they sing the incredibly moving "Ode to Freedom": "O, what joy in Heaven's fresh air." The prisoners' chorus is one of the greatest moments in opera, as magnificent in its way as the "Ode to Joy" in Beethoven's Ninth Symphony.

Back in the dungeon, Pizarro is about to kill Florestan himself when Fidelio hurls herself between them. With a pistol she menaces the cowardly governor, who retreats. And in a magnificent duet, Florestan and Fidelio, clasped in each other's arms, sing out their happiness.

It was August 14, 1944. The end of the war was approaching. Leonore sings of the ultimate victory of love over tyranny, fear, and death. When I unlocked Florestan's fetters and heard the heavenly tune of the oboe, I was flooded by a surge of pride, relief, and joy, and sang my gratitude to the Heavens above for the victory I sensed was about to come. It was one of those mystical times when I was carried out of the confines of my body to an unknown celestial realm. I must have struck a cord in the weary, starved, and exhausted audience, for they were overwhelmed along with me, and stamped and clapped and shouted and threw their hats in the air for what seemed like hours. It was a night to remember for the rest of my life.

But my triumph was also the source of a disaster. After the war was over, the Athens Opera Company decided I had "played too active a part in the last months of the occupation" and did not offer to renew my contract. It is true I had sung for Italian soldiers in audiences that included Germans and Italians, in an opera staged to please the Germans. I had even accepted food from Italian and German music lovers because my family and I were starving and we needed to survive. At the same time, I had ignored many of the enemy's rules and defied their orders. I loudly sang and played the piano by the balcony, when the Germans decreed silence. I resisted them again by walking through occupied streets to work with de Hidalgo.

I am not a collaborator in my heart. I have always hated the Germans for what they did to my people, and for the starvation, the panic, the break in my lessons with de Hidalgo the occupation brought about. But to me there is an international brotherhood of music lovers that goes beyond politics. That is who I sang for, those who love opera. This includes all those starved, lonely, homesick casualties of the war whose hearts and spirits were lifted when I sang *Fidelio*. I have a sacred mission on earth. It is to give pleasure to those who love music. If their number at times includes the enemies of our country, so be it.

I was in a rage at the Athens Opera company. I had raised the standard of their productions and brought them huge audiences, and this is how I was repaid! I vowed never to work for them again, no matter what terms they offered me. I knew the time would come when they would plead with me to return.

In October of 1944 the defeated Germans left Athens and the Greek army returned to a liberated country. All over Athens people were jubilant. They sang and danced the whole night long and threw flowers at each other in the streets. Jackie and I ran to the roof of our building and in a fit of euphoria ripped the German occupation money into tiny bits and tossed the pieces down into the street. Then we loudly shouted Greek anti-German songs to the mobs below. Little did we know that even as we celebrated our new freedom that tension was growing between ELAS, the Communist group, and the other resistance forces.

In December, fighting broke out between ELAS and its auxiliary Communist groups and the monarchists. Civil war was declared and Athens nearly fell into Communist hands. The resulting bloodshed was far worse than anything we had endured during the actual war. Thousands of people were killed, including my mother's younger brother, Filon, who was only twenty-eight years old. I think he was one of the few people Liska really loved. I felt sorry for her. Filon was a brave man who was employed by the Germans as an engineer at an air base. He became a saboteur who destroyed nine German planes by putting sugar in the gasoline. When the Communists tried to recruit him, he refused to join them, so they killed him. It was very sad, and the whole family went into mourning for a long time.

Jackie was staying with her boyfriend Milton when the fighting began, and my mother and I were imprisoned alone together in our apartment for twenty-one days. I was so terrified I was glad to have even her company. It was freezing cold, in the middle of winter, and we had no heat at all. In addition, there was no light, and after a few days, little food. We had one big box of dried beans that came to us in a carton of Red Cross rations and we ate them for every meal. I never want to see a bean again! We lived with the sound of machine guns in our ears twenty-four hours a day, along with the sirens and explosions accompanying the screams of men being murdered. Even my voice deserted me for a short while. It was the first time I could remember that I wasn't able to sing or even to study. I am extremely sensitive to sound, and I spent much of my time with my hands over my ears trying not to scream. When the sirens and the blasting stopped, I was in a rage at the Communists for interrupting my career.

Just as we got to the bottom of the box of beans, my voice rescued us again. A little boy delivered a letter from a music-loving British officer, inviting us to come to the British Embassy. If you have never seen a civil war, you cannot imagine the devastation. Whole towns and villages were demolished and people dead of starvation were decaying in the streets. The bodies were covered with maggots, and it was not unusual to see a rat feasting on a corpse. The stench was abominable, and I could not walk through the streets without holding a handkerchief to my mouth to keep from gagging. I still have nightmares in which the rats come back to haunt me. I always wake up before they start crunching on *me*.

One story in particular sticks in my mind as typical of the cruelty of the times. It seems the Red Cross didn't have enough food to feed all the children in Greece. So they went into each house and selected the healthiest child in the family, the one they thought most likely to survive, and gave milk only to that child. The story makes me flinch every time I think of it. If

Jackie and I had been those starving children, I know which one would have gotten the milk and which one would have been left to die. Liska would have seen to that.

The physical and emotional devastation I suffered during that period are engraved in indelible ink in every cell of my body. From that time on I have lived with a liver ailment, and low blood pressure of ninety at best.

I was weary of hunger, death, and destruction. In fact I was weary of Greece, for the land of my heart had betrayed me. I determined to go elsewhere and establish myself there. Elvira advised me to go to Italy, where she felt a great future lay in store for me. But much as I admired and respected her, I always believe in following my own instincts, as I did with every role I sang. My intuition has never led me astray. My mother had wrenched me away from the United States without consulting me. I knew I would never be sure where I belonged until I came back to my birthplace and made my own decision. To my great delight, my father was finally able to get through to us, and sent me a letter which included a hundred dollar bill. I decided to go to America and begin life anew.

Back to America

$\mathcal{D}$ESPITE MY INITIAL EXCITEMENT at being in the land of my birth, I found New York in the dead of winter a chilly, dirty city. I thought I would never stop shivering and sneezing. I caught one cold after another and spent much of my time holed up in a winter of a bed under a dreary pile of blankets. The only person I talked to was my father when he came home at night, and I didn't even have my birds to cheer me up. I was so lonely I thought I would die. I missed my mother and Elvira with a constant ache, and for weeks did little besides trying to fix up my bedroom with a pair of lopsided orange curtains. Oh, for the olive trees and lush hills of Greece! It was hard to believe I ever felt at home in this city of frozen filth.

My chief occupation seemed to be eating. I enjoy food as well as the next person. In fact, sometimes when I am eating ice cream or food with garlic in it, it tastes so good it actually hurts my mouth. But that isn't the kind of eating I'm talking about now. I mean the kind of gorging where I crammed food down so fast I couldn't even taste it. My stomach was an enormous open hole, a raw cavity, a crater. Whatever the hour, I kept stuffing one mouthful after another down into it. I was okay as long as food was in my mouth, but the instant I swallowed it the gnawing in my stomach started again, and back I marched to the kitchen. I didn't stop to cook but grabbed fistfuls of raw meat, stale spaghetti, whole sticks of butter, quarts of ice cream, bags of doughnuts, raw eggs, boxes of candy, whatever I could fit my lips around. This went on until I fell asleep clutching my engorged belly. Then after three or four hours of tormented sleep, I started all over again.

It took a few weeks to control the binges enough so that I could begin my crusade into musical New York. I traipsed from office to office where no one had ever heard of me and sat for hours in grungy waiting rooms hoping third-rate agents would show up. Maria Callas shrivelled into a zero.

One pudgy little cigar smoker was reading his newspaper and didn't even bother to look up when I spoke to him. I coughed and said, "Excuse me, sir, may I talk to you?" He went right on reading his paper.

Swallowing my anger, I said, "Sir, *Sir*, I'd like to speak with you."

He looked up and rudely asked, "Who are *you*?"

"I am Maria Callas, opera singer."

"Never heard of you. What have you sung?"

"I sang Leonore in *Fidelio* at the Heroditus Theatre in Greece." He grunted and was silent.

Then I volunteered hopefully, "I studied with Elvira de Hidalgo."

"Elvira who?"

"Elvira de Hidalgo, the famous Spanish opera singer."

"It must have been in the year one. Go make a name for yourself in Italy, Maria. Then I will sign you up."

"Thank you," I answered, pulling myself up to my full five feet nine inches. "But once I have made my career in Italy I will no longer need *you*."

I waited a moment and spoke again, but he continued to ignore me. Shades of my father and his newspaper when I was a child! When it dawned on me that the man was being deliberately disrespectful, a wave of dizziness swept over me. I managed to get down the three dingy flights of stairs to the street, where the world was drowning in tears of icy February rain. Then I wandered around in a wet mackintosh for hours. It was bad enough to lose my country, my teacher, and the career I had begun, but this abominable creature had wiped me out altogether. Like my father, he had denied me my identity as a singer as well as a person.

I tried to tell myself every musician, no matter how famous, has met with setbacks. By the time Bizet was thirty-four, he had written twenty-seven operas, of which only four had been published. I'll bet anything that the failure of *Carmen* contributed to his death. After the premiere of *Madame Butterfly*, Puccini heard the newspaper vendors under his hotel window yelling, "Puccini's flop." My beloved Verdi's *La Traviata* created a terrible ruckus in the audience of the Teatro Fenice in Venice, the idiots! After *Aida*, he considered his operatic career finished for a whole decade, until he wrote *Otello* in his late seventies and *Falstaff* in his eightieth year, the crowning achievements of his old age. Good old Verdi! He showed them what was what!

But, as usual, talking to myself didn't work, and I got so sick I had to go to bed for two more weeks. One night I woke from a drugged sleep cursing the bastards, vowing, "When I become famous not one of these vile ignoramuses will make a penny off me!"

All my efforts in the eighteen months I had spent in New York came to naught, including an ill-fated audition at the Metropolitan, where I was offered nothing but criticism. I know there is a story around that I turned down the roles of *Madame Butterfly* because I was too fat and Leonore in *Fidelio* because I didn't want to sing in English. It is a lie. I made it up to rescue my damaged pride. I couldn't bear the thought that others would know how badly I had failed. But I still can't get over everyone taking me at my word. Why would any struggling young singer turn down an offer from the Met? Hitler was right about one thing; people will believe anything if it is said often enough.

My "career" never looked more dismal, and time stretched ahead with an appalling emptiness. It was as if the years of success in Greece had simply vanished. All that work and all that time for nothing! For the first time I understood why people killed themselves. . . .

Nevertheless, I continued to work on my voice from eleven o'clock in the morning until midnight, singing scales and arias, studying scores of complete operas, and practicing the piano. I was grateful that I loved to sing, and the one thread woven through my life was my lifelong crusade to understand music.

My father didn't help me feel at home in this strange land where I was born. No matter which way I turned, he managed to thwart me with his disdain. "Maria, stop bothering with that opera nonsense and come sell cosmetics with me in the pharmacy," he kept repeating. He made me long for my mother, who at least encouraged my singing. Finally, I had to admit I could no longer go it alone. I swallowed my pride and wrote her a letter pleading for her to come to America. My father was making only a small salary and I certainly wasn't earning anything, so I asked my dear godfather, Leonidas Lantzounis, to lend us the money for her passage.

Since I had been away, I had forgotten how impossible Mother could be. I was soon reminded. Christmas of 1946 was a disaster. My father had developed a relationship with Alexandra Papajohn, the woman upstairs, whom he married a few years later. This did not endear him to Liska, who slept in my bedroom from the first night on, leaving no doubt where Father stood with her. They hated each other with a passion and it made me miserable to be with them. She was nasty and he was silent, and the tension between them was even greater than it had been in my childhood. I was helpless to stop them, so I stayed away from home as much as I could.

At my father's pharmacy, I met a singing teacher named Louise Taylor. For the next few weeks I went to her every moment I could sneak away from Liska. Louise's studio was a little island of security in the eye of a hurricane, and I clung to her. It was there I had a fateful meeting with Eddie Bagarozy, a lawyer who had been dabbling in opera all his life.

Bagarozy was planning to start a new project, the "United States Opera Company." I had to ask him to repeat himself when he said, "Maria, we are going to begin a tour of *Turandot* in Chicago in January. You will play the leading role." When I finally understood, my spirits soared like the trumpets opening up at the gates of Heaven at the end of Brahms's First Symphony. "My troubles are over, Papa. At last I am getting the reward I deserve," I shouted with glee, ignoring his almost imperceptible smirk. Liska, of course, was equally delighted that all "her" work was going to pay off.

Bagarozy also arranged to bring over European artists such as Nicola Rossi-Lemini, who Eddie felt would be willing to work cheaply in the depleted post-war period. The idea of being with my old colleagues again made me sing for joy all day long.

The Chicago opening had been announced for January 6th, 1947, but kept being postponed. Finally the American Guild of Musical Artists demanded a deposit to make sure the chorus and orchestra would be paid. Of course Bagarozy didn't have the money. I thought I couldn't live through it when the company declared itself bankrupt and folded. I was right back where I had started, a non-person and a failure, but now it was even more catastrophic, for victory had been snatched away just as I was ready to grasp it. Surely hell has no greater torture than showing the damned what might have been. It was back to the blankets and the kitchen for Maria!

I should have known from this fiasco that Bagarozy was not to be trusted. But I continued to have faith in him, perhaps because there was nothing else to look forward to. Or simply because I was naive. When *I* say I will do something I do it, and it never occurs to me that not everyone is like me. In the years to come, I was to pay a thousand times over for my naivete.

But even a run of bad luck runs dry after a while. My friend Nicola went looking for other work and auditioned for Giovanni Zenatello, the famous tenor who was founder of the opera company at the Arena of Verona. As its Artistic Director, he was in New York looking for singers for *La Gioconda*, and hired Rossi-Lemini to sing Alvise. "How about Maria for the title role?" Nicola brashly asked. "Sure, have her come in tomorrow," Zenatello said.

I auditioned for Zenatello by singing "Suicidio." He was an old man, but seventy years and all, he became so excited he rushed to the piano and began to sing the passionate duet between Enzo and Gioconda. He wasn't bad either; I have sung it with much worse. Since Zinka Milanov and Herva Nelli were too expensive for his company, Zenatello was happy to sign me up at what Meneghini later called a "hangman's contract." But I was delighted to work again in any capacity where I could sing. I also wanted to get away from my parents and go to Italy, and this was the only way to do it. It had been a despairing time, a frightening time, a bewildering time, a lonely time. The good results, if any, were invisible. No wonder I wanted to leave.

Mother and I had a good time selecting a new wardrobe for me, as we both felt I should arrive in Verona with some decent clothes. Unfortunately, the money my father and godfather gave me paid for only two suits and one dress, all in dark and dreary colors. Women at the time were wearing the "new look," but on me the new fashions only looked dowdy. When I look back at pictures of me taken then, I wonder how I ever let myself wear such old lady clothes at the age of twenty-three. But considering the way I had been eating, I guess they were the only ones that fit. And of course, Liska was no help at all. She hadn't the faintest idea of how to dress.

Liska stuck a warning note in my luggage emphasizing that life is full of frustration and I shouldn't be surprised when such things happened to me. The note ended with the commandment, Honor thy father and mother. I was surprised she included my father. Just before Rossi-Lemini and I left for Verona on the *S.S. Rossia*, Bagarozy waved a ten-year contract in my face. As Nicola's and my agent he was to collect ten percent of our earnings from opera, concerts, recordings, and everything else he could think of. In return, he pledged to make every effort possible to promote our careers. His wife, Louise Caselotti, would accompany us to Verona, probably to make sure we wouldn't cheat him. Distracted as I was, I signed the contract without reading it. It was an action I was to regret as long as I lived.

On June 27, 1947, the ship dropped anchor in the Bay of Naples, and I was light-headed at the thought of beginning a new life.

Meneghini

AFTER A STIFLING TRAIN RIDE, so crowded my friends Nicola Rossi-Lemini and Louise Caselotti and I had to take turns sitting on one seat, we arrived in Verona. I was so scared I shook like a little girl on her first day of school. But I was also shaking with excitement, for I was to sing *La Gioconda* for the first time. That evening I joined Gaetano Pomari, a representative of the Verona Arena, Giuseppe Gambato, a city official, Nicola, and Giovanni Battista Meneghini, an important Verona industrialist, at the Pedavena Restaurant.

Surrounded by these prominent dignitaries I again felt like a timid child, too awestruck to say a word. I ate my dinner, though. Nothing could keep me from that.

Soon I became aware that Meneghini couldn't take his eyes off me. Why is he staring at me? I wondered. Is there tomato sauce on my face? Am I supposed to cut up the spaghetti instead of twirling it around my fork? Does he think I'm too fat to sing Gioconda? I was embarrassed and, I must admit, flattered. I was surprised that any man could be interested in dull Maria Kalogeropoulos. After all, even my father wasn't.

"Battista is our local Romeo," said Signor Pomari, after telling me Meneghini had been assigned by the festival to be my official escort. I felt another moment of panic. However should I behave with a romeo, local or otherwise? I looked up at Meneghini and he smiled. A flood of pleasure gushed into my stomach, and I knew at that moment he was the one.

I had never had a lover, and erotic needs had played no part in my life. I was too busy daydreaming about becoming a great diva. As late as two months before my marriage, when I sang Kundry in *Parsifal* in Rome, I behaved like a shy virgin. When I was supposed to kiss Beirer, the Parsifal, on the mouth, I felt ashamed to do it. Would you believe, the conductor strode up onto the stage shouting, "You women are all afraid, but I am a man and I will show you how," and he kissed Beirer straight on the mouth!

Trust me, my relationship with Meneghini was not like a Hollywood romance. But I knew right away I felt safer, less frightened, and more alive in his presence. He seemed . . . well, solid, and I liked that everyone deferred to him. I liked that he was an opera lover and believed the reports he had heard about the awesome powers of my voice. I liked that he made me feel I was a genius as well as a desirable woman. For me, who was used to being admired for my voice, if at all, and not for myself, it was a dazzling combination. He made clear with an admiring glance, a thoughtful gesture, or a kind word that he liked *me*. During dinner we arranged to see a lot of each other in the course of his official duties as escort of the latest prima donna.

He walked me back to the hotel and said a gentlemanly good-bye. I was both relieved and crestfallen. "What a Romeo," I thought. "He didn't even kiss me goodnight! He was just performing his job, and was only being polite at dinner. I'll bet he thinks I'm ugly. I must have imagined his interest in me."

The next day he took me sightseeing around Verona to the amphitheatre and ruins of two gateways, the church of Santo Zeno Maggiore, the twelfth-century cathedral, and the Castel Vecchio. I was overwhelmed with the sights, the smells, and the novelty of the ancient city, as well as with being courted by an important older man. Soon he left no doubt he was interested in *me* and not just the task of squiring the new diva around town. The Italians have a way of being seductive that is irresistible. With a look of longing in his melting brown eyes, a gallantly offered arm, a handshake that lasted a moment longer than it had to, a sensual tone in his voice, he got through even to the virginal Maria.

Nevertheless, when it came to sex I remained a child throughout the relationship. I never did find it the passionate, titillating experience written about in *True Romances*. I was like Turandot, who said to Calaf, "No man will ever possess me . . . You clasp my cold veil, but my spirit is there aloft!" Somehow I managed to float above the whole encounter by filling my mind with dreams of reaching the top of my profession. I think giving in to the glories of sex meant completely losing myself, and Heaven knows, I didn't have enough self to give any away. Sex with Battista was gentle, soothing, and pleasant, and I even enjoyed it sometimes. But I wasn't really awakened erotically until I met. . . . well, that's another story.

Meneghini also introduced me to what was to become a great delight as well as a great anguish in my life, shopping. But I felt sorry for the dear man. To put it kindly, I am an indecisive shopper. My mother's thriftiness, the near poverty of my growing up years, and the extreme deprivation of the war era had made me frugal to the point of being miserly. There was no article I just picked up and bought, regardless of how much I liked it. I had to compare its quality and cost to similar articles all over town. I love a bargain, and no matter how much money I have, nothing gives me greater pleasure than an afternoon of shopping for a kitchen ware in Woolworth's. Unlike my parents, who were interested in themselves and not in me, Battista always made room for *me* and what I thought was important. Poor Titta! I'm afraid I enjoyed our lengthy shopping outings without giving his patience a thought. I can picture him nodding as he leaned upon the counter at the Five and Dime. Exasperated as he must have been, he came through the trial with flying colors.

One incident in particular shows his caring and generous spirit. During the dress rehearsal of *Gioconda*, I fell on the rocky stage of the Arena and sprained my ankle. Because I am shortsighted and did not want to wear my glasses, I didn't see an open trap door which led to the basement below the ancient amphitheatre, and I stumbled into it. I could have been killed, but fortunately there was a wooden chute down to the cellar which prevented me from cracking my head on the rocks. As it was, I survived with only a badly sprained ankle and some bruises. But I was in such pain I could hardly drag myself around the huge stage, and hobbled about while finishing the rehearsal. Titta, as I called him, insisted on sitting up all night by my bedside to take care of and comfort me, even though we were not yet married. Although it humiliated me to be so needy, I will always feel grateful to him for staying with me. He was mother, father, and surrogate husband all at once. I remember feeling that night that I would cheerfully give my life for him. If Battista had wanted me to I would even have given up my career without regret, because in a woman's life love is more important than artistic triumphs. Fortunately, he never asked that of me.

He was my devoted and loving advisor, and I knew he was entirely on my side. When I was with him I knew who I was; I was Battista's beloved woman.

He could be judgmental, too, when he thought my performance called for it. Unlike my mother, whose reproaches were like darts flying at me left and right with no time to recover between the barbs, he criticized me so gently I was able to take from him what I couldn't from anyone else.

Above all, I was comfortable with Titta. I don't think I could have lived with someone from an aristocratic background if he had considered me to be a girl from a lower class family that was beneath his. I would have been tense all the time, always afraid I would use the wrong fork or drop something that would call attention to my origins. But I wasn't afraid with my Titta and could always be myself in his presence. It was the first and only time in my life I had known unconditional love.

About the same time Titta and I became lovers, I was thrilled to begin rehearsing *Gioconda* with Tullio Serafin, one of the greatest conductors in the world. He had worked with the best singers of the day, including Rosa Ponselle. I'll never forget the first time I saw him. I had just come into Verona and stood in the Arena watching him at work in Zonatello's production. Serafin was conducting the choral scene that opens *La Gioconda*, in which a crowd is gathered in the courtyard of the ducal palace. He was a power house before them, his movements flowing like liquid gold, his face flushed with pleasure. He was involved body and soul, pointing to the singers, motioning them towards him, lifting his hands, now delicately with one finger extended, now the whole hand. Now thrusting both hands out, he pushed down on the air, now faster now slower, his body engrossed as he beat out the rhythm with his knees. Now he made an upward jerking motion of his body, now he punched the air, now gently smiling, now leaning back into the music, now reaching high to the Heavens. Then, satisfied, he relaxed and quietly said, "Thank you, people, you are remembering from the last rehearsal." I loved him immediately.

He soon became my mentor, my guide, my inspiration. He gave me the confidence to stand up for myself, to create as I saw fit and, eventually, to make my own place in operatic history. In the core of my being, he made me know I was a great diva. He brought me the greatest happiness of my career. He had an infallible sense of the potential quality of a voice when it was only in a raw state. I drank in all I could from this wonderful conductor, and pleaded for more. De Hidalgo had taught me bel canto; Serafin provided me with the opportunity to master it on stage.

He taught me there must be a justification in opera for everything you do. I learned every single embellishment must be put to the service of music, for the great composer always has a reason for everything. If you really care for the composer and not just for your own personal success, you will always find the meaning of a trill or scale that will inspire a true feeling of happiness, anxiety, or sadness in you. Maestro Serafin taught me, in effect, the depth of music. "When one wants to find a gesture or how to move on stage," he said, "all you have to do is search for it in the score; the composer has already put it into his music. And then find it within your own heart." How right he was, for if you take the trouble to listen with your whole soul and your ears—the mind must also work, but not too much— you will find everything you need right there in the music. He also taught me that opera must be a single reflex of singing and acting, and a performance is simply thousands of reflexes put together. But you can only achieve this if you have done your homework in detail. When you reach the stage, it is too late.

Communicating all you have found in a score becomes a high you can never experience any other way. At least I can't. Your wonderful drunken feeling spreads to the audience and everyone becomes ecstatic together. I have never tried drugs, but I'm sure the high one gets from them cannot compare to the exhilaration of inspired music shared by performer and public. I don't believe Heaven itself could hold any greater joy. Still, once you have finished a performance, you must look at yourself and say, "Well, this or that happened. Forget the good things and try to discover how you can improve the bad ones." That is the object of great art, to always strive upward. When you are satisfied with what you have done, there is no progress.

Superb a conductor as he was, Serafin never stopped working. I remember once I found him studying *Aida* the night before he was to conduct it.

"Serafin, you should know *Aida* by now," I said. "Why are you still looking at the music?"

He replied, "You never know a score well enough. There are things here I did not see yesterday, and today I find them." That is what music is all about; it is an everlasting search, not for power or glory but for what is deep within the notes. Thus my philosophy of life emerged from our work together, and as I got to understand the music, I also learned to find depths in myself I didn't know I had.

Serafin, like Meneghini, believed from the beginning that I was going to be a great singer, and provided the confidence that comes from the backing of a great teacher. He gave me the courage to become all he thought I could be. "That was superb, Maria," he would say about an aria in *La Gioconda*. But perhaps if you searched further," he would tactfully add, "you might find an even deeper meaning for what Ponchielli had in mind." He didn't give me the answers, but encouraged me to find them for myself within the notes and my own hidden self.

Rehearsals for *Gioconda* began in July, 1947. But my career didn't soar with this performance, even under the tutelage of the great Serafin. I was only twenty-four years old and my voice was young and strong (what I wouldn't give to have it sound like that now!) but frankly, I never felt Gioconda was one of my best roles. The plot is confusing and the characterization rather unsubtle. Therefore I only sang it twelve times. The reviews were not sensational, and I received no invitation to return to Verona.

Unfortunately, at that time I was having a great deal of trouble with my voice, which often seemed to have a thick, muffled sound, what singers call a "potato in the mouth." Hard as I tried, and long and laboriously as I practiced, the notes seemed to fall back in my mouth. My friend Nicola explained that I needed to work on my hard palate in order to place the notes forward, which would result in more resonance in my mask. The problem left me confused and frightened. After all, who was I if not a singer? But it cleared up after much effort, and I forgot all about it.

What a lucky woman I was! I had a loving man at my side who behaved like a kind and supportive husband and helped me through the practicalities of everyday living so I could concentrate on my work. And in my professional life, even though my performance in *La Gioconda* had not been the most successful in the world, I had the encouragement of one of the greatest conductors in the world, who believed in me without reservation and was teaching me what I thirsted to know. With these men behind me, everything seemed possible. There was no height, professional or emotional, I felt I couldn't reach. It was one of the few times in my life I was unreservedly happy.

But despite the attentions of these caring gentlemen, my career came to a standstill. Since Meneghini was my sponsor, I felt I could afford to be selective. Therefore I spontaneously turned down an invitation to sing *Gioconda* in Vigevano, near Milan. I felt it was a run-of-the-mill production in an unimportant town, and I was eagerly awaiting an offer from La Scala.

When you have done a few unimportant things, even though you wanted them desperately before, they begin to lose their value. You begin to wonder, "Will I be any further along in twenty-five years if I sing *Gioconda* in Vigevano now?" But to my great disappointment, no offer from La Scala came through. The assistant director listened to me sing and muttered something about vocal defects, and I went home to Meneghini.

My mood took a downhill dive, and I couldn't help wondering if I had been premature as well as arrogant in turning down the Vigevano offer. It is always hard for me to sit around, so I went to Milan and made the rounds of agents' offices again. Have you ever made those dreary rounds, dragging yourself around day after day to disinterested, often rude, petty businessmen? It was almost as humiliating as my experiences in New York. It was as if Verona had never happened. I sank inside myself like a chicken with her head under her wing, and sat chewing my nails in Milan waiting for the phone to ring.

Looking back, I can understand why I had such a hard time of it. I was a different kind of singer than they had ever heard before, and people tend to dislike anything that takes them away from tradition. The Italian critic Teodoro Celli described me as "a star wandering into a planetary system not its own." That is exactly how I felt, an alien in an alien world, when I watched the stiff portrayals of the principal singers at La Scala. Their voices were lovely, but they just stood there in the middle of the stage and sang. Who can believe in the fervor of singers who stand there with expressionless faces, arms stiffly at their sides, while vocally declaiming the extremes of passion or rage? Opera is drama expressed in music, not just vocalization. It is the communication of soul through sound. The opera of the twentieth century has become a travesty, a caricature of what it once was. We have to return to the philosophy of Malibran, of Pasta, whose voices were instruments in the service of dramatic art and not merely a demonstration of pretty sounds. The voice is the first instrument of the orchestra, and we must use it as a great violinist treats a Stradivarius, with passion as well as gentleness.

Vocal beauty must always be subordinated to emotional truth. When you interpret a role, you need a thousand nuances to portray happiness, delight, anguish, or terror. This cannot be done with only a pretty voice. Sometimes, as in the role of Lady Macbeth, it is necessary to sing harshly to interpret the truth of the music. This takes courage, but you have to do it even if people don't understand. *You* are the authority, not the audiences. If you work correctly, sooner or later they will be persuaded. And in the end, they did understand.

But for a long time they did not see what I was trying to do. They were after beautiful, captivating voices like Toscanini's favorite, Renata Tebaldi, and were not interested in emotional truths. Tebaldi was the most important rival of my whole career. Her voice was incessantly compared to mine. Those who favored mine said it was "exciting," in contrast to hers, which they called "dull." On the other hand, Tebaldi's was sometimes called "beautiful" while mine was labeled "ugly." It is true that the famous rivalry between us was largely thought up by the press. Nevertheless, she was singing at La Scala and I was sitting in Milan waiting for the phone to ring.

It was Serafin who came to my rescue. He invited me to appear in his production of *Tristan und Isolde* in Venice in December, 1947, as part of a package deal. After *Tristan und Isolde*, I was to sing *Turandot* in January of 1948. I was so happy to be working that I again signed a contract without reading it, not realizing that this time I had agreed to sing a part I didn't

know. I fearfully told Serafin about it when we got to Milan, fully expecting
him to be infuriated and to fire me.

"How can I sing a part I don't know in a month," I wailed, "especially
when I'm singing a terribly difficult role at night?"

To my surprise, he answered, "Don't worry about it. One month of hard
work is all you need." I got to work on the role right away. If this great
conductor believed I could do it, who was I to disagree?

The score of *Tristan und Isolde* is the most beautiful love story in lyric
theatre. It is a tale of tragic passion told within the framework of immortal
music. (How I love tales of tragic passion!) Tristan killed Sir Morold, fiance
of Princess Isolde, in combat and was gravely wounded himself. Isolde, a
sorceress in magic arts, carefully tended him and made him well. They fell
deeply in love, but each felt their smoldering affections were unrequited.

The opera begins on board the vessel in which Tristan has been sent to
bring Isolde from Ireland to Cornwall to become the bride of his uncle, King
Marke. Isolde is reclining on a couch on the foredeck of a vessel hung with
tapestries. Her hopeless love for Tristan has exhausted her. From high up in
the rigging the charming voice of a sailor bidding adieu to his Irish love is
heard. Isolde's eyes light on Tristan, and she gets furious at the thought that
he would deliver her to the arms of another. She calls forth the elements to
destroy the ship and everything on it. The opera is an actress's dream, in
which Isolde expresses rage, revenge, elation, and a confession of love.

As the sailors shout with joy at the sight of land, where Isolde is to be
married to King Marke, she orders her devoted friend, Brangane, to prepare
a death-potion. Tristan, thinking Isolde is about to marry King Marke,
agrees to drink the potion with her. But Brangane substitutes a magic
love-philtre, which unleashes their love to a pitch of exquisite euphoria.

In the second part of the prelude, Isolde surrenders to the rapture of
requited love. The music gathers impetus as it proceeds, is carried to a
higher and higher pitch of exaltation by upward rushing runs, and reaches
its grand climax in a paroxysm of love. I don't believe there is anything in
the realm of opera to compare to the rapturous harmonies of the duet, "Oh,
sink upon us, Night of Love." Although I had never experienced such
feelings in real life, something deep inside me knew I was capable of it, and
I sang the duet with a passion I had never known before. Do you believe in
precognition? I do, and I think my exaltation in the role was a perfect
example of it.

In the palace garden outside of Isolde's apartment, the loyal Brangane
warns her against the treachery of the courtier Melot. But the lovers, lost in
the ecstasy of their passion, pay her no mind. When the two find themselves

surrounded by the King and his men, they realize they've been betrayed by Melot. Tristan draws his sword on Melot, but is fatally wounded in the fight.

Tristan's strength sapped by the wound, his mind inflamed to insanity by his passionate yearning for Isolde, he tears off his bandages, struggles to rise from his couch, and staggers into the arms of Isolde. She folds him in her arms as he passes away. Then she collapses over the body of the dead Tristan and dies too.

Tristan und Isolde is a poignant story. My score became so smudged with tears I couldn't read the notes and had to get another copy. It breaks my heart that the lovers had to die just when they had found each other again. Sometimes I think it would have been better for Isolde never to have loved at all than to have loved and lost. But at other times I remember that I, too, have cradled Paradise in my body, and I wouldn't give up those memories for anything in the world.

My performance as Isolde was an unqualified success and made the Christmas of 1947—my first with Meneghini—the happiest in my life. It was followed in January by the *Turandot* I was supposed to have sung in America, which turned out to be a marvelous confirmation of Serafin's belief in me.

Venice was the turning point of my career. I was now a diva in my own heart and soul, as well as to the operatic world. After that, offers started pouring in, not yet from the great houses of La Scala, the Met, and Covent Garden, but they made 1948 a phenomenally successful year. My schedule included a complete tour of the great cities of Italy; Venice, Genoa, Rome, Turin, Trieste, and Florence among them.

A funny thing happened to me in Venice, where I was to sing Brunnhilde in *Die Walkure* in January, 1949. Margherita Carosio, one of Italy's leading sopranos, was cast as Elvira in Bellini's *I Puritani*. Serafin was conducting both operas. One evening when I was tired of Wagner, I started sight reading and playing around with the part of Elvira. Serafin's wife happened to pass by my room on her way back from talking on the telephone and stood at the door listening to me sing. In one of those strange coincidences which I don't believe are coincidences at all, her phone call had been from a distraught Serafin. He had just lost his Elvira, who had come down ten days before opening night with a virulent form of the flu which was spreading through Venice. Carosio had to cancel all her performances, and Serafin so far had been unable to find a replacement.

Madame Serafin said nothing about Carosio's illness, only, "Tullio is on his way here. When he comes in I'd like you to sing that for him." I had no idea why she wanted me to sing the aria, but I shrugged and said to myself, "Why not?" I sang it and he made no response. The next day, January 8, 1949, was my opening night as Brunnhilde.

That morning at ten, while I was still sleeping, the phone rang. It was Madame Serafin. "Mme. Callas," she said, "put on your robe and come down here immediately."

"I can't," I protested. "I haven't even washed yet. I need about half an hour to get ready."

"Don't bother with that. Come down right away."

I loved Serafin and could deny him nothing, so down I went in my bathrobe.

When I got there, Serafin said, "Sing."

"What should I sing, Maestro?"

"The aria you sang yesterday from *I Puritani*."

So I leafed through the score and sight read the aria. There was another man there whom I vaguely recognized as the musical director of the opera house. I stood nervously clutching Meneghini's old plaid bathrobe together as they talked. I surreptitiously ran my fingers through my unkempt hair and hoped no one could smell the sour breath of my unbrushed teeth.

When I finished Serafin said, "Maria, you will sing this role in a week."

"I'm going to sing *what* in a week?"

"You will sing Elvira next week. You will be given time off to study the role."

"That's impossible," I protested. "I have three more *Walkures* before then. The idea is ridiculous. . . . I really can't do it."

"I promise you that you can," said my mentor. And such was my belief in him that the matter was settled without any further discussion.

I didn't even know the plot of the opera which, incidentally, has the silliest libretto of the century. Elvira, a Puritan maiden in love with a Cavalier, believes he has deserted her and goes mad. His imminent execution shocks her into sanity, whereupon he is acquitted and they are reunited. It would be hard to find two parts as different as Elvira and Brunnhilde. Could I possibly learn the music, let alone the words to so difficult a role in so short a time? Could I change from one character to another without confusing the two? Wouldn't it hurt my voice to attempt so wide a range within a few days? But I was young and arrogant and my mentor believed in me. So I decided to trust him and proceed.

I sang Brunnhilde on Wednesday and Friday nights and spent all the time in between on Elvira's trills, roulades, and runs. Sunday morning was the dress rehearsal of *I Puritani*, and Sunday evening was the final performance of *Walkure*. Two days later I was singing one of the most feared roles in all of opera.

I had memorized the music by then but I hadn't yet learned all the words and had to rely heavily upon the skill of the prompter. And indeed, at least one fiasco took place. At one spot when I was supposed to sing "son vergin vezzosa" (I am a charming virgin), I sang "son vergin viziosa" (I am a vicious virgin). But to the best of my knowledge, no one noticed. Rather, despite the ridiculous libretto and the cardboard character of Elvira, my performance was considered somewhat of a miracle, and I was talked about throughout Italy. The newspapers proclaimed that not since the great Lilli Lehmann seventy-five years before had such a feat been performed. I walked around in a daze.

"This is not possible," I said to Titta. "I am just a little girl from Washington Heights. Pinch me and wake me up."

After singing four *Turandots* in Naples, I left for Rome where I sang Kundry in *Parsifal*, my third and last Wagnerian role, on February 26, 1949. *Parsifal* is the legend of the Holy Grail, the cup which caught the blood of Christ on the cross. Kundry attempts to seduce Parsifal, the "guileless fool," away from his role as champion of the Holy Grail, but at the last moment he resists her charms. She repents and humbly washes his feet and dries them with her hair.

The conflict between good and evil is one that I constantly brood over. That's why I like cowboy pictures so much; you always can be sure the "good guys" will win out in the end. I've had enough of that kind of struggle. Did goodness win out in my life? I've always worked hard, but am not sure I've won out in the end. In *Parsifal*, however, good absolutely wins out, unlike in real life, where that is not always the case.

The reviews were good and expressed surprise at the wide range of roles I could play, but I never really felt at home in the part of Kundry and was glad not to have to sing it again. First of all, Wagner's operas are usually sung in German and I don't sing in German. And secondly, Wagnerian heroines require the kind of physical stamina I'm afraid I don't have.

Which reminds me of Kirsten Flagstad's comment when she was asked if there were a secret to being able to sing Wagner's heroines. "Yes," she answered, "always wear comfortable shoes." She wasn't kidding.

But more important, I prefer Verdi, Bellini, and Puccini. They are more my style; romantic, dramatic, and all too often, tragic. I was born to sing them.

A contract arrived for me from the Teatro Colon in Buenos Aires to sing *Turandot*, but I was not to appear there until May. In the meantime, Radio Italiana broadcast a program of me singing arias from Wagner, Verdi, and Bellini.

I had only a month to prepare for my South American trip. Two days before I was to leave, I suddenly realized I would be separated from Battista for four months by thousands of miles. I panicked and thought, "Nobody can really love me. How do I know he will be here when I get back? He might change his mind about me and find someone else. Something might happen to him while I am away. His brothers hate me and are just awful to me. They think I stick with Battista for his money. They even said they'd murder him to keep him from becoming my husband. I won't go unless we are married! I will only leave Italy for Argentina as Maria Meneghini Callas."

So I said, "Titta, I want to get married before I leave or I won't go."

He answered, "Be reasonable, Sweetheart. How can I get a dispensation from the Pope to marry a non-Catholic and arrange for a wedding in just two days?"

"All right then, I'm not going!"

"You mean you'll break all your contracts and disappoint thousands of people?"

"I have no choice. I can't do it unless we are married."

Somehow he managed to get the Pope's dispensation in time to find a dark and musty little sacristy in the Chiesa dei Filippini in Verona, heavy with the smell of incense from the Cedars of Lebanon. The chapel was cramped, dusty, and littered with old statues and other church paraphernalia, but I couldn't have cared less. We were married on April 21, 1949 in a simple ceremony which made me burst into tears of joy. I knelt after the ceremony and thanked the Blessed Virgin for giving me so much happiness. No members of either family attended. Only the priest, the sacristan, and two of Meneghini's friends, for witnesses, were present. That was all right with me. I'm used to that. My family has never been with me spiritually at any other time either.

Just before we left Genoa, I sent a telegram to my parents which read "Siamo sposati e felici." My mother sent me a white bridal bouquet and a letter saying, "Remember, Maria, you first belong to your public, not your husband." Can you believe it, sending such a message to a new bride!

The day after the wedding, I cried like a baby when I boarded the *S.S Argentina* alone. But for the first time I had no doubt who I was. I was Mrs. Giovanni Battista Meneghini, a married woman, a wife, no longer a solitary misfit, no longer unloved, a normal person at last.

The Verdi Year

ON MAY 20, 1949, I opened at the Teatro Colon in Buenos Aires in Puccini's last opera, *Turandot*. He died before it was finished, and the opera was completed by the composer Franco Alfano. There is a wonderful story about the ending that I love. A sudden letdown occurs where Puccini's orchestration ends. When the great Toscanini was conducting the premiere of the opera at La Scala in 1926, he stopped the orchestra at that point, turned to the audience, and with tears in his eyes said, "Here . . . Maestro Puccini laid down his pen." Then Toscanini continued with the opera. I long to have been there.

The libretto was inspired by an ancient fairy tale from the Arabian Nights. It is the story of the cruel, ice-cold Turandot, a Chinese princess who will wed and share her kingdom only with the prince who can answer her three riddles. I think she agreed to marry the one who could answer the riddles because she never really expected anyone to figure them out. One after another the losers were beheaded, yet new ones kept popping up by the dozen. I don't believe it was Turandot's beauty alone they fell for. She was a hard-hearted, merciless person, and no suitor in his right mind would stick around her once he understood what she was like. What is there about cruelty that cements the lover to the beloved like a barnacle to a ship? I'll never understand it. The faithful slave-girl Liu says, "Tie me! Torment me! With tortures and violence belabor me! It will be the supreme offering I make to him of my love!" Is that what the torment of the lover says, "See how much I love you, how much I suffer for you?" I don't think so. At least not for me. I think it means, "I love you so much that if I have to take the pain to have you, I will."

I enjoyed playing the ruthless Turandot, particularly where she tells how she is avenging the death of her ancient ancestress, Princess Lo-u-ling. The princess was cruelly murdered "in questa reggia" (within this palace) when her country was conquered in war. I was always moved by the aria, for cold as Turandot is, she is alive in the depth of her feeling for Lo-u-Ling.

The princess's fury is woven through with moments of incredible tenderness, as when she speaks of herself as a vessel that bears the soul of Lo-u-Ling. Such conflicting emotions in rapid succession can break the most substantial of voices.

The awe-inspiring empress Turandot, who says, "I am not human; I am the daughter of heaven," becomes a flesh-and-blood woman when she falls in love. Prince Calaf rebukes the Princess for her cruelty and takes her in his arms and kisses her hotly on the mouth. That does it. "What has become of me? I am lost," she murmurs, as all her thoughts of revenge melt like a snowflake at the first ray of sunshine. She weeps in the prince's arms, the first tears she has ever shed. The magic of first kiss and first tears transforms her. From then on, the old Turandot is no more; she now lives for her man. Her metamorphosis has always moved me. Perhaps I had a premonition of what lay ahead for me.

Puccini once said, "I have more heart than mind." That is why I love Puccini so much. I adore *Turandot*. Besides being the story of my soul, it is so melodious. Despite its beauty and its hazards, however, *Turandot* requires little in the way of musical subtlety. It is not to be compared with *Norma*, for instance, which calls for dramatic accents and a complete mastery of fioritura. Incidentally, *Turandot* is the only opera I ever sang that is younger than I am. It was first performed on October 25, 1926, when I was nearly three years old.

Although I was nervous when I sang the part, I now believe my performance was better than I then thought, for a fragment of a recording from the second act with Mario del Monaco in Buenos Aires has become a collector's item. They say I sang effortlessly over the heavy orchestration, and the music critic of *The Nation* wrote "Maria Callas showed all her vocal gifts as well as her magnetic presence" in the role. I myself play the three minute segment quite often these days, although it always makes me a little sad. I like it much better than the complete *Turandot* I recorded in 1957 for E.M.I.

After *Turandot* closed in Buenos Aires, I appeared twenty-seven times all over Italy in the role of the beautiful ice princess who slays those who love her, and then I never sang *Turandot* on stage again. Singing it always petrified me, and every performance left me quaking. I prayed to God each time I sang the role that it would not wreck my voice, as it has done many sopranos. Fortunately, I was able to drop it from my repertoire before it could do me any harm. At least I don't think it did. But at this point who knows?

I spent the whole month of June, 1949, working with Serafin on *Norma,* a work of great lyrical beauty and dramatic tension. I didn't know it yet, but I would sing it more often than any other in my repertoire of forty-seven roles. On June 17, I first sang it in Buenos Aires.

Norma, the High Priestess of the Druids, has broken her sacred vow of chastity and married the Roman Proconsul, Pollione, with whom she has two children. Despite her sacrifice, Pollione has grown tired of her and fallen in love with Adalgisa, another priestess. Norma, heartbroken, sings the song of her (and now my) essence, "Ah, come back to me, beautiful, in our trusting first love . . . Ah, come back, as you were then, when I gave you my heart." The Druids are eager to go to war against the Romans, whom they hate. Norma ascends the steps of the sacred altar and tries to protect Pollione by insisting the Druids stay out of the war. She then prays to the goddess to restore peace to her people in the centerpiece of the opera, "Casta Diva." I have probably sung this aria more than any other in my lifetime, but I don't think "Casta Diva" lives up to expectations. It is lovely and melodic, but it never seemed to me sufficiently moving as a plea to the goddess for peace. Musically, it is exquisite, but dramatically, it never quite does it for me. I really don't understand why it is the most famous of all my arias.

Back to the plot. Pollione enters with the priestess Adalgisa whom he now loves and implores her to run away with him. After a terrible struggle with her conscience, she agrees.

But then she feels guilty and confesses to Norma that she has betrayed her religion for love. Norma, no mean sinner herself, is sympathetic to Adalgisa's plight until it dawns on her that Pollione is her lover. Then Norma sings another tune, "Over the waves and on the winds my burning fury will follow you; my vengeance both night and day will roar around you." Pollione is terrified of her, and has a nightmare in which he marries Adalgisa. During the ceremony darkness shrouds the sky, and Adalgisa disappears as she hears Norma's voice vowing revenge. Pollione knows her true colors, don't you think?

In her home, Norma stands over the cradle of her children, fighting an almost uncontrollable urge to kill them in revenge, and sings, "I must forget I am a mother." But her maternal love overcomes her rage, and she weeps as she embraces them. The long phrase beginning "Teneri, teneri figli" (I hold you, I hold you, children) was always an expression of infinite sorrow to me, a childless woman. As I hugged the children, their cheeks were drenched with my tears.

Norma determines to surrender her husband and children to Adalgisa and atone at the funeral pyre for her own broken vows. "A heart near death has no more illusions, ah, no more hope," she sings, with a wisdom I have only recently come to understand.

But Adalgisa realizes she loves Norma too much to run away with her betrayer, and begs Pollione to return to his wife. Norma is touched by the depth of Adalgisa's love, and the two women swear eternal friendship. How sweet! How sad! I don't think I have ever had a friend who would give up her lover for me. Is there any friend of mine I would have given up Aristo for? Not a one!

Pollione ignores Adalgesa's urging and attempts to seize her against her will. Norma, who has just arrived, finds this the last straw. In a magnificent gesture of strength and power, she pounds the sacred bronzes of the temple three times, declaring war against the Romans ("Guerra, guerra!"). Her warriors rush in and seize Pollione. She offers to spare his life if he will leave Adalgisa, but he refuses, finally showing some decency after all. "I am not a coward," he declares.

Norma's love overcomes justice and she declares herself the guilty party. To wipe the slate clean she mounts the funeral pyre. Pollione's love for Norma returns at her noble gesture, and he follows her to the pyre. They atone for their sins together, as their bodies shoot up in flames. Pollione's final song is, "Your pyre, O Norma, is mine. There, more holy, eternal love begins." So she gets him back at the end, even though she has to die for it. That's a bargain I would gladly accept.

I found myself so lost in the Druid priestess that the rest of the world disappeared. Sometimes the throes of love, jealousy, and hate swallowed me up until I forgot I was on the stage. Norma is a lot like me, a woman who is always griping and too proud to show her real feelings, but who cannot be nasty or unjust in a situation where she herself is to blame.

Norma was the custodian of a sacred art who broke her holy oath of celibacy to consummate her passion for Pollione. How well I, who broke my own marriage vows for reasons of passion, understand her yearning and her guilt! It is interesting how much these operas deal with matters of good and evil. I see I'm not the first person in the world to feel devastated by such a struggle. It is a battle we humans have fought ever since Adam—or was it Eve—bit into the apple. And when Norma discovers Pollione's betrayal, I can sympathize with the rage and jealousy she feels. After all, she loves Adalgisa, as I love Giulietta Simionato who sang the role later in Mexico. I would feel guilty at wishing her harm, yet I certainly would not want her stealing my man.

I adore the duet Giulietta and I sang in *Norma*. There is something about the contrasting voices of two women blending together, like the duet of the two priestesses, that creates a haunting beauty found in no other combination. Because Giulietta and I really care about each other, the rising of our voices in song was especially lovely.

I understand the great passion that leads Norma to want to kill her children, but I know too that something in me would not let me carry it through. At the point when I was about to kill them in performance I was taken over by a shriek from deep inside me that haunts me even now. Finally, in the spirit of Christlike, exalted self-sacrifice I, I mean she, Norma, offers herself as a victim on the funeral pyre. Although Norma seems strong and ferocious and roars like a lion, she really is weak. Yes, we actually are very much alike. The times may be different, we may wear other kinds of clothing and speak in different languages, but basically we have the same passions, the same needs, the same guilt. I am Norma, Norma is me.

I sang the role eighty-eight times from 1948 to 1965, as well as making two commercial recordings. Yet, despite my pleasure in singing perfect fioritura, cadenzas, and embellishments, I found the part the most difficult in my repertoire. And sadly enough, much as I have been praised for Norma, I torment myself that it never was as good in performance as it was in my own mind. But then that is true of all my performances.

In November, 1949, I made my first commercial recording for Cetra, arias from Wagner and Bellini on three twelve inch records. I was scared at first, because you can't tell until you try how your voice will sound on recordings. Some people don't record as well as others and anyhow you can never predict which ones the public will take to. But it turned out better than my rashest dreams. I couldn't imagine at the time how important the recordings were to become. They were the start of a whole new career that was to take my voice into millions of homes and bring me riches and further fame. The records are my children, my claim to immortality. The critic Pierre Schaeffer said it better than I when he spoke of "fragments of time snatched from the cosmos, these fragments being the grooves on the recording disks."

Serafin and I became inseparable while we were working on *Norma*, and he turned out to be the greatest teacher of my career. When I have a good teacher I practically fall in love with him. I found myself hanging around Serafin all the time, eating up his every word. "Find the rhythm and proportion," he taught me, "by singing them over to yourself as if you are talking." So that was how I always began a part, singing or talking the words to myself. Someone said I have an inborn architectural sense that tells me which word in a musical sentence to emphasize and which syllable within that word to bring out.

I treasure the remark of Nicola Rescigno, one of my favorite conductors, who said, "It is a deep mystery why a girl born into a musically unsophisticated family and raised in an atmosphere devoid of operatic tradition, should have been blessed with the ability to sing the perfect recitative." I hope my mother reads this. That should fix her boots! She thinks she did it all for me and is totally responsible for my achievements! My success is due to a genetic accident and some good luck, as well as my own unceasing efforts.

Yet when I think about Rescigno's words, I can't help but agree with him. It all seems like a fairy tale. Sometimes I'm afraid it is all just a dream and I will wake up a fat pimply teenager in Washington Heights. Other times, when the claques are hounding me or I realize I have sold my right to become a mother, it all feels like the proverbial mess of pottage. Then I *wish* I would wake up the mother of eight children in Washington Heights.

My next role in Buenos Aires was *Aida*, a story of an Ethiopian princess who was captured by the Egyptians. She is a sweet, simple soul who is deeply in love with Radames, the leader of the Egyptian army. When she sings, "Love, love! Tormenting joy, sweet rapture, cruel anxiety! In thy sorrow I find my life," I know what she means.

Amneris, the Egyptian king's jealous and conniving daughter, also is in love with Radames. She suspects Aida loves him too, and tricks her into revealing her love for Radames.

Conflict arises for Aida when Radames is chosen to lead the battle against the Ethiopians, of which Aida's father, Amonasro, King of Ethiopia, is the fearless leader.

"The sacred words father and lover . . . " sings Aida. "For each . . . I should like to pray, to weep . . . and in such cruel anguish I wish to die." Imagine if your lover and your father were fighting on opposites sides of a war! Which one would you be loyal to? The aria, "For whom do I weep? For whom do I pray? . . . I must love him, yet he is the enemy of my country!" always left me shattered and in tears. I am grateful that with all my problems with men, at least I've never been put in Aida's position.

Aida steals through moonlight and shadows to keep a rendezvous with Radames by the Nile. She is pursued by Amonastro, who tries to convince her to spy on the Egyptians and find out which road Radames' army will take. Should she refuse, he warns her, she will cause the bloodshed of her people and the fury of the ghost of her dead mother. Terrified, she agrees to betray Radames, singing "Ah, my country, what have you cost me!"

When Amonasro sang of the butchery and destruction Egypt wrought upon Ethiopia, I was hit in the stomach by a backflood of memories of the war years I had lived through. If the audience was overwhelmed, it was because I was, too. I could feel with Aida, "Ah, I remember well those unhappy days, and the mournful sorrow which filled my heart."

When I made the recording of *Aida* for EMI in 1955, Tito Gobbi played Amonasro. We sang the Nile Duet together as though it were actually happening. Some singers are so present they make everyone around them rise to the peak of their powers. Gobbi was such a person. He was magnificent in the role and brought out the very heart of me as a singer and an actress. Surprise, agony, terror, tenderness, fury, and the love of father and daughter for each other are all captured in our scene, as they never were with any of my other Amonasros. It brought back the sense of frustration and terrible longing I had felt for my own father. Painful as it was, my feelings were exactly right for the part. I will always regret that Gobbi and I never sang the opera together on stage.

In a temple on the shores of the Nile, I sang of my love for Radames and my yearning for my native land. But "Oh Patria Mia" with its grassy meadows and cool forests became a long dry patch of desert for me. As everyone knows by now, dramatic expression is my forte, and I can't say lamenting the "green hills, the perfumed shores of home" for a full five minutes appealed much to my sense of drama. I had trouble with it until I had the dream of Malibran I mentioned before. When I thought of the "blue skies, soft breezes of my homeland, where I lived out the quiet morning of my life," I began to sob, and was overcome by images of olive trees and cool valleys, the wine dark sea, the radiant blue and white cottages, and the pure white light of Greece. I had no more difficulties with the dramatic aspect of the recitative.

On the other hand, "Oh patria mia" contains a trap I never fully overcame, the battle of the high C. I could grasp C-sharp easily, but sustaining high C was always a frightening task for me. Regardless of the results, each time I prepared to sing the note I was filled with a sense of dread. I never got over it.

At the rendezvous of the lovers, Radames impulsively agrees to give up all his honors to go with Aida to her native land, where he pictures them living in ecstasy forever. Then, in a naive voice, Aida, who knows her father is listening, asks which road the army will travel on. He stupidly answers, "The Pass of Napata."

Amonasro, having heard what he needed, leaps out of his hiding place and announces he is the King of Ethiopia. He urges Radames to take sides with him, pledging Aida's hand in return. Amneris, hidden in the temple, has also witnessed his treachery. She condemns Radames, who is taken prisoner and found guilty. Amneris promises to save him if he will renounce Aida. Of course he refuses. I would, too, wouldn't you? Radames is sentenced to be buried alive.

It is interesting that the judgment scene is introduced with the same solemn theme that is part of the prelude. To me it says that Amneris's jealousy is the core of the opera. I feel Verdi respected Amneris more than Aida, and that comes across in the music. Amneris is a courageous woman. On the other hand, Aida is a weakling who betrays the man she loves because her father scared her with a ridiculous yarn about her mother's ghost. Sometimes I think I should have sung Amneris. I have more feeling for her than Aida, although in real life I have played out both sides of the record.

Radames is entombed in a vault with long arcades vanishing into the darkness. Aida has secretly concealed herself in the tomb, and when he calls out her name, as if by magic she appears at his side. Enraptured, he sings, "To die—so pure, so lovely! To die, for love of me!" They sing a final duet of love and farewell, "Oh earth, farewell, vale of tears . . . " Then they die together in each other's arms. I wish I could die in the arms of my beloved. . . .

Despite my closeness to Serafin, I was so lonely in Buenos Aires I sat in my room between performances and cried. I missed Battista terribly, and found it difficult to get through the nights without the warmth of his body beside me. It was hard to fall asleep and I woke up every morning at least an hour earlier than usual. I would curl my body around the length of my pillow and pretend it was Titta.

Then too, I really didn't like Buenos Aires. It seemed full of elegant avenues, fancy stores, and classy cars. Living there was expensive and despite my success I felt like a fish plopped down in the wrong lake. I was irritable about stupid little things like when the toast was burned. Wouldn't you be, if you went on your honeymoon by yourself?

I couldn't wait to get home. It was not that we weren't in constant touch. Titta wrote me all the time and sent lots of telegrams. And I telephoned him night and day. The cost didn't bother me, since under my contract the phone bills were paid by the Argentineans. Titta wanted to know everything about me, and the management sent him all my reviews. When my Turandot and Aida were roasted by a few critics, the dear man was able to take the sting out of the words by angrily pointing out how little the reviewers knew about opera.

It made me feel better all the time I was away that he was furnishing and decorating our new penthouse, which overlooked the Arena of Verona. He was excited about everything he bought, gilded furniture, rococo curtains, lots of wallpaper with big flowers, and best of all, a pink marble bathroom fitted with gold mirrors and crystal.

When I got home, I adored the gorgeous apartment. It was the first home of my own I'd ever had and I enjoyed every minute of my vacation. I had dreamed of being a housewife all my life, and spent loads of time in the kitchen, cooking up all kinds of goodies for Titta. Our balcony overlooked the Arena, and I could watch what was going on down there at the same time I boiled the pasta. I rushed back and forth to stir it, between scenes of rehearsals and performances. Of course I often got so involved in the opera that both the pasta and the pot were ruined. It was great fun to shop all afternoon in Woolworth's, buying spatulas, graters, cooking spoons and all kinds of kitchen utensils. I'm afraid I'm not the world's best cook, though. Titta loves German style chocolate cake, so I decided to make him one for our sixth-month anniversary. It occurred to me that I could use my new grater to enrich the icing with grated orange peels. That night after dinner, I gaily presented the cake to him with a curtsy. He eagerly bit into it and was eating awhile when I noticed a strange expression on his face.

"What's wrong, dearest?" I asked. By this time I could see he was having a great deal of trouble chewing. It seems the icing on the cake had congealed and was gluing together his teeth, but he was making a valiant effort to pull them apart and go on eating. The story of Maria's baking prowess became a standing joke between us as long as we were married. That was the last cake I ever made.

Our idyll didn't last long. I was to sing Verdi's *Nabucco* at the Teatro San Carlo in Naples at the end of the year. We had studied King Nebuchadrezor in history class at school, but I didn't find out until the end of the production that he and Nabucco were the same person. Gino Bechi, a baritone beloved all over Italy, sang the title role. I must admit I tried to steal the show from him. As you surely know by now, I am not happy unless I am top dog. A recording was made of *Nabucco* that night, the first of a complete role sung by me, showing I effortlessly sang the high C, a note marking the transition to the top of the third octave. I still enjoy the memory of the duet "Donna, chi sei?" that Bechi and I sang in the third act. We had a mighty vocal duel in it which I won hands down. After I sang a full-throated high E flat, I doubt that anyone even noticed his high A. You could hear in nearly every phrase my exultation at the triumph over Nabucco. It wasn't difficult to sing it with honest emotion.

It still makes me happy to listen to my singing of the fierce, fearless Abigaille. Even then I understood the primitive passion of envy, as Abigaille, the warrior daughter of the Babylonian king, resolved to demolish her unfaithful lover and become ruler of Babylon. Good for you, Abigaille! Would I had done the same.

That was my only stage appearance in *Nabucco*, though the second-act aria, "Anch'io dischiuso" later became one of my favorite concert pieces. I enjoyed the sheer number of notes in the aria as well as the many shades of emphasis and color it requires. To sing it well, it is necessary to experience great depth of feeling, along with an exquisite application of technique, a combination that always thrills me.

The war had not long ended, and the audience responded to Verdi's exhilarating chorus of "Va pensiero sill'ali dorate" (Fly, thought, on golden wings) in much the same way the patriotic overtones had stirred the passions of the original audience in 1842, and again years later when the great Toscanini conducted nine hundred voices in "Va, pensiero" at Verdi's grave. *Nabucco* is the story of the Jews who were under Babylonian domination, but the Italians understood the real meaning of the aria and sang with all their might of fleeing the horrors of the Nazi regime. The Austrian censorship during the war was unable to interfere with the passionate chorus of Jewish prisoners, and the song became an underground national anthem. I too had been crushed by the war, and it filled me with pride to sing the part so shortly after its end.

I began the New Year of 1950 with a performance of *Norma* in Venice. I was well received there, as in Naples, Brescia, Rome, and Catania, but I was becoming more and more disgruntled. I only wanted to sing at La Scala, the culmination of my dreams. But I heard not a word from Milan.

In March I finally received an invitation from Antonio Ghiringhelli, the infamous manager of La Scala, whom I despised, and who, I'm afraid, returned the compliment. The offer was far from the one I wanted, for I was to replace the ailing Renata Tebaldi in *Aida* on April 12. I took the job, because however unsatisfactory the conditions, it was a debut at the world's premiere opera house. But I vowed never again to sing in Milan as a replacement for anyone. Either I would sing because I was wanted for myself or I wouldn't sing at all. I am nobody's understudy.

I'm afraid I wasn't too pleasant to the press, who swarmed all over me when I arrived in Milan. I resented being hired as a replacement and was not gracious about it. I am known as a haughty woman, and it has caused difficulties for me on many occasions, including this one. I was determined to maintain my dignity, and not act as if I was being handed a gift from the gods.

"Are you excited about singing at La Scala, Madame Callas," they asked.

"Oh yes, La Scala, splendid opera house. Of course I am delighted. It is a fine theatre. But I am nearsighted and for me all theatres look alike."

"Are you happy about the public, Madame Callas?"

"The public? They are no different here than anywhere else. If I sing well they applaud me, if I sing badly they hiss."

"How about your voice, Madame Callas? People are saying you sing inconsistently."

"They can say whatever they want to. I sing the way I sing."

"What about your life? Is it a good one?"

"My life! What life? I move from hotel to hotel and live out of suitcases. People envy me for my trips around the world. Some trips—I travel from one theatre to the next one."

When I look back now, I am amused at my arrogance. I'm afraid I didn't endear myself to either the press or the people of Milan. This might have contributed to the cool reception I received from Ghiringhelli and the critics. The truth is that the audience at La Scala was different from any I had faced before. I was terrified to be singing in front of diplomats, ministers, visiting dignitaries and their wives, bedecked in designer splendor and dazzling jewels, and I didn't do my best work. In spite of that, Meneghini and I fully expected an offer of a contract from La Scala. When I realized it was not forthcoming, I collapsed like a deflated balloon.

Nevertheless, I had made my debut at La Scala at the age of twenty-nine. It had been adequate if not earthshaking, and I was famous all over Italy. My confidence soon soared again, and I knew beyond all doubt the day would come when I would return to La Scala on my own terms.

After La Scala, I sang two more *Aida*'s in Naples and left for a 1950 tour with the Opera Nacional of Mexico. I have already spoken of the fiasco with my mother that took place there, and I'd just as soon not think of it again. Believe me, I have all I can cope with now, just trying to think about my present problems.

I was singing the duet "Mira O Norma" in my first piano rehearsal with the conductor Guido Picco at the Opera Nacional when the assistant manager, Carlos Diaz Du-Pond, came by. This duet has always been a favorite of mine, and I have received compliments on it from many critics.

Du-Pond was equally impressed. He immediately phoned Antonio Caraza-Campos, the manager, and said, "Come here right away; Callas is the finest dramatic coloratura soprano I have ever heard in my life, and I heard Ponselle's Norma at the Met." Caraza-Campos rushed right over, carrying the score of *I Puritani*, in which the aria "Qui la voce" expresses the essence of melancholy. He asked me to sing it so he could hear my E flat. I replied, "If you want to hear my E flat, you must engage me next year for *Puritani*." How about that?

I made my Mexican debut on May 23 at the Palacio de las Bellas Artes. It was to be a four-week visit. We opened with *Norma*, in which my great friend Giulietta Simionato was singing her first Adalgisa, Kurt Baum was Pollione, and Nicola Moscona was Oroveso. Both Giulia and I were ill and not at our best. Even "Casta Diva" did not do it. I said to Carlos, "I'm not surprised at the cool reception; people don't like my voice on a first hearing and must get used to it." He explained that South American audiences prize high notes. So later in the season I sang a D flat at the end of the second act and received an ovation for it. That showed them who Callas is!

Norma was followed on May 30 by *Aida*, in which the duet between pleasant little Simionato and me reached proportions I never expected. In fact it grew to a full confrontation. The two of us were competing for Radames in the opera, as Amneris's jealousy of Aida is the mainspring of the story. "I love him, with a mad, desperate love which is killing me," she sings. "Vengeance cries out in my heart." But in real life we wanted to prove who was the better singer, and our competition certainly fueled the duet in a way I'm sure heightened the scene. Giulia is a lovely woman who I had never before thought had an ounce of maliciousness or jealousy in her body. That just goes to show you can never really know anybody.

I saw another example of this side of Giulietta during our *Aida* in Mexico City the next year. Antonio Caraza-Campos, the general director of the Opera Nacional, invited Giulietta and me to his home. We were all angry with Kurt Baum because he kept holding the high notes long past the time he should have. To get even with Baum, Caraza-Camos proposed that I substitute a high E flat at the end of the Triumphal Scene. I would soar up an octave and hold a full E flat all the way to the end of the orchestral finale. "If you do," he said, "the Mexicans will go crazy." I refused, first of all because the note was not written there by Verdi, and secondly, I am careful not to annoy my colleagues. But unlike most prima donnas who would have a fit if I tried such a thing, my devilish friend Giulietta urged me to do it. "Cara per me, da il me bemolle. ... This could lead to some fun!" She turned out to be right. But devilish or not, I have rarely seen such generosity as Giulia's on or off the stage.

At the May 30 performance, Kurt Baum irritated the cast by holding on to his high notes until his eyes popped. I'd had all I could swallow of him. So at the intermission, I said to Carlos, "Please go to Simionato and Robert Weede (who was singing Amonasro) and ask them if they would mind if I sang a high E flat. Now an E flat *in alt* in the Act Two finale of *Aida* is more than just a high E flat in any other opera. It is a scene of dazzling impact in the style of grand opera. To sing the note, I had to compete with a vast choir and full orchestra with blazing trumpets. I don't mind telling you few sopranos will try it, because they would be drowned out by the magnitude of sound. But I am always ready to take a risk if I feel it will benefit me and the production, as well as sneak in a little note of revenge. So in Act Two I soared upward an octave and held on to a full-voiced E flat all the way through the end of the orchestral finale. The tone cut through the discord of the scene like a bolt of lightening across a summer sky. Both the audience and Kurt were dumbstruck, and he later shouted he would never sing with me again. Now I ask you, do you think I cared one whit whether he did or he didn't? I had a great time. After all, I inherited an instinct to enjoy the upper hand from my mother.

In Giulietta's and my duet in *Aida*, however, there were no holds barred. "Vieni, o diletta" (Come, dearest friend) began as a duet between the two of us, but later Radames makes it a threesome. In it, Amneris feigns friendship for Aida, but expresses her jealous hatred in asides. Even though Giulia is a wonderful singer, I'm used to being top dog in every opera I sing. To my surprise, we ran neck and neck throughout the duet. Even worse, it was one battle I'm not sure I won. Never underestimate the power of a woman, no matter how harmless she may seem!

I am happy to report the production was one of my best *Aida*s. But take my word for it, you don't want to hear about our third Mexican opera, *Tosca*, except to know it was conducted by an idiot, Umberto Mugnai, with the clown Mario Filippeschi for a tenor. I am still embarrassed to have my name connected with it.

The production of Verdi's *Il Trovatore* was also interesting. Did you ever see the opera done without the Act Four duet? It happened in Mexico that June 20, 1950, on opening night. Leonard Warren was sick and they had to omit the aria. They brought in Ivan Petrov from New York for the second and third performances.

It was also a first for another reason; I had to prepare for it all by myself. Serafin wouldn't help me because he said he refused to give advice on a production someone else was conducting. I love the man, but I don't think that was nice of him. It turned out not to matter, however. I sang the most blazing, passionate Leonora of my career. Looking back now, I would say there was an element of spite in it. I had to do well! My cabaletta was called a true *tour de force*, as it included powerfully executed trills, finely accented *staccati*, a faultless D flat, and another high E flat. So there, Tullio Serafin! Who needs you?

After signing a contract for the following year, I left for home and Meneghini. I was so exhausted from the demanding schedule I had to take a break of three months before singing *Tosca* in Salsomaggiore on September 22. Then on October 2, I sang *Aida* in Rome, where I was also preparing my first role in comedy, Fiorilla in Rossini's *Il Turco in Italia*. I was sick and tired of playing melancholy heroines who were either poisoned or stabbed, or who killed themselves and/or suffered the catastrophes of the damned. I wanted the fun of playing a light, cheerful role for a change, even though I have been accused of not having any sense of humor. Therefore I was delighted to read the following review in *Opera* of the October 19 performance: "Maria Callas was the surprise of the evening. She sang a light soprano role with the utmost ease, making it extremely difficult to believe she can be the perfect interpreter of both Turandot and Isolde."

The opera was suggested to me by Luchino Visconti, a famous producer and Italy's foremost director of films, who later was to become a significant person in my life. He first heard me in *Turandot*, but it wasn't until my *Parsifal* that he really became interested. He used to kid me by saying, "You had a little Circasian stool on your head." In 1951 he sent me a cable saying, "All my warmest congratulations after having heard you with the greatest of pleasure on the radio yesterday." In 1953 when I appeared for the last time in *Aida*, Visconti told me he was enchanted by my marvelously oriental performance. "But you need someone to design hats for you that don't fall down over your head," he joked. I found his philosophy of opera much like mine. He, like Wagner, believed in singing as a form of acting. I took to him on first sight. I'm funny—the moment I see a person, I can tell if he is going to become important to me. People don't believe it when I tell them that, but trust me, something inside of me just knows these things. That's how I was able to tell right away Battista was the one. Thus with Visconti I instantly realized our relationship was going to be special, and soon found out the fascination was mutual.

I'm no intellectual, but when Visconti and his friends talked politics, revolution, art, music, and the new morality, I sat there spellbound. I loved him, and listened with excitement to everything he said. When a person loves, areas open up that were never of interest before.

But when you burn the candle at both ends, sooner or later you end up with no light at all. That's what happened to me after *Il Turco*. Just three weeks after its last performance, I was back in Rome singing Kundry on a radio broadcast of *Parsifal*. In between, I had also been adding Elizabeth in Verdi's *Don Carlo* to my repertoire. I have always been too driven to know when to rest and have to be forced to give in to my all too human bodily needs. I also was in terrible conflict about the breakup with my mother, and worked even harder to keep from dwelling on it. Be that as it may, no one stopped me from driving myself and I collapsed with jaundice. I had to leave in the middle of a rehearsal and didn't recover in time to sing the role. All performances of *Don Carlo* in Rome and in Naples had to be canceled. I wish I had a mother . . .

Meanwhile, Italy was preparing to celebrate the fiftieth anniversary of Verdi's death. I was looking forward to participating by singing my first *Traviata* for the Teatro Comunale in Florence, with Serafin conducting.

I guess it will be no surprise that this time Serafin and I were having difficulties. I was irritable with him for not helping me on the *Trovatore* in Mexico City, and my exasperation erupted into our first quarrel. He had complained at the dress rehearsal about my dressing "too casually" and not behaving like a prima donna. As if it is clothing that makes a singer! It was the prelude of many arguments to come.

I had found out in Mexico that I could get along without Serafin very well, because I had done as well on my own as under his guidance. I have always felt my intuition is far more dependable than any of my mentors' teachings, and this was another proof I was right. I had learned everything he had to teach me, and I guess I just fell out of love with him. Then, too, I had Visconti now to learn from.

Although it is always pleasant to win a point, I was disappointed the reviews found nothing extraordinary about either my performance or the production of *Traviata*. When the final curtain came down, however, Serafin and I acknowledged the applause hand in hand and all our difficulties seemed forgotten.

"Here was a great accomplishment," Serafin said, "and it surprised many." Including him.

Insult in the Midst of Success

$\mathcal{T}$WO WEEKS AFTER THE FLORENCE *TRAVIATA*, I sang the role of Leonora in *Il Trovatore*, in Naples. I never liked the part even though she sings some exquisite arias, because nobody ever really understands what the opera is all about. So I was happy to leave Naples to sing *Norma* in Palermo.

When I arrived there I received an urgent phone call from Ghiringhelli. Renata Tebaldi was ill again and the frosty La Scala manager who smiled only with his mouth invited me to take over her role in *Aida*.

Ha! I thought, I have him just where I want him! I've always known some day he would need me and I wouldn't be there for him. They say revenge is sweet, but it is better than any candy.

"No," I answered haughtily. "I will never grace the stage at La Scala again until I am invited to be a permanent member of the company." I knew it would just be a matter of time until he came around.

It took a bit longer than I expected. But a funny incident happened in between. Ghiringhelli had told Gian Carlo Menotti he could cast anyone he wanted to sing Magda in *The Consul*. Menotti said, "I have chosen Maria Callas."

"Oh, my God!" Ghiringhelli cried. "Never, never, never! I know I promised you any singer you picked would be acceptable to me, but I will not have Maria Callas in my theatre unless she comes as a guest artist." Menotti came to see me and begged me to accept Ghiringhelli's terms. But I absolutely refused and said to him, "Mr. Menotti, I want you to remember one thing. I *will* sing at La Scala, and Ghiringhelli will pay for this the rest of his life."

It happened on May 26 right after I opened at the Maggio Musicale in Florence singing Elena in *I Vespri Siciliani*. I received a telegram from Ghiringhelli congratulating me on the performance and saying he would be coming to Florence to discuss my engagement at La Scala. Now the shoe was on the other foot. I had hugged the fantasy of singing at La Scala to my breast for a long time. Why shouldn't he experience a bit of the torture he had put me through? So I made good and sure whenever Ghiringhelli wanted to see me, I was unavailable. After my third Elena, he came backstage and offered me the honor of opening the 1951/52 season at La Scala as a full-fledged member of the company. In addition to Elena, he invited me to sing Norma, Constanza in *Il Serraglio* and Elisabetta in *Don Carlo*. Mohammed had come to the mountain, and I was not going to relinquish the pleasure of seeing him defeated one moment before I had to.

"I will not sign," I said haughtily, "unless I can also play Violetta in *La Traviata*." He needed me. I ask you, what else could he do but agree?

My contract included three leading roles, thirty performances the first year, and 300,000 lire (practically $500) per performance. I raised my arms to the mighty chandelier of Bohemian glass with its three hundred sixty-five lamps and gloated. It was a glorious victory, the greatest triumph of my life. Nothing feels as good as having a childhood dream come true, especially when someone has done everything he could to keep it from coming about! Knowledgeable fans of opera ruminate from yesterday to tomorrow on the reasons Ghiringhelli disliked me from the beginning. Some say it was because he couldn't control me like the others, but I don't think so. There were other divas, certainly one I know of, not to mention any names, who had him wrapped around their little fingers. Others have conjectured that he, like me, comes from a modest background and doesn't want to be reminded of it. Another theory I've heard is that I was Serafin's protegee, and Ghiringhelli doesn't like Serafin. In fact, the conductor has not worked at La Scala since the year Mr. G. was first appointed.

I think the reason he hated me is so simple I wonder why no one else has thought of it. I sang for the Italians and Germans during the war, and for that reason was asked not to return to the Athens Opera Company. Ghiringelli is a European Jew whose parents were victims of the Holocaust. In my opinion he has always held it against me that I performed for the enemy, even though I have repeatedly said I was not a sympathizer of the Nazis or Communists. I can't think of any other reason why a man should hate me so much before he even met me. Then too, why would it have been all right with him if I sang as a guest of La Scala and not as a permanent member?

In *I Vespri Siciliani*, Verdi had advised that the aria in which Elena urges her fellow Sicilians to rise against their invaders, "Courage, come, courage, Bold sons of the sea," be sung *con calma*. Well, I sang it calmly enough on the surface, but underneath was the churning feeling, "Yes, I'll sing it all right, but you're not going to like it!" Surely I can be forgiven a special pleasure when I performed *I Vespri Siciliani* in Milan. Yes, revenge is the sweetest pleasure of all!

Between the sixth and seventh performances of *Vespri* I traveled to Parma to appear in a performance of *La Traviata*. A few memorable events occurred there, two of which were regrettable and one delightful. As they say in America, I'll give you the bad news first. The first act prelude began with de Fabritiis, the conductor, taking a few measures on the fast side, which led to hissing from the galleries. That always upsets me, although I take great pains to make people think I don't care. Then Ugo Savarese, the baritone, got a frog in his throat. That idiot! You'd think he would know by now how to take care of his voice! And the ultimate horror, I had a serious problem with my nemesis, a high C. Despite all that, my performance was a triumph, topped off by an incident that gave me great satisfaction. Elizabeth Schwarzkopf, the great German soprano, came back stage after the performance with a moving tribute. She said she would never sing Violetta again. "Why should I?" she asked. "I have seen the perfect Violetta."

Of course there are those who say she never sang the part well anyway, was "miscast and vocally cold," and wasn't giving up very much. Nevertheless Schwarzkopf is a great diva and I felt honored by her deference. She is what I call a big person.

All of a sudden everybody wanted me. Athens, New York, and Verona were all bidding for my services, and Covent Garden was trying to get me to sing *Norma* in 1952. My major ambition in life had come to pass, and I was now the leading prima donna in Italy. I couldn't have been happier and to make things even better Battista and I were to leave for another Mexican tour and my father was coming, too.

Would it strain anyone's patience if I were to say that I work hard, probably harder and longer than any other artist? It's not as though all this acclaim was just handed to me. Audiences should be aware of the tedious work, tension, fatigue, self doubts, and love that go into every insignificant word or note, not to mention the gestures and expressions that are an essential part of the role. My only desire is to fight for art, no matter what it costs me. I can't bear it when singers take their work casually and do a sloppy job, like some people whose names I won't mention. It is disrespectful to themselves, to their colleagues, and to the audience. I have been called temperamental by many impresarios, but I will always be as difficult as necessary to achieve the best.

Why am I telling you these things that you probably know already? I want to make sure you understand that I deserved my success and nobody ever handed me anything for nothing. (Attention, Liska!)

The music critic Henry Wisneski understands what I have tried to do. He said in a review of *I Vespri Siciliani*, "Callas gives the impression of projecting one long uninterrupted musical thought, and sings with an exquisite thread of shimmering sound." Yes, that is what singers should work to do, to project one long uninterrupted musical thought. And the only way to do that is by working incredibly hard for as long as it takes to get the results you need.

I am never happier than when lying in my bed and studying a new score, with my little poodle Toy under my arm. I spend a great deal of time there. But the preparation of a role is not enough. No matter how thorough, it must be backed up by courage. Before the curtain goes up, friends and colleagues can do everything possible to support an artist. But when the curtain rises, the only thing that matters is courage, the courage to act on impulse, the courage to go on with the role no matter how frightening or malevolent the circumstances. Or perhaps it is something deeper than courage; it is an unlimited faith in the Divine Protection.

People always ask, "What is it that makes you such a great actress, the envy of many famous leading ladies, and causes critics to compare you to Bernhardt and Duse?" Well, I have a secret for you. I was and am a woman of the theatre, but I am not an actress. I never act; I feel. I will not sing a single note or make a solitary gesture if it does not echo some inner truth. When I work on a character, I always ask myself what I would do if I were in her place. That's the way I learn how she feels. But if something does not come from inside me, it rings false to me and therefore to the audience and I won't do it. I don't think they ever can be fooled. I am not acting my characters; my characters are me.

In other words, you must transform yourself in a role, but at the same time you must manage to remain your own person. Then each character will be unique. People have said I have a thousand voices, and it always makes me happy when I hear my Norma, my Tosca, my Violetta, my Lady MacBeth, my Medea, my Madame Butterfly all differ from each other. I guess I can do that because not only do I have a thousand voices, but a thousand selves. Each role dips into another aspect of Maria Callas.

What makes me different from other singers is that I am not just a voice, but am able to transform myself into the characters I play. It has been said that I enter into their souls. I don't believe I could do that if I were frozen into one identity. I suffer from what the French call "the deficiency of one's excellency" in that what makes me weak as a person makes me strong as an artist.

In Mexico City, I was feted and applauded, and given every tribute by the press, along with every available cultural honor. But best of all was the presence of my father. How happy I was at the curtain calls when I saw him standing in the first row and applauding! You remember he didn't like opera (goodness knows I've said so enough) and felt I never would amount to anything as a singer. Imagine what it is like to have a parent who has always put you down do an about-face and applaud you. It was second only to the surrender of Ghiringhelli and La Scala. Maybe it was even more important.

When I got to Mexico City I found they had scheduled an extra performance of *La Traviata* which I had not agreed to. It makes me want to scream when people think they can force me to do what they want just by publicizing that I'm going to do it. Nobody can do that to Callas! I immediately cancelled the performance.

Have I mentioned that my husband was always thinking of money? In Mexico he insisted I be paid in gold dollars. It was funny to see him stashing away the loot in a bulging black bag he had bought for the occasion. He looked like a corpulent little country doctor.

My next stop was Sao Paulo in Brazil. But I was exhausted from the hard work, the excitement, and for some reason I do not understand, the lack of sleep. My legs were badly swollen, and since I had been ridiculed before about their size, you can understand why I did not care to appear on stage like that. Especially in *Aida*. I cancelled all my performances of it in Sao Paulo, but consented to appear in *Traviata*, alternating as Violetta with Renata Tebaldi. Since the opera is set in Paris around 1700, I didn't have to worry about costumes revealing my legs.

When I arrived in Rio de Janeiro, I was shocked to be greeted by a press singing the praises of Tebaldi's Violetta. Of all the sopranos in opera, Tebaldi was the closest to being my rival. Neck and neck triumphs increased the tension between us. As anyone who knows me realizes, I do not take competition lightly. When one more journalist asked me what I thought of her singing, I blurted out, "She has a lot to learn." The press made hay of my impulsive remark and never allowed me to forget it. The camp became divided, and pretty soon the musical world began to separate into Callasites and Tebaldists.

At a benefit concert at the Teatro Municipal in Rio on September 14 at which both Renata and I were to take part, the conflict between us came to a head. I was to sing "Sempre libera" from *Traviata* in the original key and she the "Ave Maria" from *Otello*. I sang my aria and promptly left the stage, as any good colleague would do. Renata had the gall to sing not one but *two* encores. This is illicit behavior among singers, unless it is previously agreed upon. Believe me, in this instance it was not. Renata said the encores were in response to the audience's demands. Can you believe the nerve of the woman? I was in a rage, and broke off all relations between us.

If you've ever had to work with someone you're not talking to, you know how uncomfortable that can be, especially if the two of you are cramped together backstage in a small space. You try to look away, but whatever your eyes fasten on, you find the other person is looking there too. Mostly we ignored each other, but sometimes at a professional or social occasion, it was impossible to do so. Once at an after-dinner discussion, we exploded like two fishwives. The other guests had a field day. I'm sure it made the party for them.

To make a bad situation worse, I was fired by the director, Barreto Pinto, at the end of the opening night performance of *Tosca* in Rio. Pinto, a man of one of Brazil's wealthiest families, was described by Battista as a repellent-looking, small, toothless man whose head was set way down in his shoulders, and who gave an impression of being dirty. I must admit, he was pretty disgusting-looking, not to mention his revolting character. According to Pinto, I was dismissed because of unfavorable reactions of the audience to my *Tosca*, but we knew better. I believe Renata Tebaldi was behind the decision to fire me. Even though I insisted on being paid for my unsung performances, it was humiliating to find my replacement for *Tosca* was none other than Tebaldi herself!

When I walked into his office to collect my pay before leaving, he insulted me further by saying, "So you want money on top of glory, eh?" I was fuming at the outrage and couldn't help myself. I picked up a bronze ink stand from his desk and was about it hurl it at him when a secretary rushed forward and wrenched it out of my hand. I don't know who was luckier, Pinto or me. I might have gone to jail, but he could have been killed. Too bad he wasn't. It might have been worth it.

I returned to Italy, but the unpleasant memories of Rio rankled for a long time and prevented me from enjoying my wonderfully successful year. Could anyone forget such an insult, even in the midst of triumph? It festered inside of me and felt like an infected tooth were rotting in my heart.

Some Thoughts About My Work and Me

ALTHOUGH I AM CRITICAL OF MY WORK and seldom felt I did my best, on rare occasions a performance stands out in my mind as adequate. I remember with pleasure a Martini-Rossi concert I gave on February 18, 1952 at the RAI auditorium in Turin, where I sang arias from *Macbeth*, *Nabucco*, part of the Mad Scene from *Lucia*, and my favorite, the Bell Song from Delibes's *Lakme*. It was fun to mark and shade each note with what must surely be the longest-breathed legato in operatic history. I had a wonderful time finding tones to sound like the "Magic bells of the enchanter." That's the way I played as a child, fooling around with the notes of a song until I could make it sound like any instrument I wanted, a violin, a clarinet or even the drums. I remember how I giggled when my neighbor Martina stuck her head out her door and yelled, "Who is playing that beautiful violin music, Liska?" It was me singing, of course. I enjoyed the rendition of the Bell Song so much I still love listening to the recording of it.

On April 2, 1952 I appeared at La Scala as Constanza in *Il Ratto dal Serraglio*. The audience liked it but I didn't. It is a fiendishly difficult role, which took a great deal out of me without giving much back. In the first aria alone I had to sing twenty high C's and eleven high D's. This was the only Mozart role I ever played. It's not that I haven't been offered a number of other Mozart operas. In fact when Rudolf Bing asked me to do the sorceress, the Queen of the Night, in *The Magic Flute* at the Met, I told Battista, "He's crazy! I have enough trouble reaching High C, without stretching my voice another octave!" I also refused to sing *The Magic Flute* in English for the Met. First of all, except for Weber's aria from *Oberon*, "Ocean! thou mighty monster," I do not like to sing in English. For some reason the soft Italian tones are more conducive to making me feel the music in my heart and body. And secondly, I really do not care for Mozart. At the risk of shocking everyone, I consider him dull. His music never makes me feel anything. A master technician, yes; a man of the heart, no.

After the last *Norma* at La Scala on April 14, 1952, I left for the Comunale in Florence, where I sang three performances of *Armida*. Rossini wrote it for his wife, Colbran. He must have hated her! It is another punishing role, which includes the most demanding variations in Act Two, "D'amore al doce impero." I also had to sing chains of triplets of extraordinary difficulty, exacting arpeggios, and a taxing ascending and descending scale of two octaves which I enjoyed only because it was fun making sounds like rippling water. It is an almost impossible part, full of roulades, trills, runs, and leaps. In the final twelve-minute scene, I spanned almost three octaves. And I had to learn all this in five days, sandwiched in between *Norma* at La Scala and *I Puritani* in Rome!

By the dress rehearsal, the night the performance is traditionally viewed by the press, I knew the music but unfortunately forgot some of the words of the recitative, and the prompt box was not yet ready. So I had to be lugged back off the stage and have the orchestra play the entrance music again.

You'd think I would be upset by this, tyrant that I am to myself. If I had messed up the music, it would have stabbed me in the heart. But I just don't care as much about the words. If I miss them, I simply make up new ones. The libretto is not the main thing; the heart of the opera is in the music. This must be true for the audience too, for my Armida created a sensation and nobody seemed to give a damn whether I remembered the lines or not.

You will recall during my first Mexican tour, Antonio Caraza-Campos, the general director of the Opera Nacional, had asked me to sing the aria at the end of the Triumph scene in *I Puritani* so he could hear my E flat. I replied, "If you want to hear my E flat, you must engage me next year for *Puritani*." He loved that story and told it at parties everywhere. He had gotten the point that Callas no longer has to audition. On May 29, on my third Mexican tour, he finally got to hear my E flat in his production of *I Puritani*. I trust he found it worth waiting for.

Nevertheless, except for the marvelous tenor Giuseppi di Stefano and me, the performance was a disaster. The conductor, Guido Picco, seemed to be half asleep and I have rarely seen less involved musicians. My particular voice needs the textures and overtones of a fine orchestra to highlight and underline it. A good example is the Easter Hymn, "Inneggiamo il Signor non e morte" in *Cavalleria Rusticana*, in which Christ has arisen and triumphed over death. I can't tell you how much I love this aria and listen to the recording of it again and again. I am proud of the way my voice rings out loud and clear over the powerful tones of the orchestra. I have heard many divas sing the opera and most of the time during the hymn the voice of the soprano, even that of my gifted friend Giulietta Simionato (although I hope she never reads this), is all but swallowed up by the orchestra.

Incidentally, I find great pleasure in soloing with a good orchestra and chorus behind me. We are like one big happy family enjoying life together, which, of course, my family and I never did.

But at this performance of *I Puritani* cooperation between musicians and singer was not forthcoming. I do my work conscientiously and expect professionals who appear with me to do the same. It is infuriating to have one's performance ruined by an incompetent orchestra and supporting cast. The human voice as it converts breath into sound is a glorious combination of wind and string instruments, the most eloquent of all musical instruments and the most difficult to master. I am a perfectionist and cannot bear to see the finished product treated shabbily. When I don't like something, I have never been one to mince words on the subject. People have always said of me, "There goes Maria again, spouting off at the mouth!" I'm afraid I chewed out the musicians rather badly after the first performance, and they will never forgive me for it. But I have no doubt they deserved it.

On June 10, I sang Donizetti's *Lucia di Lammermoor* for the first time. I've always wanted to sing it because it reminds me of when I was ten years old and listening to Lily Pons singing the Mad Scene on the radio. I insisted she had strayed off-pitch. A friend of my mother, Mrs. Theopolous, was listening with us. She claimed the lady was a great star and a child like me should be more respectful. I stuck to my guns, declaring, "I don't care if she is a star, she is still singing off-key! Just wait and see, one day I'm going to be a star myself, a bigger star than her." So I hoped for a long time to make my prediction come true.

I guess it did, for the great Toti dal Monte, the reigning diva of the role during the entire interwar period, came backstage to say she had sung Lucia all those years without having really understood it. We fell into each other's arms in tears. It is moments like these which make all the *sturm und drang* worthwhile.

In the opera, Lucia's brother, Lord Enrico, wants her to rescue him from his financial problems by marrying the wealthy Lord Arturo. She refuses, for she loves Edgardo, Enrico's enemy. Edgardo comes with the news he is being sent to France on matters of state. In a sensitive, tender scene by a fountain, the lovers promise eternal fidelity. They sing "Verranno a te sull' aure" (Zephyrs will bring you my ardent sighs) in which Lucia hopes that when her sighs reach Edgardo on the breeze, he will drop a tear of remembrance on the ring she has given him. The tenderness of di Stefano's "Ah, Lucia!" when he declared his love for me always broke my heart.

In the meantime, Enrico has proceeded with plans for Lucia's wedding to Arturo. The captain of the Guard intercepts Edgardo's letters to Lucia and produces a forged letter suggesting he is in love with another woman. Believing her lover is unfaithful, Lucia sings, "The moment of my death is at hand. His faithless heart now belongs to another." Since all is lost anyway, she decides she might as well marry Arturo.

Just as Lucia is signing the marriage contract, Edgardo dashes in. He believes she is false to him and leaves, cursing her and her family.

The bride and bridegroom have retired to their rooms after the marriage ceremony when word comes that Lucia has gone mad and killed her husband. She clutches a bloody dagger in her hand and appears disheveled and distraught among the still-celebrating guests, who scream out in horror. The Mad Scene follows, in which she sings of her joy as she anticipates the ecstasy of a reunion with her lover. The scene is incredibly lovely. It makes you see why Lucia went mad. Who wouldn't prefer imagined beauty to an unbearable truth? At the end of the scene she falls back dying.

Edgardo has been told by the people of Lammermoor that Lucia has gone crazy and is calling his name as she is about to die. Knowing he cannot live without her, he cries out to Lucia in Heaven he is coming to join her and stabs himself.

I think of poor Lucia, in love with Edgardo and forced to marry another. She is so devastated it drives her mad. I can understand loving a man so much you would die if you couldn't have him. I have loved like that, too.

The whole audience, including the normally blase orchestra, went wild and called me back for sixteen curtain calls and a twenty-minute standing ovation. I am always involved emotionally in my roles but something happened at this performance that I had never experienced before. I was singing the Mad Scene, which ends with an E" flat. My body seems to grasp the truth long before my brain catches on. There must be something in Donizetti's music about going mad that I know only with my heart, for when I got to my dressing room, I began to cry, and got so hysterical I couldn't stop sobbing for over an hour. Everyone was frightened, including me.

Incidentally, I never read Sir Walter Scott's "The Bride of Lammermoor," which the opera is based upon. The book is not important; it is the music that matters. After all, Donizetti's genius, not Sir Walter Scott's, created the Mad Scene. It is true that words are the springboard, but the really crucial thing is what the composer does with them. There is nothing Scottish about the way Donizetti interpreted Lucia. In the opera, she became a universal character, which is what I sang.

On June 28, I played Puccini's *Tosca*, and repeated it on July 1, my final appearance in Mexico City. I wasn't happy with my performance, although it was called electrifying and dramatically plausible. It was a work in progress and not until 1964 in Covent Garden, under Zeffirelli, was my interpretation anywhere near my satisfaction.

At the end of the performance the orchestra played an old Mexican farewell song, "Las Golondrinas." The musicians, the audience, and I all wept. It was good to have played Mexico City again, but I knew I would never come back.

On July 19, 1952 I returned to the Arena of Verona in the role of my Italian debut, *La Gioconda*. I cannot speak of the Verona Arena without mentioning that my first performance under the midnight stars was a once-in-a lifetime experience. Built during the first century, the arena is an enormous stone structure seating twenty-two thousand people. The massive casts and spectacular staging made possible by the vast theatre are breathtaking. The scenery is built into the tiered layers of stone and lights up when the audience files in. Singing there under the open sky is an event of unsurpassed beauty and grandeur.

Despite the splendor of the setting and my profound enjoyment of the role, I have reservations about the opera itself. I've never met anyone, including myself, who understands Arrigo Boito's complicated libretto, but I will try to explain it as best I can.

Barnaba, a spy for the Inquisition, plans to win the ballad singer, La Gioconda, who arrives leading La Cieca, her blind mother. I have always found the scene between Gioconda and Cieca moving. There is a deep love between mother and daughter ("She of my life has been the angel bright") which makes Gioconda tenderly care for the blind woman in her old age.

Gioconda is seeking Enzo, whom she loves but who does not love her. Barnaba waylays her to declare his love. She is indifferent to him and manages to break away. The spurned lover gets his revenge by fabricating a story to a boatman that Cieca has thrown an evil spell over him. The boatman swallows the tale and attacks the old woman, who is saved in the nick of time by the arrival of Enzo.

Alvise, a leader of the Inquisition, arrives with his wife, Laura, whom Enzo is in love with. The good-hearted Laura pleads with Alvise to protect La Cieca. But Barnaba fabricates a second lie that Laura is planning a visit to Enzo's ship that night. Enzo hurries to the ship with excitement to greet his beloved. The betrayer Barnaba then informs Alvise that his wife Laura is planning to meet Enzo on board his ship. God, this opera is complicated!

Gioconda overhears them and weeps bitterly. Yet despite the anguish of unrequited love, she has her mother to turn to. "Place your hand upon my heart, Mother, and feel how great is my woe," she sings. Hand in hand they go off, "one grief of two griefs making, sharing each other's woe." It is the kind of relationship I will never have with my own mother, and the scene always brings tears to my eyes. It makes me feel in my heart how much I have missed. Grief, no matter how catastrophic, is bearable if a woman can be comforted by her mother. It makes me sad to think of all the times in my childhood I suffered alone.

Laura and Enzo plan to sail at dawn. The duet between the rivals, Gioconda and Laura, beginning with "E un anatema" (Curses on you!), is the high point of the opera and perhaps the most passionate scene I've ever sung. Gioconda says her name is vengeance and denounces Laura in fury. I sang it in a manner so real it scares me every time I hear the recording we made of the production. There is a truth in it which came from the marrow of my being. Gioconda says she loves this sailor "as the lion loveth blood," in contrast to the pallid Laura, who loves him "like a celestial dream." That is the way I love, like Gioconda! Other women, not to mention any names, love, if at all, like Laura.

Alvise decides the unfaithful Laura must die. He orders her to drink poison and leaves. But Gioconda remembers how Laura befriended her mother and substitutes a narcotic for the poison. Of course no one notices or stops her. The heartbroken Enzo angrily denounces Alvise, who has him arrested. Gioconda still loves Enzo, and feels she will do anything to save him. She tells Barnaba she will give herself to him if he will release Enzo. When he agrees, Gioconda is happy she has saved Enzo but knows she has no choice but to kill herself.

Enzo arrives and Laura revives. Gioconda helps the joyful couple to escape. She is just about to swallow poison herself when Barnaba approaches. She pretends to yield to him, but instead pulls out a dagger she has hidden on herself and, with a grisly gasp, stabs herself and dies. But Barnaba has his revenge, as he cries into her dying ears that he has murdered her mother.

Who thinks up these stories? Why do all the heroes and heroines have to die so tragically? Would you believe, since 1948, I played eighteen different women one hundred and seventy-three times who died or killed for love! Surely some people must live out their lives and die happily together. Sometimes I get so sick of these tragedies I'd like to chuck them all and spend every day watching cowboy pictures and eating ice cream cones for dinner.

There are a number of moving moments in the opera, especially when I plead with Alvise in "Pieta, pieta" to spare my mother's life. I must still have some feeling somewhere for my own mother, because the passage always moved me. The section where I tell Barnaba, "Go to the devil, you and your guitar!" blazes with wrath. When I sang it, I always thought about whichever man I happened to be angry with at the moment, like Ghiringhelli. There was always someone, I'm afraid. Whoever he was, it felt great to tell him off. Since operas at the Arena begin at a late hour and end well after midnight, my greatest fear was that no one would stay for the last act to hear "Suicidio," my most important aria. I needn't have worried. Unlike a few of my other fears, this one proved groundless. Not one person ever left the theatre until the opera was over.

When I sang "Suicidio," it always brought to mind thoughts about the morality of people taking their own lives. I am preoccupied with that idea, but I don't want to talk about that now, except to point out some uncanny resemblances between my life and La Gioconda's. She is a singer in love with a sailor, who left her for the wife of a senator. I don't have to explain who the sailor in my life is, nor who was the wife of a senator. And La Gioconda dies for love.

Are these really coincidences, or is there some fiendish master plan designed to mould me into the heroines whose lives I have sung? Or could it be that there are psychological traits we share that get us into similar messes? Who knows? Certainly not I.

Nevertheless, it pleased me when the participants of the Processo Alla Callas noted my portrayals contained psychological perspectives from the period of Freud and Kafka. I've always been told that, psychologically untutored as I am, I have wonderful insight into human nature. I like to believe it is true, and that my intuition, in my singing at least, leads me deep into the bottomless pit of the human soul.

Despite my contract with La Scala, 1952 brought no notice of a production of *La Traviata* from Ghiringhelli. I longed to sing the role and thought it essential to appear in it at La Scala. I decided Mr. G. was shilly-shallying around long enough and it was time for some strong tactics. So I had

Meneghini write Ghiringhelli that if there was no production of *La Traviata* this season I would cancel the *Norma* scheduled in a few weeks. He responded with a special delivery letter saying "every problem with Madame Callas will always be solved with the utmost cordiality." Yes. And I am the Queen of Romania.

He quickly scheduled a meeting in his office. He said La Scala was not able to produce *La Traviata* that year, but promised a new production of the opera for me the next season. Although it was not staged for another three years, Ghiringhelli managed to sweeten the loss nicely. He brought out his checkbook and wrote out my full fee of 1,400,000 lire for four performances.

On November 8, 1952 it was a thrill to make my debut at the Royal Opera House with *Norma*. Covent Garden was the third major house I appeared in, after the Colon in Buenos Aires and La Scala in Milan. It was the first time *Norma* had played there since Ponselle sang the title role in 1929.

Speaking of Ponselle, she is one of the few sopranos I admire, and I've been told my voice has something of the same quality as hers. I've looked up to her ever since I was a child, when I listened to her records and tried to understand how she sang. I would imitate her technique until I could sing an aria the way she did; then I would put aside her style and work on my own. We have sung many of the same roles, like Leonora in *Il Trovatore*, *Gioconda*, Giulia in *La Vestale*, Violetta in *La Traviata*, Maddalena in *Andrea Chenier*, Leonore in *La Forza del Destino*, Elizabetta in *Don Carlo* and, of course, *Norma*.

Some people are born complicated; I, like Norma, was born simple. I try to reduce problems in both life and art to their basic elements, so I can see clearly what I have to do and concentrate on solutions. Of course if you simplify, you must face up to what you find. It is not always pretty, as when Norma understands Pollione's love for Adalgisa, for she has to take the consequences. To simplify, like Norma, you must have courage. She defied the rules of a society she didn't believe in, to love and live with Pollione. And she was able to face her vengefulness and murderous feelings for her children. That takes real courage.

Anything that's complicated bothers me. I don't like modern music because it is all so convoluted. I sing the old music where, as Sir Thomas Beecham said, the melody is good, with tunes. If the public cannot keep a tune in its head after it has heard an opera, that opera is a flop. What can you sing after you've heard a rock concert?

I also believe in self-discipline and a degree of self-restraint. When

Pollione attempts to seize Adalgisa against her will, Norma declares war against the Romans. For even though she still loves Pollione, she loves honor more. But her love for him overcomes her wish for revenge. She proclaims herself the guilty party and sentences herself to the funeral pyre. Despite her passionate nature, Norma turns out to be a straight-laced lady after all. That *is* simple, don't you think?

I deceive no one. What you see is what there is. Norma also deceived no one, and I, like her, am a moral person in that I see what is right and do not evade it. When I say "yes," I mean "yes," when I say "no," I mean "no." When I say I will do a thing, I do it. For example, I don't need to sign a contract. I dislike even the thought of one because it means your word is put into question. But I do not claim to be a "good" woman; that is for others to judge.

My moral convictions and principles, which are somewhat unusual in opera, made trouble for me among my colleagues, especially the women. Of all the divas, only my little Simionato really likes me. I am respected and feared by them, but not liked. I'm sorry about that, even though I pretend not to care. It often makes me sad and lonely, but I can only be who I am.

Sometimes I don't recognize the woman called Callas written about in the newspapers. Paid booers hired by my enemies try to destroy my reputation. Agents wishing to bring in their artists put claquers in the galleries to hiss me and applaud their clients. They want the newspapers to report, "Callas is on her way out—they hissed her again last night. X is a rising star—the audience applauded her like mad." Others hiss who are not paid. With them at least it is a sincere expression of emotion—and they have a right to do so. But it hurts me when top artists trying to interpret musical masterpieces are denied the proper atmosphere to do their best. It seems not so much unfair as brutal and immoral.

Theatre managers tend to think in terms of package deals. One might say, "I want X to sing *La Traviata*." So he goes to her agent who says, "You may have X to sing *La Traviata* if you will take Y to sing Alfredo and Z to sing his father, and agree to the casting of several small parts." Maybe the manager thinks Y and Z don't go well with X or perhaps he wants to cast the small parts with unknowns. But if he wants X for *La Traviata*, he has to take the rest too. I do not like these package deals. I stand on my own merits and am interested in working only with people who do likewise.

If I cannot sing what I want with whom I want with those who want me for what I am, I won't sing in public at all. But the press gives me bad publicity because of it; they say I am a tiger who is impossible to work with. But I do not do it for myself. I want the best standards, the best work, the best company for my art. Music is the deepest means by which one person can communicate with another; it is humanity at its best, the highest level mankind is capable of reaching. I will not knowingly take part in its degradation.

I guess I'm saying that in our own way, Norma and I have integrity, as well as courage. She did what she thought was right, even if it killed her. I, too, will not mouth what people want to hear in order to avoid trouble.

I remember the moment I first stepped onto the Covent Garden stage to sing *Norma* and thought my heart had suddenly stopped beating. I had gotten such fantastic advance publicity I was afraid I never could live up to it. Then I remembered that in my heart I am a queen, and got lost in the music.

For when all the drudgery is over and the problems worked out, a glorious moment comes when the mind recedes and intuition takes over. One enters a second state in which one feels enormous, larger than the theatre itself. One glides through the air, propelled by some sublime instinct, I know not from where. Then the aches and pains, the strain, the frustrations of preparing a role disappear, and one is carried along on the joy of creation. One becomes a vessel for the glorious inspiration of the Grand Creator Himself.

At other moments of course, one feels small, dirty, ashamed, and would like to run away. At those times, the performance must go on anyway, one must continue to sing, to act, to create. Those are the times that try my soul.

But at this moment at Covent Garden, I spiraled to the heavens in the role, so deeply involved I can hardly remember the details. The public senses when such a thing happens, and ascends on high with the performer. In this instance, their approval was overwhelming. They went on applauding until Ebe Stignani, who played Adalgisa, and I were forced to encore the Act One duet.

On December 7, less than two weeks after my Covent Garden *Norma*, I opened the season at La Scala with my first performance of Verdi's *Macbeth*, under the direction of Victor de Sabata. Although I had long been fascinated by the idea of playing her, Lady Macbeth is a difficult role both vocally and dramatically, and my performance had almost no precedent. The mezzo soprano Pauline Viardot appeared in the original version of Verdi's *Macbeth* in Dublin in 1859. Knowing this gave me moral support, as Viardot was the sister of my beloved guide, Maria Malibran. I have always regretted that my great forerunner never attempted the role.

Verdi was a lifelong student of Shakespeare and read and reread him all his life. *Macbeth* was a work special to his career, and as it turned out, for mine too, even though I sang the role no more than a few times. Although Francesco Maria Piave wrote the libretto, Verdi preserved the story and main incidents of Shakespeare's tragedy. Naturally, he had to simplify the wording and limit the number of characters to fit the requirements of opera.

Verdi understood the psychology of Lady Macbeth very well. He said she must look "ugly and wicked, with a harsh, choked, and black voice, the voice of a devil." I followed his instructions to the best of my ability, especially in the hand-washing scene, where the ugliest sounds ever recorded came out of my face. Verdi's understanding of the queen makes me think he must have known a real Lady Macbeth type. If you can't find something or someone in your own life that echoes a role, I don't see how you can possibly write or sing it.

Lady Macbeth gave me a chance to express the hidden, black, satanic parts of my nature, my overriding ambition, the murderous wishes I have tried to conceal all my life, my terrible guilt, which I sometimes fear will drive me mad, my occasional manipulations to get what I want; all the feelings I wouldn't tell my best friend if I had one. Yes, I can even understand being ambitious enough to want to kill to achieve my heart's desire, although my conscience would never let me do it.

The world of opera is not unlike the primitive world of Macbeth, where the philosophy of "foul is fair" reigns. Most singers are reluctant to depict such sordid human emotions on stage. Yet they are feelings all of us have at times, if only we are honest enough to admit it.

The backbone of the part is divided into four solo arias. The first shows the lady in all her power, as she majestically provides the courage Macbeth lacks and provokes him to murder King Duncan. The greed of her ambition dominates the second part. "La Brindisi," the drinking scene, is set within the drama of the banquet, where the drinking song expresses fright, violence, and hysteria, as she tries to hide her husband's guilt from the startled guests. The fourth aria, the famed sleepwalking scene, exposes her mental derangement in all its nakedness.

She has to demonstrate at least six kinds of thoughts in that scene, each one completely different. An ambitious lady, she has persuaded her husband to kill the king so he could take over the throne. But she is tormented by her conscience and the guilt drives her mad. A crazy person, of course, is not logical. First she talks about the bloodstains on her hands and is terrified she can never wash them off. Then she jumps to, "Come now, we must get ready to receive these people, everything is fine." The scene cannot be performed in a straight line as some singers might do, but has to be broken up into many different ideas. Next she abruptly asks, "Why are you afraid to go in? . . . How could you be such a coward? Shame on you!" Then she switches her thoughts again to, "Who could have imagined in that old man there could be so much blood." Her mind wanders one moment, is terrified the next, and then becomes controlling. How could anyone communicate all this in one mode of voice?

Although the doctor speaks to her, the Lady does not hear him. She is completely distracted, cannot look at anything because she is so wrapped up in washing the blood off her hands. She realizes with horror that she can never atone for her guilt and it drives her mad. Verdi has marked this section triple piano, and it should be nearly husky in quality, almost eerie. Have you ever been so petrified you can only whisper because you are afraid people will hear you? I have, many times. There is an eruption followed by a pianissimo when she grows quiet with terror. When you have these outbursts in an opera, you have to be careful it doesn't erase the pianos.

The passage suddenly becomes lyrical when the Lady seduces Macbeth. She must have been a sexy lady. When she says, "Come, don't be afraid, let's go to bed," he cannot resist her. However, she goes on to another frame of mind in which she hears a knocking at the door. In the first act there was a knocking at the door when people entered to say, "God, we have found the king dead!" This and the whole sleepwalking scene are memories of the past. How can a mad woman with bizarre thoughts leaping from one to another be portrayed in a direct, graceful melody, as some critics would have me do? The whole idea is ridiculous. Verdi helps the singer break up the action with his diminuendos, crescendos, and allargandos.

It was gratifying to be called back for seven curtain calls after this scene, which for La Scala is a lot. Many people could not cope with what one critic called my "almost inhuman vocal qualities," but surely this was because of their own limitations, not mine. This was one time when the thunderous ovation at the end of the performance and the glowing comments of critics drowned out the voices of the dissenters.

Yes, I felt good, but it was not always that way. Sometimes in the middle of a performance in which I disappointed myself, I would ask why go on doing this? I don't have to work. Why torment myself this way? Somebody once said, "I think: therefore I am." With me, it is "I sing: therefore I am." I sing because I am Maria Callas and that is the only way to be me.

But it exacts a terrible price. To be a singer at the top of one's profession is to live with frightening pain and loneliness. I cannot always sing top notes in the way expected of me. I am a human being. If you haven't been in this position, you can't imagine what it is like to have people always demand the impossible of you. You must forever demonstrate your superiority or be regarded by them and yourself as a failure.

When I feel I fall short in a performance, the torture is so painful I cannot bear it. It is as if taut steel bands rigidly restrain what is in my heart. I fight and struggle and scream, but I cannot break through the bonds and reach my feelings. It is like a nightmare in which you run and run, but your legs can't move. It is a nightmare I cannot wake up from, because no matter how bad it sounds I must go on singing. When I feel this way, I want to hurry home and bury my head under my pillow until the harrowing metal bands dissolve in the night.

For a singer, the never-ending search for perfection is particularly brutal. If a musician gets ill, he knows his instrument is reliable. But our instrument is our voice, so if a singer gets sick, her voice does, too. When she is terrified, so is her voice. We cannot be allowed even a cold or an injury like any ordinary mortal, or the voice will reflect it. Since we are all human, our voices, unlike the musician's instrument, always have to cope with this or that. Yes, the life of a singer is the most excruciating of all.

Nevertheless, at those rare moments when the voice reaches its pinnacle, you are transported to those mysterious realms which are the closest a human being can get to Heaven. You, like Michaelangelo's Adam on the ceiling of the Sistine Chapel, have been touched by the finger of God. Then the *sturm und drang*, the pain, the torment, the fear, the fatigue, all, all is forgotten, and you soar with the ecstasy found by less fortunate people only in Paradise.

But you cannot do good work alone, as was made clear in the performance of *I Puritani* in Mexico. It is important to have a great conductor help with the orchestra, as well as a fine stage director and hard working, talented performers. That is why it hurt me so much when my sometime friend Giuseppe di Stefano did whatever monkeyshines he felt like, no matter how much it interfered with a performance. A good operatic production consists of teamwork and requires sacrifice, seriousness, knowledge, and faith in the Creator. Without it, a production is no more solid than an aging dandelion that blows away in the wind.

Humiliations and Triumphs

I LOVE THE SILENCE AT THE BEGINNING of a concert the instant before the orchestra begins to play. I always hold the quiet for a few seconds longer than necessary, just to savor the awesome vacuum created when thousands of people become still as death. No one ever sneezes or coughs or fidgets until I sing my first note. It is a moment alive with potential; anything can happen. My performance could rise to the heights I've always dreamed of but have never achieved, the way it is in my head sometimes when I'm working alone. On the other hand, I'm terrified the performance will be a catastrophe. My throat will close up and only a squeak will come out, or my voice will be weak and wavery or off pitch. I will forget the score and stand there dripping with sweat until I am engulfed in a puddle of humiliation. I will be frozen in my muscular prison, in agony as I vainly try to get in touch with my feelings. I reach out my arms and cry "Help me, help me!" but no one is there. Or the prompter is there but is reading the newspaper and pays me no attention. Or as in a nightmare I have sometimes, I am standing on the stage ready to sing, open my mouth, and cannot remember which opera I am supposed to be singing in. Or worst of all, the audience will laugh themselves silly at some unidentified imperfection, and I will die of shame.

I have been laughed at on stage several times. I remember each incident as if it happened a few minutes ago. An obscene episode probably orchestrated by Renata Tebaldi's claque happened once at the curtain call of *La Traviata* at La Scala. My kind supporters had deluged me with bouquets of roses and a rain of flowers. In the middle of all of them a bunch of radishes and turnips was hurled onto the stage. Fortunately, I am shortsighted as a bat and didn't see the demeaning display at first, and bowed and waved kisses to the audience at the curtain call with what I am told is my usual grace and charm. Even after a gasp of embarrassment arose from the viewers, I pretended I hadn't seen the vegetables. I thank the Lord Almighty I didn't give the perpetrators the satisfaction they wanted. But when I got home, I screamed and cried for hours, and experienced a panic at each curtain call for weeks after. I am a sensitive woman, despite my reputation for being a tiger. This show of hostility attacked me at my core, and it took me a long time to get myself back. It didn't help me get over it that Meneghini kept muttering, "One indignity after another!" I've never felt so disgraced in my life, on stage or off.

No, that isn't true. I had a worse experience. I still can't bear to think about the most awful ordeal of my life, until the trouble with Aristo, that is. Before I was thirty years old, I was extremely heavy, and my fat legs plagued me throughout my youth. Even now, when I receive compliments on my sveltness, I'm not happy with the shape of my legs. I try to cover them up whenever possible, even when I am wearing a bathing suit on the beach. If you have seen the photograph of me on Ibiza taken by Aristo in which I have on a bikini, you will note that I am holding a wrap down the side of one leg. Incidentally, I love that photo and think my figure looks fabulous in it. Did you notice my flat stomach?

Back to less pleasant memories. When I appeared in *Aida* at the Arena of Verona, several elephants were led on stage as part of the setting. One of the critics wrote "it was impossible to tell the difference between the legs of the Elephants on the stage and those of Aida sung by Maria Callas." I was only twenty-eight years old and at my most obese, with all the normal young woman's sensitivity to appearance. I thought I couldn't live through the mortification. I have experienced great cruelties before and since in my lifetime, but never have I been so mortified as on reading that review. If the critic had stripped me naked and beat me publicly I couldn't have felt more violated. It was as though a great fire started in my chest and flared through the rest of my body. The flames raged on and on until I almost passed out from the pain, but there was no relief, even though I cried for days after I read the article. Even now I often think of the incident and burn with shame. Many is the time I have shouted that I hope the fiend burns in hell! May his arms and legs be twisted into corkscrews and his teeth be wrenched out one by one! May the Good Lord scourge him for his brutality to an innocent young woman trying to do her best for her art.

But despite my anguish, something good came out of the incident. It taught me to bear the unbearable, to live with shame and rage without collapsing, a strength that was to serve me well later in my life. As I always say, what doesn't kill you will make you strong. More important, the calamity helped set off one of the major changes in my life. I determined never again to open myself up to humiliation by exposing an ugly body for all the world to see.

I had been thinking for a long time that my horrible figure prevented me from singing many roles I would have enjoyed. Can you imagine *Madame Butterfly* played by a heaving two hundred thirty-seven pound woman dripping sweat all over the stage? I can't. I was also preparing to sing *Medea* and it seemed to me a gaunt face was necessary to portray her as I saw her. My face was too fat and I needed the chin line for certain hard phrases, cruel phrases, tense phrases. And I felt—as the woman of the theatre I was and am—that I required these necklines and chin lines to be thin and pronounced. I darkened my neck color and all that, but it is nonsensical to think such subterfuges can fool anybody. There is no way to mask a hundred pounds of flab! I wanted to be a dramatic as well as a vocal success, and the lean and hungry look I required was just not there. I was tired of dragging around the heavy, lumbering carcass of what was supposed to be a beautiful woman. I thought, *If I'm going to do things right, and I've studied all my life to put things right musically, why don't I just diet and get myself into decent shape?*

A person who has never been obese cannot possibly fathom the humiliation and inconvenience of having to leave a movie theatre or needing to pay for two airplane seats when one cannot fit into a single seat: of sitting ungracefully with one's chafed legs spread wide apart so they won't smart, of having salesgirls in dressing rooms look with disgust at the blubber bulging over one's corset, of huffing and puffing on a short walk when one is unable to keep up with a person twice one's age. Then too, I suffered from many headaches and fainting spells, which I attributed largely to my surplus poundage.

The New Year of 1953 was fast approaching, and what better time than New Year's Eve to make a resolution to lose weight? A good friend of mine says, "Other people say they will do things and they don't. Maria says she will do them and she does." Thus it happened that I began the famous diet of green salads and raw meat designed to make me the sylphlike creature of my dreams. I am so jealous of people like Audrey Hepburn who are naturally thin that I determined to have a figure just like hers. Nobody who has not been fat will ever understand the constant hunger and temptations I've lived with ever since. Do you know what it is like to *always* be hungry? There was never a moment the gnawing in my stomach stopped. I never got used to it, no matter how long I stayed thin. I wouldn't wish such torment on Renata Tebaldi. Once I was so starved for something sweet I ate a whole box of massotocci, my favorite candy. I tried to throw up afterwards, but am not able to do so at will. I cried for hours and promised myself never to gorge again if I died of hunger. And I didn't—not for a few months anyway.

It is widely said that my first performance of Cherubini's *Medea* in Florence on May 7 made operatic history. *Medea* is known as a "musician's opera," and Brahms himself described it as the greatest piece of dramatic art in music. I love it, and my creation was one I'm proud to remember. It calls for a ferocious combination of voices and orchestra and is one of the most difficult roles ever written. The great Giuditta Pasta called it "that grand fiendish part," and few sopranos have been able to master it. It is said Julie Scio, the French creator of *Medea*, died after fatally injuring her lungs while singing the role. Clara Stockl-Heinefetter tried to sing it and went insane. *Medea* is a tale of a lusty, revengeful woman, and her savage and tender passions are too raw for most people to bear.

Naturally, I became anxious when I heard all these stories, but soon realized I could sing the role without harming myself. Instead of a boring classical heroine no one was interested in, my Medea became a woman of torrential passion.

I suspect everyone in their heart of hearts would like to experience deep emotions, although most people are embarrassed to show it and freeze up. But that is not my way. Everybody both on stage and off should learn to overcome their shame and let others know how they really feel. I've taught myself to do that more and more in my work and in real life. If I don't like something, I say so. When I'm angry at someone, I don't hold it in. My friends are not always happy about it, but it certainly clears the air. As a result of my willingness to expose my deepest emotions, this little-known opera became a huge box-office success.

Medea came from a savage tribe; she was a primitive Colchian princess who practiced black arts. I saw her as fiery, apparently calm, but intense. Yet I feel her rage should not be primary, because in opera emotion without intellect is no good. You would be a wild animal and not an artist.

The happy time with her beloved, Jason, is past. A goddess and a beast are at war with each other in her body. Within a few moments, she goes from the most beautiful, tenderly sung memories, "We dreamt of heavenly joys on earth, joined together by a sacred, eternal love!" to a malicious declaration of hatred, "Inspire me, O Cholchis, with your cruelest horrors! . . . . Medea, in leaving will tear your heart out!" In the first act, I tried to disguise Medea's rage as much as possible with tenderness and love for Jason. But little by little I dropped her pretenses until by the third act she became a cauldron of evil. Norma agonized over taking her children's lives but couldn't bring herself to do it. Medea not only did it but gloried in the murder. The audience saw vengeance, flaming jealousy, raw evil.

Other divas have moved audiences by projecting fear, rage, love, desire, sorrow, and ecstasy. But I don't believe any singer before me ever communicated naked hatred. Difficult as it is to accept for most people, it is part of the repertoire of human emotions and belongs in a work of art. I see myself, like Medea, as a person familiar with the tenderest of passions, as well as the apex of hatred, and worked at pulling those feelings out of the hidden wells of my deepest self. In the process of learning about Medea, I reached depths of hatred I had never known before.

Rudolf Bing, manager of the New York Metropolitan Opera, was in the audience that night. He indicated he would like me to sing for the Met, but my increasingly bad-tempered husband made it more and more difficult for Bing, particularly in terms of how much money he was asking. The negotiations soon fell apart. Meneghini told the press, "My wife will not sing at the Metropolitan as long as Mr. Bing runs it. It is their loss."

I said to him, "I don't know what's with you these days, Battista. Who is the prima donna around here, anyway? Why don't you learn some English and social graces instead of worrying about money all the time?"

He answered, "Sweetheart, I am just trying to do the best I can so that we can have money for our old age."

I said, "But Titta, I am only thirty-one years old!"

I was not happy. The productions of *Aida*, *Norma*, and *Trovatore* in London in June were done with shabby sets and a bevy of untalented performers. Even the magnificent reviews and spectacular ovations I received were not enough to change my black mood. Maybe living on vegetables and electrical massages made me irritable. And after all that deprivation, what did I have to show for it? I wanted to look like Audrey Hepburn, but I still looked like Kate Smith.

Ghiringhelli came in for his share of my anger, too. Since I had opened the opera season in 1952, Mr. G. with his misguided sense of justice decided it was only fair that Renata Tebaldi open the new season, with *La Wally*. Hmmmm, fair! What does he know about fair? It would only be fair if the better singer were to open the season! I didn't care for the competition between us and thought this would be a good chance to show the public the feud was mostly a product of the media's imagination. Also I missed her and wanted to repair our friendship, as I'd always thought of her as a kind and tranquil woman before our "feud" erupted. So I attended opening night at La Scala and ardently and conspicuously applauded Tebaldi from where I was sitting in Ghiringhelli's box. I felt smacked in the face when I opened as Medea a few days later to find Tebaldi conspicuously absent. It just goes to show which one of us is more competitive and which one holds the grudges!

When I feel hurt I get angry. So naturally, when I was asked by a reporter how I compared myself with Tebaldi I answered, "I am built by an unknown artisan, but my instrument is played by Paganini. She is a Stradivarius played by an amateur." Angry, yes. Mistaken, no. But at least I was a little nicer to her than the time I compared myself to French champagne and Tebaldi to beer! Or was it coca cola?

The public's response to my performance of Medea in Florence had been so overwhelming that Ghiringhelli had felt forced to include it in the new season. He did it by replacing Scarlatti's Mitridate Eupatore. But the switch turned out to be a nightmare for the director, Margherita Wallman. First of all, she had great problems with the sets, costumes, and staging, all of which were of inferior calibre. To make matters worse, Victor de Sabata was stricken with a heart attack ten days before the opening.

I wondered, "Why is God doing this to me? Didn't He know I needed Victor?" No other conductor could be found to step in so close to the performance. Fortunately, Leonard Bernstein was just coming to the end of a long Italian tour. Even though he had never worked in an opera before, had never even heard of Cheubini's Medea, was exhausted from his long tour, and suffered from acute bronchitis, he agreed to undertake the job.

It is interesting how we found him. I had heard a fascinating concert of his on the radio, and found out the name of the conductor. Ghiringhelli, who had never heard of Bernstein, refused to consider him, but when I pressed him (and I do know how to press people) he reluctantly contacted Bernstein.

Lennie later confessed to me that he had been afraid to "meet the tiger," especially after he decided to cut one of my major arias after he became acquainted with the opera. He was afraid of getting me angry. It always amuses me when people are afraid of me, because I know what a frightened little child I am underneath. I find it hard to believe they can't see through me, because there is a space about as thick as tissue paper between the tiger and the defenseless baby. But Lennie was in for a pleasant surprise, for he and I loved each other from the beginning. I found his keen wit, good manners (which I couldn't help but compare to Meneghini's boorishness), and sense of drama irresistible. Lennie himself told a reporter he was absolutely amazed that I immediately understood the dramatic reasons for the transposition of scenes and the cutting out of my aria in the second act. "Callas?" he said. "She was pure electricity."

By this time, I had begun to lose weight, but not too much yet. Miss Wallman said I looked like one of the caryatides on the Acropolis, one of the carved women who stand like pillars supporting the temple. She felt my extra weight gave the characterization a quality of antiquity I would lose if I got thinner. I'm glad she thought so, but I believed I would gain more than I lost in the role with the clean lines a weight loss would bring to my face and chin.

A bizarre incident happened once during the Act One duet in which Medea begs Jason to return to her and their children. As I started "Dei tuoi figli," an awful hissing sound came from the gallery. It escalated like the roar of a tornado and soon filled the entire auditorium. When I reached the place in the score where Medea censures Jason with "Crudel," I was so furious I stopped singing and glared straight into the audience. Then I flung my second "Crudel" right in their faces. Everyone was quiet after that and there wasn't a peep out of a one of them. Incidentally, I still don't know what caused the hissing, unless it was one of Renata's awful claques.

A comment by the great Greek director Alexis Minotis, who had sought to recapture the long-lost style of expression and gesture used in the time of Aeschylus, Sophocles, and Euripides, thrilled me. I am most proud of my proficiency as an actress. I have studied voice with the masters, but my dramatic ability is pretty much of my own creation. When Minotis saw me kneel in a frenzy and beat upon the floor to summon the gods, the very gesture he had directed his wife, the great actress Katina Paxinou, to do in the play, he asked me why I had done it. I said I felt it would be the right thing at that moment in the drama. He went on to say he couldn't understand how I had thought of it. He knew that as an American girl I had never seen the classics, and after the Germans occupied Greece during my stay there, theatrical activities were practically nil. Minotis came to the conclusion these things simply flowed in my blood.

Another incident that still gives me great pleasure happened during a run of *Medea*. A beautiful young singer named Teresa Berganza was playing her first role, my maid Neris. She sent me the following letter about an incident I didn't even remember:

"Dear Maria: Thank you for what you did for me in *Medea*. You gave me so much of yourself on stage I couldn't help giving back to you. You never tried to upstage me or steal the limelight. Instead, you showed me how to act Neris so I could emulate you. At moments I dare to think I even sounded like you. When the aria I sang to you, "Only my heart is open to my grief/ Wherever you go I will follow you faithfully" stopped the show, you remained completely still until the applause stopped. It makes me cry every time I think of it. I have never known such a generous person, certainly not in opera. You are a great lady and there is no way I can thank you except to give you my eternal love and gratitude."

Isn't that a lovely letter? And from a woman singer yet!

Besides being a passionate person, I identified with Medea in other ways. Because I am torn between America, Italy, and Greece, I never really feel at home anywhere. Medea cried out in Pasolini's film, "I look at the sun with my eyes and they do not recognize it. I touch the earth with my feet and do not recognize it." Like her, I am a drifter without a real home who must "wander sadly from land to land seeking peace without ever finding it!" And like her, I somehow found the strength to cut emotional ties when it was necessary to proceed with my life.

The Milan presentation of *Medea* turned out to be one of my most successful performances and I count it among the great days of my career. I sometimes run through it in my mind and am sad I will never sing like that again. But the recording captures me at my best, and I am happy it is preserved for posterity.

I Lose a Mountain of Fat

1954 WAS THE YEAR of my greatest success at La Scala, with thirty-one performances of five operas different in style and technique. I was getting more and more rave reviews, with success beyond my wildest imagination. But for me that was not the big news of the year.

The most wonderful thing that happened to me was that I became the woman of my dreams. I lost sixty-two pounds between *La Gioconda* of December, 1952 and *Don Carlo* of 1954. The change in my appearance set off a mysterious transformation of my personality as well. As a stout woman, I had played at being a grand diva, but never really believed I was. With my new figure I became that person. I no longer had to act the part of a grand lady, and then go home and cry because I invariably messed it up, like the time I was asked to pour tea at the home of the Duchess of Windsor in Paris and dropped the lid of the silver teapot in the bone-china cup. Being slender brought the strangest sensations; one day I felt fat and ungainly, the next day beautiful and sexy.

I had never been interested in clothes because I looked so awful in them. An old tent dress and scuffed shoes were good enough for me. Buying a new dress was torture and I avoided it until absolutely necessary. The year before I had gone to Biki, the granddaughter of Puccini and Milan's leading fashion designer, but she refused to dress me unless I lost weight. Now that I was slender, I went back to her again. Like a starving person let loose in a supermarket, I went on one wild shopping binge after another. Would you believe I bought twenty-five fur coats, forty suits, two hundred dresses, one hundred fifty pairs of shoes, and three hundred hats? Instead of a dumpy child of immigrants, I became a woman of high fashion. I still can't believe my eyes. Serafin couldn't believe his, either.

Meeting him for the first time after my weight loss, I said, "Good morning, Maestro Serafin. How nice to see you again!"

He answered, "I'm happy to hear it, lovely lady. But do I know you?"

"Maestro, it's me, Maria! I'm Maria gotten thin! Don't you recognize me?"

"My God, so it is! What happened to the rest of you, Maria?"

I answered, "I'm leaving it to the other divas, Maestro."

But let me tell you, achieving one's most secret fantasy is not all joy. Sometimes it brought terror to my heart. One day when looking in the mirror, a memory from my adolescence came back to haunt me.

It was hot and humid, as only New York City can be in August, and I was dripping with sweat. I was standing in front of the looking glass of the medicine cabinet of our small bathroom crowded with the curlers, face creams, cosmetics, and assorted paraphernalia of three women. Part of the mirror was covered with steam and reflected a bizarre image back to me. I shut my eyes in order not to see it, but the eerie likeness pierced my fused eyelids. It comes back to me still.

Well I recall the pustules bloody from squeezing, the fat face, the big nose, the coke-bottle glasses. Who is that ugly creature? Why is she in my mirror? Surely it is not Cecilia Sophia Anna Maria Kalogeropoulos, the pretty little girl who lives in my house and comes running when she is called.

Maria, Maria, Ma-ria-Ma, ri-A-Ma, I said over and over until the syllables made no sense. What does it mean to be called Maria? I answer to that name and yet I haven't any idea what it means. To be a certain person, what is the meaning of that? Does anyone know? Certainly not my mother, who was so busy dragging me around to contests and auditions she couldn't have cared less. If I had asked her she would have answered, "Don't be silly, of course you are Maria." Definitely not my father, who was so absorbed in his own troubles that half the time he didn't know I existed. Not Jackie either, she was too wrapped up in her clothes and her boyfriends to pay any attention to her kid sister. I shivered in the hundred-degree heat, and almost passed out in front of the mirror. That pimply, fat-faced, long-nosed stranger simply couldn't be me. I would not permit it; I would stay the pretty little girl forever.

Today I look in the mirror again. This one is an elegant designer original, trimmed in pure gold. I see a tall, slender women with a face characterized by hollows and carved lines. Could this sophisticated lady be the awkward fat girl with pimples of so many years ago? Surely not: Nobody could change that much. Is her name Maria, too? Maria, Maria, ria-Ma, ri-Ama, who are you, Maria? Sometimes I don't recognize you any more than I did that pathetic teenager in Washington Heights. People call me Maria and I answer, but I still am not sure who I am. I had gotten used to being the fat girl with the legs of an elephant, had even gotten fond of her, since the world paid homage to her talents. But I don't know this slender, fashionable lady. I still wake up at night and remember the ghost in my childhood mirror. At least I had gotten used to her face. But this stylish creature who wears French designer clothing, who is she? Sometimes I think I'd rather have the pimples.

When I first lost the weight I was terrified to be this stunning new creature. *Something horrible will happen to me. The fates will be jealous; they will destroy me.* My mother used to tell us about Phaethon, son of Helios, who insisted on driving the sun's chariot against the better judgement of the gods. Phaethon, screaming, was cast down from the skies into the river. I was petrified by her tales of vengeful gods punishing mortals who dared defy them by turning them into stags, boars, and stones. Liska would do that to me if she could. It would be better, I thought, to turn back the clock and be fat clumsy Maria again. At least then I would be allowed to exist.

But my anxiety eventually receded into the background and I became free to enjoy my hard-won victory. Thus the high point of my career that year came not from the raves over my performances, but in the second act of *Alceste* when I could be lifted above the heads of three bearers and carried aloft into the temple. Souls admitted through the Pearly Gates certainly feel no greater ecstasy than I did at that moment.

I first performed *Alceste*, the Queen of Pharae, on April 4, 1954, when I was thirty years old. She was elegant, stately, dignified, and graceful, the perfect role for my new svelte self. I was amused when I met the conductor, Carlo Maria Giulini, for the first time in two and a half years. He didn't recognize me either. He hadn't seen me since I had sung Violetta under him at Bergamo, so I guess it was hard for him to find the fat grungy peasant girl in the body of the slender aristocratic-looking woman. Christolph Willibald von Gluck's *Alceste* had never been performed at La Scala, even though it was first staged in 1767. *Orfeo ed Euridice, Armida,* and a single performance of *Iphigenie en Tauride* had been produced, but the magnificent works of Gluck had been given nowhere near the number of presentations they deserved.

For conductor Giulini, director-choreographer Wallmann, designer Piero Zuffi, and me, our work represented something sacred. In Zuffi's enchanted designs, austere columns supported a frieze copied from antiquity, silhouetted against a sky washed with color. We never limited ourselves to getting the music together and establishing the tempos, but went as far beyond that as we could. We searched for the meaning of each word, the value of each note, of each pause. We looked for reasons a phrase went in one direction rather than another. These are the fundamentals of great art and the only basis on which to perform a role such as Alceste. But most of all, I sought to capture the heart of the character within the spirit of the composer's music.

Always a hard worker, I surpassed even myself on this production. I lived for the opera twenty-four hours a day. Margherita Wallman, the director, asked me to come to the rehearsals of *Alceste* at twelve o'clock, but when she arrived at the theatre in the morning she was surprised to find me already there.

"Dear," she said, "you don't have to be here before noon, because I have to do the staging of the chorus." I was surprised that she was surprised. Like the eager girl who knocked on de Hidalgo's door before eight o'clock, I always attended all the rehearsals of every production I was in. Margherita should have understood that I had to know the complete opera in order to feel it as a whole. How else could I sing the role in depth? This certainly is true of so beloved a work as *Alceste*.

For all of us who brought *Alceste* to La Scala, it was a labor of love. When an artist prepares a project as difficult as this, he is wrapped up in it with every aspect of his mind and body for many weeks, and is glued to the orchestra, the instruments, the singers. The opera forms a private little world around him as the story is retold. This enclosed sphere became my life and was the only thing I found exciting or even interesting. Anything outside of it felt boring, irritating, and a waste of time. I remember once Margherita brought Grace Demetriadis, an old acquaintance from Washington Heights, to my dressing room to see me. You'd think I'd be thrilled to show off my new self and career for her to take back to my old neighborhood, after all they'd put me through. But no, after feeling a twinge of sweet revenge, I couldn't wait until she left and I could get back to my music. That is the manner in which I work. Such absolute dedication precedes the birth of all real works of art.

Thus I came to understand the world of Gluck and the quality of Alceste. I loved my role and tried to approach it with humility, sympathy, and passion. Alceste was a great and majestic queen, a woman of classic nobility. Do you wonder how a little girl from Washington Heights could play a woman of royal stature? I'm going to give away my secret. When I needed to feel most regal, I thought of my mother as I saw her when I was a child.

Alceste is an opera derived from Greek mythology. Greek subjects stir up great passion in me. They bring up primordial images of my heritage, my ancestry. The great classic gestures of the early Greek tragedies came naturally; I did not have to imitate them, for they came out of something deep inside me.

Alcestis was the devoted wife of Admetus, who lay dying. Apollo begged the fates to spare Admetus. They made a nasty bargain with him. They would permit Admetus to live if he could find someone to take his place. Alcestis volunteered. (So would I, in a case like that. Wouldn't everybody who loves?) But the gods apparently were so moved by Alcestis's sacrifice that they granted life to both husband and wife. The opera ends with the victory of love celebrated in a dance, as Admetus and Alcestis sit on the throne. Of course, I am so myopic I couldn't see a thing. But I enjoyed the triumph of good over evil and, for a change in an opera, outwitting the Grim Reaper. Most of all, I loved singing the celebrated aria, "Divinites du Styx," in which Alceste defies the deities of death. In those days I could afford to . . .

The tremendous weight loss meant I could finally sing a role I had been studying for four years. A week after *Alceste*, I played the regal Elizabetta di Valois in Verdi's *Don Carlo*. She was forced to marry the aging King Philip the Second of Spain, although she and the king's son, Don Carlo, were in love with each other. The world must be filled with jealous women, opera is so full of them. Princess Eboli, also in love with Don Carlo, allowed jealousy to get the upper hand and informed the king of the love affair. The King handed the Don over to the Officers of the Inquisition, who dragged him to his death as the curtain fell. Another tragic ending to a beautiful romance. Is that the way life is for all of us?

My costume of black, silver, and white, designed by Nicola Benois, was inspired by the paintings of Velazquez. It was intended "to suggest the drama of a woman cruelly struck by fate." I studied the figures in the paintings Benois had worked from and attempted to emulate their posture and expression in my role. According to Benois, "It was a terrible, black moment in Spain's history, a time when even kings wept." This is what we hoped to capture in our production.

Don't you think it is ironic that the rave reviews were for my physical transformation and not my singing? All those years and all that work and all the critics saw was my figure!

Some of the critics were not impressed with my portrayal of the sweet Elizabetta and felt I would have been better cast as the jealous Eboli. Perhaps that is why I sang Elizabetta only five times, though it is preserved in one of my favorite recordings.

I have said before that even though I achieved fame and fortune I never really performed as well as I wanted. That is the reason I was always upset by a bad review, or even an unenthusiastic one, for then I was sure my mother's poor opinion of me was correct and my self-doubts justified. "This is not right" or "That is wrong," she constantly pointed out, and the critics are just like her. I never stopped working, because I was always afraid the next time I would fail and my entire empire would collapse. In contrast to my mother, Battista was a great help to me at such moments. He would stand in the wings whispering words of reassurance. "Go on, Maria!" he would urge. "There is no one like you. You are the greatest!" I must have believed him, at least for the time being, for he got me through many an emotional crisis. Wasn't it wonderful that I picked someone to marry who was so different from my mother?

Despite the lackluster reviews of _Don Carlo_ and my revived self doubts, I was thrilled to be given the title of "La Regina della Scala" at the end of the year. This was a special honor, not the least because my old rival Renata Tebaldi had also given some brilliant performances that season. It must have been painful for her. Actually, I felt sorry for her. After I win a competition I always feel compassion for my fallen rivals. I know how they must feel.

While I was singing _Don Carlo_, I was also recording _Norma_. Many people had been nice to me on the way up. Here I saw a chance to repay their kindness. Fortunately, I was able to influence casting and the selection of conductors. Thus I could arrange for Serafin, who was not officially connected with La Scala, to conduct most of the operas we recorded with their orchestra and chorus. And I was happy to make sure Nicola Rossi-Lemini, Serafin's son-in-law, was cast as Oreveso. The power to help my friends is a source of great satisfaction to me and is one of the things I enjoy most about my success.

The dramatic weight loss also resulted in my first legal dispute. I didn't know then that it was to be the first of many, and undertook it with enthusiasm. As I have said, I am a moral woman, and will fight immorality passionately when it is directed against me.

In February of 1954, the Pantanella Pasta and Flour Factory published an advertisement using my name without my permission. It said, "In my capacity as the doctor treating Maria Meneghini Callas, I certify that the marvelous results obtained in the diet undertaken by Señora Callas were due in large part to her eating the physiological pasta produced in Rome's Pantanella Mills." It was signed by Dr. Cazzarolli, Battista's brother-in-law and a friend of long standing, who had been best man at our wedding. I was immediately besieged by a host of phone calls and letters demanding to know more about "physiological" pasta, whatever that may be. I lost weight through starvation and my own will power, nothing more! Anyone who has been around me much knows I cannot bear being used. I was in a rage at Cazzarolli's exploitation of family and friendship and demanded a public retraction and apology. It was not forthcoming, as he no doubt felt they could get away with it because of the family connection. I was also furious with Battista throughout this whole thing because, although he denied it to the end, I suspected he had secretly given his brother-in-law permission to use the advertisement. Under the circumstances I had no choice but to bring suit against the company.

Unfortunately for me, the owner of Pantanella was the nephew of Pius the Twelfth, and made various efforts to influence me to drop the action. When I persisted, the Pope summoned us to the Vatican.

"You are Greek and grew up in America," he said, obviously trying to get on my good side. "Yet the way you speak Italian one would say you are from Verona. I congratulate you on your *Kundry*, which I heard on the radio. But I am sorry you did not sing it in German."

As I am not Catholic I was not intimidated by the Pope and disagreed with him vehemently, since I feel Italians get a great deal more from their beloved operas when they are sung in their native language. All the while poor Battista was squirming at my side and nudging me under my coat to shut up.

Then came the real purpose of the meeting. The Pope looked deep into my eyes and said, "I read the newspapers from cover to cover. Nothing escapes me. Not even your legal fight with the Pantanella Company. We should be grateful if you come to a speedy agreement, in a manner in which the Pope could be left in peace."

Meneghini assured him we would.

Shocked and furious that so mighty a man as the Pope would use his holy office to try to rescue his nephew from the consequences of his illegal behavior, I ranted at Battista as soon as we got outside. "This has nothing to do with the Pope," I shouted. "I'm not going to let those crooks go scot-free because he wants them to!"

I was furious because I knew Battista, and I was sure he permitted his family to do this to me. Battista is a weak man, who isn't able to say no to his relatives. This was a further example of my increasing disillusionment with him.

The case dragged on for the next three years, until the Pantanella Company was forced to pay legal expenses and damages and publish a letter of retraction. They accepted most of the judgement but appealed the part about the letter. Sure. As long as they could keep from retracting it, they could continue to cash in on their "physiological pasta!" Meneghini managed to talk me into allowing them to skip the public apology. But as soon as the Pope died, I saw no further need to grant them any favors and insisted on a full public apology. This was eventually confirmed by the courts, and Pantanella and Dr. Cazzarolli were ordered to publish a letter of retraction.

So justice triumphed after all, above so-called religion, family, and the protests of my husband. I told you I am a moral woman. There is justice. There is a God. I have been touched by God's finger.

My next goal was to repeat, or better yet, exceed my European triumph in America. During an interview with the American magazine *High Fidelity*, I said, "Every year I want to be better than the year before. Otherwise I'd retire. I don't need the money. I work for art." Well, perhaps that was not entirely true. I liked the money, too.

Since I had been wanting to launch my career in America for some time now, I welcomed Lawrence Kelly and Carol Fox's offer to appear in the revival of Chicago's famous opera house. Unlike the Met, the young entrepreneurs were so eager to have me they agreed to whatever I wanted, including $12,000 for six performances, my choice of repertory, *Norma*, *Traviata*, and *Lucia*, and the casting of my friends, Gobbi, di Stefano, and Rossi-Lemeni. If I had to pick the musical apex of my life, I would say the Chicago tour was it. These were the days I could sustain an E flat for ten seconds or more. Pandemonium broke out at my performances, where I worried the explosive applause would shatter the chandeliers. I received twenty-two curtain calls after *Lucia* and the aisles were packed with fans shoving toward the stage. I could hardly walk through the downpour of flowers. The press blockaded me, admirers swarmed around me, and balls were given in my behalf. The reviews were all superb, like the one by Claudia Cassidy who wrote, "She sang the 'Casta Diva' in a kind of mystic dream, like a goddess of the moon briefly descended." I was feted as the ugly duckling turned swan, the American dream come true. But no dream I ever dreamed surpassed the miracle of my Chicago tour.

Best of all, my father stood by my side and saw it happen. It seems even the Sphinx can be moved. When I saw tears roll down his cheeks, I knew I had proven myself in his eyes and the eyes of God.

But remember my mother's story about Phaethon and the jealousy of the gods? I should have known that sooner or later they would make me pay for my success.

For all during the triumph of the tour trouble was brewing underground. As you may recall, I had thoughtlessly signed a contract in 1947 with Eddie Bagarozy that granted him the right to be my sole representative, including a ten-percent share of all my fees and the expenses he was supposed to have incurred on my behalf. Would you believe $300,000! He couldn't have spent that much on me if he had purchased the Met outright! Rossi-Lemeni, who had signed the same contract, had the foresight to pay Bagarozy a few thousand dollars to get him off his back. But my tight-fisted husband was unwilling to part with a dime. So I immediately issued a statement that Bagarozy had gotten me to sign under duress, had done nothing at all for my career, and therefore had no claim on me whatsoever.

Nevertheless, the lawsuit dragged on interminably and caused me endless distress and fatigue. At some points, I was so upset by it I tossed around all night and couldn't even work. It was a good three years before the infected thorn in my side could be pried loose.

I had changed my body, a project everyone thought was impossible. That gave me the courage to begin a greater enterprise, as I brought all my energy to bear on transforming classical opera. I had a wonderful vision of awakening its deadness, like the resurrection of Christ. I wanted to show that drama in opera is simply the material of real life magnified a thousand times. Instead of exhibits of stiff vocal declamations, opera needs to ooze life, sweat, and blood, and I wanted to bring it about. To do so I needed to put the singer back as chief interpreter of the composer's music. This was not new thinking: every great operatic advance in the past, including the works of Verdi, Wagner, and Gluck, was geared toward establishing emotional interest in music. They belonged to the Romantic era of the nineteenth century when music was full of feeling, which, I don't have to tell you, is my favorite period. In my day and age, I had to do it alone, as the stilted stance of other opera stars and the limitations of conventional conductors fought me every step of the way. Most singers just stood like corpses in the middle of the stage and sang.

To help me accomplish my goal I had to find allies. I discovered one in Luchino Visconti. Because he helped bring about my vision, I loved him with all my heart for a time. He always thought I was *in* love with him, but that was not the truth. He was homosexual, and how could any normal

woman be in love with a homosexual? But even though I was thirty years
old I had a violent school-girl crush on him, because he was my mentor who
taught me how to act. As a singer I had placed myself at Serafin's feet. Now
as an actress I sat at the feet of Visconti. I wanted him to help me become as
great an actress as a singer.

Luchino was a nobleman, a duke, one of Italy's most notable film
makers, and a distinguished director in the Italian theatre. This excited me,
because, frankly, I hadn't encountered too many noblemen in Washington
Heights.

Luchino says I fell in love with him and followed him around like a
schoolgirl. He thought I was possessive, and jealous of his homosexual
lovers. Didn't the man realize I am a Greek? That is the way Greeks love,
passionately and primitively. He became a part of me. I was not *in* love with
him, but only loved him. I repeat, I was not in love with him! Anyway, when
he got to know someone well he had terrible manners. He often behaved
boorishly, even worse than Battista. Somehow he believed his nobility gave
him the right to use vulgar language and ignore me when he felt like it, like
when he hung around his homosexual pals. I learned all I could from him,
and when he had no more to teach me, I got tired of him and his affected
ways. So much for our so-called love affair!

Despite the ins and outs of our personal relationship, the man accomplished miracles. When he took on Spontini's *La Vestale*, it was the first time
a professional of his stature had ever directed an opera. The revival of the
opera, which I had requested after twenty-five years of neglect, opened the
La Scala season on December 7, 1954. The production was overwhelming,
with its massive three-dimensional sets and historic costumes. It created a
frenzy and broke all records at La Scala. We didn't know it then, but it was
eventually to change the history of opera.

I never acted better than under Visconti's guidance. He was a connois-
seur of art, and indeed, helped Battista and me choose paintings for our new
Milan home. He based many of my stances and gestures in the opera on
classic paintings by Canova, Ingres, and David, and together we studied the
poses of great Greek and French actresses. He wanted to transform me into
a classical actress, with the grand and eloquent gestures typical of those
times. The man is a genius, and, perhaps because I loved him, I was able to
take his suggestions almost before they were out of his mouth.

Arturo Toscanini, then a very old man, was sitting in a box with Victor
de Sabata at the premiere. As the French say, the more things change the
more they stay the same. Shades of my performance when I was thirteen on
the ship coming over to Greece! When a deluge of red carnations poured

down on me at the end of the second act, I picked one up with a bow and offered it to Toscanini. The tumultuous applause said the audience approved as much as they had when I presented the carnation to the ship captain so long ago.

Speaking of Toscanini, I have a sad truth to tell you. I have never gotten over the fact that he preferred Tebaldi to me.

La Traviata, My Crowning Jewel

MY FIRST PERFORMANCE IN 1955 was supposed to be *Il Trovatore*, with Mario del Monaco as Manrico. But three weeks before, he had sung Giordano's *Andrea Chenier* at the Met with great success. He persuaded Ghiringhelli to substitute it for *Trovatore* only five days before the opening. At first I was seething. What is it with these men? If I had suggested changing the opera five days before production, Ghiringhelli would have screamed and hollered and it would have been plastered all over the papers that Callas was pulling another one of her stunts! But let two men get together and do what they will and all is well with the world! After a bit, however, I calmed down and thought it might be fun and a challenge to learn the part of Maddalena di Coigny in five days, just like in the old days.

As usual, I should have listened to my instincts. The performance was a total disaster. The concentrated rehearsals for *Chenier* on top of the grisly schedule of the last six months showed in my voice, and my worst nightmare came true. When I got to my biggest aria, "La mamma morta," my voice wobbled and got out of control on a climactic high B. Besides my own mortification, the audience behaved atrociously, booing and hissing and whistling enough to drown out the applause. The wonderful compliments of the composer's widow and the enthusiasm of the critics couldn't begin to make up for my humiliation. I was furious, and knew right away the demonstration had been led by Tebaldi's claquers.

As a result, I roared at the press, "If the time comes when my dear friend Renata Tebaldi sings Norma or Lucia one night, then Violetta, Gioconda, or Medea the next—then and only then will we be rivals. Otherwise it is like comparing champagne with cognac. No—with Coca-Cola." Of course I was never allowed to forget my understandable outburst, which I'm sure will be quoted to the end of time. When I opened in *Medea* a few days later in Rome, Tebaldi's crew were out in full force to pay me back for my assault on their heroine. The most ironic thing about the substitution of the operas is that I was blamed for the whole incident on both sides of the Atlantic. Everyone was sure it had been at my insistence that the operas had been switched. Callas can never win. If my enemies don't see to it, my friends will!

I was so upset by the unexpected turn of events that I returned to Milan sick in body as well as in heart. I had a painful boil on the back of my neck the size and color of a juicy Italian plum, and my doctor ordered complete bed rest. The opening of Bellini's *La Sonnambula*, directed by Luchino Visconti, had to be postponed two weeks, to the utter delight of Leonard Bernstein, who was thrilled with the eighteen rehearsals he got instead of the one usually earmarked for the conductor.

I worked on the part all the time I was in bed. There is a special reason I enjoy singing Armina; it was one of my dear Malibran's favorite roles. It is sweet, simple music that I love.

Armina and Elvino are set to wed in a village courtyard when an unknown Count arrives in their midst. He goes to sleep for the night, and Armina sleepwalks into his room. Elvino finds out and gives her the gate. Then Armina walks in her sleep again over a fragile bridge. (Which, incidentally, had everyone in the opera and probably the audience terrified that shortsighted Callas would break her neck! They didn't know how carefully I had marked out every step in my mind.) Elvino then understands why Armina was found in the Count's room and joyfully embraces her as she awakens.

How simple, after the convoluted plots of *La Gioconda* and *Tosca*! And what joy to sing in an opera where I was not a killer, a murder victim, or a suicide!

At the end of the opera when the lovers are reunited, all the lights on both the stage and auditorium, including the famed great central chandelier, were turned up full flood. The last bars of my final aria, "Ah! non giunge" were blanketed in a swell of bravos and applause. It was a moment that fills me with happiness every time I remember it.

Incidentally, although I've never walked in my sleep, I can understand the state of mind that makes someone do it. Once after I finished some Pasta E Fagioli before a performance of *La Sonnambula*, I was so out of this world that I carried the empty bowl up the stairs to my bedroom. I didn't realize it until Battista ran after me and took it out of my hands.

Visconti is a magnificent director. He helped turn my character into a reincarnation of the nineteenth century ballerina Maria Taglioni, who inspired his conception of the part. Somehow, with his superb talent, he made me, a woman of five feet nine inches, appear small and graceful. He even taught me ballet positions and how to take little ballet steps. "A sylphide tripping on a moonbeam" is how the designer Piero Tosi remembers me in the role. I never in my life thought I could look like a sylphide, on or off of a moonbeam. Visconti helped me sing the part of an unsophisticated girl with what was called a high degree of artistry. It is not easy to convey both attributes at the same time. The performance was another great Visconti-Callas triumph. There is no doubt in my mind that Visconti was a genius, and I am grateful to him.

All the time I was working on *La Sonnambula*, Meneghini was furnishing our brand new home on the Via Michelangelo Buonarroti, where a four-story house was being turned into a palace. It made me feel like I was truly the prima assoluta of the world. What a long way I had come from Washington Heights!

Battista was also negotiating with Lawrence Kelly for a contract with the Chicago Lyric Company for a second season there. Because he knew they were desperate for my services—indeed, without me there would have been no Chicago season at all—Battista gave them his usual hard time. He made Kelly give me everything I wanted, including a unique proposal that would protect me from further ravages of Bagarozy. I remember playfully telling Kelly that he should sign up Renata Tebaldi too. "Then your audience will have the opportunity to compare us, and your season will be even more successful." To my surprise he took me up on my proposal.

Speaking of Tebaldi, she really wasn't much competition anymore. She sang Verdi's *La Forza del Destino* on April 26 at La Scala, but it was the last time she appeared there until December 7, 1959. I guess she decided La Scala was not big enough for both of us. Poor Renata! But to the victor belong the spoils.

For my fourth opera of the season I tried something different from my usual gloomy heroines. On April 20, 1955, I took on the comic role of Fiorilla in Rossini's *Il Turco in Italia* at La Scala. I ordinarily am not a funny person, but one who steeps herself in serious work, so I was afraid to try the silly opera. But it turned out to be lots of fun. It is the story of the young wife of the aging Don Geronio, who flirts with the visiting Sultan as she wanders about the house raving about the joys of infidelity. She not only has an old husband, but is soon to pursue the wealthy Turk. It must have been a premonition of things to come, for I really got into the spirit of things. At one point I even danced a little tarantella and at another spontaneously took off my shoe and hit Zaida, my rival, with it. I was told the public was quite aware of the age of Meneghini, and it added extra spice to the production for them. And, I must admit, for me too.

The opera was directed by Franco Zeffirelli, with whom I had a little tussle about my costumes. He set the opera in the period in which it was composed, but I was upset by the bulky folds of my skirts and the way I was always draped with a scarf that covered up my midriff. "All that dieting," I complained to him, "and you give me a waistline up to my neck!" I snuck around to the seamstress and got her to lower the waistline, but that devil Zeffirelli made her hike it back up again.

On May 28, 1955, I concluded the season with *La Traviata*, a drama of the romantic era, in the most beautiful production of my life. The music is incredibly sweet and the aria "Vanne...lasciami" (Go...leave me) in which I say goodbye to Alfredo is the most poignant aria I ever sang. I had played Violetta before at Bergamo and Sao Paulo but this time around was a different story. Carlo Maria Giulini, the conductor, spoke for me too when he said he was overwhelmed by its beauty every time he looked at the performance. "What transpired on stage was truth, life itself," he said.

For Giulini, Visconti, and me it was a creation from deep in our hearts. Working together for weeks, our growing insight helped us discover new colors in my voice, hidden nuances in Verdi's score, and creative ways of expressing what we learned. We uncovered a stillness at Violetta's core which set the tone for my characterization and led to the final fragile style of the dying woman. It was thrilling to unearth an ever richer understanding of her sacrifice and deep-seated pain, and to discover a silence in my own core I never knew was there.

Violetta Valery is a courtesan who has never been in love. As we saw it, she is afraid that if she gives in to love she will have to give up her selfish desires to do as she pleases, go where she chooses, and make love with whomever she fancies. When you don't have much of a self to begin with, it is frightening to give over to another person what little you've managed to hold on to. I know . . . it took me a long time to allow myself to love.

When Violetta cradles her face in her hands and sings, "Oh, Amore" from deep inside herself, we know she cannot keep from falling in love with Alfredo. This was acted out in an exquisite scene in which I, carrying a bouquet of violets, backed off when Alfredo declared his love for me. Then as I surrendered to his embrace, I slowly dropped the violets to the floor.

Violetta leaves her life of pleasure and moves with Alfredo to her home in the country, where they are ecstatically happy. Unfortunately Alfredo is broke, and Violetta is forced to sell her jewels to afford their country life. When he finds out, he rushes off to Paris to raise some cash. In his absence his father, Germont, arrives and, in a scene many feel is the essence of *Traviata*, pleads with Violetta to give up Alfredo. Germont says she is jeopardizing Alfredo's future, as well as his sister's. For Violetta has been a prostitute, and the fiance of the pure and innocent young girl will not marry her if he knows Alfredo is living with Violetta. She sympathizes with Germont's dilemma, and out of her deep love for Alfredo as well as a feeling of mercy for the purity of his sister, agrees to leave him.

The scene in Act Two in which Violetta renounces Alfredo is sheer poetry and probably the most moving I've ever sung. It was a rare night the audience was not in tears along with me. The aria "Amami, Alfredo" where Violetta takes her leave of Alfredo broke my heart every time I sang it, and the words will haunt me to the grave:

> . . . you love me, you love me,
> Alfredo, you love me, don't you?
> I needed tears—
> Now I feel better
> See? I am smiling at you—see?
> I shall always be here near you, among the flowers.
> Oh my beloved,
> Love me always, Alfredo,
> As I love you.
> Farewell, my love!

Just putting down the words makes me cry.

Violetta writes Alfredo a letter saying she no longer loves him, which he believes. She returns to Paris and her former mode of life, where she grows desperately ill with consumption.

Perhaps more than any other role, I understood the character of Violetta. I had to play Violetta so that she was transformed from an egotistical woman who lives for her own pleasure to one who develops a genuine capacity to give. Although she has formerly led a life devoted to her own enjoyment, her selfishness is transcended through love. She becomes a truly heroic woman who renounces love out of a great generosity of spirit, even though she is sapped of her *raison d'être* when she loses her lover.

As Violetta lays dying, she reads a letter from Alfredo's father, who says Alfredo has learned of her sacrifice and is returning to her. He rushes in and embraces her, but it is too late. She sinks rapidly and dies in his arms. It took me years to develop the role so her illness became apparent in my voice and she could grow progressively weaker as the opera proceeded.

I finally understood it to be a question of breathing. One needs a clear throat to keep up the tired-sounding speaking and singing. Later, in a London production, my voice broke for a moment on a top A at the end of "addio del passato." It was exactly the effect of dying I had been trying to get for years. If I had used a little more pressure in my breathing the effect would have been ruined. But of course there were always the critics who said, "Callas is tired. She is over the hill. She can't hold a top A anymore." How ridiculous! How could a dying woman sing big, clear, high notes? But my mother taught me early enough that people who are out to criticize will always find grist for the mill. Let them say what they want. I have to do what I have to do. The meticulous, careful work in *Traviata* was done not for success in the public eye, but for theatre in the most profound sense of the word.

I got many marvelous reviews, including some that compared my performance to the great beauty of Greta Garbo's *Camille*. This time it was mostly Visconti who got the criticism. To please me and show off my new figure to better advantage in the costumes of the day, he had changed the action to a *fin-de-siècle* background. He said that with my tall, newly slender body, I would be a vision in a gown with a tight bodice, a bustle, and a long train. He was severely attacked by the traditionalists for this small departure from the composer's stage directions. And when he had me throw off my shoes before "Sempre libera," and God forbid, wear my hat and coat while dying instead of lying back in bed, he created a commotion. Such conservative thinking is the product of small minds. It was just this kind of creative imagination that made Visconti a great director.

I have said that Visconti, Giulini, de Nobili, and I worked together like a dream. But in any cast, there is usually one member out of step with the rest. This time it was my good friend and preferred singing partner of a lifetime, Giuseppi di Stefano. He has a unique voice with an incredibly sweet timbre I would recognize anywhere, but he relied on his God-given gifts and worked as little as possible. He joined our rehearsals when Visconti wished to show him the intimate love play he had conceived between Violetta and Alfredo. But Pippo was bored with the opera and was always late and disinterested, or didn't show up at all. I became angry with him once and shouted, "It is a lack of respect for me and also for you!" It didn't help.

He did listen to me another time when he failed to appear at a rehearsal.

A friend of mine was singing her first Tosca at the Chicago Lyric Theatre, and to her shock found she had no co-star. She phoned me in a panic. "What shall I do, Maria? Di Stefano is not here and doesn't answer his phone. My big chance is ruined. I can't go on without a leading man." I called his hotel and asked an Italian waiter to stand outside Pippo's room and shout, "If you don't show up immediately at the rehearsal you will have to answer to Callas." He went.

But there is just so much one can do. He is one of those people who never grow up. At one rehearsal he wore one of those atrocious American trick ties in which you press something and a snake jumps out. Visconti and I were not amused.

It must be something inherent in the tenor character. Caruso had a similar sense of humor, if I may dignify it by calling it that. Once, in the last act of *La Bohème*, when poor Mimi was dying in the middle of her iron bed, the Bohemians pushed it to the center of the stage. A gasp went up through the audience as a gleaming white chamber pot put there by you know who was revealed for all Covent Garden to see. I don't imagine Nellie Melba, who was playing Mimi, was amused either.

Di Stefano was resentful of our long and arduous rehearsals, and all the attention I was getting, and after the first performance walked out of the theatre, the production, and the city! We had to replace him in the next two performances with Giacinto Prandelli, and I vowed never to speak to di Stefano again. Of course, like other such vows of mine, it didn't last. But I certainly meant it at the time.

Di Stefano could have been as great as any opera star before him, even Caruso, if only he weren't such a spoiled brat. He was not only a great singer but a great actor, and a dream lover on stage. The love scenes we sang together in *Traviata, Lucia,* and *Un Ballo in Maschera* are the most exquisite of my career, and never fail to move me when I hear the recordings. I often found myself day dreaming that we had a child together. What a magnificent voice a child of ours would have been born with!

To express appreciation for the marvelous season at La Scala and in particular for my performance in *La Traviata,* Ghiringhelli surprised me with an elegant hand-wrought silver mirror. I could hardly believe that this man who had hated me and made our lives difficult for such a long time would give me a beautiful present. He actually smiled with his eyes when presenting it to me. I was genuinely moved and accepted it as graciously as I could. I guess even the worst of us have some redeeming feature.

I spent July learning Puccini's *Madame Butterfly* for my coming Chicago tour. I took lessons from the famous Japanese Butterfly, Hizi Koiyke, on how to unwind my complicated hairdo so I could let it fall at the exact moment I commit suicide. Most of the singers who have the voice for the part are not capable of portraying a fifteen-year-old girl. A child lives inside of me beside the passionate woman, and I was able to sing both.

I sang the role of Cio-Cio-San for the first time in August for the recording microphones under Tullio Serafin, along with *Aida* and *Rigoletto*. And guess who sang the Duke of Mantua in that one? That's right! It was none other than my dear friend Giusepppe di Stefano. He is so cute and so talented I forgave him his tantrums in Milan. Also, I needed him.

In August, I was elated at the visit of my beloved friend and teacher, Elvira de Hidalgo, who had been teaching at the Conservatory of Ankara, Turkey for the last few years. It was as if no time at all had passed between our visits and we were as close as ever. But then I had never really felt far away from her. We always corresponded, and I kept her in touch with all my engagements and, less happily, my problems. She never failed to come through with wise and caring counsel. I was delighted to be able to share my triumph as Violetta with her. She couldn't have been happier if she had done it herself. And, indeed, part of her had.

She was the only one I told of my increasing dissatisfaction with Battista.

"He sleeps in front of the TV all evening, and doesn't share my quest to understand human nature and the ways of the world, Elvira. He has nothing to teach me anymore and he bores me."

Elvira, wise woman that she was, said, "Be careful, Maria! You are expressing the kind of feeling that breaks up marriages."

I laughed, and said, "I never would leave Titta because he is so good to me. But I can tell you this, Elvira. Sometimes when I look at him I have to turn away, because I can't stand his ugly beer belly and his greasy balding head."

Elvira could only shake her head sadly.

In September I sang a few *Lucias* under Karajan at the Stadtische Oper in Berlin, with much the same cast as had appeared at La Scala. An excellent recording was made of it and many people feel it is one of my best. Nevertheless, the performance worried me. I sounded thinner and paler than at La Scala. My voice didn't surmount the orchestra in the stretta, and I had to conclude the cadenza without an E" flat. And, ominously, there was no applause from the audience. At La Scala when I sang the E" flat, pandemonium broke out. I hoped it was merely a stroke of bad luck, and it, too, would pass.

The final performance of *Madame Butterfly* in Chicago was the prelude to one of the worst nightmares of my life. I hate to think about it, but my story is incomplete without including at least some account of that miserable experience.

I opened as Butterfly on November 11, 1955, after having sung *I Puritani* for the last time, as well as *Il Trovatore*. Until the Bagarozy episode, my visit was a dream come true. All of the "creme de la creme" of Chicago courted, wined, and dined me, and treated me like the divine being they thought I was. Would you believe, box-office lines stretched the length of the theatre, around the corner, and over the bridge to the *Daily News* building! No engagement could have been more delightful, as it seemed the whole city strove to honor me and give me pleasure. I really tried my best to be nice, too, because I wanted to repay their kindness. (Incidentally, I hate the word "nice." It is so . . . so nothing a trait!) Carol Fox and Lawrence Kelly had pleaded with me to give an extra performance, and in my new efforts to be "nice" I agreed. But the third performance of *Butterfly* turned out to be a disaster and the tragic end to my love affair with Chicago.

The applause that night went on interminably, and I was eager to leave and get home. I had just come off the stage, tired but elated, when a man wearing a felt hat and white raincoat like Humphery Bogart rapped me on the shoulder and poked a paper into my kimono. I was indignant at this invasion of my body. How dare he? Surely a more dignified method of presenting something to a prima donna could be found! I was also bewildered and couldn't figure out what he was giving me. At first I thought maybe he was a crazy, or perhaps there was a review or something he wanted me to see.

Trying to fight him off, I said, "How dare you touch me? I am Maria Callas. Who are *you*?"

He answered, "I don't care if you are the Queen of England, lady. I am Marshal Stanley Pringle. This is a summons issued by Edward Bagarozy for you to appear in court."

I screamed, "I will not be sued! I have the voice of an angel. No man can sue me! Chicago will be sorry for this!"

It turned out that Bagarozy was suing for the $300,000 he considered ten percent of my earnings since 1947. Apparently he smelled blood, with all the publicity going on about me.

What a moment to humiliate me, after one of the great triumphs of my life! I was infuriated and continued screaming at him. Of course the paparazzi picked just that moment to photograph me in the most hideous picture ever taken of me. It didn't help that my garishly made-up Butterfly mouth was twisted with rage. The picture was reproduced all over the world and I never was able to live it down. It marked a turning point in my relationship with the public, and is responsible for the terrible reputation that has haunted me ever since.

It was all so unfair! I was the abused one and I was attacked for being a witch! When a person gives her life to the public she shouldn't be left to the mercy of any unprincipled person who happens to come along! I had a clause in my contract requiring the Lyric Theatre to protect me from harassment while I was in Chicago. They failed to keep up their end of the bargain. Nobody shielded me from the indignity, and I never got rid of the suspicion that I had been betrayed by the management of the Lyric Theatre. As a result, I vowed never to return to Chicago.

What an awful way to end the year of my greatest triumph! Mother was right once in a while after all. Whom the Gods would destroy, they first make proud.

Underground Rumblings

1955, AS THEY SAY IN AMERICA, was a tough number to follow, considering the triumphs of *La Sonnambula, La Vestale,* and *Traviata.* Compared to 1955, 1956 was a disaster. It started out well enough, with twenty performances of *Traviata* at La Scala held over from the last season again proving the most exciting productions of the year. But after that, one fiasco followed another.

Of course, the time the bunch of radishes was thrown at my feet will long be remembered, but I don't care to think about *that* again. And have I mentioned the horrible story making the rounds, thanks to my esteemed colleague Mario del Monaco? Since the Bagarozy incident in Chicago, people are willing to believe anything about me. I'll never understand it. I'm given a summons in an atrocious manner by a liar and a cheat and the world rises up in arms against *me*! Lord have mercy on me.

After one of my January *Norma*s in Milan, Mario, who was playing Pollione, told the newspapers I kicked him on the shins in order to steal a solo bow. Can you believe it? Everybody who has ever worked with me knows how scrupulously fair I am with my colleagues. I never even hold a note on stage beyond what is customary without getting their permission. Mario said he had insisted Ghiringhelli allow no solo curtain calls and I kicked him in the shins so I could rush on stage and take my bow alone. He was just getting even with me for a dispute he had with Meneghini. Battista, in his increasingly quarrelsome stance, had gone to the claque chief, Ettore Parmeggiani, and given him the business for an unreasonable display of enthusiasm by del Monico's so-called admirers. Parmeggiani went and complained to del Monaco, who charged up to Meneghini shrieking, "You and your wife don't own La Scala, you know! The audience applauds whoever deserves applause!" Ha! Anyone who has heard his Pollione knows his heavy-handed metallic rendition could never bring down the house! To add to the unpleasantness, he kept squawking at me off stage every chance he got until I hid behind the curtain when I saw him coming.

When I got home that night I listened to a record of *Norma* that had something wrong with it. It sounded like the shrieking of two mating cats. It made me laugh so much I listened to the whole thing. That's what Mario sounds like when he screeches at me, a mating cat.

I next appeared in *Il Barbiere di Siviglia* on February 16 at La Scala. That was another catastrophe, put together with spit and scotch tape. It was an old stock production revived without finesse or imagination. I thought because I did well as Fiorilla in *Turco* that I would be just as effective in another comic role. I had another thing coming. I guess I need a director like Zeffirelli to bring out the light touch in me. I am such an earnest, serious person that sometimes I sound heavy-handed even to myself. My performance as Rosina went over like a soggy pizza. It was a disaster all around. Carlo Giulini said it was so bad he conducted with his head lowered so he wouldn't have to see what was happening on stage.

We closed the Milan season on June 3 with Giordano's *Fedora*, the last of six performances conducted by Gianandrea Gavazzeni, an exciting new addition to the staff of La Scala. The play by Victorien Sardou was once a vehicle for Sarah Bernhardt, but hadn't been performed since her death. At the time the play was a shocker, because of its open approach to unwedded bliss. But by the time we presented the opera, it had lost much of its shock value, although, believe it or not, I still am not in favor of extramarital relations. I was coached for the role by the great Russian actress, Tatiana Romanov, and was pleased to be told I had grasped the elements of the Russian acting style extremely well. She said no singer had ever sung Fedora with so much nuance, color, and subtlety. But wouldn't you know, the kind of criticism I got was, "Even if she is not the greatest singer, she is certainly one of the world's greatest actresses."

Actually, there is an element of truth in that review. If I am pushed to describe my talents, I would say I am not so much a singer who acts as an actress who sings. I always worked to inflect my words so they added natural color to the music. And in every role, I tried to adapt my voice to the character. Perhaps the best examples are *Butterfly* and Gilda in *Rigoletto*, in which I sang in a "little girl" voice at the beginning of the operas. While my colleagues know how conscientiously I always worked at understanding the music, my acting came from the soul, and I always knew instinctively what to do.

On June 12 the entire Milan company trooped to Vienna, where the majestic Staatsoper, which was severely damaged during the war, was celebrating its first season after the reconstruction. Our production of *Lucia di Lammermoor* was the high point of the "Festwochen." Herbert von Karajan, the conductor, was the power behind the scenes. As a boy, he had traveled a hundred miles, partly on foot, to see Arturo Toscanini conduct the opera, with the great Toti dal Monte singing Lucia. It had been the goal of his lifetime to return to the Staatsoper with me singing the role. Happily, the festival fulfilled his ambition. Further proof that nothing makes for greater happiness than having your childhood dreams come true.

No, despite our great success in Vienna, it wasn't a good season. To top it all off, I was getting worried about my voice. When I sang *Il Trovatore* for EMI in August, the recording took ages to make. My voice was unsteady and I was finding I could not depend on it to stay in focus or to remain under my control. I said to myself, maybe it is because Battista and I had been on vacation on Ischia off the coast of Italy and I hadn't rehearsed enough. After all, I'm not even thirty-three years old! That's much too young for a voice to go downhill. Then I decided perhaps it was the role, and determined never to sing it in the theatre again.

Speaking of vacations, a delightful thing happened when I was the guest of honor at the Seventeenth Annual Motion Picture Festival in August. Only someone who was a fat, pimply teenager can appreciate this one! I was lying under a tent talking to Carla Mocenigo, a friend from my Venice days, when two young men approached and asked us out for the evening. I pointed to Meneghini who was sleeping beside me, and said, "I'll have to ask my father." And they believed me!

You may have noticed that the name of Serafin is absent from the three recordings I made in August. That's because I was furious with him. He was supposed to use me in the *Traviata* he made for EMI, but because I had contracted with Cetra not to rerecord *Traviata* until 1957, he went ahead and recorded it with Antonietta Stella singing one of my favorite roles. You'd think a man who claimed to love and value me so much could manage to wait a year, after all the beautiful performances I gave him. I considered it an impertinence and a gross betrayal of both friendship and musical etiquette and vowed to make no more recordings with Serafin.

At last the big event I had been waiting for all my life! I finally got to sing at the Met. I arrived at Idlewild Airport with my husband, two secretaries, and my poodle Toy. (If you are wondering how it was that Toy was still alive, all my dogs are called Toy. This one was Toy number two. Or was it three? I never can remember.) I was happy to find my father waiting there, along with Public Relations man Dario Soria, representatives of the Met, and an attorney in case any legal difficulties arose. This time Georges didn't have to find out about my arrival by reading the passenger list of Greek immigrants, for the papers were full of my debut at the Met. He was scrupulous about saving every speck of information in the papers about me, and had no difficulty finding out about my arrival. That's how he showed his love, by saving all that stuff, although he never did seem to appreciate my singing. Some people are opera lovers and some are not. I'm learning as I grow older to forgive him for being himself.

We opened at the Met on October 29 with the perennial *Norma*, five of them, and then went on to two *Toscas*. Despite my yearning to sing at the Met, I was terrified. The more important something is, the easier it is to mess it up. I kept asking Bing, "Is New York really anxious to hear me?" I had so many memories of rejections by New Yorkers it was hard to believe that this time they actually wanted me. Bing said later he'd been struck by my "girlishness, the innocent dependence on others that was so strong a part of her personality when she did not feel she had to be wary."

Me dependent? Me? I'm the most independent person I know. How else could I have the courage to walk on stage with my knees knocking before thousands of people who would be delighted to see me fail? But I was relieved somebody saw the insecure little girl beneath my pose of sophisticated diva. It is so much me I don't understand why everyone doesn't see it all the time.

Just as I was about to relax and think I could repeat my European success, *Time* magazine came out with my picture on the cover and a mortifying four-page story about me. *Time* had given a questionnaire to my so-called friends and colleagues. Many of them replied with a vengeance, some out of jealousy, and others to gain notoriety. Worst of all was my mother's response. She gave them an excerpt of my misguided letter to her that said if she couldn't make enough to live on, she should jump out of the window or drown herself.

I was also outraged by *Time*'s statement that I was "a diva more widely hated by her colleagues and more wildly acclaimed by her public than any other living singer." Of course they dragged out the old chestnuts about Renata Tebaldi, Mario Del Monaco, and, even though we had made up and he was again recording me, Maestro Tullio Serafin. But I must admit it rankles that my colleagues, especially the women, don't like me. It is because they are jealous of my status as prima assoluta of the world, and I am different from them. If I am right in my method of singing, then they are wrong, and their whole careers have been bungled. It is much easier for a diva to dislike me than to accept that she has devoted a lifetime to mediocre singing.

As if I hadn't paid enough for my impulsive remarks, New York now made me pay in blood, and in self defense I stayed in almost complete seclusion at the Hotel Sulgrave on Park Avenue. The newspapers were vicious, for I had dared defy the myth of American mothers and apple pie. I stood behind the curtain literally shaking, until Dino Yannopoulos, the director, had to push me out on the stage. He said, "I promised to deliver a prima donna and so I will; after that it is up to you."

When I made my first entrance as Norma, the audience was in a deep freeze. The applause I got was piddling, compared to that given Zinka Milanov when she swept down the aisle to take her seat. I ask you, how do you think that made me feel? I was the leading lady come triumphantly home to New York, and they applauded Zinka more for just walking down the aisle! I might have looked unruffled, but I was so nervous I was in far from my best voice. Even "Casta Diva" did not succeed in warming the audience up. Fortunately, such things make me angry, and I knew I had to win them over if I were to live with myself. And impress them I did. I didn't have to act much to portray a suffering, somber, broken-hearted Norma. As I got into the second act I felt the tide of the audience gradually shifting and it gave me the necessary jolt. In the moments of my final sacrifice in the opera I knew I had won the battle of the Met. Sixteen curtain calls confirmed my success.

"Now that this is over," I told my friends as I emerged from the enthusiastic embraces of Meneghini and the reception line of my eager admirers, "I can relax and get down to work."

An interview I gave reporters after my third Met performance reflected my more relaxed state. My speech, they said, was charming and informal and "except for an occasional quaint turn of phrase and some random Italian intrusions, still retained many colloquial Americanisms." This pleased me because I was born and brought up (mostly) in the United States, and somewhere in my heart I guess it is still my homeland. After all, I still count in English.

But the feud with Tebaldi persisted, despite my best efforts to squelch it. She was furious at the old story quoted in *Time* in which I said, "She's got no backbone. She's not like Callas." She answered with an indignant letter, "The signora . . . says I have no backbone. I reply: I have one great thing she has not—a heart."

While I was reading the letter Battista came into the room and said, "Maria, why are you crying?"

"I'm not crying," I said.

The night of my thirty-third birthday I opened with the first of five performances of *Lucia di Lammermoor*, the final opera of my long-awaited New York engagement and the high point of my visit. I love to perform on my birthday, when there is always the hope of a new beginning both on stage and off. Although the sets of the Donizetti opera had been gracing the stage of the Met for decades, and it was painful to compare them to the sumptuous settings of the Milan and Naples productions, I determined to hold my tongue and not ruin my anniversary celebration. I did mutter to Battista, however, that the monstrous well which covered half the stage looked like an old oil tank.

The memory of *Lucia* I love the most was a conversation with the Italian stage director Sandro Sequi. He compared the movements of my arms in the Mad Scene to the wings of a great eagle. He said I moved them slowly, like a great plane taking off in the sky. They didn't seem airy like a dancer's arms, but heavy and weighted. When I reached the climax of a musical phrase, he continued, my arms relaxed and flowed into the next gesture like a great eagle in motion. The image of my arms as the wings of a majestic eagle comforts me in the darkness of the night when I feel more like a pigeon whose survival depends on crumbs thrown by soft-hearted strangers.

Of course there were other sorts of remarks after *Lucia*. One rotten critic heard high notes "like desperate screams" and another said I "barely struck the top E flat before toppling over." Criticisms were coming thick and fast. Much as it grieved me, I had to at least consider that my voice was giving out on me.

An unpleasant incident also happened at one performance when the baritone, Enzo Sordello, held a top note a lot longer than he was supposed to, thereby giving the impression I was out of breath. The malicious story of the latest Callas "scandal" circulated that I had lashed out at him on stage. I was supposed to have said, "Basta!" which means "enough" in Italian, and this was overheard by the audience. I don't have to tell you what they thought I said. Fortunately, Fausto Cleva, the conductor, knew Sordello was responsible for furthering the impression the press and audience got, and therefore had him fired by Bing.

I had risen to the rank of diva assoluta, I had sung in all the great opera houses of the world to the huzzahs of the mighty, I had achieved all my worldly ambitions and was even a multi-millionaire. I had convinced my father, Ghiringhelli, and Bing that I belonged at the top. Where was I to go from there? There is no place higher than Mount Olympus. And even if there were, I no longer could deny that at the youthful age of thirty-three my voice was beginning to betray me. I'm the kind of person who always needs a challenge. So it was time to look for greener fields. I found them in a manner no one could have foreseen.

Elsa Maxwell, the Hearst newspaper woman and famous party-giver, much preferred her friend Tebaldi to me. Maxwell had written in her column that she was disappointed in my performance of *Norma*, and my "Mad Scene" in *Lucia* had left her "completely unmoved." Her herculean efforts to boost Tebaldi's reputation at the expense of mine served as a red flag to me, and I accepted an invitation to a ball at the Waldorf Astoria to aid the American Hellenic Welfare Fund in order to meet her.

When we were introduced by Spyros Skouras, the Greek film magnate who had invited me to the ball, Maxwell said she thought I'd be the last person on earth who wanted to meet her. "On the contrary, Miss Maxwell," I responded, "you are the first one I wanted to meet because, aside from your opinion of my voice, I esteem you as a lady of honesty who is devoted to telling the truth." I trust she didn't notice my fingers crossed behind my back.

This seems to have had the effect I wanted. After that this monstrously unattractive lady who led a lonely, loveless life fell in love with me and followed me around like a lost child. From that moment on, she retracted everything malicious she had said about me in the papers. The damaging statements in her columns disappeared like magic. Through her I was invited to appear on many television programs and to attend the most elegant balls of the season. Our relationship was to bring changes into my life that could not have been predicted by the Delphic Oracle itself.

For a while I took advantage of her company, partly because the woman had so much power to make or destroy a reputation. She was the reigning queen of party-givers when I was still sitting in elementary school in Washington Heights. Furthermore, I knew she could open up fairy-tale worlds for me of yachts, royalty, and billionaires.

But there was another reason for me to be kind to her. I know what it is like to be fat and unloved, and how much a generous word or action meant to me when my figure was not much better than Elsa's. Unfortunately, after a while her gushy declarations of love disgusted me, and I made sure I was never alone with her for even a few minutes. It was only a matter of time before I had to reject her completely.

On December 21, the morning of the day we were to leave for Milan, I had to testify before the Supreme Court of New York about the Bagarozy case. My attorneys stated that the lawsuit was nothing more than a scheme to harass me. It was intended to force us to pay an unjustified sum of money to avoid the expense of further litigation. Attorney Angelo Sereni contended that a similar suit against Nicola Rossi-Lemeni had been settled for $4,000, in sharp contrast to the $300,000 claim against Callas.

Sereni's move was countered in court, and nothing was resolved. I testified that Bagarozy had done nothing whatever to further my career. Indeed, he was the one who had failed to live up to the conditions of the contract. "My husband owns me as my manager," I said. I cannot bear to be exploited and was determined to fight to the finish.

A court action was scheduled in Chicago and to make it worth our while both financially and musically I accepted an engagement for a benefit concert to be given by the Alliance Francaise for Hungarian Relief.

At this time another chapter was about to unfold in my relationship with Elsa Maxwell. She was busily arranging an elaborate fancy-dress ball in my honor for Venice high society in 1957. It was to set off the worst press explosion I had yet experienced.

Society Queen

1957 WAS THE YEAR OF MY ARRIVAL as a society queen. Something deep within me was as gratified by this success as by my professional achievements. I suppose when one persists in seeing oneself as an unloved, homely child, one will always crave the recognition of the elite. The peak of my new "career" took place at the Waldorf-Astoria at a regal ball, where I was dressed as the Egyptian Empress Hatshepshut, with two strong men carrying my train. Homely child or not, I felt very natural, covered with emeralds worth three million dollars hired from Harry Winston. Let me tell you something, I took as great pains with that costume as any at La Scala or the Met. To you tell the truth, I enjoyed it even more, because I had all the glory without any of the worry or the work. I didn't have to do anything except show up to hear the cheering of the crowd.

I laughed out loud when I saw Elsa. What a joke! She thought she was disguised as Catherine the Great. As if anyone would be fooled!

But eventually the fun was over and I had to return to work. Ironically, the court case which had brought me to Chicago was postponed and a new date set for the fall. I planned it to coincide with my San Francisco concert.

On the way back to Italy I stopped in London on February 2 to sing *Norma* at Covent Garden. Even before I got there the reviewers were busily trying to decide whether the loss of sixty kilos had damaged my voice. The consensus was that my voice was at its peak. The response was so overwhelming at the second performance that John Prichard, the conductor, was forced to break with tradition and allow Ebe Stignani and me to encore "Mira, o Norma." We held hands in front of the stage and sang the first encore at Covent Garden in twenty years. Both of us were in tears when it was over. Nevertheless I received one of the greatest shocks of my life when I opened the *Daily Express* and read Noel Goodwin's review. He wrote that it obviously took effort for me to produce a D at the end of the Act 1 trio and predicted my career would be over in five years. The review was the first real outside reference to my mortality as a singer. A *frisson* slid down my windpipe all the way to my stomach as I read it. Was it possible all this acclaim was a fluke, a whim of the crowd, a passing swell through the oceans of time? Would I would end up being the unlovable creature I always felt I was, disliked and ignored by everyone? Somewhere inside me I was not surprised. No wonder I took such infinite pains with every note, every nuance! I always suspected that each performance would be my last. Be that as it may, I knew I would not take defeat without a fight and resolved to battle to the finish to hold on to my empire.

In March I sang six performances of *La Sonnambula* under Antonino Votto at La Scala which brought me much praise, although the production as a whole left much to be desired. It was supposed to be a revival of Bernstein's production, but Votto seemed able to produce only a pale carbon copy. Although maybe after Bernstein anything would look pale.

It was followed at La Scala on April 14 with the first of seventeen sellout performances of Donizetti's *Anna Bolena*, the "Tragic Queen" of England, the "rose without a thorn." It was a beautiful, haunting production full of atmosphere that set a new standard for operas of the early Romantic period. *Bolena*, which was unfamiliar even to Italians, was directed by Lucino Visconti. He did fairly well with the critics this time, although he was accused of concentrating on the figure of La Callas to the point of making the opera a one-woman show. But that's what it is anyway.

As the opera began, I slowly walked to the footlights and sang the lovely nostalgic cavatina of recollection, "Come innocente giovane" (How young and innocent). My husband, Henry VIII, has fallen in love with Seymour, my beloved lady-in-waiting. I have lost him to my cherished friend. Surely there is nothing more painful than betrayal by a loved one. I feel a stab in my stomach when I think of it. How right that Giulietta, a superb singer whom I love, who at times has given me real competition, sang the role. Our duet together was so real I almost forgot we were on the stage.

As with other operas based on a real person, I have been asked if I studied the historical background of Anna Bolena. I have to answer no. I can't even remember how many wives Henry VIII had. Neither they nor the real Anne Boleyn interest me, because the Donizetti heroine and the real Anna had nothing in common. It is from the music alone I get my insight for my roles.

In the opera, Lord Richard Percy, my first love, arrives. The corrupt king has us watched to give him an excuse to divorce me. Percy tries to make love to me, and even though I resist him, the king accuses me of adultery. If I confess to adultery, the king will divorce me; if I tell the truth, I will die. Seymour pleads with me to lie and confess my guilt, but that is something neither Anna nor I could ever do. Jane begs for my forgiveness for stealing my man. In a noble gesture like that of Norma, I pardon her. I feel pretty big about that, but it makes her feel even worse, because although she has deceived me, she still loves me. Visconti, Gavazzeni, Benois, and Simionato all said my duet with Seymour in which she admits she is my rival for the throne was one of the most thrilling moments they ever experienced in the theatre. In that production I reached the pinnacle of my art.

It is strange the brief moments that return to haunt us. As I run away from my pain into delirium, Rochefort, played by Plinio Clabassi, sings, "Anna!" He sings only this one word, "Anna!" But the tenderness, the compassion, the sadness in his voice come back to me now and bring tears to my eyes.

I reached the peak of my powers as a singer and actress in the final scene at the Tower of London. Imprisoned in the Tower, a deep subterranean chamber with barred windows, I go insane. I imagine it to be my wedding day and sing the aria full of tender memories, "To the sweet native castle guide me." In the original arioso based on "Home, Sweet Home," I make my final peace.

At the end, in the forceful cabaletta "Copia iniqua," I denounce the guilty couple. My voice soared in trills that rose from B flat to F sharp, so that the "Vendetta" was hurled out over the audience until they were mesmerized in their seats. That night I broke the record for La Scala's curtain calls; the audience applauded me for twenty-four full minutes. Sometimes I feel frightened at the strength of my own powers.

It makes me think of Arachne, the girl in Greek legend who was turned into a spider because her pride in weaving angered the gods. I can't afford to have the gods angry with me; life is difficult enough as it is. But even though the idea of such mystical powers terrifies me, it thrills me. How could it not?

Elsa Maxwell came to see me perform in *Anna Bolena* at my invitation. The moment she stepped off the plane at the Milan airport and into my waiting arms was indelibly captured by photographers. The caption underneath the photo was "Ecco i due tigri" (Behold the two tigers). I am a little embarrassed now at having our embrace preserved for posterity.

Ifigenia in *Ifigenia in Tauride* on June 1 was my twentieth production at
La Scala and my second and last Gluckian role. I didn't realize at the time
it would be the last production Visconti and I would do together. After that
we never seemed to agree on anything. As a matter of fact, we didn't even
agree on *Ifigenia*. He placed the opera in the middle of the eighteenth
century in an elaborate rococo style.

"Why are you doing it like this?" I kept asking. "It is a Greek story and
I am a Greek woman. I want to look Greek on stage." He said the Greece I
was talking about was a far-off Greece, and he wanted the opera to look like
a Tiepolo fresco come to life. Tiepolo or no Tiepolo, I didn't care for the
costumes. I would have preferred a classic Greek gown of white cotton,
crossed over the breast and twice around the waist by a silk cord, and gold
sandals. I didn't like the production or my performance, even though
Benois designed the sets and Visconti thought it was the most beautiful
opera he had ever done.

I worry about myself. Sometimes I fall so in love with people I can't stay
away from them. And then, poof, I'm finished with them! There was my
mother, Meneghini, Serafin, and then Visconti. Of course, when I remind
myself about Aristo, the love of my life, I stop worrying. There is nothing
flighty about my love for him. Although I might have been better off if there
were . . .

I got another stab in the back after *Bolena*, this time from the critic
Michael Scott, who said, ". . . her voice has lost much quality, the tone has
become thin and horny, as if the stuffing had been knocked out of it. It not
only lacks sufficient variety of color but it is not as smoothly produced as
. . . in her other Gluck venture, *Alceste*, three years before." Drop dead,
Michael Scott! Are you the same as you were three years ago? For an
authority on music you are remarkably stupid. *Ifigenia* is a very different
opera than *Alceste*, and anyone who knows music is aware it has far less
color in it!

On June 19, when I sang the Act 1 scene from *La Traviata* and the Mad
Scene from *Lucia* at a concert at Zurich, he was at it again. "We hear how
much thinner her voice is becoming, how her upper register is growing ever
wavier, and the top notes even more chancy." Why, oh why did he persecute
me? I hate you, Michael Scott!

Two days later, my wounds were covered over a bit when President
Gronchi presented me with the coveted title of Commendatore. Despite the
fate of Arachne and her spiders, I was filled with pride.

Elsa took me on a three-day tour of Paris and the high and mighty of
society, including tea with the Windsors, cocktails at the Rothschilds,

dinner at Maxims, and the races with Aly Khan. He is supposed to be a great romantic and a notorious womanizer, but both he and his horses left me cold. Elsa was a phenomenal hostess and I enjoyed being feted and admired by the Parisian aristocracy. It was nice to have a champion of her size. (Ha! And they say I have no sense of humor!) When she was told about an anti-Callas lobby, she wrote she could hardly believe anyone would spread poison about one of the most touching individuals she had ever known, and nothing could destroy the supreme art of Maria Callas.

I left Paris exhausted, though I had a long summer ahead of me. I had to give a concert in Zurich and another one in Rome, two *Sonnambula*s in Cologne, and thirteen days of recordings, including *Manon Lescaut*, a rather silly opera I had never sung before. All of this was followed by six *Turandot*s. I know I said I wasn't going to sing it again because it has ruined many voices, but I wanted to see if doing a recording was less harmful than singing it in a theatre. I'm still not sure.

Elsa wanted me to come to a party she was giving for me in Venice in September, but I was supposed to go on tour with La Scala and was conflicted about accepting her invitation.

The performance of my heart in August was my return after twelve years to Greece, where I was to sing two concerts at the Herodes Atticus Amphitheatre in Athens. But I can never do anything without everybody making a big fuss. The political opposition accused the Karamanlis government of neglecting the needs of the lower classes by paying an opera star so much money when people were starving. Nobody mentioned that I had offered my services for nothing and the organizers of the concert had haughtily refused.

Even worse, the government was so worried another unpleasant incident would occur that they promptly ushered my mother and sister out of the country. Of course, this added to the Greek image of Callas as the "bad daughter," for which they had never forgiven me.

People say I am a tiger. They don't know I feel more like a baby lamb, a little Greek baby lamb. The first concert was scheduled for August 1, but I was suffering from nervous exhaustion and was terrified at the thought of appearing before twenty thousand cold and hostile Greeks. I wavered back and forth until I realized I just wasn't strong enough to face them in the hot dry weather, so I canceled the concert. Unfortunately, it was not announced until one hour before the performance was scheduled, and bus loads of angry people stampeded the amphitheatre.

When I came on stage for the second scheduled concert, it was like smacking into a wall of ice. The hostility of the audience was so evident it almost stood by itself. I was so terrified I couldn't stop shaking for ten minutes. But apparently they liked my singing, for when I got to the Mad Scene from *Hamlet*, the frost thawed and a deluge of approval poured over the footlights from the audience to me.

As I stood there listening to the applause thundering through the amphitheatre, I felt like a goddess on top of Mount Olympus, a Divine Being granting pleasure to thousands of mortals seated below. To them I wasn't singing opera, I wasn't singing a concert; I was singing Callas. They all arose as one to give me an explosive ovation, almost thirteen years to the day after I had made my first triumph there in *Fidelio*. I sang the second part of the Mad Scene for an encore, but didn't feel up to rescheduling the concert I had missed.

But of course my nemesis, Michael Scott, had to ruin my homecoming. He said, "Her voice is no longer what it had been only a year before when she sang the RAI concert." Didn't that man have anything to do but follow me around the world? He reminds me of something that happened to my mother when I was a little girl. We were in a butcher shop picking out a chicken. Liska kept turning it over and over and poking into all its openings. The butcher said to her, "Lady, could *you* pass such a test?"

I next returned to Milan to prepare to sing Amina in *La Sonnambula* at the end of August at the Edinburgh Festival, the only British festival of international importance. I was utterly exhausted and the thinnest I've ever been. My collarbones stuck out when I wore an open dress and my blood pressure was dangerously low. In fact, the doctor insisted I cancel all my engagements, warning I had lost too much weight and my entire physical system might collapse. But I knew another cancellation so soon after the Athens fiasco would bring on a hullabaloo, which my career couldn't afford. My generally poor health made me feel much older than a woman of thirty-four, but then my health has always been fragile.

I took a week off to rest in Buonarroti and then left for Scotland to sing Amina. In spite of my physical condition, I managed four performances which the reviewers praised, but of course my friend Scott had to say my voice was "threadbare." I must admit the role is difficult because you have to control yourself so much and sing softly throughout. Perhaps that is why I never sang Amina again.

Despite my success, the Edinburgh Festival resulted in one of the greatest scandals of my career. The program listed a fifth *Sonnambula* which did not appear on my contract. I knew I was not capable of singing it and decided to leave after the fourth performance. Well, you would have thought I had thrown a bomb right into the middle of the esplanade of Edinburgh Castle! It was hailed as "another Callas walkout" all over the world. It was so unfair! I had never agreed to a fifth performance and had clearly informed Ghiringhelli I would sing only four. But never my friend, he refused to stand up for me and issue a public statement that it wasn't my fault.

I kept asking myself, "Why, Maria? Why are other singers like Tebaldi allowed to be sick all they want but you must always be Superwoman?" It was as bad as living with my mother. No matter what I did she always found something wrong with it. Once in sewing class at school we had to embroider a picture of an American eagle. I worked hard on mine, and the teacher thought it was beautiful. I proudly brought it home to show Liska. She looked at it with a frown and zeroed in with her forefinger on the one stitch I had dropped. Leave it to the whole world to zero in on my dropped stitch and overlook the eagle.

I sometimes think people sense that underneath the poised diva is a vulnerable child, and they are all standing there with a giant whip waiting for an excuse to flail away at me. Is it possible I provoke their attacks?

The racket might have died down except for Elsa Maxwell's ball in my honor in Venice. I thought that since I was flying to the warm south anyway I might as well attend the party. After all, partying is different from singing a strenuous role like Amina. I'd worked so hard my whole life I felt entitled to have a little fun.

But of course the pictures of me at the ball appeared in all the newspapers. Sometimes I take terrible pictures in which I look like a witch, long nose and all, but wouldn't you know, the photographs of me at the party looked glowing and positively radiant! The press found my presence there outrageous and demanded to know how I could spend all night at a ball if I was too exhausted to sing. Elsa didn't help any when she told the press, "I have had many presents in my life . . . but I have never had any star give up a performance for a friend."

It soothed my spirits a bit that I was the belle of the ball and everyone there looked at and admired me. And among those looking at and admiring me the most was Aristotle Onassis. . . .

Before I knew it, Ari had managed to inveigle the seat next to mine at the dinner table, and placed a motorboat at our disposal for as long as we were in Venice. And for the next seven days, wherever I was he appeared next to me as if by magic. Everybody noticed but Battista. I found it flattering and pleasant, but for the time being, nothing more.

I had contracted to open the San Francisco Opera season in September, when my doctor advised against it. I was willing to disregard his orders for Elsa's exciting party, but not for the stress, the strain, and criticism of another opening night. The more fame you have, the more responsibility is yours and the smaller and more vulnerable you feel. I simply couldn't go through another ordeal at that time; I didn't have the physical or emotional stamina. So I sent a telegram to Kurt Adler, the director of the San Francisco Opera, canceling my scheduled performances of *Lucia* for September, but offering to honor my contract for October for *Macbeth*. I was stunned when he canceled all my San Francisco appearances and referred my case to the American Guild of Musical Artists. The Guild is important to musicians because it has the power to keep us from appearing on stage anywhere in the United States. I felt, "Oh my God, not another court procedure! Why is the whole world picking on me?"

No wonder I was upset. The last hearing of the Bagarosy lawsuit was scheduled for New York on November 5. After all the harassment, hearings, summonses, and strain on my nerves, the case was finally closed twelve days later. They settled out of court. I gave them a few thousand dollars just to get them out of my hair. I was sick and tired of being a chronic courtroom character.

I shrugged off the San Francisco fiasco and decided to rest quietly in Milan for a week with Battista and my dogs. I made only one trip abroad, when I flew to Dallas to give one of my best concerts for a long time. I must say, at one hundred and seventeen pounds I looked superb, and my dramatic black velvet dress showed off my shape to its best advantage. Even though it had been several years since I had lost weight, I had not yet gotten used to being slender and was as delighted by my new figure as a teenager. Will I ever get over feeling like a pudgy and pimply child? I doubt it. I ended the concert with my *pièce de résistance*, the Tower Scene from *Anna Bolena*, which, of course, brought the house down.

On the plane back to New York with Elsa I got one of the great jolts of my life. I knew she loved me and was unusually affectionate with me. She followed me around all the time from Chicago to London to Milan as if she were my shadow, and swamped me with phone calls, telegrams, and letters. She sent me intimate letters that sounded like they came from a lover. She wrote pages and pages with stuff in them like, "Maria, the only thing that sends me into ecstasy is your face and your smile." I got so tired of the letters I started giving them to Battista, saying "Here, you read them for me." But, child that I was, I thought what she did for me was out of admiration and friendship. It never entered my mind she wanted anything more from me.

On the airplane out of Dallas the steward seated her next to me. I groaned inside, because I'd had enough of her and wanted to rest. So I was quiet most of the way. About an hour out of New York, she said to me, "Maria, this is hard to say, but I have to talk to you. You know I love you, don't you?"

I answered, "Of course, Elsa. I love you, too."

"No, Maria, you don't understand. I don't just love you, I am *in* love with you." I stared at her and said nothing. Innocent as I was, what she meant was beginning to get through to me.

"My dear," she went on, "do . . . do you think you could love me, too?— I mean in that way?" She lifted up her grotesque face and I saw her puckered old eyes melting with love.

Now even a moron couldn't fail to get her meaning. I was so stunned I opened my mouth to answer and not a word came out. Since I want to be honest here, I must admit I was disgusted as well as shocked. It was not only that her sexual leanings were the farthest thing from my own, but she was a homely woman, one might even say repulsive. Battista said she was the ugliest woman he had ever met. I didn't want to hurt her, because I know how sensitive a fat person can be. She was also a powerful woman and I didn't want her for an enemy again. So I swallowed hard and tried to be tactful.

"No, dear," I said, "I'm sorry, but I'm afraid I don't feel the same way as you. That is not my way of life."

Then she got angry and began to yell so loud it must have been heard all over the plane. In fact, I'm sure that rumors starting about our relationship came out of that conversation.

She shouted, "Don't worry, Maria, you have squelched my love for you forever. I'm completely over you now. Rest assured I won't bother you again. But what I have against you is that you could have crushed my feelings before it was too late. It was hateful of you to lead me on the way you did. You used me when you needed me and now you have no further use for me."

How does one answer such charges? Perhaps she was right that my silence encouraged her and made her feel her affections would be returned. But I really hadn't understood and was just trying to be nice, which I knew she wouldn't believe in a million years. There was nothing further for me to say. I could only be silent.

But I'm afraid poor Elsa had not stifled her feelings for me after all. She

came to Rome to see my *Norma* and then to Milan for *Anna Bolena*, she kept
sending me letters about how much she had done for me, and then she told
an interviewer for *Cosmopolitan* magazine we had been acquaintances for
only a few weeks and I was not the kind of woman for friendships or
affection of any kind except with my husband. Big deal! I was never worried
about that anyway. Nobody who knows me would believe I shared her
interest in women. I don't even like them.

Thus my "friendship" with Elsa Maxwell ended. But she had left me
with a legacy. She had introduced me to the rich and famous of the world
and changed my life forever.

On December 7, I opened the La Scala season with the first of five
performances of *Un Ballo in Maschera*. I love this role, even though it doesn't
call for the technical skill of Verdi heroines like Lady Macbeth or Violetta
and takes a back seat to Riccardo's character. Amelia is a more modern
musical figure than any other of the composer's heroines, and the most
human. In one aria alone, in the second act, she expresses love, tenderness,
fright, panic, sadness, and resignation.

Even though Amelia and Riccardo are deeply in love, they agree to
sacrifice their happiness to do what is right. It always makes me cry that
Amelia was so decent she was able to refrain from possessing the one she
loved for the sake of her conscience. She must have something in her
character that is missing in mine.

The opera was performed by a great team and staged in a stark realistic
manner. Gianandrea Gavazzeni was the conductor, Margherita Wallmann
the producer, with stage designs by Nicola Benois. My sometime friend
Pippo was at his best, which is very good indeed, and the duet we sang
together in Act Two was eloquent and lyrical. Unfortunately, as I had
mentioned before, we had had a difference of opinion and were still not on
speaking terms. The rehearsals for our love scenes were extremely embar-
rassing for both of us. I am a direct person and dissembling comes hard to
me. If you've ever had to kiss a person you hate you will understand what
I mean. You'd rather spit at them but you have to go on kissing them. But
by the time of the performances, professionals that we are, we were able to
play the love scenes with tenderness and conviction. I don't believe anyone
guessed we hated each other. Despite our success, however, it was the last
time we were to sing together until our ill-fated tour in 1973.

The production was particularly important to me because I had been
promised a debut as Amelia at La Scala in 1947 and waited in vain for the
telephone call that never came. That had been a terrible blow to me, among

the worst in my life. I waited ten years to play Amelia at La Scala, and I never sang it anywhere else.

Thus ended 1957, a year that marked a turning point in my life. Although I had a number of stunning successes, including the triumph of *Un Ballo in Maschera*, I no longer could kid myself that my voice had not deteriorated. I had also experienced a number of catastrophes that continue to haunt me to the present day. But I had been introduced to "la creme de la creme" of society, which feted and adored me as much as the operatic world. One way or another, I was determined to hang on to the tiger.

La Scala Cools Off

*W*HEN I OPENED THE NEW SEASON OF 1957-58 at La Scala as Amelia in Verdi's *Un Ballo in Maschera*, I worked diligently to correct the flaws in my voice. On the way back to Milan I stopped off in Brussels to visit Château Ixelles, the house of Charles de Beriot, the beloved violinist husband of Maria Malibran. I never cease to marvel that my dear predecessor had the same first name as I. When I stood holding a bouquet of flowers next to a bust of her, I felt her presence surrounding me. At Chateau Ixelles I found the same atmosphere of silence and absolute serenity I had experienced at her grave side, and it gave me a feeling of inner peace. I treasure the photo Battista took of me standing there.

On New Year's Day in Rome I awoke with a cold and found myself voiceless. I was horrified and went to bed right away, hoping the illness would clear up before the performance of *Norma* scheduled for the next evening. Meneghini called the Sovrintendente, to whom I suggested getting a substitute. "Absolutely not!" he bellowed. "It is the opening night of the year and the President of Italy, Giovanni Gronchi, and his wife will be there. There is a sold out house and you must sing!" I said I would see how I felt. Battista called the doctor, who put me on all kinds of medication. The next day I felt better and the doctor confirmed an hour before the performance that I was well enough to go on.

While singing "Casta diva" at the beginning of the opera, I realized my voice was in abominable shape and sounded muffled and unpleasantly shrill in the upper registers. The audience sensed I was not well and was silent, except for a few obnoxious hecklers who shouted "Go back to Milan." In the middle of the song I felt my voice dying altogether and I had no choice but to leave the performance at the end of the act. Backstage I was in a near state of collapse and decided I couldn't continue with the opera. Battista, and Elsa Maxwell, who had returned to hear me sing *Norma*, agreed I shouldn't continue. In the meantime Wallman, the stage director, and Santini were pleading with me to go on with the role, even if I just walked through it without singing. I didn't even deign to answer *that* suggestion. I vacillated back and forth for an hour, and then the president and his wife left their box and an official announced from the stage that I was not well and could not continue the performance. The audience was seething, and came out into the street whistling and shouting abominations at me.

When I got back to the hotel I immediately wrote a letter of apology to the president and his wife, explaining about my illness. Many people had followed me out of the auditorium to the hotel and staged a near riot, stamping and yelling under my window all night long. An argument between pro- and anti-Callasites nearly turned into a brawl. But that was only the beginning of the ruckus. It even extended to parliament, with the episode sparking a debate on the mismanagement of opera houses. The newspapers, of course, had a field day; anything they could get on Callas they chewed to death. This time they behaved like a starved wolf leaping on a carcass.

It was announced by the Rome Opera that if Callas had been too ill to sing on Monday, she wouldn't be able to sing on Tuesday and Wednesday either. I was replaced by the little-known soprano Anita Cerquetti. Eventually I would win a suit against the Rome Opera filed by Meneghini, but for the time being I was forced to leave Rome, defeated and despondent.

It wasn't all bad, however. Friends and colleagues, including Visconti, continued to support me and express their sympathy. I appeared on television to explain my departure, where I said, "I had such a reaction from the public . . . I never had so many flowers and so many letters . . . I know that I really am loved."

For ten years all my free time, my days off between performances, and even the few holidays we had taken for my health had been devoted to my voice. I had spent time on vocal exercises and practiced my beloved piano every day. And for ten years it seemed to have paid off in the progress I made in my career.

But what the public did not know and what I was able to admit to myself only belatedly, was that my voice was leaving me. It was the most painful ordeal of my life. To know what an aria should sound like, indeed, to have sung it that way many times before, and to feel one's voice not responding to the directions from one's mind is a nightmare. Surely Hell could think up no worse torture for the damned. Every time I stepped upon the stage, I shivered with panic. I was afraid my voice would wobble, my range further contract, and my upper register sound shrill. I feared the colors I saw in the eye of my mind would not be translated into song, or the whole aria would be spoiled by excessive vibrato. After I finished singing, the agony of knowing I had failed was sharp as Tosca's knife and ripped me to bloody rags for days. It wouldn't go away, no matter what anyone said to console me. In fact, their compliments only made me feel worse, for I knew in my heart they were false. I could only go to bed with my suffering and stay there until the pain subsided. My mistakes have tormented me from the beginning, but there was always the hope that the next performance would be better. When I was young, I was willing to sing with a cold and trust myself to get through the performance all right in spite of it. But I couldn't do that anymore, and I was less and less able to subject myself to the emotional agony of singing badly.

It was hard enough when *I* knew my voice was failing, but when it was spread across the headlines of the world for all to see, my humiliation was unbearable. On January 22, 1958, I sang a concert in Chicago, a city I love dearly where I had made my American debut. This was my last performance there, and the reviewers who had always been among my supporters left no doubt they knew my voice had deteriorated. Dettmer, of the *Chicago American*, always one of my greatest admirers, wrote that I was "in big vocal trouble, how serious only she is equipped to measure." He said my voice was "strident, unsteady, and out-of-tune," and worst of all, "seems to have aged ten years in one." The pain was too much to bear. I died. I didn't think I would ever feel anything again. I was thirty-four years old and I was dead.

But to my great surprise and elation, the tide began to turn in my favor, and I began to feel once more. When I appeared at the Met in *La Traviata* on February 6, the critics let up on me and I began to feel the whole business of my voice declining had been nothing but a terrible nightmare. The reception New York gave me was even warmer than I had received during my first season there, some even claiming I was the best Violetta heard at the Met in years and it was my finest performance to date. The reviews weren't all good, of course. They never are. Paul Henry Lang in the *Tribune* praised my "brilliant acting" but went on to deplore my lack of a "true and beautiful voice." Then he griped that Barioni and I both sang flat in the Act 1 duet, "Un di felice." Leonard Bernstein wrote to the *Tribune* disputing Lang. He said Barioni had sung sharp but Callas sang in tune. How nice to be defended for a change by a knowledgeable friend!

I had another little tussle with Bing in which he fussed about my fee for twenty-six appearances in New York and on tour for the 1958/59 season. "You already make more than the President of the United States," he said.

"Then let him sing!" I answered. My mind was eased when Bing had me sign the contract. It began to look like the soothsayers were all wrong and Callas wasn't finished yet.

Whatever one could say about my professional life, my social career was taking off. After every performance and on nights when I wasn't working, I flung myself into the life Elsa Maxwell had introduced me to. Parties, restaurants, expensive jewelry, and the *crème de la crème* of society became my passion, my *raison d'être*. Battista was beginning to become a casualty of my glittering new life. He didn't speak English and refused to learn. At parties he embarrassed me by falling asleep. After a while I left him home as often as not and was happy to be away from him. He continued to manage my career, but not much else. His feelings were hurt but I didn't care.

From New York I stopped in Madrid on March 24 to give a concert at Cinema Monumental. From that time on, I sang more and more concerts and fewer and fewer operas. During the rest of 1958, in marked contrast to previous years, I sang only four complete operas. The rest of my performances were concerts. It was far less work to prepare them than the operas. I sang a wide variety of arias, and was spared the nerve-wracking ordeal of complete performances. Since I had far more control over my choice of arias in concerts than in operas, I chose less demanding works and therefore didn't have to worry as much about my voice. It was a good compromise and seemed the solution to my vocal problems. This regime satisfied the huge crowds who lined up to hear me sing. They didn't care if I sang operas, they didn't care if I sang concerts; they only wanted to hear Callas. They were happy to see me, I was happy my career was not over, and Meneghini was happy that the money kept pouring in.

In the meantime, something funny was going on between Ghiringhelli and me. His behavior changed completely. It was not like when he was purposely cold, when he didn't want me in the company at La Scala. It was more as if he didn't see me, or looked right through me. One night when Battista and I were seated at a table in Biffi, he walked right by us. I could swear he pretended not to see me. It gave me the creeps and made me feel I didn't exist. With my history, I don't take well to being ignored by men. I think he never forgave me for the canceled Roman performance or for attending Elsa Maxwell's party in Venice. He repeated all the time that prima donnas come and prima donnas go, but La Scala remains. I was afraid he was hinting that I was on my way out.

La Scala seemed to be cooling off, too. I had to work much harder to gain their admiration than formerly. In the April 9 performance of *Anna Bolena*, the audience was also cold. The claquers were out in full force and threw radishes and tomatoes and even an old shoe onto the stage. Whatever one says about the crudity of people in the United States, the audiences there are composed of ladies and gentlemen who never behave as badly as that. In the third scene, when the guards came to arrest me, I swept them aside and swooped down to the footlights where I hurled "Giudici! ad Anna! . . . Giudici!" (Judges! For Anna! . . . Judges!) directly at the audience. They went wild and after the opera it was necessary for police in the streets to keep them under control.

But that is not the worst of the story. When we got home to Via Buonarroti we found our garden gate smeared with excrement, as was the pathway. The walls and front door were covered with graffiti, and we got one obscene phone call after another. One, accompanied by a weird shrieking laugh, is burnt into my memory. "Is this f___ Maria Callas? How would you like to eat my s___? Hah hah hah hah hah." I screamed and slammed the phone down, and we took it off the hook, but even Battista's curses couldn't soothe me. The police paid no attention whatever to our complaints. We could only conclude they were in on the vandalism, maybe even contributed to it. I was terrified and bewildered. What had I done to deserve such punishment? I was only trying to practice my art as best I could. Battista and I were afraid to stay there even overnight, so with hurting hearts we left for our retreat on Lake Garda. Of course Toy came with us. I needed him near me. Only my dogs could be trusted not to betray me.

Who was responsible for such an outrage? Could it have been the Tebaldi claque? Would they go that far, to defile my home with feces and obscenities? Were people protesting the diminution of my vocal powers? I didn't know. I only knew my heart was growing heavier by the moment. I wondered if it was safe to stay in Italy under the circumstances and even if it were, was it worth enduring such hostile and degrading experiences. I seriously considered leaving opera altogether. I was tired of feeling like the mountain nymph Echo, who dared talk back to the goddess Hera and was punished with the loss of her own voice.

On May 19, I played my first new role at La Scala in more than two years, Imogine in Bellini's *Il Pirata*. It went well, but there were two trouble spots that plagued me. The first was the sustained high C, which I solved by placing less pressure on my voice, and having the conductor, Nicola

Rescigno, speed up the tempo. The second difficulty was between the orchestra and me in the aria's final set of rising scales.

I didn't know it at the time, but it was to be my last new role ever. I later found out it had been common knowledge I wouldn't be returning to La Scala the next season. I guess if I had wanted to, I could have read the message in Ghiringhelli's snub at Biffi. But did he have to be so cruel about it? There is no doubt the man is a monster!

I got my revenge on him (as I knew I would) in *Il Pirata*, when I sang "La vendete il palco funesto" (There, behold the fatal scaffold). By some strange coincidence the word "palco" in Italian means both scaffold and theatre box. I stalked across the stage and spat the line straight at Ghiringhelli's box! I'm sure there wasn't a person in the auditorium who didn't get my meaning. I savored that. It gave me a warm glow all through my middle, starting with a little spot in my stomach and radiating out like the rays of the sun. It is warming me up now.

He got back at me, however. At the end of the opera, when fans usually swarm all over the stage and me with their excitement and good wishes, Ghiringhelli had the fire curtain lowered and the lights dimmed so they couldn't get to me. But he wasn't counting on the love of my fans. They followed me out into the street and across the piazza to Saveni's restaurant in the Galleria. As they say in America, you can't keep a good man down. Or woman, for that matter.

Another disaster happened the day before the third performance. I began to bleed and had to have an emergency operation for hemorrhoids. The sharp pain felt like the hook torture applied to Mario in *Tosca*, and I was angry that Battista couldn't have the surgery for me. I was terrified I would have to cancel the May 28th performance. Anybody else can be sick or be operated on and bow out of a performance, but not Maria Callas! So with throbbing derriere and gloomy spirits I dragged myself to the theatre and sang the opera on schedule.

I knew I couldn't stay with La Scala any longer. When the theatre where you work continually harasses you and treats you rudely, it is physically and morally impossible to devote yourself to doing your best work. For my self-protection and dignity, even if I were to be rehired I had no choice but to leave La Scala. Callas will not be treated that way!

I knew leaving there would be traumatic for me. I had felt homeless all my life, shifting from America to Greece and back to America throughout my childhood and adolescence. At the age of thirty, I had finally found a professional and emotional home in Milan. Giving it up was a terrible defeat and I knew in my heart it was just the beginning of many such reverses.

On June 10 I sang the Mad Scene from *I Puritani* at Covent Garden in front of the Queen at the centenary of the theatre. They couldn't have been nicer, Lord Harewood even giving me his private office for my dressing room. The concert was shining with stars, but I outdid them all and was called back eight times. One newspaper called me the star of the week. I tried to feel happy about it, but after all, I had been fired from La Scala, the opera house of my dreams. The defeat was never far from my mind.

After the performance I tried to curtsey to the Queen, but my shimmering black sheath was so tight all I could manage was a bow. I hope she didn't mind. All she did was smile at me, even though she spoke to the others. I felt bad about it. Didn't she like me? That's me, always a fish in the wrong bowl, no matter how high I swim in the water!

I left London for Milan and two months of supposed rest at Lake Garda. But I was bored and restless. Battista was no company or intellectual stimulation: all he did was work on my fall and winter schedules and accounts of how much money I'd made. I was as lonely as when I was a child and my father wouldn't be with me.

I had agreed to do two recordings in London, a nationwide concert tour of America, and *Traviata* and *Medea* in Dallas in the fall. Rudolf Bing wanted me for twenty-six performances in three operas, but I couldn't make up my mind about it. To tell the truth, I was terrified of appearing at the Met. It is one thing to go sour in Dallas, but New York is one of the great opera centers of the world. I was tired of being attacked by the New York press, and of having to seduce the sophisticated audiences into submission. I was never good enough for my mother. I dreaded my inner knowledge that the time would never come when Callas would be good enough just as she was.

On my arrival in New York on October 7, Rudolf Bing and I got into an immediate controversy. We had agreed on a series of appearances in February, 1959, and he scheduled me for a new production of *Macbeth*, which delighted me. I had not sung the opera since 1952 except in concerts. But singing an aria is not the same as an entire opera. *Macbeth* had been one of my greatest successes and I hoped a new production would be an impressive demonstration of my talents this time as well. The problem arose with the second opera Bing had chosen. He wanted me to sing *Traviata* and *Macbeth* on alternate dates, with little time in between. Although I hated to admit it even to myself, my voice in 1958 was not what it had been in 1949, when I sang *Die Walkure* one night and *I Puritani* the next. I knew I no longer could sing roles demanding such different qualities of voices on alternate nights, and felt he should make another suggestion. He refused, saying the Met was a massive organization and couldn't change its plans so easily. How dared he treat Callas that way? Didn't he realize I had the voice of the century? He had never liked me, and I soon realized it was a diabolic manoeuver to contribute to the destruction of my career.

I left for my American tour, still not having come to a decision. I played Birmingham, Atlanta, Montreal, and Toronto before flying to Dallas on October 31, where I was to sing *La Traviata* and *Medea* at the State Fair Music Hall. Throughout the tour, I kept receiving telegrams and messages from Bing insisting I make a decision. Nobody treats Callas that way! When I am bullied and harassed, I become even more stubborn and do the opposite of what is demanded. Thus I refused to commit myself to the Met for the 1959 season.

In Dallas, at the Civic Opera Company, where we were received like royalty, the predicament with Bing exploded. First I received a telegram from him demanding that I accept his dates and conditions. When I didn't answer, I received another on November 6 canceling my contract. Then he issued a nasty press release, saying, "I do not propose to enter into a public feud with Madame Callas, since I am well aware that she has considerably more competence and experience at that kind of thing than I have. Although Madame Callas's artistic qualifications are a matter of violent controversy between her friends and foes, her reputation for projecting her undisputed histrionic talents into her business affairs is a matter of common knowledge." That was highly uncalled for vindictiveness! I consider Bing a sadist, a Hitler in a tuxedo. I had only asked him to change the dates of two or three performances! After all I've done for him and the Met, surely he should have obliged. Battista was going to sue him, but we were told that legally Bing was in the right.

"Too bad!" I said at a party that night, when I found out about my defeat. "I was put on earth to offer art to the public, and that is why they love me. Mr. Bing was hardly very cooperative." I didn't want to sing any more lousy *Traviata*s with decaying sets anyway!

The fiasco was great for business. The rest of our tour had the air of a circus about it. It seemed everyone in the country wanted to see for themselves what the singing battle-ax was like. People who couldn't tell bel canto from a bean bag lined up and fought in the street for tickets. Battista was in his element as he shovelled in the cash. How could the $18,000 the Met offered us be compared to the $10,000 per night we were raking in? I've never seen Battista so happy. He told me of a dream he had in which I was shaped like a thousand dollar bill. I'm not surprised. More and more I thought he just cared about me for the money I made, and not for myself at all.

Despite the success of the American tour, I was beginning to feel the effects of Bing's action. On December 4, I celebrated my thirty-fifth birthday in Milan, where I looked forward to a bleak winter, almost devoid of engagements, except for one.

On December 19, I sang in Paris for the first time. They welcomed me with adoration. After the cold bath I had received in Italy and from Bing, their adulation warmed my heart. I know how the Allies must have felt when they marched through the Arch of Triumph. My victory made me want to walk through it singing, "Ritorna vincitor" from *Aida*. I have always been happy that I won the heart of Paris before Mrs. Kennedy—I will never call her "Onassis!"—when the President told the Parisians he was the man who had accompanied his wife to Paris. "Only the French have tried to understand me," the headline in *Le Figaro* quoted me on December 17. Believe me, that's no exaggeration. Although many of the world's finest theatres were now closed to me, I had conquered Paris in a single performance, and I was satisfied, even as I thrust away the knowledge that my voice was crumbling to bits.

My engagement was at a gala charity concert for a Legion d'Honneur, in which the seats sold for the highest price ever charged at L'Opera. Present were numerous government ministers, the Begum Ali Kahn, the Rothschilds, Charlie Chaplin, Brigitte Bardot, Francoise Sagan, the Windsors, Jean Cocteau—and Aristotle Onassis. The house was completely sold out and I gave my fee of $10,000 to the Legion d'Honneur. A special program sold for twenty dollars, and with it patrons were given my new record, *Callas Sings Mad Scenes*, a lottery ticket for a fund-raising activity, and a sachet of perfume. The concert was followed by a sumptuous dinner for four hundred and fifty guests in one of the grand ballrooms of the Opera. The evening was a tremendous success and was televised in nine countries, so the whole world could share my triumph.

The morning of the concert I received a huge bunch of red roses, with good wishes in Greek, signed Aristotle Onassis. Another huge bunch of red roses arrived at lunch, also with good wishes in Greek, signed Aristotle. And just as I was about to leave for the opera house came another bunch of roses, also with good wishes in Greek. This time there was no signature on it. I knew who had sent it . . .

Aristotle Onassis and Me

1959 WAS TO BRING ABOUT a transformation of my secret self as drastic in its way as the changes that had taken place in my body.

The year started off not so differently from 1958. After spending Christmas in Italy, I returned once more to the United States, where I gave the last recital of a Sol Hurok tour on the eleventh in Saint Louis. This was followed by a concert in Philadelphia to commemorate the one hundred and second birthday of the Academy of Music.

On the twenty-seventh I returned to New York to sing Imogene in Bellini's *Il Pirata* at Carnegie Hall, under the auspices of the American Opera Society. Many of the reviews were glorious, including one which thanked Rudolf Bing for leaving the gap in my schedule which allowed me to accept the Society's invitation. But the reviewers, of course, were not unanimous in their accolades. My main adversary, Michael Scott, still following me around the world, took up his battle cry again. I was heartbroken to read, "Her voice has become thin and raw. It has lost so much quality that the only analogy this feat conjures up is that of a turkey gobbling." Did he have to be so heartless? Even though I knew inside that my voice had deteriorated badly, I tried to convince myself it was my judgement that was critical, and to listen instead to the voices of the adoring crowd. By slashing off the scabs, Scott exposed a fatal wound and left me writhing in agony.

Do other people hurt as intensely as I do? No sooner have I recovered from one laceration than another arrow darts out of nowhere to pierce my serenity. There is scarcely a moment I am not smarting from something or other. I remember thinking when I was eleven years old that a single day never went by without something happening to hurt my feelings. Either the teacher would slight me or one of the children make a nasty remark. I always acted as if I didn't care because then it didn't hurt so much.

No one ever thinks when they tear me down, Is this woman hurting? Is

there someone there to hold her hand? That's why I always get so aggres-
sive. I've been hostile ever since I was a child, in order to protect myself. Like
Joe McCarthy and Indian Joe, who kicked people first before they could kick
him. I'm the batboy in the circus everyone throws baseballs at.

The day after Scott's review, I was honored by Robert Wagner, the
mayor of New York, with a citation "to the esteemed daughter of New York,
whose glorious voice and superb artistry have contributed to the pleasure
of music lovers everywhere." How ironic that the city whose opera house
banished me was now honoring me with a citation of esteem!

I forgot to mention that something good happened on January 27th,
1959. I went to the AGMA offices on Broadway to defend myself against
charges about my cancellation of the San Francisco opera I had contracted
for. I spent two miserable hours justifying myself before the cross examina-
tion of twenty solemn judges. Apparently my stacks of medical records
convinced them I had been unable to perform and I got off the hook with no
more than a reprimand. I was permitted to sing *Il Pirata* in concert at
Carnegie Hall after all. Thank God for small favors!

I returned to Milan with a professional engagement book that was
practically blank until March 16, when I was set to record *Lucia* in London.
The gaps in my schedule were wide enough to get lost in. I had to go back
ten years to find an April in which I had not sung. The hiatus turned out to
be both bad and good for me. On the one hand, it is painful to live with the
rejection of one's colleagues, especially when one has been prima donna
assoluta of the world for over ten years. On the other hand, I needed the time
to work on the problems of my voice.

On April 21, Battista and I celebrated our tenth wedding anniversary at
Maxim's in Paris. I wore a stunning fitted evening dress of black matt satin
with a stole of the same material. My only jewelry was a pair of pear-shaped
diamond earrings Battista had given me for our anniversary. A chinchilla
wrap was casually draped over my shoulders. I rested my hand over his
through most of the dinner, and kissed him in the restaurant, wishing to
keep up the pretense of a perfect marriage. Believe me, I did some of my best
acting that night at Maxim's. At the end of the evening the violins serenaded
us and the whole restaurant applauded. I told the newspapers, "I could not
sing without him present. If I am the voice, he is the soul." From there we
went to the Lido and continued "celebrating" until the early hours of the
morning. It makes me laugh to think how easily people are fooled!

The real story is that for some time I had been wearying of Meneghini.
I wondered why I'd never noticed how self-involved, scheming, clumsy,

and narrow he was. He had no interest in art, philosophy, or ideas, not even opera, except for the contents of the cash box. In fact, I thought if I heard one more word from him about money I would scream! He spoke no languages but Italian, and was never willing to learn. That put him (and me) at a real disadvantage in American, French, and English society, in which we spent much of our time. He embarrassed me by falling asleep at the events we attended, even my concerts. Can you imagine how it looks to have the husband of the prima donna start to snore in the middle of her most important aria? I'm surprised the papers never got hold of it. They would have had a field day! He hadn't aged well at all, and seemed to have become coarser and less sophisticated as he grew older, almost like a clown. He never managed to dress smartly. Or maybe it's just that no suit would look good on a homely, elderly peasant type. Since I had become so svelte, the thought frequently crossed my mind that I deserved a more dashing, exciting man.

On June 17, after a fabulous performance of *Medea* at Covent Garden, we attended a reception at the Dorchester where we met Aristotle Onassis again. I was ready . . .

He had organized a party for me which literally left me gasping. Meneghini and I were millionaires, but compared to Onassis, we were poor relations. He invited forty people to come to the opera as his guests and then one hundred and sixty to a party at the Dorchester. It was more lavish than any ever given for me, even by Elsa Maxwell. The ballroom was decorated entirely in orchid pink and overflowing with matching roses. I had often heard the expression, "Your wish is my command," but this was the first time I had seen it in action. Ari never left my side and no request of mine was too small for him to grant. When I casually mentioned that I liked tangos, he rushed up to the band leader with fifty pounds in his hand. That was one hundred and forty dollars in American money, and twice the weekly salary of the average Englishman. After that nothing but tangos were played all evening. I found out later that my "wish" had been a fortunate one, for Carlos Gardel, the great Argentine singer of tangos, had been the idol of Ari's youth. We didn't leave the Dorchester until after three o'clock in the morning. In the foyer, the three of us were photographed in a hug, Aristotle on one side of me and Meneghini on the other. How prophetic that shot turned out to be!

Ari kept inviting me all evening to come and cruise with him and Tina on the *Christina*. He was hard to resist, and poor Meneghini didn't offer much competition. For a little girl from a lower middle class neighborhood in Washington Heights, it was a fairy tale, a dream come true.

But most important of all, for the first time in my life my head was filled with erotic fantasies. I was so overwhelmed with images of making love with Ari that I could hardly concentrate when anyone else was talking to me. It was frightening but oh, so exciting! As Battista and I left for our limousine, I murmured to Ari that I would consider the *Christina* trip and give him my decision soon. I didn't know it yet, but the die was already cast.

Impatient as I was, I had a concert at the Holland Festival and four *Medeas* in London in July before I could get back to Ari. I wondered how I would ever get through the next few days. Time only seemed to exist when I was with him; the rest was just an abyss to be vaulted with one continuous fantasy, where I obsessed about all the things I would like to do to him and have him do to me.

My fantasies would always start with our trip on his boat. Menenghini would be tired and Ari would ask me if I wanted to go for a stroll around the deck. I would sound reluctant, and he would know just how to coax me so it sounded like his idea and not mine. We would breathe in the sea air and become heady with the salt spray on our faces. He would gently kiss me and move away, but I would no longer be able to contain myself and would grab him. We would kiss passionately, furiously, with our tongues deep in each other's mouths. I never kissed Meneghini that way. In fact, kisses always seemed so intimate to me I was rather disgusted by them. But the thought of tongue kissing Ari was very appealing. As I was to find out soon, when you really love a man, anything goes. Then, just when I felt I couldn't stand the tension any longer, Ari would suggest that we go to his stateroom for a drink. I would agree, again sounding reluctant, of course, and we would stroll down to his quarters, looking unconcerned with each other if we passed any of the staff or other guests. When we got inside the door of the stateroom, we would be so impatient we would pull off each other's clothes and fall right down there on the floor. He would kiss my entire body starting from the top and going on down. At times the excitement of my fantasy became so intense I was frantic to see Ari and get relief. I hardly recognized prim and proper Maria in this newborn sex-crazed creature.

I gave a joyous concert, in which I sang an aria from Act 1 of Ernani with a new passion, especially the lines:

"Ernani, Ernani, bear me away
from that abhorred embrace.
Let us flee if love permits
me to live with you;
through caves and desolate wastelands,

my footsteps will follow you.
Those grottoes will be
an Eden of delight to me."

When I drove to the Hotel Amstel with Peter Diamand, the director of the Holland Festival, I told him I had to talk to him without Battista. Just in case it was necessary, I said, I wanted him to keep my fee for me and not deposit it in the joint Meneghini account.

"What melodrama, Maria!" Peter declared.

"Not melodrama, Peter. Drama," I answered him. I had already made up my mind. In spite of Meneghini's protests, we were going cruising on the *Christina*. How could I do otherwise, in the shape I was in? Battista gave in, of course. He always did when I insisted.

Every time I thought of Ari's warm black eyes drinking me in, I was thrilled anew that I was thin. I went shopping in Milan, where I spent millions of lire on bathing suits, vacation outfits, and lingerie. A sophisticated friend told me later that a woman always buys new lingerie when she is about to have an affair. She was right, but I wasn't ready to admit it yet; I told myself I just wanted to look nice on the trip.

The three-million-dollar sea palace was as large as a football field. On board were Winston Churchill, his wife and daughter, and many other well-known Greek, American, and English personalities. I don't have to describe the *Christina*, because by now everybody knows about the palace on the sea that was Onassis's home. Suffice it to say I ran about the ship like a schoolgirl, exclaiming at each new discovery, now the solid-gold fixtures shaped like dolphins in each bathroom, now my enormous, beautifully decorated cabin and marble bathroom with adjoining boudoir and limitless closet space for all my beautiful new clothes (a suite, incidentally, which I never used later unless Ari and I had a fight), now the real El Greco in Ari's study, the fabulous jewelled Buddha, the swimming pool decorated with a mosaic reproduction of a fresco from the Palace of Knossos, the huge oak-paneled lounge with a majestic grand piano at one end and a lapis lazuli fireplace at the other, and Ari's private bathroom, which looked like a temple, the bath inlaid with flying fish and dolphins, an exact copy of the one in King Minos's lost Palace of Knossos in Crete. Ari, who had fussed over every detail like a housewife, was in raptures over each of my enthusiastic outbursts. The ship boasted a crew of sixty, including two chefs, one French, one Greek. The guests were given a choice of menus, but I was still eating mostly raw meat and salads, so I didn't really appreciate them. Of course I am known for sneaking bits of food from everyone else's plates, so I got at least a sampling of the fine cuisine.

The trip was literally an eye opener for me, a staid Italian matron who believed in fidelity and monogamy. I was shocked to see many of the guests sunbathing without any clothes on, and some of them openly playing around with other people's mates on deck. Aristo was one of those walking around naked. He was hairy like a gorilla, Battista said. My reaction to his nudity was the second sign that I was becoming another person. I have always been a bit of a prude, so much so that I wouldn't sing the Dance of the Seven Veils in Richard Strauss's *Salome* because she had to take off her clothes. But when I saw Ari walking around like that, I began to giggle. I had never seen a nude man besides Battista, and I couldn't tear my eyes away. The sight of him exposed like a vulnerable child thrilled me so much I forgot all about my ideals. I only wanted to touch him. My fantasies about making love with him escalated until they kept me awake all night.

My enthusiasm was not shared by Meneghini. He got crabbier and crabbier the further along we got in our voyage. He was interested in neither the ship nor the other guests, and spent his time whining to me about the way people were slighting him. Of course he never mentioned that he was the only person aboard who spoke neither French nor English. I found his griping and endless criticism of Aristo increasingly irritating. I kept comparing his sluggish demeanor with Ari's vigor and passion for life, and Battista fell far short. He was only nine years older than Ari, but he behaved like his grandfather.

For me, it was a magnificent three-week voyage. I liked the person I became when I was with Ari more than I had ever liked myself before. I felt like a beloved woman, and it warmed the place deep inside my diaphragm where I live.

Our plans were to stop first at Portofino, a toy port on the coast of Italy, and then go on to Capri for sight-seeing. Then we would sail from the Mediterranean through the Aegean Sea to the Gulf of Corinth. From there we planned a sight-seeing trip of Delphi, sailing on to Izmir, the Turkish name for Ari's boyhood home, and then on up to the Dardanelles to Istanbul and home again.

I was drunk with the fresh sea air, the cloudless blue skies, and the company of Onassis. For a few days I tried to attribute my glow of happiness when I was near him to our common Greek heritage, but it didn't take long for me to stop kidding myself.

By the time we reached Piraeus, the weather became so stormy that Meneghini and most of the other guests got seasick and took to their staterooms, leaving Aristo and me practically alone. We sat in the deserted games room basking before the fire in the lapis lazuli fireplace. The sparkle of the flames lit up the deep blue of the lapis, and was reflected in eyes as black and round as Greek olives. The room was dimly lit, and once in a while was brilliantly lit up by a flash of lightening. Once during such a flash I saw my own eyes mirrored in his. I was scared at first, but then thought, his eyes, my eyes, what's the difference: It's all the same to me. Then I was filled with the most heavenly feeling, like a baby who has just been fed.

The motion of the ship on the stormy seas rocked us back and forth so that I was almost in a trance as we sat there talking all night. We spoke mostly in Greek, or, rather, Ari did. He told me all about his boyhood, where he came into the world seventeen years before me in Smyrna near the coast of Turkey. Later he had the captain stop the ship there so he could show me the house where he was born. He spoke about the Greek quarters where he was brought up, and of his father and uncle, who were flourishing merchants of cotton, tobacco, and anything else that would grow in the Anatalyan area. Then without making a play for sympathy, he described his mother's death during a kidney operation when he was only six. He spoke of his father's subsequent remarriage to his aunt, and of his beloved grandmother. He also said he had been a choirboy and boasted with a beguiling smile that he, too, had a good voice. I found him enchanting, and knew other women did, too. He had been a ladies' man from the time he pinched his English teacher's bottom and was suspended from school. He was incorrigible from the beginning, and made love for the first time when he was only thirteen. When I think I was twice that age when I had my first sexual experience, I am embarrassed.

He also told me of the horrors in his life during the Second World War. They far surpassed mine. Earlier, he had lived through the Turkish attack on Smyrna and saw thousands of Greeks tortured and killed, and survived his father's arrest and the atrocities that followed. He described how at age sixteen he rescued his father from the cruel Turks, who massacred one million Greeks in Turkish Asia Minor between 1918 and 1923. Then he told me about crossing the sea in a filthy boat crammed with a thousand immigrants in steerage until his arrival at Buenos Aires on September 21, 1923. It amazes me that six weeks before I was born, Ari was already a seasoned man on his way to success. He soon started his career with a Buenos Aires telephone company and, by the time he was twenty-four, had become Greek vice-consul general in Argentina. Shortly thereafter he arranged to buy the two Canadian ships with which he began his stunning career.

On August 4 we dropped anchor at the foot of Mount Athos, where something happened that was to change my life forever. We were received by the Patriarch Athenagoras. Ari and I knelt side by side to receive his blessing. Speaking in Greek, he called us "the world's greatest singer and the greatest seaman of the modern world, the new Ulysses."

When he thanked us for the honors we had brought to the Greek world, my eyes filled with tears. It was as if he were performing a solemn marriage ceremony. Somehow I felt that he had brought me God's permission to be together with Ari, and my last resistance crumbled. After that we were man and wife in my mind, and a few hours later, in our bodies.

That night there was a party at the Istanbul Hilton for the guests of the *Christina*. Meneghini said he felt too tired to attend and remained on board the ship. When I returned at five in the morning, he was waiting up for me and demanded to know why I was so late. I knew I couldn't keep up the pretense any longer. "I am in love with Ari," I said.

A week after the *Christina* had docked in Istanbul, Battista and I left the ship on one of Onassis's private planes and flew to Milan, and then promptly left for Sirmione. I wore a bracelet with the initials TMWL (To Maria With Love) engraved on it, which I didn't remove for many years. After I had declared my love for Ari, Battista and I argued ferociously night and day and I'm sure our voices carried all over the ship. But I guess poor Titta had given up by the time we reached Sirmione, or else he was emotionally exhausted, for we sat together in silence.

Parting from Ari left a hole in my chest, which I filled by fantasizing the whole night long in Sirmione that he would come get me. To my great surprise, to say nothing of Battista's, at nine o'clock the next morning we heard a voice outside my window singing, "Maria, Maria!" It was Aristo. He told Battista, "I've come to marry your wife." Yes, dreams do come true . . . sometimes.

At four o'clock in the morning, I left with Aristo for Milan. He then flew to Venice to discuss divorce with Tina.

For the first time in my life, I was madly in love with a man who was in love with me. It was too much to take in all at once. I was flooded with so much feeling I felt I couldn't stand it another moment. Then I would remind myself that despite the blessing of the Patriarch Athenagoras, I was having an affair with a married man, and this would calm me down a bit. I appeased my conscience with the knowledge that Ari and I would both try to get divorces and marry as soon as possible.

People said my whole personality changed, that my sharp edges melted and I became a softer, gentler person. Even poor Battista said I was a different woman. Why not? For the first time in my life I was happy. I had the feeling of having been kept in a cage so long that when I met Aristo, so full of vigor and zest for life, I did become another woman. So much so that I hardly recognized myself. Would you believe that even Ghiringhelli succumbed to my new temperament? When we met to discuss my recording *Gioconda* at La Scala, the iceman actually thawed. He even smiled with his whole face when he asked me to return to La Scala on my own terms and to sing anything I wanted. I arrived in Milan on September 2 in wonderful spirits to begin rehearsals for the new recording.

My happiness was somewhat flawed by the press and photographers, who persecuted me mercilessly. The throngs of press people were so numerous and unruly that I needed physical protection to keep from being mauled. On one occasion they caught Ari and me dining tête-à-tête at the Rendez-vous in Milan, and at three o'clock that morning we were photographed going into the Hotel Principe e Savoia arm in arm. In order to increase my chances of getting a divorce by mutual consent, my lawyers insisted I issue a statement to the press saying: "I confirm that the break between my husband and myself is complete and final. It has been in the air for some time, and the cruise on the *Christina* was only coincidental. . . . I am now my own manager. I ask for understanding in this painful personal situation. . . . Between Signor Onassis and myself there exists a profound friendship that dates back some time. I am also in a business connection with him. When I have further things to say, I shall do so at the opportune moment."

As I have said, I am a simple, moral woman. I despised living a lie, which no one believed anyhow.

Aristo was also attacked by reporters, but he was much more honest than I. "Of course," he said, "how could I help but be flattered if a woman with the class of Maria Callas fell in love with someone like me? Who wouldn't?" Dear Ari! Always frank, always forthright! How could I help but be flattered if a man with the directness of Onassis fell in love with someone like me?

On September 10, as soon as the *Gioconda* recording was finished, I rushed to the Milan airport to board the private plane Ari had sent for me. From there I flew to Venice, where I excitedly boarded the *Christina*. Aristo triumphantly marked my arrival by setting off the loud, blasting siren announcing the departure of the *Christina*. Only two other guests were along this time, Ari's sister, Artemis, and her husband Theodore Garoufalidis.

Tina was not on board. She had taken her children a few days before and fled to Paris to the home of her father, the respected Greek ship owner Stavros Livanos. Aristo, who was upset about the children, had followed her in his private plane to make a half-hearted gesture of reconciliation. But Tina was not about to forgive him for the public humiliation he had put her through. This left Ari free to do what he really wanted, which was to sail on the *Christina* with me.

What a dream voyage it was, with both of us relaxed and at peace with ourselves. Our love was just what the Good Doctor had ordered. We soaked up the sun all day and then swam for hours in the sun-drenched Mediterranean. Then we would make love all night, reaching peaks of pleasure that went on and on almost beyond endurance. At last I knew what the Hollywood movies were about. It was the first time in my life I felt happy to be alive. If I were lucky in my earlier life, I might have felt moments of joy here and there, but they were greatly outstripped by periods of misery. In fact, if someone had told me it was possible to experience a feeling of bliss most of the time, I wouldn't have believed them. On the *Christina*, however, I felt full of happiness the whole trip, except of course on the few occasions when Ari and I had a fight.

Luxuriating in my new happiness left me unwilling to give up one minute of it. I was so immersed in the timelessness of the present that I paid no attention to my career. I was sick and tired of being a sexless nun and was relieved to leave the hard work behind me. Nevertheless, I was shocked at the end of the year when a newspaper compared the number of appearances I had made pre and post Ari. In 1958, I gave twenty-eight performances of seven operas in six cities all over the world. As the whole world was to see later on, my professional decline continued, so that in 1961 my schedule showed just five performances, all of *Medea* at Epidaurus and La Scala. The descent escalated even more rapidly in 1962, when I only sang *Medea* twice at La Scala. And in 1963 I gave no performances at all. In 1964, sadly enough, I made the last stage appearance of my life. The cold figures offered proof in black and white of the dreadful decline of my career.

Why did my career go downhill so rapidly? Biki, Milan's leading fashion designer, and others say Ari destroyed my life. I don't think that is a fair statement. It is true that he didn't want me to sing, but I didn't have to give in to him. Whatever his shortcomings, he can't be blamed for that. The truth is, life for me began at nearly forty. I couldn't bear to be away from him for one moment, and in the beginning we spent every waking hour together. We Greeks are possessive people, and I wanted to hold on to every bit of him he would allow. Then too, I must confess I didn't want to give him the opportunity to find a replacement for me.

And perhaps most important of all, I had been having trouble with my voice since 1955, when, ominously, it wobbled and got out of control on a climactic high B during "La mamma morta." I was so upset by the decline of my voice that I couldn't bear to practice, and rarely did so. Thus any hope of recovering my vocal powers was lost, for singers are like athletes in that we have to keep on exercising if we are to retain our prowess.

I have another theory about the loss of my voice that no one else has mentioned, despite the thousands of words spent chewing over the problem. (As if it is anybody's business but mine!)

When I first went to de Hidalgo, I sang mostly in the middle range. By sheer hard work and persistence, we extended my ability and constructed the top and bottom ranges. This fact was not lost on critics like Howard Taubman, who wrote in the *New York Times* that my voice gave the impression it "was formed out of sheer will power rather than natural endowments." Taubman was probably right. Singers like Rosa Ponselle were born with more natural aptitude than I. Doesn't it make sense that the last ability to be developed would be the first to go, particularly when I was no longer practicing?

Something similar happened with the incomparable Giuditta Pasta, a great singing star who combined technical virtuosity with an almost hypnotic presence, a combination it has been said is descriptive of my abilities as well. The early deterioration of Pasta's voice makes me think my theory about the decline of my own voice is correct. She became famous in 1822, when she was only twenty-four, and remained the diva for the next ten years. According to Stendhal, she was a mezzo who forced her high tones, and later paid for it with her career.

But despite the degeneration of my voice, I was thirty-six years old and happy for the first time in my life. I ended 1959 feeling, along with Blanche Dubois in *A Streetcar Named Desire*, that "Sometimes there's God so suddenly."

Fun and Games with Ari

*I*F I EXPECTED OUR PARADISE to last indefinitely I soon found I was mistaken. Like all heavenly sojourns on earth, my utopia was short-lived. Or perhaps it would be nearer correct to say it became erratic, as a new phase of our relationship began. Like many men, Ari became much more difficult once he had me for his own. Now he played hard to get. Gone were the days of the Dorchester when every wish of mine was his command. Now his pleasure became central to mine. To my despair, he spent time with his wife, trying to woo her back. He began to dine with other women, like Jeanne Rhinelander, who was named as correspondent in Tina Onassis's divorce suit. He behaved like a typical Greek man and I a typical Greek woman, whose philosophy is that a man cannot really change himself, but a woman must be able to transform herself to suit her man.

He often became withdrawn and perverse, staying away for as much as a week, not even phoning when he didn't feel like it. Nor would he answer my calls. I would be in a panic for days at a time that he didn't love me and I would never have him again. What a comedown for the prima assoluta of the world! He had all the power in the relationship: I could only sit and wait. Once in a while I would hate myself for being his slave, and find the courage to visit a friend, see a movie, anything not to be waiting for him. He must have been telepathic, because that was the exact moment he always picked to phone me. When I got home, I would call him right back, only to find that he had left and was not available for days. I felt desperate until I could contact him. He knew how to cure me of going out when he was away.

Then suddenly, for no reason I could understand, he would begin to phone again every day and send me flowers. Or he delighted me by showing up unexpectedly or sending for me. I was so happy to see him I overlooked being hurt and angry and jumped into bed with him at the first opportunity. When we did get together, our sex life was on a different planet, and made up for all his mistreatment. Each return was another honeymoon that left us moaning in ecstasy.

It was uncanny how he was able to sense the very things he could do to me that were most painful. With his ability to read minds, he would have made a great psychic. He never was affectionate with me when people were around, never took me in his arms or gave me a kiss, because he knew I needed public recognition from him. He acted like I was some casual acquaintance he had just picked up in a bar. He often treated me even worse; he was rude and humiliated me in front of others. He forgot all about my thirty-sixth birthday, although I suspected his neglect was meant as some form of punishment for my wish to marry him. It felt just like my mother's rejection of me at my birth. I need to be with someone on my birthday who is happy I was born; otherwise I feel unwanted and unloved. Down in the dumps, of course, I called my old reliable Meneghini, even though we were in the midst of divorce proceedings, and spent my birthday with him. It was good to be with a man again who lived his life only for me. But it was Aristo I loved and Aristo I forgave, as I was to do time after time for nine long years.

Onassis wasn't my only problem in 1960. I was disturbed by difficulties with my voice during performances. The reviewers picked them up, of course, but I could generally manage to convince myself the trouble would pass. I knew this pitch or that note was wrong, but felt during my good moments there was nothing I couldn't cure with persistence and hard work when I got around to it.

1960 brought the first indication of real catastrophe. It began with a sore throat, which spread to my sinuses and made it remarkably painful to sing. I needed not so much to sing as to know I *could* sing, so I would go into the music room on the *Christina* and sit at the grand piano and try to sing something, anything at all. The pain would begin immediately. It felt like a knife had been impaled in my throat and sliced all the way up my windpipe to my head. Sometimes it seemed the knife was twisting around in my temples, at other times as if a huge anchor was being swung at my forehead. The pain was so sharp I had to stop singing instantly. I would try again day after day until even the thought of singing gave me a migraine. So I would quit for an hour or even a day or two, and then try to resume my practice, each time with the same agonizing results. I was in a panic, and tried now this doctor, now that medication, now this new teacher, but with no outcome but frustration and despair. I felt like the helpless Butterfly imprisoned in the net of a gigantic manipulation; there was nothing to do but bang myself against the wall as long as the headaches raged away. I noticed I often had trouble with my voice when I was unhappy. In fact, I once told an interviewer, "Only a happy bird can sing." And a happy bird I was not.

As a matter of fact, I was often miserable, in spite of the many exciting interludes with Ari. I was frequently deserted by him, particularly when I needed him the most. I was in a panic about my voice. And to top it all off, Liska's book, *My Daughter Maria Callas*, came out, in which she played the dramatic role of injured and abandoned mother. She should have gone on the stage; if she was half as good on it as she was on television I would be known as Liska Callas's daughter!

According to Liska, she was all but starving and I refused her a crust of bread. Imagine what it does to one's self-esteem to be humiliated by your mother in front of millions of people! It left me with a gaping hole in the middle of my stomach and, I must admit, a tingling on my buttocks.

I understood very well what she had in mind. She expected me to make a big ruckus about her book, and the resulting publicity would seduce many readers into buying it. She exploited me when I was a child, and I was determined not to let her do it again. So I refused to answer reporters' questions about what I thought of the book and pretended to take no notice of it. I told anyone who asked me that I had never read it. As a consequence, after the first flutter of interest it sank like a rock in the sea. It is a bad book. That's where it deserves to be, buried at the bottom of the sea. Thank God not many people read it. God is on the side of the righteous. Sometimes, anyway.

Things with Ari settled down a bit, and he began to spend more time with me. Although he never explained his change of heart any more than his game playing, I suppose he realized he cared about me and felt less trapped. Not surprisingly, my headaches disappeared. Ari was the only medicine I needed. Once again I was elated, and as Tina went about getting her divorce, my fantasies changed from erotic ones to those of being his wife and bearing his children.

"I don't want to sing anymore," I wrote my godfather. "I want to live like a normal woman, with children, a home, and a dog." Of course, as I said before, whatever I most wanted from Ari was the one thing I was sure not to get. But I didn't know yet he would never marry me, so I lived for years in a fool's paradise, always believing some day my dreams would come true.

We talked a lot about getting married. In fact, on August 10, when he said once more that he would marry me, I made an announcement to the press. Would you believe he told reporters it was just a childish prank and purely my fantasy! Once again I was humiliated publicly but was a good little girl and said nothing. How I had changed from the Xanthippi, that shrewish wife of Socrates, who was married to Meneghini! I should have insisted Onassis marry me then or else. He would have done so at that time, if not marrying me meant losing me. But apparently I got enough from him when he was being his loving, loveable self to keep going. And really, I had no choice. He was my life.

It boosted my image of myself that the crew considered me mistress of the ship, for Ari had instructed them to do anything I asked. Once, though, I ordered a picture of Tina removed from the games room, and he commanded it be put back. I should have realized then I was living in a fool's paradise. The crew loved it that I came down to the kitchen every day and tasted and appraised the various Greek dishes. The whole crowd gathered around me as I sampled each of the foods, and awaited my exuberant responses to each mouthful.

I was fascinated with everything about Ari, and often sat in when he and his associates held their conferences. This was a side of him I completely respected and I frequently listened in awe of his brilliance and business sense. I was glad to be interested, for it brought us closer together. He asked for and valued my advice, too. I was the only woman, Ari told a friend, with whom he could discuss business affairs.

Keeping up with that man was like being spun around in a tornado. It was a job in itself, and even if I had wanted to, there was no time for a career. I visited Via Buonarroti very little in 1960 and no longer thought of it as home. My home was where my heart was, with Ari, and we began to look for a new residence together.

If you think that means all was well with our relationship, think again. Ari behaved like a pasha. Never mind that I was queen of the opera. When he didn't want me along on the voyages of the *Christina*, he had no compunction about kicking me off. His excuse might be that he had important business engagements he didn't want me to attend, or he didn't want to embarrass the Churchills, who were fond of Tina, with the presence of his concubine. (Imagine him calling me his concubine, I who loved him more than life itself and would have joyfully married him the minute our divorces came through, if only he had asked!) Other times he had no excuse at all, only that that was what he felt like doing. Winston's wife Clementine once said to me, "When Winston and I got married he said we would be one person. But he never said that one person would be he." I know what you meant, Clementine!

Meanwhile, Tina was going about getting her divorce, in spite of Aristotle's pleas for a reconciliation. Something else good came out of their last meeting. Tina agreed to drop her New York divorce suit and to go for a quickie in Alabama, which meant a lot less messy publicity for Ari and me. I was overjoyed when he agreed to look at a chateau with me in Eure-et-Loire. The divorce came through a month later; the chateau never did.

It was 1960 and my career was getting shakier and shakier. My voice continued to give me trouble, and Ari wouldn't let me practice around him, so I wasn't able to correct what might have been changed. I recorded some Verdi arias for EMI in London in July, but they sounded so dreadful I refused to allow the recording to be released. Then I left for Belgium to give a concert in Ostend. The morning of the performance I woke up and was horrified to find I could hardly talk, let alone sing. The concert had to be canceled and I left Belgium terrified that I had agreed to give two performances of *Norma* in August in Greece. I couldn't sleep for weeks. How could I sing a whole opera when I couldn't even record a decent aria? Yet I knew I had to overcome my fears for better or for worse, because it had almost a religious significance for Ari that his mistress score a triumph at historic Epidaurus.

He put everything else aside for me for those weeks and we were deliriously happy again, as we spent almost all our time together. We had some of our best hours playing in the water. We both loved to swim, and chased each other merrily over and under the swells like children. I tied my long auburn hair into a knot, and we put on flippers and goggles and dived deep into the Mediterranean. It was lovely to kiss among the colorful fishes and ferns, where the rest of the world seemed but a dream. It gave our love an eery storybook quality that comes only when you get your heart's desire. We shot up triumphantly waving shells and urns. One of our finds was a broken terra-cotta vase I still keep on top of my bureau.

When I felt he loved me, everything seemed possible. Once when we were racing over the waves, I had a funny thought. I was doing the crawl. I thought, everybody thinks it is a miracle Jesus walked on water. Isn't it as much of one that I can crawl on top of it?

Aristo kept strange hours, often turning night into day and day into night. This was fine with me, as I've always been a night person. If he spent the whole night talking business, I worked on my *Norma* score. Then when he was ready for bed in the early hours of the morning, I was there too. When he was alone with me and in the mood, nobody could make me feel as loved and valued as Aristo. He had a way of looking deep into my soul as if he were I and I were he, as if we two were the whole world and nothing else existed. Being with him when he was loving was pure bliss. What he offered was the feeling of being totally cherished. His constant presence that summer reassured me that I was loved and gradually my confidence began to return. He even gave me emotional support for my singing, allowing me to practice during those weeks and complimenting me on the results. It began to seem possible after all that I could sing *Norma* at Epidaurus.

The performance on August 24 turned out to be one of the peak experiences of my life. When I was a child and my mother told me stories of the ancient amphitheatre in the Peloponnesus, I dared to dream that someday I would sing there before my countrymen. The stone seats of the theatre are built into the hillsides, and its beauty and sweeping majesty make it an awesome sight. In ancient times the area also served as a spa, where patients went to be healed. They would go to sleep in the abaton and dream of cures prescribed by the god Aesclepius. I hoped singing there would cure me of my ailments, both physical and emotional.

But in my life, nothing is perfect. The gods make sure of that. On August 17, my first night at Epidaurus, a violent thunder storm poured down from the heavens just as the overture was about to begin. Twenty thousand people surged out of the amphitheatre back into the cars, buses, and boats that had brought them the sixty miles from Athens. Twenty thousand people were heartbroken at the disruption. But at least this time no one could blame *me*.

On August 24 I returned to the greatest standing ovation ever heard at Epidaurus. Imagine how it felt to see Aristo sitting on the front row with my father, both men proud and happy to have their Maria bringing honor to their beloved country! It was literally a dream come true.

I gave a performance at the apex of my art; I had never sung better, nor with deeper and more powerful feelings. Norma was more complex and many-sided than I had ever sung her before. When I sang to the children, my heart and soul went out to them with a mother's emotion more profound than any I had ever known. Greek subjects have always stirred in me the bottomless passions of my ancestors, but my relationship with Aristo added wisdom and tenderness to my performance. I knew I was exposing my inner chaos in all its nakedness, but was gratified that I could use my personal tragedy to deepen my art. Norma is a high priestess and at the same time a vulnerable woman. Who would know better than I the extremes of her character?

The performance began at sunset and the magnificent darkening sky was soon shimmering with starlight. Because the amphitheatre has perfect acoustics, I could feel my voice reaching to the top row of the worn stone steps. When a laurel wreath was placed on my head at the end of the performance, I could sense the thunderous applause raining down on me all the way from the most distant seats. It was as if I suddenly had twenty thousand friends who loved me, all of them Greek. I was so carried away I didn't know what to do with my feelings. I could only stand there immobilized and speechless. When I was crowned with that laurel wreath, I fell on my knees and sobbed my gratitude to the audience and to God.

Ari and I were deliriously happy after my triumph at Epidaurus, so much so that I forgot I had to sing another *Norma* in four days. We spent the interim sightseeing, sunbathing the whole day under the sweltering sun, and celebrating all night long in nightclubs.

I always have to pay for my achievements with some suffering, either emotional or physical. The day of the performance I came down with a raging fever and felt terribly weak. The doctors insisted I remain in bed, but sick or well I was not about to miss the second night of my triumph. I dragged myself to the amphitheatre and out onto the stage. Strangely enough, once I opened my mouth to sing, my illness completely disappeared. It was the ancient healing power of Epidaurus working its magic again. I was so grateful, I gave my ten-thousand-dollar fee to create The Scholarship Fund for Young Musicians. I wanted young, talented artists to share the miracle of singing under the shining stars at Epidaurus.

We spent three restful, relatively quiet months on the *Christina*, where I was preparing to open the La Scala season for the first time in three years with Paolina in Donizetti's *Poliuto*. The anxiety and panic I went through before singing my usual repertoire had become too much for me to bear, and I selected the simplest, least demanding role I could find to open the season. Paolina, second in importance to the tenor Corielli's character, was a relatively minor role. My panic subsided as I looked forward to working with Visconti again. I felt he would help me through the ordeal of opening the La Scala season.

But whom the gods would make humble they first make proud. I was badly shaken when Lucino withdrew from the opera. He explained he was protesting the Italian Government's censorship of his movie *Rocco and His Brothers* and his production of the play *L'Arialda*, and would no longer do any artistic work in Italy. He apologized for leaving me in the lurch, and sent me his admiration and hugs and kisses. I wanted to shriek, "Stop! Stop! You can't do this to me! I am Maria Callas, prima donna assoluta of the world!" Instead I sent him a sympathetic letter expressing concern for his predicament. I don't know why I was so nice, considering I felt as if I were standing on the edge of a precipice. After thirty months of absence, I was frantic at being left on my own to face the opening night at La Scala, with Ari, Princess

Grace and Prince Ranier, the Begum Aga Kahn, Erich Maria Remarque and his wife, Paulette Goddard, and the usual fashionable Milan audience in attendance.

Sure enough, the reviewers were like vultures, and after the fifth performance I was a mess. I knew I couldn't expose myself to their attacks much longer without being destroyed to the core, and determined to sing less and less in the future.

Paolina was the last new role I was ever to risk. After that, I appeared onstage in only three operas, my old reliables, *Norma*, *Tosca*, and *Medea*, and those only rarely.

The Declining Years

I WAS NOT SCHEDULED TO SING at La Scala for another year. In the meantime, I moved to Paris, which I had loved since the first time I sang there. I recorded my first French recitals in March and April of 1961 with Georges Prêtre and the Orchestre National de la RTF at the Salle Wagram, singing a lighter program than I was used to, more that of a mezzo soprano. It included the Habanera from *Carmen*, Gluck's "J'ai perdu mon Eurydice," and "Pleurez mes yeux" from Massenet's *Le Cid*. The success of the recording convinced many people I should begin a new career as a mezzo. They said many divas like Regina Resnik changed from soprano to mezzo and then had fabulous careers, and I was much too young to give up a profession in which I had been so successful. Nellie Melba sang *La Bohème* from a wheelchair into her sixties, so I suppose I could have done it too. But I was tired. I didn't feel much like a tiger anymore. And besides, there was Ari.

At first I lived at the Hotel Lancaster, Rue Berri, but soon moved to an apartment at 44 Avenue Foch. My choice of address wasn't a coincidence. Ari had an apartment at number 88, and Maggie van Zuylen, an old friend of Ari's who was to become an intimate confidant and advisor about my problems with him, lived at number 84. Michel Glotz, the head of Pathé-Marconi, the French counterpart of EMI, had also become a good friend, as was my conductor, Georges Prêtre.

My work revolved more and more around my cruises on the *Christina*. I couldn't be away from Ari for long without becoming a nervous wreck, so I would undertake an engagement only when it didn't interfere with his plans. Thus, as soon as I finished the Parisian recordings, I left for a cruise out of Monte Carlo. And after my concert at St. James Place on May 30, where I was restless and not in good voice in spite of the fact that it was attended by the Queen Mother, I immediately fled from London for another cruise.

I enjoyed relaxing on the ship and living my life around Ari. Gradually, without even noticing it, I practiced my music less and less. It was only when Zeffirelli called my beautiful fingernails to my attention that I realized how long it had been since I'd practiced at the piano. When Princess Grace said that I hadn't even sung exercises for the entire three weeks she had been aboard, I was too embarrassed to admit the truth. Instead I blurted out, "I don't need to practice."

I don't have to tell you this didn't bode too well for my August 6 performance of *Medea* at Epidaurus. When I got there I rehearsed without stopping for four days and nights before the opening. I even slept in a room in the Museum of Epidaurus to allow its spirit to seep through me while I slept. Apparently the gods themselves came to my rescue. The opening night was my greatest triumph in Epidaurus. There were seventeen curtain calls, and twenty thousand spectators on the stone steps, on the surrounding hills, and even sitting up in the trees. My father and sister—yes, I had allowed Georges to bring Jackie on condition that Liska didn't come along —were there. Only Onassis was missing. He said business had kept him away . . . It always takes me days to recover from singing a tragic role, but this time in spite of my great success it took me longer than ever.

I had an unsettling setback in London three months later, in November, when I recorded a series of arias from Bellini's *Il Pirata*, and others of Donizetti and Rossini, with the Philharmonic Orchestra under Tonini. The recording was a disaster. My voice lacked both fluidity and range, and I allowed only the *Pirata* to be issued, and then not until 1971. My voice was leaving me, along with my heart.

My last appearance of 1961 was at La Scala, where I appeared for the first of three performances of *Medea*. This time I wasn't scheduled until four days after opening night. Even so, it was good to appear with Minotis producing, Schippers conducting, and my old friends Simionato and Vickers singing with me. It seemed like old times . . . almost.

I was not in good voice in my first-act duet with Jason on opening night, and am the first to admit I couldn't give it the intensity it required. But I didn't deserve what happened. From the top of the gallery came a ghastly sound like the hiss of a cluster of snakes. It spread like an atomic bomb through the whole auditorium. Nevertheless, I kept on singing until I came to the point where Medea condemns Jason with the word "Crudel!" which means "Cruel man!" I'd had enough of cruel men to last a lifetime, and knew I had to do something if I were to keep whatever dignity I had left. So I hauled the old Callas up out of nowhere, stopped singing, and glowered deep into the auditorium. I hurled my second "Crudel!" straight at them, paralyzing the audience into silence. When I sang "Ho dato tutto a te" ("I gave everything to you") I shook my fist at them. Take my word for it, there wasn't a peep out of them the rest of the performance. I felt good because I had found Maria Callas again, at least for the time being.

Three *Medea*s were scheduled, and after the second performance the pain in my sinuses was so acute even the air exerted a pressure on them. I was forced to go for an operation before I could sing the third *Medea* on December 20. Onassis didn't show up at the hospital during the operation or my convalescence. He sent me some chintzy carnations, which I promptly threw into the wastebasket. The press reported our relationship was kaput, and I was afraid they were right. Heartbroken and dismayed (Crudel! Crudel!), I joined him in Monte Carlo for Christmas. Fortunately or unfortunately, *la passione dei sensi* rescued us once again and kept the relationship, decrepit as it was, going for six years longer.

On February 27, 1962, I sang a concert at Royal Festival Hall in London, which included my familiar friends "Ocean! thou mighty monster" from *Oberon* and "Pleurez mes yeux" from *El Cid*. The English press, which usually felt I could do no wrong, turned into a school of sharks who smelled blood and criticized even the lighting and the lay audience. They said the ambiance reminded them of pop singers and nightclubs. Nevertheless, everyone else went into raptures over my performance and gave me a standing ovation that even the orchestra participated in. All except Ari, who wasn't there. . . .

Next I did a ten-day tour of Germany in March, where I sang a similar program, and then went to London in April for a mediocre recording of mezzo arias, of which I allowed just the Rondo Finale from *La Centerentola* to be published.

While in London, I got the news that my mother had made a suicide attempt. I know her. It was designed to get me to rush over to the United States for a sentimental reconciliation. I understand her too well to be taken in by her histrionics.

Then I received a notice from the New York City Department of Welfare that my mother had applied for public assistance and I was responsible for her support to the extent of my ability to contribute. I was furious with Liska for her book, her hawking of Callas dolls, her constant whining to the press, and her interminable attempts to force me to give her money. I was also certain her "suicide" was at least in part an effort to embarrass me publicly. Nevertheless, I knew I had to do something or the press would descend on me like vultures. So I wrote to my godfather giving him permission to make a settlement with the Welfare Department. I agreed to send her two hundred dollars a month on condition she keep her mouth shut. Of course she didn't, but as with my mother and every other aspect of my life, there was nothing I could do about it.

It was the principle of the thing that bothered me, not a scarcity of money. Although my divorce from Meneghni was not to become final until 1966, he had filed suit for a legal separation in 1959, in which Judge Cesre Andreotti awarded me Villa Buonarroti, most of my jewelry, and Toy. Meneghini was allowed to keep Sirmione and all the other real estate we owned jointly. All of our other valuables were divided equally. It was a fairly equitable settlement, and I was satisfied with it.

I went to New York on May 19 but didn't visit Liska. How ironic that I flew there to help celebrate President Kennedy's birthday at Madison Square Garden, where I sang the Habanera and Seguedille from *Carmen*. This was my first interaction with the Kennedys. Unfortunately, it was not to be the last.

On November 4, I broke my five month vacation from singing to appear on television in an ITV Golden Hour from Covent Garden. I sang "Tu che le vanita" from *Don Carlo*, and the "Habanera" and the "Seguedille" from *Carmen*. Everybody loved my new hairstyle and said it made me look youthful and radiant. According to the papers, the most memorable thing about my performance was that while I was singing, my heavy diamond bracelet fell off my arm. The press made a big fuss that not a flicker of my eyelids gave any indication of awareness I had dropped it. Then they raved because I bent down and picked it up at an opportune moment. From such moments is fame forged.

Since I was working little, I had much more time to spend with Aristo and his friends. Our social life intensified and we went out gallivanting every night until all hours of the morning. We attended star-studded parties with the elegant Riviera set, the races, and dinners at Maxims, and appeared at Greek nightclubs where, for the first time in my life, I began to drink a glass or two of wine with Ari. As Tinca says in Puccini's *Il Tabarro*. "When I drink I don't think. When I think I don't laugh."

I loved Ari as he was and accepted all his weaknesses along with the qualities I admired in him. He, on the other hand, was constantly trying to change me. For example, he didn't like the way I dressed and had the gall to phone Biki during my fittings to make sure my new clothes would be to his taste. He said I looked plain in my glasses. Since I'm unable to tolerate contacts, I walked about the ship half blind, holding my glasses in my hand. He didn't like my long hair which had always been my glory, either, so he sent me to Alexandre in Paris, who cut my hair while I kept my hands over my eyes. To my surprise, I loved the short, bouncy hairstyle he created, and thought it made me look younger and more sophisticated.

Ari was now frantically running around with a host of people who had entered his life after his divorce—I think he was trying to escape from the pain of it. Ari doesn't like to be a loser and this was one battle he had lost hands down. He had gotten to the point where all he looked for was excitement. He didn't even care about making money anymore. "After you reach a certain point," he said, "money becomes unimportant. What matters is success. The sensible thing would be for me to stop, but I can't."

Wearying a bit of all this social life—despite my bouts with Elsa Maxwell, partying did not come naturally to me and I did it to be with Aristo—I began to work on my voice once more. Perhaps I hoped to find the real Maria Callas again. Somewhere in all this gadding about, I had lost her. It is said I am a singer with a thousand voices. I think I am a soul with a thousand selves. Sometimes I feel that only on the stage am I a real person. In different operas I discover parts of myself I have never met before. In *Fidelio*, I found out what it is like to be a man. In singing *Carmen*, I learned what it feels like to take men the way men take women, and to be a loose woman who inflames men while her own vanity streams like ice water through her veins. I learned about the depths of hatred in *Medea*. As a singer I entered lives I could never know any other way and in this way grew as a person. I miss it. I am a whole human being only when I sing.

In 1963, for the first time since my career began in 1946, I sang no operas. Instead I planned to do some commercial recordings for EMI in Paris in May and then to begin a six-concert tour of Europe that would take me to Berlin, Dusseldorf, Stuttgart, London, and Paris, and would end up in Copenhagen in June.

The arias I sang were familiar to me and not difficult, for example "Casta diva," "O mio babbino caro," and Muzetta's "Waltz Song" from *La Bohème*. But I wasn't enjoying singing anymore. When you are young, you like to stretch your voice. You enjoy singing and relish every minute of it. It has nothing to do with ambition; you sing because you love to. If you sing out of pleasure, it brings on a high, almost like getting drunk. The audience senses your happiness and joins in. But on this tour, I sang simply because I had contracted to and got no satisfaction from it. I was told at times my voice sounded lifeless and tired. I'm sure it is true, because that's the way I felt. The tour seemed to last much longer than the five or six weeks it actually took. In fact time yawned and seemed to stretch out for half my lifetime. My old feeling that my head was encased in cotton wadding came back. I have never been able to describe it to anyone. The closest I can come is to say I couldn't find the feeling of being myself that allows one to feel comfortable in the world. I sang my way through the concerts as if in a dream, fighting to get my vision into focus, like trying to pull myself out of a deep sleep to return to the surface of consciousness. I wore the disguise of a singer, but my heart was with Aristo.

At night, I would try to hold myself back from the twilight of drugged sleep, where frightening dreams pursued me. Like Puccini's *Manon Lescaut*, "I tremble and sorrow without knowing why. Ah! I sense something ominous! I quiver before unknown perils . . . " Then, after hours of battling, a dream of Ari and some faceless woman would sneak through the mist. A beautiful, aristocratic woman with dark hair? Her image sought me out in my sleep and I would wake to keep her away. In the dark hours of the night it seemed to me death would not be so terrifying, only a long, quiet rest . . .

I needed to be with Aristo all the time. Yet the thought of stopping singing altogether put me into a panic. That's who I was—a singer. I didn't know anything but music. What else could I do but continue, even though I couldn't bear to be away from him and it broke my heart each time I sang.

Prince and Princess Radziwell had become great friends of Onassis. Lee Radziwell was the sister of Mrs. Kennedy. That connection and that summer marked a turning point in my relationship with Ari. Lee left the *Christina* to fly to Mrs. Kennedy's bedside, where she had just given birth to a baby, Patrick Bouvier Kennedy, who died two days later. When Lee returned to Athens, she told Ari and me at dinner how desolate and distraught her sister was. Ari immediately offered Mrs. Kennedy the use of the *Christina* for her convalescence. Lee excitedly phoned Jackie to tell her about the invitation. She eagerly accepted, although I must say that neither the President nor I shared her enthusiasm. President Kennedy objected to his wife's cruise because Onassis had been indicted during the Eisenhower administration for conspiring to defraud the American government of taxes on surplus American ships. He had to pay the government seven million dollars to get off the hook. And I—I had vague anxieties I didn't understand. I only knew I felt desolate and lonely at the thought of Mrs. Kennedy's presence on board, and strangely enough, found myself trembling with fear.

I fought and screamed, but to no avail. So I announced I would not go on the cruise with that woman. "Well," Ari said, "in that case I won't go either." But of course the First Lady and her sister insisted, so Ari went, which both he and I had known all along he would do.

I didn't mind so much that he stocked the ship with eight varieties of caviar, vintage champagnes, fresh fruit flown in daily for her from Paris, and had expanded the crew to include two extra hairdressers, a masseuse, and an orchestra for dancing at night. After all, she was the First Lady. But I still can't bear to think they might have spent the night in the lounge talking in front of the lapis lazuli fireplace. And worst of all, he took her to Smyrna and showed her where he had grown up.

I was seething, and wouldn't talk to Ari for days after she returned to the White House. It took all the sweet talk of our close friend Maggie van Zuylen to get me to reconcile with him. I allowed myself to enjoy our brief reunion, for Ari had to leave soon for a business trip. On November 22, just after he had returned from his cruise, he went to Hamburg to launch a tanker. While there he heard the news of President Kennedy's assassination. He immediately flew to Washington to be at Mrs. Kennedy's side. According to him, he livened up the wake with his crude buffoonery.

Then he flew back to Paris to celebrate my fortieth birthday. I should have been suspicious that he bothered.

It must have been an innate sense of survival that persuaded me to return to my singing, even though I had not appeared in an opera for a year and a half, nor made any recordings in the last six months. So in December, 1963 I struck three new albums at the Salle Wagram in Paris. My voice was not what it had been, and by then I could only sing inside a narrow range. But within those limitations I sang "The Willow Song" and "Ave Maria" from *Otello* most effectively, and enjoyed singing such arias as "Ocean! Thou mighty monster" and Beethoven's "Ah, perfidio" once more.

This gave me the courage to try opera again. That and my dear friend, Zeffirelli, who looked after me like a baby, and did all he could to raise my shrinking self-esteem. I returned to the stage January 21, 1964 in his production of *Tosca* at Covent Garden. Although my voice had grown lighter in the past ten years, my skill as an actress had matured so that the six performances as well as the television concert of Act Two were among the finest I have ever given. My experiences with Ari helped me bring a fresh sensuality to the role, as well as new depths of jealousy and anguish. It was pure joy to work with Zeffirelli again, along with Tito Gobbi, the finest Scarpia I'd ever sung with. We were so absorbed in our roles during the dress rehearsal that when the back of my wig brushed against a lighted candle and caught fire, I went right on singing. Tito rushed across the stage, threw his arms around me, and covertly put out the fire. He thought I hadn't noticed it, but I whispered "Thank you" between arias. Another time, I didn't realize that the blade of the sliding knife I was supposed to stab him with hadn't slipped back into its holder. I saw it only after I had drawn blood, just in time to keep from plunging it into him. He gasped an unnerved "Oh my God!" and went right on singing.

With the triumph of *Tosca* behind me, I regained my confidence enough to appear in Zeffirelli's production of *Norma* in Paris on May 22, 1964, for the first of eight performances. I was thrilled with my success in Covent Garden and needed to further prove to myself that my vocal problems were a thing of the past. This was particularly important as my relationship with Onassis grew more and more impossible. Singing was not what I wanted to do, but what I *had* to do under the circumstances.

It was an exquisite production, designed by Zeffirelli to bring out my new softness. It was set in a vast forest in which the color of the leaves changed with the seasons. I was dressed in graceful floating silk and chiffon gowns of cream, pink, apricot, and lilac, and people said I looked younger and better than ever. But the production was not a total triumph for me. At the second performance I collapsed on a high C" in the last act, I who had sung a high F in Rossini's *Armida*.

"I'm going to stop kidding myself," I thought, when the house rose in an uproar. "The audience certainly isn't fooled." I raised my hand for silence and motioned to Prêtre who was conducting to start over again. This time I had no difficulty with the note. It was an unheard of act, but I was happy to have pulled it off. Nevertheless it was the last new production I would ever attempt.

Aristo was sweet about the fiasco and ushered me off to Skorpios as soon as the opera was over. I had to leave shortly to make the long-planned complete recording of *Carmen*, with Georges Prêtre. The sessions seemed interminable. I longed to get out of the hot city and back to the *Christina*, where we had one of our best summers yet.

It was a funny thing about Ari: He behaved like two different people around me. When I was successful, he often brought me down and humiliated me in public and diverted the attention away from me onto himself. For instance, we were with some friends in a night club, and a woman singer began to perform. I said to my friends, "My reviews for *Tosca* were wonderful again. I hope that means my voice troubles are over. Don't you think so, Ari?"

He ignored my comment and said, "Don't you think that singer is wonderful, Maria?"

"Yes, dear, she's good."

Ari said, "But don't you think she's *very* good?"

I answered, "Yes, Ari, for a nightclub singer, she's very good."

But sometimes when I was dejected and beaten down, he seemed to feel the need to protect me and shield me from further pain. He would hold me in his arms at night, matching his length to mine, and I would rub my face against his, weeping, surrendering my consciousness to his, as if trying to inject him with my pain so I could sleep. Then all would be healed, and I felt like Lucia di Lammermoor, who sings about her lover, Edgardo:

> He is the light of my life,
> solace to my torment.
> And when in raptures
> of burning passion,
> he swears eternal love,
> he talks from the heart.
> My anxieties are forgotten,
> my tears become joy.
> When I am near him,
> the very heavens
> reveal themselves!

How could a man differ so much from one situation to the next? But perhaps I understand it after all. He was sympathetic to my pain unless *he* had been the one to cause it. Then he enjoyed ripping me to shreds.

I think about him all the time. And now I have come to another conclusion, the kind only someone who loves can arrive at. Ari picked up and left whenever he felt like it. No need of mine or scheduled event, no matter how important, could keep him from bolting away. Even at our best times, that was the chief bone of contention between us. He reserved the right to change the rules of the game whenever it suited him. I remember that his mother suddenly died and left him when he was young. That is what Ari did to me; he left me in shock each time, causing me the agony her disappearance must have caused him. Her death put him through the tortures of the damned, and he did the same to me until the end.

A revealing incident happened as we were trying to escape photographers at a nightclub in Athens. "Why do you keep chasing us?" Ari asked one photographer. "Why do *you* keep running away from *us*?" the photographer asked in return. "Ah, but that is my trick," Ari answered. "If it was too easy to take our pictures, none of you would have bothered." Despite his success and his billions, in his heart he remained a poor abandoned boy who felt he had to play tricks to hold on to those he cared about.

Poor Ari! Poor Maria! Life is so sad. It is a terrible disappointment to me. It is tragic that loved ones die, our lives pass us by, fame and fortune come to naught, fantasies rarely come true, and unlike fairy-tale endings, the prince and princess rarely live happily ever after. And if they do, it is not with each other.

On July 6, 1964, I began a complete recording of *Carmen*. Some say the part was written for me and I would have ruined it for singers ever after if I had performed the opera onstage. Be that as it may, I never did. Many people, including Zeffirelli, tried to persuade me to sing it, but I always refused. First of all, I am embarrassed to admit, Carmen displays her legs, and I have never gotten over my humiliation of being likened to an elephant in that first *Aida* so many years ago. Secondly, and perhaps more important, Carmen is a role any soprano can sing. It doesn't take a Callas. And I never have been happy with the character of Carmen, who approaches men the way men solicit women. In my soul, I have remained a puritan, despite my relationship with Ari. When I don't respect a character, I don't like to sing the role. Nevertheless, I'm happy to have made the recording, and enjoy listening to it from time to time even now.

In 1964 I celebrated my tenth anniversary of being thin by having a silk gown copied from the one Audrey Hepburn wore in "Breakfast at Tiffany's." Sleeveless and black, it was cut just like hers, even to the asymmetrical shoulder straps. I wore it during a concert I gave in Paris. I wonder if anyone noticed. Probably not. Funny how something can mean so much to one person, and not matter a tinker's damn to anyone else.

Despite my victory over flab, which is still unbelievable to the little fat Maria inside me, it was not a good year. But compared to what was to come, it was a picnic.

The End of the World

ETWEEN DECEMBER 3RD AND 4TH OF 1964 I made my second recording of Tosca, with Berganzi and Gobbi, under Prêtre, and then began to prepare for eight *Toscas* at the l'Opera in Paris. Zeffirelli's entire production had been brought over from London, and was a complete triumph again. It had been a long time since I had experienced anything like it, and I wanted to prolong the high. So unlike my usual custom, I agreed to add a ninth performance.

I flew to New York the next day, where we repeated our tour de force at the Met on March 19, with Fausto Cleva conducting. The sets were so old they actually shook during the performance. There was not a single stage rehearsal, with just one piano run through in a dark and gloomy studio, and I had been given no choice in the conductor. Nevertheless the performance was a phenomenal success. On the Thursday evening before the performance there was already a long line of standees with sleeping bags and blankets, and a large sign hanging on the front of the opera house saying, "Welcome Home, Callas." On opening night, a huge crowd was waiting outside, hoping they could get tickets at the last minute, and watching for celebrities. A few minutes before the curtain went up there was a smattering of applause from the audience. But this time it wasn't for me; Mrs. John F. Kennedy had arrived to see the opera.

At my first cry of "Mario" offstage, a gasp rose up in the audience, who greeted me with an ovation that lasted four full minutes. There were sixteen curtain calls at the end of the performance at 11:40. It had been scheduled to finish at 10:40, but the audience had cheered and applauded for a full hour. Maria Callas reigned again. It was a lovely welcome home after seven years away from the Met, and I hoped it meant the problems with my voice were left behind forever. Little did I know it was the last time I was ever to appear at the Met.

I am sitting here now looking at a portrait of me taken in 1955 when I was thirty-two and singing *La Traviata* at La Scala. I am standing there quietly looking into myself. I look gentle, guileless, and loving . . . yes, loving. That is the real Maria Callas. And I think how unlikely it was that this innocent, tender creature who shook and had hysterics outside of Major Bowes Radio contest when Liska dragged me there when I was eleven—I think how improbable it is that I should have reached the peak of my profession to become the prima donna assoluta of the world. It was truly the "Impossible Dream" come true. Who would have believed it and not been taken for a madman?

Would I have changed my destiny if I could? No, then I wouldn't have been Maria Callas. The diva is me.

That reminds me, Kiri Te Kanawa, a rising young opera star from New Zealand came to see me. She sang a lovely *Marriage of Figaro* at Covent Garden and seemed to be headed for the top. She is the Tebaldi type of singer rather than like me, as she is more gifted at producing "golden tones" than dramatizing the music. She is also one smart lady. Less than thirty years old, she already wanted to know how I thought she should preserve her voice so as to make it last. She didn't actually say, "You fool!" but it was implied. Otherwise why come to see *me*? Well, why shouldn't young divas learn from the mistakes of older singers? I've always been generous with young vocalists, although I must say that's not what the media picks up about me. I saw no reason not to be helpful with her too, even though her philosophy of singing irritates me and it has seen its day. I told her if her aim in opera was to be long lasting she should always play it safe. She should ruthlessly limit her range and the roles she accepted, make sure to space her performances so as not to get overtired, and refrain from flitting all over the world to keep up with the demands of her public. In other words, she should take every safeguard Maria Callas did not.

As for me, if I had to do it over again and were Kiri's age, would I, too, play it safe, so as to have my career continue to my last dying gasps? No, I wouldn't, even though it is agonizing to watch my voice deteriorate to a soggy piece of cardboard. When I hear my old recordings it breaks my heart that Callas will never sing that way again. But my aim was always to be the best soprano, not the longest lasting. And that is what I became. I've been told I have single-handedly changed the course of operatic history, and I believe that is true. I am proud of my achievements, and have long had a dream that my reputation, like my beloved Malibran's, will live after me through the ages. I couldn't do that and hoard my talents, so I was reckless with them from the beginning. For instance, take 1949, when I was Kiri's age. How could I have sung the role of *Turandot*, the ruination of many fine voices, twenty-seven times, if I had been trying to preserve my voice? As I correctly predicted years ago, when you burn the candle at both ends, you often end up with no light at all. That's what happened to me after *Il Turco*, when my frantic schedule caused me to collapse with jaundice. Nevertheless, just three weeks after its last performance, I was back in Rome singing Kundry on a radio broadcast of *Parsifal*. In between the two, I had also been working on Elizabeth in Verdi's *Don Carlo*, and was preparing to celebrate the fiftieth anniversary of Verdi's death by singing my first *Traviata* for the Teatro Comunale in Florence. Reckless, yes, fool, no! I have earned my place in history, and it was not acquired by sparing myself.

On May 14th I sang *Norma* again, this time in Paris under Prêtre. As usual, I gave everything of myself to the role. Zeffirelli, the producer, pleaded with me to avoid unnecessary vocal challenges. I answered, "I can't, Franco. I won't do what Anna Moffo does in *Traviata*. I won't skim through my music. I have to take chances even if it means a disaster and the end of my career." I could have done as he suggested and left out the high notes, as I did in Kansas City in *Lucia*. But when I did I felt the audience was cheated, and my conscience wouldn't allow me to do it again.

On the opening night of *Norma* in Paris on May 14, 1965 I was in bad shape, both physically and emotionally. Heavily medicated as I was, I could barely walk to the stage. I am just a person with all of a human being's fears. When people only see you sparkling under the limelights, how can they know you? How can newspapermen understand you? How can anyone sense the mountainous tidal wave of fear, the barricade of agonizing stage fright I had to bat my head against every performance? My strength was fading fast, and it didn't hold up to the end of the run.

It was especially important to me to sing well at these performances. My friend Giulietta was appearing in Paris for the first time, and it was critical that I sing the duets with Adalgesa acceptably. I did not want to spoil Simionata's debut in Paris.

On the fifth performance, I collapsed at the end of the third act and had to be carried unconscious to my dressing room. The curtain was brought down, never to rise again.

I was supposed to sing five *Toscas* at the end of June in Covent Garden, but I knew I would never be able to do it, so I telephoned the general administrator, David Webster, a few days before the scheduled performances to tell him my health wouldn't allow it. He flew to Paris to talk me

into appearing at one of the performances, a charity gala on July 5 which the
queen would attend. I did my best, but even though I had been up the whole
night before practicing *Tosca* in full voice, I no longer was able to project my
voice properly in the theatre. It was an unbearable ordeal for me.
Brokenhearted, I decided this was the last performance I would sing on the
operatic stage. I was forty-one years old.

Why me? The contralto Vittoria Tesi, born in 1700, was still singing until
well into her seventies. Adelina Patti's career spanned forty-five years. Lilli
Lehmann was forty before she sang Fidelio, Norma, Isolde, and Brunnhilde,
almost sixty when she first appeared in *La Traviata*, and sang Donna Anna
at the Salzburg Festival at the age of sixty-two! I was supposed to have had
one of the most glorious voices of the century, and here I was with a broken,
run-down rag of a voice at age forty-one.

Why? Is there some fiendish master plan designed to mould me into the
tragic heroines whose lives I've sung? Instead of art taking the place of life,
as it has done before, my life is now replacing art. I have always been a good
woman, even, in my own way, a religious woman. What have I done to
deserve this fate?

Just when I needed him the most, Aristo became impossible, and we
had our worst summer together yet. Ingse Dedichen, his lover during
World War Two, told a friend that Ari had beaten her up until she looked
"like a boxer who has lost a fight." He told her afterward that every Greek
without exception beats up his wife. "It is good for them," he said. "It keeps
them in line."

He never beat me physically—he probably knew that was the one thing
he couldn't get away with, either in my eyes or those of the world—but his
treatment of me was almost as brutal. No curse was too vile to hurl at me,
no words of abuse too insulting. It is mortifying even to repeat them.

"Shut up, Maria!" he said. "You are only a stupid dame whose nose is
too big, with glasses that make you ugly and legs that are too fat. You are just
a cunt with a whistle in her throat who is good only for fucking."

I said, "Ari, must you humiliate me in front of people?"

He answered, "Don't tell me what I can say, Miss Whistle-in-the-throat.
I'll say what I want when I want to say it. If you don't like it you can always
leave."

He always made sure to insult me in front of people, to make my
humiliation that much more painful. It hurt as much as when my mother
spanked me in front of my sister's friends and the sting lasted as long. Once
Zeffirelli told Ari it was very distressing for my friends to see him treat me

that way, but Franco's words had no more effect on Ari than a summer breeze can budge the *Christina*.

One day after he had made a particularly brutal remark, I looked at him. Would you believe his face had the same tight little smile as my mother's when she was hitting me?

Maybe I'm kidding myself, but I feel the deeper Aristo became involved with a woman, the more terrified he became. It turned him into a little boy who was scared he would lose his beloved. When he played the bad guy, he didn't feel like a helpless child who could be hurt at anyone's whim. He was the one doing the hurting. There is no more powerful way to hold onto someone for life than to be cruel to them. It creates an excitement and a bond no amount of pure loving can do. I know. I was married to a kind man. I never loved him the way I do Ari.

I tried to be patient and understanding, but it was becoming more and more difficult. Especially since there was nothing in my life but Ari. The sense of nothingness inside me when he was not with me terrified me and caused me to screech like a fishwife when we were together.

Zeffirelli wanted to make a film of *Tosca* with me, and came to Skorpios several times that summer to discuss the project. The prospect was intriguing. I wondered if it were possible for me to begin a new career as a movie star at my age. He thought I could become as fine a screen actress as Greta Garbo. Aristo discouraged the plans by demanding I be paid an incredibly high fee. When I gave my opinion, he humiliated me again by shouting, "Shut up! You know nothing about these things. You are nothing but a nightclub singer." The film was never made.

Aristo was having his own problems with his old friend Vergottis, who later sued him, and with Prince Ranier, who was trying to unseat Ari as the person with the controlling interest in the State of Monaco. Ari loved his power over the principality, and gloried every time he took a step into Monaco. It was the crowning jewel of his life. In a brilliant move in 1966, the prince created 600,000 new shares in the company in which Onassis had a controlling interest, and offered to buy out any shares of the existing shareholders at the market rate, thus giving Ranier and his stockholders complete control over the destiny of his country. This ousted Ari from his position as the most powerful man in Monte Carlo. He appealed to the courts and lost. A defeated man, he left Monaco, not to return until shortly before his death.

When Ari is upset and vulnerable he becomes most vicious. Ranier kept Ari on his guard for months, as the confrontations and intrigues continued. The suspense created an atmosphere like the stillness before an electrical storm. His moods were like an elevator, soaring when he thought he was winning, and taking a nose dive when his treasures floated out of his grasp. Believe me, it was not easy. While he was away I sat there quivering until his return, waiting to find out what my own mood would be. For how Ari felt about himself was how he treated me, and the way Ari treated me was what determined my mood. Would he be angry, curse, and push me away, or would he be tender and loving, and plead with me to hold him in my arms? Would I be happy, would I be sad? It all depended on Ari.

When he was feeling good he would speak again of our marriage, and then forget all about it when he was upset. I got sick of all his talking, and also of the difficulties in getting my divorce in Italy. In April, 1966, I decided to renounce my American citizenship. According to a Greek law passed in 1946, no marriage of a Greek citizen is valid unless the couple was married in a Greek Orthodox church. By becoming officially Greek, my marriage to Meneghini became nonexistent all over the world, except for Italy, and I was free to remarry.

When I announced this to the press, of course they asked Aristo if we were going to marry. He answered, "All along, we have explained we are very close, good friends. This new event changes nothing. Of course, I'm very happy her seven years of struggle have ended so well. It is wonderful for her to be a Signorina again." Like my mother, he loved to expose me publicly, but he chose the whole world for an audience.

Of all the possible times of my life it could have happened, I picked the moment when our relationship was at its lowest point to become pregnant. Nevertheless, I was thrilled, and thought perhaps it would bring us closer together. I couldn't wait to tell Ari. I wanted to have a baby more than I ever wanted anything except him, and the thought of bearing the child of the man I loved filled me with tenderness. I should have known better. As I have said and said, anything I really wanted with Ari was what I was sure not to get.

I said, "Aristo, I have great news. I am going to have a baby."

"You are *what*! Why should I want another child? I already have two."

"But Aristo," I pleaded, "I have always wanted a child. It is a miracle I'm pregnant at all at the age of forty-three. If I don't have this baby, I'll never have another."

"Have it then," he said, "and it will be the end of our relationship."

I had to make a choice, so I had the abortion. After that I knew I would never get what I needed from this man. It marked the end of our love affair, even though we stayed together, more or less, for a few years longer. But from the moment I made the decision to abort, we never stopped fighting.

I didn't know what to do, because I felt about him the way Norma did about her children, "At once I love and hate my children! . . . I suffer on seeing them, and suffer if I do not see them." I couldn't live with him and I couldn't live without him. So I compromised and got my own apartment.

I was forty-three years old and except for hotel rooms when I left the *Christina*, had never had a place of my own. I always wanted to live in Paris, and since Ari was not about to move in with me, I decided this was a good time to buy my own apartment at 36 Avenue Georges Mandel, and furnish it the way I wanted. For the first time in my life, I could call myself "head of the household," as they say in America. It was a good feeling. The apartment was decorated in vibrant shades of blue and orange by the famous designer, Georges Grandpierre. The formal Grand Salon was complete with a Steinway Grand piano, Louis Quinze furniture, a Regency inlaid rosewood and violet wood commode and pagoda, a silk petit-point carpet, and grand Renaissance paintings by Fragonard, Bassino, and Sevastiano del Piombo. It was elegant and lovely, but nobody ever sat in it. The heart of the home was my bedroom and bathroom. The outstanding piece of furniture in the bedroom was a large eighteenth-century Italian double bed with an elaborately carved headpiece, which had been a present from Meneghini soon after we were married. I had been comfortable in it for ten years and I was delighted to have it in my new home. But my favorite room was the gigantic bathroom of pink and white marble, with a settee and armchair covered in orange velvet, where I talked on the telephone, listened to my recordings, and received my friends.

The staff consisted of my maid and confidante, Bruna, who had been with me when I was still living with Meneghini, Ferrucio the butler, and Consuelo, the part-time cook. Bruna worked for me for twenty years and turned out to be the best friend I ever had. She loved me unconditionally, was there for me night and day, did exactly what I wanted, sometimes even before I knew I wanted it, and always put my needs first. Too bad I didn't have someone like her when I was growing up! I wouldn't be in the shape I'm in today.

The summer of 1967 was the last Aristo and I were to spend together. It began well enough, with me impatient to get to Skorpios. I felt hopeful that once we were there we could renew our relationship. It turned out to be the saddest and most futile of all our times together. Ari was having his biography written by Willi Frischauer, and in spite of his initial reluctance, had become thoroughly involved in it. To my disappointment, Frischauer was invited to Skorpios too. Soon Aristo was spending all his time with Willi and practically none with me. Even their mealtimes were shared, when they remembered to eat at all, and I was made to feel like an unwelcome intruder. Of course I was in a continuous rage, all but consumed by little green-eyed monsters. I returned to Paris unrefreshed and more worried than ever about the relationship.

The confirmation of my fears came when Ari's servants, George and Helen, told a friend they had been ordered to spend an entire evening in their rooms while Ari entertained and cooked for a "special guest" himself. I knew Aristo had been having affairs all along, but like all Greek women, I felt I had to accept this as part of the terms of the deal. But I knew intuitively this incident was different, and I remained agitated and anxious, despite the fact that he called me every day, from whatever part of the world he happened to be.

I soon found out who the "special guest" was. The newspapers reported seeing Ari and Jackie Kennedy dining together at El Morocco, 21, Dionysis, and Mykonos with his daughter Christina, Nureyev, and Margot Fonteyn. Gossips were already listing him among Jackie's possible suitors. I couldn't kid myself any longer about the seriousness of the affair when I found out he had kept in touch with her since 1963 and, as he did with me, carried on long telephone talks with her from all over the world.

One conversation between the two of them came back to me and particularly rankled. We were in New York together and he had called Jackie, who invited him over for a drink. "I'd love to," he answered, "and I have Maria with me." "In that case, sorry, perhaps another time," was her response. When I overheard the call I thought perhaps she didn't like me, but it soon began to make sense.

The crisis came when I returned to the *Christina.*

Ari said, "Maria, I want you to go back to Paris and wait for me there."

"You must be crazy, Ari. It is August. Nobody goes to Paris in August."

"You *have* to go."

"I have to? What are you talking about?"

"I'm having a special guest aboard and you can't be here."

"And who is so special that I can't be aboard?"

He didn't answer, but it didn't matter. I already knew the answer.

"I'm leaving you," I said.

"Don't be silly, Maria. I'll see you after the cruise is over in September."

"No, Ari. You don't understand. I said I'm leaving you. You are never going to see me again." And I left, never to return. There was nothing else to do. As Medea said in Pasolini's film, "It's useless. Nothing is possible anymore."

Jackie was given my suite on the *Christina*, a space that was reserved for special guests like Churchill and me. I knew every detail of their life, from breakfast in bed to the daily cocktail hour to lunches and dinners aboard or on islands where the ship docked. I knew the staff missed me, no matter how excited they were about entertaining the wife of a former president. There was not one moment I wasn't on the *Christina* in spirit watching the two cavorting together. Dante's Inferno had nothing on me. There was no way I could sleep without taking pills. Oh, Amelia, I think of your words in *Un Ballo in Maschera*, "What remains for your unhappy heart/ What's left, once love is gone?"

I didn't know what to do with myself while they were cruising until Lawrence Kelly invited me to go to America with him and Mary Mead Carter. So I went, just to keep my mind off Aristo. We knocked about from one place to the next, but I don't even remember where we went, I was so obsessed with *them*. When I returned to Paris, I got the news I prayed I would never hear. Ari's butler, dear soul, called to tell me Aristotle and Kennedy were going to be married on October 20th.

That was in 1968, and Lord knows how I managed to survive. In my head it is all one black swirl. I had been part of a unit with Aristo for ten years, and for ten years before that with Meneghini. I didn't know how to be a separate person. About that time, I had a dream that I was riding alone on a bicycle built for two. That's exactly the way I still feel.

EMI wanted me to record *La Traviata* with Luciano Pavarotti at the Accademia Santa Cecilia in Rome. I was tempted—I thought perhaps I could have found my identity as a singer again, and it would be fun to sing with Pavarotti. But I knew neither my voice nor I was up to it.

I didn't know what else to do with myself, so I decided to make a movie. The famous film director, Pier Paoli Pasolini, asked me to film *Medea* with him beginning in June, 1969. The idea stirred up the eons of Greek drama smoldering in my blood. After all, the one part of my identity that has never left me is the knowledge that I am a Greek. I was excited for a time, and enjoyed making the movie. For a little while I even thought I might live again. But the film turned out to be a disappointment. It did well in the reviews and the art houses, but it was not a popular success. It soon became apparent I was not going to be the next Garbo.

In the meantime Ari was not doing so well either. Jackie was bleeding him dry with her lavish buying sprees of jewelry and clothing and he was beginning to realize she was taking him for a fool. He kept calling and sending me flowers, but for a long time my pride was too hurt and I refused to talk with him.

He kept saying to my staff, "Put Maria on the phone."

The servant would reply, "Mme. Callas is not in."

He would shout so loudly I could hear him in the next room, "Maria, I know you are there! Pick up the phone right away! I want to talk to you."

I laughed out loud and hoped that he heard me.

Finally in 1969 we met at a party given (and, I'm sure, arranged for that purpose) by Maggie Van Zuylen, and little by little, we began to see each other again. He was my heart, my soul, my insides. Without him I was a transparent ghost, without any substance. I even carried around a bag of gravel in my purse for a while, to make sure I didn't float away. How could I possibly resist seeing him again?

The climax came after we had spent four nights together, when he took me to dine at Maxim's for the whole world to see. I was ecstatic, my love and I were together again and *she* was just another paramour to be forgotten. But the lady had other ideas. When she saw the newspaper photos of us dining together with blissful smiles, she was furious and flew immediately to his side. She insisted he repeat the drama of the day before at Maxim's, but with her in my place. He went without missing a beat. The next day I was admitted to the American Hospital at Neuilly with the diagnosis of "over-dose of barbiturates."

"Oh Lord," I prayed, "grant me the mental and physical strength to bear this agony. I don't ask for much. I'll be satisfied with one year, one good year like it was. It's the beginning again . . . that's what I'm terrified of, returning to the beginning. Oh Lord, please don't let me go back to my miserable beginnings, when I hardly existed at all."

After I got out of the hospital I made up my mind to get off the see-saw of moods Ari kept me on, no matter how much it made me suffer. No more, I thought. I've had enough! Better to stay down than to be built up to the skies and then cast down again. I would rather hope for the worst and be surprised by the best.

Many people asked, "A beautiful woman like you, and world famous? How come you haven't gotten interested in any other man?"

First of all, I hadn't gotten over my heartbreak, and felt, rightly, as it turned out, I never could. I was Ari, Ari was me; no other man fill could fill that space. Another man wouldn't be me. And secondly, I had been hurt so savagely I closed myself off. The less open you are, the less you are hurt. Then, even if you meet someone who might be good for you, you clam up because you're scared, so you never find out if it could have worked out. Ari spoiled my love life and my hopes and dreams for a family. How could I trust another man not to do the same?

For the first time since Ari's marriage, I returned to Greece, this time as the guest of Perry Embiricos on his private island of Tragonisi in the Aegean. Perry was a friend of Onassis, and Onassis had introduced me to him. To my surprise, who should show up on the island but Aristo! He greeted me with a kiss, and from then on we resumed our relationship. Without him I was nothing; with him in my life I had at least part of myself back. When it wasn't possible to eat a whole loaf, I found crumbs could keep me alive.

I flitted around for a year or two, filling up time between his visits by participating in lots of ceremony and protocol. Standing next to the French secretary of state, I cut the ribbon initiating the Nocturnes du Faubourg Saint-Honoré; and as the official guest of Madame Furteva, the Soviet minister of culture, I judged the finals of the Tchaikovsky Competition. I sat next to Ghiringhelli in his box at La Scala on opening night, when the audience broke into applause with cries of "Ritorna Maria." But I didn't do anything I considered worthwhile until 1971, when I was invited by Peter Menin, president of the Julliard School of Music, to give a series of Master Classes at the school.

I gave twenty-three classes between October 1971 and March 1972 for twenty-six students handpicked by me out of three hundred applicants. For twelve weeks, twice weekly, they took turns singing scenes and arias from the standard repertoire. I have always been interested in helping young singers with their careers. My aim here was to bring out the individual personalities and talents of each singer, not to stamp out miniature Marias. The classes were audited by a star-studded audience, including Lillian Gish, Tito Gobbi, Elizabeth Schwarzkopf, Ben Gazzara, and Franco Zeffirelli, who paid to watch. The main thrust of my teaching was the complete union of word and music. I wanted to teach the students how to dramatically develop a character from one scene to the next through the use of the sung word. I went through every major opera I'd ever sung and showed them how I had looked for the essence of each character and made that the core of the role. "Make love to the music," I told them, "because that is the only way to make it come alive." I said I considered myself privileged because I've been able to bring truth from deep in my soul, to give it to the public, and have it gratefully received. Not everyone can do that. It is one of the greatest powers in the service of the greatest of the arts—music. I wanted to help my students rejoice in that glory, too.

The series was a great success and I could easily have developed a new career as a teacher and lecturer. But although I enjoyed playing Elvira de Hidalgo for a while, I really didn't see myself as a teacher. Interesting as it was, it left me feeling empty. I don't know who I am, but I know it is not a teacher. I used to be a singer, but apparently I am not that anymore. I used to be Aristotle Onassis's lover, but I wasn't that anymore either. I could only say, along with Medea, "I am someone else now."

Perhaps teaching didn't take for me because no junior Maria Callas showed up. I remember with amusement Meneghini's answer when he was asked if he intended to make another diva his protegee. "Just give me someone with the heart and soul of Callas, her determination, her talent, her spunk etc. etc., and I'll make you another Callas."

These days I have to smile when I think of Battista. The longer I knew Aristo, the better Titta began to look. He was kind to me and I could not have become La Callas without him. I'm struck by how different he is from my mother, who always takes all the credit for my career. I guess I'm learning to forgive Titta for what I've done to him.

Evidently I had regained enough confidence and self-esteem from the success of the master classes that I was willing to try again, both romantically and professionally. My old friend Giuseppe di Stefano was in trouble, because his daughter was dying of cancer and he needed money badly. I'm good at comforting people (Damm Ari! He took advantage of that quality in me when his son died, but would he do the same for me? No!) and helped Pippo live through her death. This made us close for a while, and we even became lovers of sorts. Then we made a duet recording of Verdi and Donizetti duets for Philips in St. Giles, Cripplegate. Unfortunately, it wasn't good—Pippo and I spent all our time arguing instead of rehearsing—and I refused to allow the record to be released. In 1973, we decided to produce *I Vespri Siciliana*. Like Aida, when I'm involved with a man, I submerge myself in his personality. I forgot I was prima donna assoluta of the world and allowed di Stefano, who is not the most sophisticated of men, to take over. Nobody knew what was going on, including me, and the result was chaos.

You'd think I would have learned by then that we weren't an effective team. But no, he was my lover and I was grateful to him for distracting me, at least part of the time, from thoughts of Ari. So after *Siciliana*, I let Pippo talk me into taking a concert tour with him to help pay his daughter's expenses.

Speaking of being lovers, after the first time we made love I cried for hours because he wasn't Ari. Why couldn't I fall in love with Pippo instead?

Common sense would tell you we were much better matched than Aristotle and I. But no, the only time sparks flew between us was onstage. Compared to Ari, Pippo was like American white bread to me, a woman who loves to sink her teeth into a crusty European loaf. But then who understands the needs of the human heart?

We didn't stay lovers for long; I was unhappy that he was married and, anyway, I was never really excited about him as a lover. Making love with him just didn't do it for me. But then I guess after Aristo, nobody could have satisfied me.

Our tour covered many of the great cities of the world. It began in Hamburg on October 25, 1973. I sang many familiar arias, including those from *Carmen, I Vespri Siciliani,* "Suicidio" from *La Gioconda, Tosca,* and *La Bohème.* We followed up with appearances in Berlin, Dusseldorf, Munich, Frankfurt, and Mannheim, singing much of the same material. We next sang a concert in Spain, two in London, one in Paris, and still another in Amsterdam, stopping for a short rest in January in Italy, after performing at a hospital in Milan.

We picked up our itinerary in February in America, playing, among others cities, Philadelphia, Washington, Boston, Chicago, New York, Detroit, Dallas, Miami, and Columbus. I was often forced to appear alone, as di Stefano was frequently "indisposed." Other times he couldn't decide whether to sing or not until the last moment. It was sad to hear what had become of Pippo's magnificent voice and I suppose people felt the same way about me. While on tour I was horrified to read one review which said we barked at each other onstage like two dogs. Be that as it may, I had my own vocal difficulties to deal with, and the strain was frightful. I've always been my worst critic, and the pain of each appearance was a descent into Hell. It was all I could do to drag myself to performance after performance. But, woman of the theatre that I am, I crushed my grief to my heart and went on singing. Yes, the audience applauded wildly, and I appreciated it. But it was the legend not the singer they applauded now. Sometimes I think they would have clapped if I had come on stage clucking like a chicken. I know when I am through. On November 11, 1974, at a city in Northern Japan called Sapporo, I made the final public appearance of my life. Callas will never sing again.

By this time Pippo and I were getting along badly. I knew he loved me, but his daughter's illness kept him terribly anxious throughout the trip, and he hadn't much left over for me. Our angry outbursts were growing more frequent and the times between them less pleasant. I couldn't wait for the tour to be over. When we ended it we also aborted our sexual relationship.

Thus my last love affair ended at the same time as my career. Nevertheless, I was able to hang on by the tips of my fingernails until March, 1975, when Aristo became critically ill with incurable myasthenia gravis.

Onassis

 HAD BEEN GETTING DAILY REPORTS about his progress from my friend Vasso Devetzi. Her mother, by a terrible coincidence was being treated for cancer in the room next to Ari in the American Hospital in Paris, where he had gone for surgery. He never recovered consciousness, and was kept alive for five weeks by a respirator and intravenous feedings.

"He had his blood replaced today," Vasso said. Another time, she informed me Jackie had spent a half-hour at his bedside. "He is in an oxygen tent," came the next report. "His daughter Christina has not left his bedside all night." My lover was dying, and I was kept from his side. My suffering sliced me to shreds. The doctors said it could go on for weeks or even months. I knew I couldn't wait any longer or I would die too. So on March 10, I rented a house in Palm Beach and flew out of Paris with my staff, Bruno, Ferrucio, and Consuelo.

On March 12, I received my last report from the American Hospital. Aristo was dead. Only now, as I write these notes am I able to remember how I felt.

It must be a mistake, I thought. Not Ari, it must be someone else of the same name. I turned on the TV and frantically switched the channels. The news was on every one. He had died of myasthenia gravis in the Eisenhower wing of the American Hospital in Paris. At least *she* wasn't by his side. I couldn't cry, I couldn't do anything. I must have been in a state of shock. My knees buckled and I passed out and fell to the floor. I don't remember how long I lay there, but when I came to, my heart was pounding frantically. I tried to stop its terrible rhythm so I could stand up.

After I managed to pull myself to my feet I had a sensation I'd never felt before. It was as if my stomach had dropped into a pit of blackness. The darkness spread and engulfed me like thick black smoke so I couldn't move. I stood there looking out the window of 12 Golf View Road in Palm Beach for hours. I watched the procession of trucks roll by, garbage trucks, laundry trucks, air-conditioner trucks, liquor-store trucks, locksmiths trucks, florist-delivery trucks, all had the look of objects seen under water. I had the sensation of floating through a dream, borne helpless and unresisting to a frightful end. I must prepare my will, I thought idly.

Some people were standing outside the house staring into the windows and I hid behind the sheer white curtains. It was as if the clouds had stopped in the heavens. I wondered why the earth continued to turn on its axis. I looked out and saw the traffic lights had changed and changed again and traffic continued to roll by as if nothing had happened. Why does it keep going? I asked myself. Doesn't everyone know Aristotle Onassis is dead?

What shall I do? What shall I do? I said aloud, crying at last. How will I get from one minute to the next? He was the core of my life. Whatever will I do without him?

I was slowly dying from the loss of my career. He had flashed into my life like a bolt of lightning across a dark summer sky; where there'd been nothing, suddenly there was Aristo. Four little lines from "La mamma morta" in Giordano's *Andrea Chenier* tell the whole story,

> "It was during that sorrow
> that love came to me! —
> a voice filled with harmony —
> and said "Live still! I am Life!"

For ten years, he has been my life's blood, my mainstay. My career, my friends, I care nothing for any of them. Only *he* exists for me. People are nice to someone as miserable as I, but their generosity means nothing. Can you understand that? Everyone is considerate, thoughtful, and loving. But it means nothing, nothing.

If I hadn't met him I would have had to invent him, so necessary was he to fulfill my destiny. I had squelched the essence of my soul all my life in order to become what Mother and then I had wanted for me, the prima donna assoluta of the world. But the deepest part of me was buried until I met him, when I could say, along with Elena in *I Vespri Siciliani*, "O beloved dream, O sweet intoxication! My heart leaps with a love unknown!"

Was I upset that I had ruined his marriage or he mine? No, I was no home breaker, nor was he. His wife, Tina, was going to leave him anyway. My marriage with Meneghini had been going steadily downhill for years. It was something that had to happen. Ari had to come along for me to live out my destiny.

He was small and dark and his features were ugly, but when he smiled at me the whole world changed color. And when he kissed me a wave of sweetness I had never known before swept over me and I wanted more, more, more. He could do anything he wanted to me and I loved it all. For years, I never wanted to get out of our bed.

What was the power of this squat, elderly gnome that enabled him to win the affections of the wife of a president and the world's greatest diva within a few years? Some say it was money. I don't agree. Money is nice. It is pleasant to be rich and to be able to spend it as lavishly as he did. But I am a millionaire in my own right and Meneghini had plenty of cash, too. Rather, Aristo looked deep into my soul and saw what I had hidden even from myself, the unawakened desires of a passionate woman. In return, his melting black eyes promised to open the gates of paradise, a promise only he knew how to deliver.

When we first made love I couldn't believe it was happening to me. After all, I had been married for ten years, and sex was not important in the marriage. I was not interested in men, in interminable bouts of love making, in submitting myself to the domination of another. I had stood apart from my body, unwilling to subordinate myself to my husband. He said I kept myself virginal, untouched, always under control. That was all right with him. He was happy just to be around me.

With Ari, I was open, exposed, raw, helpless, terrified. I knew he was going to hurt me badly, but I couldn't stop, didn't want to stop. My heart began to pound as if it knew something the rest of me did not. I clutched and clawed at him, petrified of losing control, yet desperate to give it up. He went on as if unaware of my terror. I behaved like a mad woman, my face awash with tears, bucking, heaving, sweating, struggling, slurping his saliva, licking his sweat, wanting to bite through his shoulder to the bare bone and savor his blood, writhing with pleasure beneath his body. I clutched at his shoulders, his back, his hair, scratched his face, hit him with my fists, crying out time after time like some unearthly animal. I lost all consciousness of a self; his body or my body, his rapture or mine, what did it matter, it was all the same to me. He must have been the world's best lover. Engrossed in his own pleasure, he never neglected mine. When it was over, I cried like a baby in his arms, "Don't leave me, don't ever leave me, I'll be good."

This isn't possible at my age, I thought in a rare moment of clarity; it is too fantastic, too glorious. Surely I will be punished for it.

Sometimes I feel like I'm two women encased in one body. One is the elegant diva, world famous, feted and envied by many. This woman speaks four languages, and is poised, reserved, and sophisticated. When I speak of my art, I am the epitome of the self-confident professional. Just underneath, however, lies another woman who is profoundly Greek, a raunchy, smoldering, outspoken, earthy, even common peasant. This one speaks like a Greek, natural, unassuming, unpretentious. She's the one in love with Onassis. Being Greek is what we have in common. Greeks are passionate, demonstrative people, in anger as well as in love. When we speak we use our hands and our hearts, and are incapable of Anglo-Saxon reserve and objectivity. Greeks consider it an illness not to feel deeply about everything, and have an unflattering word for such people; *nero vrasto*, which means boiled water. When I am around Aristo, the Greek in me comes alive and La Callas is dead and forgotten. My *nero vrasto*, which is there in my television interviews for all to see, completely evaporates.

Beyond our small, intense universe, nothing seemed real. My past, my career, all else became irrelevant. I have never known anyone like him. He is . . . was . . . my *raison d'être*. The thought of him—his sensual mouth, his earthy voice, his gentle touch, his masculine smell, his hairy body, his lusty love-making—sends a surge of dizziness across my head. He was my nucleus, around which the rest of me revolved. How can I live without a center? Whatever will I do without him?

Now I implore whatever Gods may be to anoint me again with that divine happiness, that utter ecstasy, that luminous, virginal innocence that inundated my body. I beseech God, Christ, the saints, Fate, the universe itself to reenergize my depleted body with that luminous glow. I have known pure love. I have known physical rapture. Surely Heaven above holds no greater bliss than experiencing both together. Love with Aristo has spoiled me, Lord; I can settle for nothing less. Listen to me please, I entreat You, or I will surely die.

Crudel! Crudel! Why, Aristo? Why? Wasn't my love enough for you? I was like a good wife to you, a good lover, a good mistress, a good friend. I did whatever you wanted. If you had said to dive off the decks of the *Christina* into the pitch-black waters of the Aegean at midnight, I would have done it. I would gladly have died for you. I never lied or covered up the truth. Maybe I didn't tell you everything. I didn't complain to you when I felt fatigued or ill the way I did to Battista; I knew you wouldn't have put up with it. But what I did tell you was always the truth.

I gave up my career for you. True, my voice had gone, but I could have fought to bring it back. I put up with your eternal abuse. You mistreated me, as you did your wife and your children. Crudel! Crudel! You attacked me as a woman and mocked my voice, you spoke to me in language that made the sailors blush. But I never stopped loving you. Not even when you made me have an abortion.

I have always wanted a child desperately. Next to you, it is what I would have liked more than anything in the world. It is a way to begin one's life over again and do it right this time. As Medea said in the movie, "Give life to the seed. Be reborn with the seed." But you wouldn't let me. You said, "I don't want a baby by you. What do I need another child for? I already have two."

Crudel! Crudel! The decision was torture. It took me four months to make up my mind. That little baby pulled out of my womb in pieces, slaughtered before it had a chance to take its first breath! I am like Lady Macbeth, who would do away with her "blessed babe." I was a fool to go along with you, Aristo, and I despise myself for having given in. But I was afraid of losing you. Think how different my life would be today if I had stood up to you and had the baby. I would have a child ten years old now. Every time I go past a girl of that age, I think, "My daughter might look like that today." I would have had a reason to live.

I used to love singing Puccini's *Suor Angelica* when I made the recording with the Philharmonic orchestra for EMI in 1954. Sister Angelica, who entered a convent to atone for her sins, mourns the death of the baby she was forced to abandon. She longs for death as her only hope of reunion with her child.

> "Little hands
> crossed on the bosom,
> little hands unable to caress me!
> Oh thou art dead, without knowing
> how much thy mother loved and adored thee! . . . .
> Oh tell me when shall I see thee in heaven?"

But now I can't listen to *Suor Angelica* anymore. It is too painful.

I used to talk to the baby in my tummy. "And how are you this morning, my little darling? Did you have a good night's sleep? Some day soon, I'll know without your telling me, for you'll be kicking me when you are awake. I can hardly wait for that first kick." I drank orange juice and milk to make her grow strong and healthy. I did exercises every day to make her delivery easy, even after I knew I was going to have the abortion. And I dreamed of her future, a future that was never to be. If the nurse brought the baby to me and it turned out to be a boy, I would never say, "Take him away! I don't want him!" I would grab him up and hold him close to me for ever and ever. My daughter, if it was a girl, would be called Maria, after me, and she would look like the pretty little girl I was before I got fat, except for an exquisitely chiselled nose like those on the rarest of cameos. She would have inherited my talent. I would have rocked her and sung lullabies to her before she went to sleep. I would have taught her everything I know about music from the time she was in the cradle. I would have spoken to her in song. I would have had her singing scales before she could even talk. She would have become the greatest opera singer the world has ever known, better than me, greater than Malibran. How could she have missed, with me as her mother?

But no! Strike that plan, Maria! Whatever are you thinking of? I would not do the same thing to her that Mother did to me. My child would *not* have to be an opera singer. I know what it is like to lose one's childhood to a career that isn't one's own idea. I wouldn't have made her do anything she didn't want to. I would have seen to it that she had the happiest childhood imaginable. I would have bought her all the toys she wanted, gotten her a little puppy like Toy for her own. I would never have given her a sister, to take away the limelight from my darling. I would have hugged her and kissed her all day long and at night she would have slept in my arms. I would have watched her diet carefully and not fed her spaghetti and ice cream, so she wouldn't have gotten fat as an elephant. And I never, never would have slapped her, as Liska did me. We would have been so happy together, my daughter and I. It's what I've always wanted. How sad that my dream will never come true.

I'll tell you what I never told anyone before. In the third act of *Norma* in the scene where she contemplates the murder of her children, the long D-minor phrase beginning "Teneri, teneri figli" developed into an elegy of bottomless grief for me. That and the aria in the last act, "I must forget I am a mother," broke my heart each time I played my recording of it after the abortion, for I never failed to think of my dead baby.

Leonore's words in *Forza del Destino* keep pealing through my mind, "Madre, Madre, O Holy Madre, hear my prayer, Forgive my sin appalling . . . Repentant here I'll make amends, I'll make amends. . . . In mercy hear my fervent plea! Forsake me not, forsake me not. . . . "

My bottomless sorrow is for the child I had to kill to please you, Aristotle. Crudel! You made me murder her! You took away my dream. I'll never forgive you for it. I wish I had never had a voice. I wish I had never met you. Then I would have become a housewife in Washington Heights with a houseful of children.

Sometimes, Aristo, I think you were my pleasure and my punishment all rolled up in one. You loathed my singing and wouldn't let me practice anywhere around you. When Churchill asked me to sing for him on the yacht, I said no because I knew you wouldn't like it if I did. You mattered a lot more to me than Churchill did. You put me down and humiliated me cruelly in front of people. When I asked you how you liked my new hat, the creation of the designer, Biki, you answered, "Either you cut your nose off to match the hat or you get a bigger hat to match your nose." When you screamed at me, "Shut up! You are nothing but a nightclub singer" in front of Sandor Gorlinsky, my London agent, I quietly left the room. When you said, "What are you? Nothing! All you have is a whistle in your throat which no longer functions" I still was silent. But your abuse of me, no matter how crucifying, never stopped me from loving you. In fact, like Elena in *I Vespri Siciliani*, "My greatest sorrow was to have to hate you."

I turned my cheek when you took other women to our bed, because I knew there could be no relationship unless it was on your terms. I didn't even object aloud when you threw me off the *Christina* to bring *her* on board the first time. You said it was not fitting that your "concubine" be present when a president and his first lady came aboard. Ha! Since when did you ever do anything because it was fitting?

I was a fool to have gone off in hurt silence. I should have howled and shrieked and threatened. I should have refused to go, I should have made you carry me off the ship kicking and screaming. Maybe that would have stopped you. But I doubt it. You always did what you wanted, no matter how many people were hurt. Your mother spoiled you rotten, and so did I. Instead of behaving as you deserved, I went to a hotel in Athens and literally clutched the telephone wire. It comforted me because I knew if I had to I could call you. The wire was my umbilical cord, my lifeline.

In the scene in *Medea* in which she watches Jason betray her by taking Glauce as his bride, I broke into sobs. My tears were real ones, my sweetheart; believe me I was not acting. "Sola, perduta, abbandonata." Like Puccini's *Manon Lescaut*, I am "Alone, lost, abandoned in this desolate land! Ah, alone, forsaken, I am a deserted woman!"

You never cared what people thought of you. And you never really believed you couldn't have both of us, did you, that I wouldn't be sweetly waiting on the isle of Skorpios for you to tire of your new plaything. And you were right, weren't you. That is exactly what I did.

You loved me, Aristo, I know you did. You said so over and over again. With that melting look in your olive-shaped eyes, who could doubt you? Certainly not I, who needed to believe you. You told me you had never really loved anyone before. And I believed you. I believe you still. You were just a collector of famous women. How like Scarpia in *Tosca* you were! "Power!" he sings. "The thing I desire I must conquer! I possess it and soon discard it,/ Seeking other pleasure." The only way you could have *her* was to marry her. But it was only me you loved, wasn't it? That's why you came back to me after your so-called marriage went kaput. Then I was happy my suicide attempt (after you again deserted me for her) had failed. Oh, I know, the American Hospital at Neuilly told the newspapers it was an overdose of barbiturates, that I had used more and more sleeping pills and simply lost track of how many. They lied. But you and I know the truth, Aristo, don't we. I hope that knowledge helped destroy your marriage.

It all happened so fast, so quickly, your betrayal of me. One day you were mine and the next day—hers! I don't understand. How could you, Aristo? I'll never understand it. Without you, I feel like Medea when Jason rejected her in the movie, "I am someone else now. I have forgotten everything. What used to be reality no longer is."

Jackie, Jackie, the name haunts me. How could he? He loved me, not her. What diabolical need drove him to take on another? Was I not woman enough for him? We belonged together. How many times in our bed did he whisper I was the heart of his Greek heart, his joy, his comfort when he was hurt, the rock upon which he stood. I did everything he wanted. I even gave up trying to sing again when he said, "Why do you have to work? I have enough money." No woman could do more. But it was not enough for him.

The strains of "Amami, Alfredo" (Love me, Alfredo) from Act Two of *La Traviata* keep going through my head. But it has new words:

> Love me, Aristo.
> Love me, Aristo.
> You love me,
> don't you really?
> Oh don't you?
> My Aristo, do you love me? . . . .
> Oh my beloved,
> Love me always, Aristo,
> As I love you.
> Farewell, my love!

Over and over I keep repeating the aria. I pray to God, "Do with me what You will, but give me the strength to bear what you send me and to survive it."

What irony that the two women who have destroyed my life are both named Jackie! Or wasn't it a coincidence at all, but just Ari's intentional climax of our sadistic love affair? But could anyone carry a perversion that far, to marry the wife of the slain president of the United States, just to torment the one he loves? Or did his cruelty merely add extra spice to his romance? The second Jackie! The one who shared my sister's name. He couldn't have thought of a more effective method of torturing me were he the Marquis de Sade.

Here I am fifty-three years old, the age my mother was when I wrote her to jump out the window. A coincidence? Maybe. But I don't think so. I am a half century and a continent away from my beginnings, an accomplished woman, cultured, famous the world over, some say the greatest diva since Malibran. Many people would die to be in my shoes. And yet, in the stillness of the night, I find the wound of my childhood is bleeding anew; Ari ripped off the scab. He made me see the truth. It was not his fault he left me. It was because of the person I am. *My mother was right not to love me; I am not a lovable person.* I fling myself back and forth in my empty bed to get away from the truth. The sheets are rumpled like a hot heap of rags, but my agony continues.

I know now on a deeper level what I have always known: My mother never loved me. I came out of her body uninvited. Jackie is the child of her heart. I gave Liska what she wanted, no daughter could have tried harder. I devoted my life to it. But she still loves Jackie more. And there is nothing I can do about it, any more than I can change the fact that Ari married someone else. I am helpless to keep my life from being ruined.

Whatever happened to me? I was supposed to grow up and get married and have children. Now my life is over and I can no longer tell myself it will come about. I'm through waiting. I'm everything now I will ever be. Maria Callas is finished. Whatever my success as a singer, I'm a failure in the game of life. My mother never loved me and Aristo didn't either. The two Jackies are the winners. Like Radames in *Aida*, "Life is hateful to me. The source of all joy is now dry, every hope is gone. I only wish to die." There is no hope for me, ever. I don't want to live.

In operas, I've played many heroines who die for love—and that is something I can understand. My life is an opera. The strains of "Suicidio" from Act Four of *La Gioconda* keep going through my mind. Isn't it miraculous how much it foretells Maria Callas's ultimate aria?

> "There is only suicide
> now left me!
> Stern fate forever
> of hope has bereft me.
> I the last accents
> of destiny hear,

Bear my cross!
Know the end draweth near.
Bright is the day,
The hours gayly flying!
Lost is my mother;
Love lies a-dying.
Conquer'd by jealousy's
Terrible fever,
I drop exhausted;
Sink down forever!
The end is nigh!
If Heaven prove kind,
Ere long in the grave,
Repose I may find."

But here's my problem. I am afraid to die, and when I finish this memoir I'll be faced with the task of killing myself. Every morning I wake up in despair that I am still alive. Every day that passes I thank God there is one day less to live. I have made up my mind. It is no longer a question of *if*, it is only a question of *when*. There is no turning back, although I still am terribly frightened. But then being afraid has never stopped me from doing what I wanted before, from leaving home to facing the terror of a hostile audience to separating from my husband to being the concubine of Aristotle Onassis. I'm certainly not going to let fear stop me now when I have nothing to lose. Nevertheless I can't stop shaking.

Come on, Maria. The only thing left unfinished in your life is this memoir. There is nothing else for you on earth. You've had it all and now you have nothing. You lost your weight, you lost your voice, then you lost Onassis. It is pathetic to listen to you sing now. There is no reason to live longer with grief and loneliness your only companions.

All right, it is decided then. When I finish this memoir I will finish with my body, too. So be it.

After I wrap this package and send it off to you, Alma Bond, I will go to my stately bedroom and put on the sexy black negligee Aristo loved. I will take the picture of Malibran with me and lie down on the bed Meneghini gave me. I will play my recording of "Vissi d'arte" (I lived for art, I lived for love) and soar to the skies one last time. Then I will breathe out a prayer to Heaven above for my quick release from this vale of tears. And I will take the cache of pills I have hoarded since Aristo died and swallow them one by one until my pain and I disappear forever.

Don't grieve for me, Dr. Bond. Please understand that this is the natural conclusion to my life, something that had to be. When I lost my voice, I lost myself. I found a new identity as the lover of Aristotle Onassis. He rescued me from nothingness and saved my life. Our relationship was not, as many believe, a wild and destructive veering off course. That course had already disappeared by the time we met. When I lost Ari I lost myself again for the last time. There is nothing left but my pills . . .

Postscript

ACCORDING TO MENEGHINI, in June, 1956, Zeffirelli wrote a curious letter to Maria. He said he had met Marlene Dietrich, one of Maria's greatest admirers. The actress told him that patients in American hospitals continually play Maria's records because they have discovered that her voice calms them down and gives them confidence they will recover their health. "That is not surprising," Zeffirelli continued. "We who love her have known that for a long time."

I had a personal experience with the curative powers of Callas's voice which makes me believe without question that Dietrich's story is true. One night recently I was sick in bed, and lay there clutching an aching stomach. I turned on a Callas CD to divert me from the pain. I must have fallen asleep, because in my dream state, I saw a lovely white figure, with flowing auburn hair singing "Casta Diva." She seemed to be in a cave somewhere, perhaps Turkey, where she had passed out while making the film, *Medea*. The voice that poured out of her was love, pure love. It filled my body and settled in my stomach. I awoke and found to my surprise that the pain had completely disappeared.

Callas told her students at the Masters' Classes she taught at Julliard that they must make love to the music. Perhaps that is the secret of the mystery of Maria Callas's success. She was great because she made love to the music and the people for whom she sang. Maurice Sendak in *In The Night Kitchen* says, "I'm in the milk and the milk's in me. God bless milk and God bless me!" That's the way it was for Maria when she sang. The love poured out of her as lavishly as Evangelia's milk must have flowed for the lusty infant. We who listen to her can feel that love in our hearts, if not in our heads. She would have liked that.

Ode to Maria

Sing, sing to us, oh diva,
sing to us in unknown tongues
of enchanted lands
where passions peak,
where stately beauty reigns as queen
and we, like blind men,
look to you
to open the gates
of Valhalla.

Sing a lustful song of love
to slither our hearts
with swells of joy,
sing of evil that
shrivels our souls
til we dissolve into dust.
Sing of grief so black, so thick
we dare not enter
the murky deep
lest we abide there forever.

Sing, sing with pride, oh diva
that inflates you like a prancing rooster
before his obliging hen.

Higher and higher you soar, oh diva
through moving sunlight
and billowing clouds,
thru membranes of terror,
thru mantles of bliss,
always at home
in the house of the dead
in the anteroom of death.

While I,
with borrowed shadow wings,
from some heroic mythical bird
in unilateral harmony
float along
beside you.

Sing on, sing on, my diva,
reckless heart and steadfast soul.
Would I, your shadow,
hold the key
to unlock the door
of Nirvana.

— Alma H. Bond

Bibliography

The Callas Legacy, **John Ardoin**, Charles Scribner, New York, 1977 (1982)

Callas at Juilliard: The Master Classes, **John Ardoin**, Alfred A. Knopf, 1987

Callas, **John Ardoin and Gerald Fitzgerald**, Holt, Rinehart & Winston, New York, Chicago, San Francisco, 1974

The Octagonal Heart, **Ariadne Thompson**, Riverside Press, St. Louis, 1976

Those Fabulous Greeks: Onassis, Niarchos and Livanos, **Doris Lilly**, Cowles Book Company, New York, 1970

Aristotle Onassis, **Nicholas Fraser, Philip Jacobson, Mark Ottaway & Lewis Chester**, J.B. Lippincott Co., Philadelphia and New York, 1977

Maria Meneghini Callas, **Michael Scott**, Northeastern University Press, Boston, 1991

Maria Callas: The Woman Behind The Legend, **Arianna Stassinopoulos**, Simon and Schuster, New York, 1981

Maria Callas, **Jurgen Kesting**, Northeastern University Press, Boston, 1990

My Daughter, Maria Callas, **Evangelia Callas**, Fleet Publishing Company, New York, 1960

Sisters, Jackie Callas, St. Martin's Press, New York, 1989

Callas: La Divina, **Stelios Galatopoulos**, London House and Maxwell, New York, 1970

Callas: Portrait of a Prima Donna, **George Jelinek**, Dover Publications, New York, 1986

Diva: The Life and Death of Maria Callas, **Stephen Linakis**, London, 1981

Maria Callas: D'Art et D'Amour, **Jacques Lorcey**, Paris, 1983

Callas—As They Saw Her, **David A. Lowe**, The Ungar Publishing Company, New York, 1986

My Wife Maria Callas, **Giovanni Battista Meneghini**, Farrar Straus Giroux, New York, 1982

Maria Callas—A Tribute, **Pierre-Jean Remy**, London, 1978

Maria; Callas Remembered, **Nadia Stancioff**, E.P. Dutton, New York, 1987

Maria Callas: The Art Behind The Legend, **Henry Wisneski,** Doubleday, New York, 1975

Kobbe's Complete Opera Book, **Gustav Kobbe,** edited and revised by The Earl of Harewood, G.P. Putnam, New York, 1972

The Last Prima Donnas, **Lanfranco Rasponi,** Alfred A. Knopf, New York, 1982

Vincenzo Bellini, **Leslie Orrey,** 1987

The Operas of Puccini, **William Ashbrook,** 1985

The Man Verdi, **Frank Walker,** 1982

The Met: One Hundred Years of Grand Opera, **Martin Mayer,** Simon and Schuster, New York, 1983, The Metropolitan Opera Guild

Early Romantic Opera, **edited by Philip Gossett,** Volumes One and Two, Garland Publishing, New York and London, 1983

A Knight At The Opera, **Sir Rudolph Bing,** G.P. Putnam, New York, 1981

5000 Nights at the Opera, **Sir Rudolph Bing,** Doubleday and Company, Garden City, NY, 1972

Opera: What's All The Screaming About?, **Roger Englander,** Walker and Co., New York, 1983

The Opera, **Joseph Wechsberg,** Macmillan Company, New York, 1972

Introduction to Opera, **edited by Mary Ellis Peltz,** based on *Opera Lover's Companion* and *Opera News* (publications of The Metropolitan Opera Guild), Barnes & Noble, New York, 1962

The Story of A Hundred Operas, Grosset & Dunlap, New York, 1940

The Authentic Librettos of the Italian Operas, Crown Publishers, New York, 1939

A Song of Love and Death: The Meaning of Opera, **Peter Conrad,** Poseidon Press, New York, 1987

Enjoying Opera, **Olga Maynard,** Charles Scribner, New York, 1966

The Splendid Art of Opera, **Ethan Mordden,** Metheun, New York, 1980

The Angel's Cry: Beyond the Pleasure Principle in Opera, **Michel Piozat,** Cornell University Press, Ithaca and London

In The Night Kitchen, **Maurice Sendak,** Harper, 1970

Opera Today, Meirion and Susie Harries, St. Martin's Press, New York, 1986

Great Singers, Kurt Pahlen, Stein and Day, New York, 1974

COMPACT DISKS:

"Callas in her Own Words," John Ardoin, Eklipse Records Ltd., EKR P-14, 1996

"Maria Callas at Juilliard, The Master Classes," EMI Records Ltd., 1987

Author has included only critical biographic sources from the many books, articles, CDs, and films researched.

ARTICLES:

"Callas Remembered," *Opera*, November, 1977. Recollections, tributes and commentaries by Tito Gobbi, Carlo Maria Giulini, Lord Harewood, Rold Lieberman, Sir John Tooley, Margherita Wallman

"Autobiography of Maria Callas," Anita Pensotti (in installments), *Oggi*, Jan. 10, 1957

"Maria Callas," Recorded Reputations, The Earl of Harewood, Music Magazine, April, 1993

"Kiri at 50," Lesley Garner, Music Magazine, London, March, 1994

VIDEOS:

"Interview with Maria Callas," PBS, 1994

"Callas In Her Own Words," John Ardoin, Eklipse Records Ltd., 1996

"Callas Reveals Herself," Callas, Di Stefano, Mischa Elman, Svetlana Berlosova, Donald McCleary, Jose Greco, Georges Prêtre in a gala. Boheme, Carmen (2), Don Carlo & songs, 1962

"Conversations With Callas," with Lord Harewood & "Callas in Paris," (1965) Manon, Sonnambula, Schicchi and interview in French & "Norma" (highlights)

"Tosca," Act II with Callas and London, Mitropoulos conducting & interviews

"Medea," film starring Maria Callas, Pier Paolo Pasolini

"Interview with Aristotle Onassis," PBS, 1994

Author has taken some liberties with the dates of Michael Scott's reviews, as well as with the early appearance of Kiri Te Kanawa in *Marriage of Figaro* at Covent Garden.

Acknowledgments

I would like to express my deep appreciation to Mr. John Ardoin, distinguished music critic of the *Dallas Morning News*, biographer, and dear friend of Maria Callas, who was kind enough to critique this manuscript and to share his memories of Callas with me. His approval made me feel more secure about the publication of this book.

I also wish to voice my gratitude to Lawrence Janos, Karen Leonard, Emily Lowe, and Sam Maxwell for reading early versions of this book. I found their constructive criticism and suggestions most helpful. In addition, I want to thank Judith Gaddis, Richard Hardy, Paul Hardy, and Holy Trinity Church in New York City for providing me with information about Maria Callas and/or Greece. Although many libraries contributed to my research, including the Music and Art Library at Lincoln Center, I found Marianne Duchardt of the Monroe County Library, Key West, Florida, particularly generous and helpful with her time and expertise. A special brand of thanks goes to my friend and ex-student, Dr. Donna Bassin, for her brilliant connection of Maurice Sendak's *In The Night Kitchen* with the lushness of Callas's singing.

About the Author:
Alma H. Bond

Dr. Alma Halbert Bond, a psychoanalyst, is a member of the International Psychological Association, and a fellow and faculty member of the Institute for Psychoanalytic Training & Research.

In 1991 she retired from a highly successful practice in New York City to write full time. Since that time she has had six previous books published, including *Who Killed Virginia Woolf? A Psychobiography*, Human Sciences Press; *On Becoming a Grandparent*, Bridge Works; *Is There Life After Analysis?*, Baker Book House; *Dream Portrait*, International Universities Press; *America's First Woman Warrior: The Courage of Deborah Sampson*, Paragon; *Profiles of Key West*, Poho Press.

Her articles have appeared in numerous prestigious psychoanalytic journals, and is a regular contributor to *Psychoanalytic Books*. Interviews by Dr. Bond have appeared in various Florida newspapers and magazines. Two of her most recent articles in print are "My Memories of Marlon Brando" in *Remember Magazine*, and "The Romance of the Golden Greeks: Maria Callas and Aristotle Onassis," in *Greece Travel Magazine*.

The author's admiration for and fascination with the life of Maria Callas led to the research and writing of *The Autobiography of Maria Callas: A Novel*, the latest of her books to appear in print.

Dr. Bond was the wife of the late screen, stage and television actor, Rudy Bond. She is the mother of three, and grandmother of five. Her son, Jonathan Bond, is Chairman of the prestigious New York advertising agency, Kirschenbaum & Bond. She makes her home and writes her books and articles in Key West, Florida.